NIMBUS

"Hell on Earth"

'There's something in the rain, and it wants
the dark in you to come out.'

TONY
MARTURANO

a Different Angle

First published in the USA and Canada by Trafford
Publishing. 2001
ISBN 155212568-8

First published in the United Kingdom by Glacyk
Publishing. 2001
ISBN 0-9540137-0-0

'Hell on Earth' edition Published in the United Kingdom
and the rest of the world by a Different Angle. 2016
ISBN - 978-0-9540137-5-2

Cambridge, UK

Author's Note

After many years of writing scripts for the stage, I would never have dreamed of writing a novel.

Then, one day, one of my dearest friends suggested that I turn my hand to writing a book. I rewarded her by laughing. "Me? Turn my hand to writing books? I'm a dialogue guy; I write scenes and put words in the mouths of characters."

She looked at me, knowingly.

Two years later, after turning in a couple of hours each morning before leaving for the office, devouring every bit of spare time I could steal, I'd completed the first draft of Nimbus.

Like many authors when they first finish a book, I copied and sent extracts to every British publisher I could find.

None were interested. And, like many before me, I felt demoralised; I had turned in all of these pages, and for what?

A few months later, I found myself in conversation with a friend. She was bemoaning the fact that she'd received rejection letters from a series of jobs she had applied for.

I left the room, returned moments later with what appeared to be a whole ream of paper, and I dropped these sheets in her lap. "That's rejection," I said.

So, we made a pact. She wouldn't stop hunting for the perfect job, and I wouldn't stop honing Nimbus and looking for ways to find it a home.

Nimbus was published in 2001.

My friend found the perfect job (albeit a bit sooner!).

When I agreed to write a novel, I made a pact with myself that, if I was going to write a book, then I wanted to write about something that would truly scare the reader, some everyday thing that would go on to terrorize an unsuspecting public.

And, of course, living in England, I didn't need to look very far for inspiration.

I remember, when I received my first fan message that told me that the reader would *never go out in the rain again,* I knew my work was done.

Now, over a decade later, I find myself in the enviable position of revisiting the Nimbus characters, my old friends, with whom I shared my first writing adventure, and it has been a fantastic experience to be able to look at the journey with fresh (some would say wiser and more experienced) eyes.

Fully revised (and edited by my new and most eminent editor) with some added never-read-before scenes, sex, action and horror, this book is most definitely one of my favourite works, and I'm hoping it will become yours, too.

So, buckle up and strap yourself in because there's a reason why I've dubbed this edition of Nimbus - 'HELL ON EARTH'.

Tony Marturano, Cornwall, November 2015

For Bella, without whom…

PROLOGUE

Icelandic Coast – 200 km Northeast of Reykjavik

After ten minutes of flying over Iceland's barren region, the helicopter approached the glacial perimeter, where erupting geysers and bubbling mud lakes cooled into a winter wonderland of snow-capped mountains, gurgling brooks and green valleys.

Up ahead, the sky was steely blue, and bubbling with angry cumulonimbus clouds.

Stefán looked out of the window and smiled as the ground sped beneath them like a moving canvas.

The more he thought about his wife, and what she had told him over breakfast that morning, the more his heart beat with joy. He had waited a long time for this day and, finally, it had arrived; he was going to be a father.

He blinked watery eyes as another snow-capped hill erupted from the horizon.

The pilot gunned the engine and the chopper climbed upward.

Beyond the hill, the Glacyk Chemico complex nestled inside the valley like an absconding armadillo. The three square miles of white hexagonal buildings, satellite dishes, radio masts and giant chimneys – all encased in a twelve-foot-high electrified fence – resembled a moon base.

Specialising in the development and production of pharmaceuticals, ChemiCo owned some of world's leading drug brands. Its latest project was rumoured to be a major breakthrough in psychotropic medicine. One that the corporation's mission statement claimed would *"change the treatment of mental disorders, forever."*

Details of the revolutionary new drug remained highly classified. In fact, Glacyk ChemiCo, a fraction of the size of its global sister plants, had been awarded the research and development because of its remote and discreet location.

The pilot spoke into his mouthpiece, identified himself, and requested authorisation to land at one of the four giant helipads that marked each corner of the facility.

A few minutes later, the helicopter dipped and began its descent over a concrete platform, marked H - North.

Stefán unbuckled his seatbelt, thanked the pilot, and stepped out of the craft, instinctively stooping to avoid the whirring blades. He breathed deeply as he took in his surroundings. The valley was dusted with snow in stark contrast to the sky that was dark and atmospheric.

He made this journey every morning, but it had never looked as beautiful as it did today; he was the happiest man in the world. He cheerfully greeted the driver of the waiting jeep, and climbed into the passenger seat. Behind them, the whirring of the helicopter's engine grew louder until the machine climbed back into the gathering gloom.

After a short drive, the jeep pulled up alongside a flight of steps. At the top, two armed guards in black duffel coats stood to attention outside of a set of giant double doors.

Stefán climbed the steps and said, "Morning."

"Morning," one of the two replied. Then, noticing the smile on his face, he added, "You seem happy this morning."

"I am," Stefán said, holding up a barcoded identity card to the close circuit camera above the doors. The lens zoomed in and a laser scanned him, the image and the code.

"Oh yeah? Something we should know?" the guard asked curiously as the doors buzzed open.

"Yes, there is," Stefán beamed as he entered the building, "but I'm not going to tell you."

Inside, the main reception area was large and lavishly furnished, with dark grey marbled floors and walls to match. The décor captured the essence of the desert in the form of two giant cacti whose roots were imbedded in large troughs of sand. They stood, like the giant pillars of an ancient coliseum, on either side of the room.

Stefán nodded at the security guards behind a sizable granite reception desk. They sat, caps pulled tightly over their foreheads – one of them greeting visitors as the other watched like a bird of prey, his eyeballs fixed to the bank of monitors in front of him.

At the elevator situated to the side of the lobby, Stefán swiped his key card through the reader.

As the lift descended into the bowels of the complex, he allowed his thoughts to drift back to his wife and her smile. The beautiful smile that had accompanied that morning's news.

Less than a minute later, a bell sounded and the doors swished open. He stepped out of the lift and hummed as his footsteps echoed around the dimly lit corridor, until he stopped in front of a pair of doors upon which a plaque read, "TURBINE 3000 - AUTHORISED PERSONNEL ONLY."

Because of its remote location, Glacyk ChemiCo couldn't connect to the national grid, and thus needed to produce its own energy in order to power the various offices, as well as research and development laboratories. The T3000 did this with extraordinary efficiency. The generator was unique. It had been designed by ChemiCo's own engineers, and had the capacity to generate enough electricity to power a small town.

He placed his right hand on a glowing red panel and, after a few seconds, it beeped and turned green. Then, with another swipe of his card, the doors opened to a murmur of voices and ringing telephones.

The walls of the control room were made of electronic monitors and gauges of all sizes. In front of these were computers on desktops, all manned by men in white overalls.

It was 8:00 a.m.

Hinrik, a young man in his late twenties who was wearing a grey overall, glanced up from the tablet he was holding. "Morning."

"Good morning," Stefán replied. "Anything exciting happen?"

Hinrik thought about the question and then, without taking his eyes off the screen in front of him, offered, "No, not really. We had a minor problem with B in the early hours, but nothing serious."

"What happened?" Stefán asked.

Here we go. "Nothing much – thought we had an alarm in one of the coolers but it stopped before we could even trace it."

"Did you run diagnostics on it?"

"What for? There wasn't a fault."

Stefán forced an incredulous laugh. "Hinrik, it's standard procedure. There could be other faults in the system."

Hinrik breathed deeply, handed the tablet to him, and said, apathetically, "Well, my shift is over now. What you do is entirely up to you."

Running the diagnostics programme would mean shutting off one of the generators and running the plant at half-power for a minimum of five hours. Management hated these delays, as they meant that many activities would have to be halted.

The mantra was that a few hours of delay for them could mean a massive advantage for their competitors.

Across the room, Tómas, one of the newest and youngest recruits, was making notes when, suddenly, a beeping sound demanded his attention. He looked up to see that the green status indicator on his monitor had turned yellow, and a small window had popped up out of nowhere and begun to scroll an endless list of data he didn't understand.

It had never done anything like this before.

He scanned the room, but his managers seemed deep in conversation. He glanced back at the computer monitor and attempted to read some of the text. The words "ERROR 99" headed it, but after that came a jumble of numerical data which meant absolutely nothing to him.

Panicked, he called to Hinrik.

"Hold on a minute," his manager replied, distracted as he proceeded to argue his case

"But, Sir…"

"I said hold on a bloody minute!" Hinrik barked.

Mr. Know-it-all had decided to make him look stupid by suggesting that they run diagnostics now. That would mean filing a report detailing exactly how and when the error had originally occurred, which had been during his shift.

"Listen, Stefán. I know you think I was promoted early. Earlier than you, and if that's the source of some resentment for you, well, that's your problem. But I got this promotion because somebody thinks I'm up to the job, and if you don't think so then…"

"…I didn't say you weren't up to the job, Hinrik. I am just…" Stefán stopped in mid-sentence as he locked eyes with Tómas. The boy was sweating, his eyes wide.

He walked over to him. "What's wrong?"

The yellow status indicator had turned red and the beeping was now a loud shrill.

"Get up," Stefán ordered.

Tómas gratefully obliged.

Stefán took his place and immediately began to work the keyboard.

Hinrik joined them. "What the hell's going on?"

There was silence, except for the clicking of the keyboard and the alarm buzzer.

"Are you going to answer me?"

"I don't know yet," Stefán replied calmly. "Looks like there's something wrong with one of the coolers."

"What do you mean?" Hinrik asked, snatching up the tablet and tapping buttons until…

…His heart skipped a beat. It was the same error he'd seen earlier. Only this time, it was constant. He considered sharing the information, but decided against it.

By now, others were aware of the commotion and had abandoned their screens to watch as Stefán proceeded to key in various command strings, his fingers working fast. His face was calm and composed.

The computer's screen scrolled data in response to his keyboard interrogation.

Then, pausing as he took in the information, Stefán said flatly, "We need to shut down the turbines. Call Williamson and tell him what we're going to do."

His words weren't pointed at anyone in particular, but Tómas would have been very pleased to carry out his instructions.

"We can't call him – he's not here," Hinrik said.

"Then we'll have to shut it down anyway."

"Hang on a minute," Hinrik interjected, playing down the seriousness of the situation. "You can't shut down the entire plant without authorisation."

"Watch me," Stefán replied as more lights changed from green to yellow and the room filled with a cacophony of alarm shrills and buzzers.

He looked at a bunch of keys hooked to Hinrik's belt, and their eyes met.

"Give me the keys."

Hinrik shook his head. "Oh no," he breathed. Suddenly, he was filled with dread. Things were getting too serious. "I can't let you do it. We don't even know what the problem is yet."

"Don't be an idiot. The data speaks for itself. The turbine is overheating. We need to shut it down now."

Nevertheless, Hinrik shook his head again. It was apparent that he had made a serious error in judgement. If Williamson learned of this, he would most certainly be fired, and then what would he do? Jobs like this, around here, were a once in a lifetime opportunity.

"Hinrik!" Stefán shouted, as if to awaken the young man from a trance. Then gently, he continued, "This is serious, Hinrik. I need those keys right now."

Behind them, Tómas and the others were watching the battle of wills, each silently urging the man to comply.

As if he had heard them, Hinrik reluctantly unhooked the keys from his belt and threw them at Stefán, who caught them with his right hand. He tapped various commands on the computer, waited, and then tapped some more before leaving his chair and hurrying over to the far side of the room. There, he fell to his knees and unlocked a small metal cabinet underneath one of the desks.

A yellow sticker with a bolt of lightning and the words "Authorised Personnel Only" branded the door. He opened it, revealing a panel of colour-coded push-buttons and one black handle.

In that moment, the lights dipped, a loud siren sounded, a red light at the centre of the ceiling flashed, and a recorded female voice played over the public address system…

"Attention, this is an emergency. All personnel are to evacuate the building immediately. Attention, this is an emergency."

The voice repeated itself like a demented robot.

"Oh my…" Hinrik breathed. "We're going into meltdown!"

Tómas was frozen with fear as he watched his colleagues kicking and clawing at each other as they scrambled for the exit whilst, on the floor in front of him, his managers grappled for exclusive access to the cabinet.

"Shut it off! Shut it off!" Hinrik yelled.

The siren blared, the red beacon flashed, and, somewhere, someone was screaming in agony.

Tómas put his hands over his ears in an effort to block out the noise and his terror as he slowly slumped underneath one of the desks, drew his knees up to his chest, and began rocking himself gently.

Hinrik lashed out and hooked Stefán in the jaw, sending him reeling backward. Then, reaching into the cabinet, he clasped the black handle and began to pull it down.

"NO! Off, first… Hinrik, close the circuit first or you'll blow us sky high!" Stefán shrieked, tugging at the man's shoulder. But Hinrik was determined. He pulled the black lever down as far as it would go.

That was when Tómas closed his eyes and prayed for the Lord to forgive his sins.

The wolf froze and watched with unblinking eyes as the humans ran, screaming, from the building, but it was too late.

The first explosion ripped through the entrance lobby, propelling the double doors outward, mowing down the security guards on the steps. The next one erupted upward, catapulting red hot debris into the air and flames out of cavities, like fire from a dragon's mouth, incinerating anything and anyone within its reach.

A satellite dish from one of the nearby buildings whistled like a firework as it was blasted thirty feet into the air. It returned to Earth, crushing a man in a white coat and dyeing the snow crimson.

The explosions continued until the whole valley was ablaze, and all that remained of Glacyk ChemiCo was a pile of rubble and fire.

The wolf whimpered as the sun was eclipsed by great clouds of green-tinted smoke that raced towards the sky, seeking and merging with the smog high above the troposphere.

1

Widemouth Bay – Cornwall, England – 06:59 a.m.

The crimsoned glow of the rising sun peeked over the horizon as his trainers splashed through the salty water, leaving the surf to nip at his heels.

"19.5 Miles", an automated voice spoke over the pounding bassline of the music through his earbuds.

The sweat glistened on his face, his heart pounded and his lungs were screaming at him, yet Blake Hudson felt exhilarated. This was his favourite running track, but it wasn't made of polyurethane, but of natural firm, honeycomb sand, that stretched into a ten-mile arc of the bay. There were no spectator stands, just a rocky cliff face and a stunning moving canvas of the aquamarine ocean and the cotton-balled sky.

Just another mile, Blake, and you'll have broken your own record. Come on! Come on!

He ran almost every morning and lifted the occasional dumbbell for definition, and this maintained an athletic body that complimented short black hair, big hazel eyes and an angular stubbled jaw. He was handsome, but not aware of it, despite the regular attention he received from members of the opposite sex.

A beep sounded in his ears and then the same automated voice announced, "News alert."

"...Ministers have rejected calls to change the law that allows journalists and voters to expose wrongdoing and incompetence in public bodies. A commission set up by the government last summer to review the freedom of information act is due to report today, and more than a thousand people have died in an explosion at a chemical plant in Iceland. The cause of the tragedy remains unknown, but unconfirmed reports suggest that a power surge may have been responsible for the disaster, from which there were no survivors. I'm Elena Parker. This is Southwest Radio, and now with today's weather, here's Andrew Jarvis."

"Thanks, Elena. Well, easy forecasting today. It's going to be

a warm, sunny day for most of Great Britain. In fact, I've just been told that it's going to be one of the warmest May days recorded since 1932. But make the most of it, because it looks like bad weather is on the way. Meteorologists have picked up a large band of cloud over the Atlantic Ocean, and it's heading our way."

"Thanks, Andrew. It's three minutes past seven. Time for a sports update with..."

Blake pulled the ears buds from his ears and docked his phone in the dashboard of the Range Rover, and then he spoke to the cabin, "Open trunk." Instantly, the hatch hummed open to reveal an equipment-crammed interior.

The inventory was essential and always the same:

1 electronic D.O.M (Dissolved Oxygen Metre)

1 ammonia Test Kit, 2 Eye wash bottles

1 pair of Wellington Boots

1 pair of Gloves

1 life Jacket

2 crates of small sample bottles (with colour-coded caps)

2 wooden stakes

1 inflatable oil boom

2 bales of writing pads

1 hard black case, containing an array of tools (including a couple of flares, a strapped down Stanley knife, and a pack of PH sticks).

On top of the case was a face-towel and a pair of clean trainers. He wiped his hair and face with the towel, and then changed into the trainers.

As he bent down to tie up his laces, he paused, catching sight of the bay. It was cradled between two huge, rugged cliff tops, upon which nested several colonies of seagulls. Occasionally, a group of them ran sorties to and from the ocean.

Blake squinted into the early morning sun and watched the waves break on the shore. It was a canvas snapshot, and it reminded him why many artists flocked to this part of the country.

He paused his panting recovery in favour of one full inhalation of the fresh morning air. He was content. Moving here was undoubtedly one of the best decisions he had ever made.

At thirty years of age, Blake Hudson had achieved much, but he still wanted more from life. He had taken a job with the Cambridgeshire County Council as an Environment Officer not long after graduating from Cambridge. Shortly after that, he'd applied for and won a position with the Environment Agency.

It was when he'd been assigned to assist with an investigation into a potential mercury contamination incident, in the Southwest, that he'd discovered his love for Cornwall.

Within weeks, he had sold his Cambridge home and put down the deposit on an abandoned lighthouse at Stony Point. He spent the next year partially contracting and personally putting in the hard graft needed to convert the building into the perfect home.

He glanced at his watch, redeposited the towel and then hurried to the front of the vehicle where he assumed his positioned in the driver's seat and started the engine.

As he drove, he made a mental note to call his parents. His mother had already left him two messages that would undoubtedly be about whether or not he planned on visiting over the weekend.

His parents, both retired, lived in a handsome Georgian house in Stowe, Buckinghamshire. They were very proud of their only son, and although Giles Hudson's dream of Blake graduating in politics, and following in his footsteps as a Member of Parliament, was not being realised, he wasn't disappointed. In fact, Giles took every opportunity to praise his son's achievements, and cherished the bond between them.

The Range Rover rounded a bend in one of the many narrow roads that snaked through the Cornish countryside and revealed the lighthouse up ahead. Its poise was regal, as if it had naturally erupted from the rocky cliff face on which it stood.

Despite its circular architecture, the lighthouse was spacious inside. The entrance lobby led through an archway to an extended area that was the lounge. The furniture was dark, modern, and set off nicely against the virgin white walls that were adorned by various black and white photographs of the coastal area.

A door at the opposite end of the room led to a kitchen, a utility room, and a downstairs toilet with a tiny window that offered an appetising view of the rocky shore.

A spiral metal stairwell led to the bedroom on the first floor, where a custom-made bed sat to one side, flanked by a door that led to a relatively small bathroom that was awash with daylight streaming in through a large circular window. A fitted wardrobe ran the opposite side of the bedroom. Next to that, a balconette framed an azure ocean.

Blake's office was on the second floor, where the thin glass that had once run the circumference of the building had been replaced with double-glazed windows in a PVC frame. A sliding glass door led out onto the balcony that offered spectacular views of the coastline.

Like the rest of the building, the office walls were white, displaying a series of dark picture frames that showcased diplomas in various subjects. A small desk sat to one side of the room. On it stood a large flat screen computer monitor. Opposite this was a small leather divan. Next to that, a telescope peered out of the balcony doors.

In his bedroom, Blake seemingly spoke to the walls, "Music on!"

He showered as a thumping baseline resumed and echoed throughout the building.

2

Plymouth College – Plymouth, England – 11:00 a.m.

Blake, now dressed in a dark blue suit, glanced discreetly at his watch. He was half an hour into the lecture and wondered if any of the students had actually taken in anything of what he had just said.

A hand fluttered up at the back of the classroom. It led to a gangly looking young man.

"Yes?" Blake asked.

"I've got a question."

"What is it?"

"A moment ago you talked about the effects of acid rain in northern Europe, and said that we were responsible for a large amount of it. I'm not sure I understand why."

Blake smiled, and moved to the front of the desk and leaned back onto it.

"Well, most of you, I'm sure, are aware of the infamous smog that smothered the whole of London in the early 50s."

Blank faces.

"OK. So, for those of you who aren't... In the winter of 1952, London was plunged into what seemed to be a permanent fog – only it wasn't. It was a chronic smog, caused by the over-burning of fossil fuels such as…"

"Coal!" An excited blonde girl interrupted from the front row.

"Coal, that's right," Blake agreed.

The girl smiled, sweetly.

She was attracted to Blake. He had been aware of this ever since he had started giving lectures here, two months ago.

"And what else?" He offered the question to the rest of the class.

The blonde girl, Clare, jumped in again, "Discharge from power stations."

"Correct. It became just as bad as any other major epidemic. Four thousand people died, whilst thousands of others were hospitalised. It took the appalling death toll from the killer fogs of 1952, and a great deal more, to bring about legislation to clean up the air over London. Finally, in 1956, the Clean Air Act put an end to smog by banning the use of coal, for domestic heating purposes, within London. It didn't, however, legislate for other damaging pollutants. Chimneys were simply built taller. So, for decades, much of the pollution that would have mimicked the smog of 1952 was simply being dumped further afield, over the rest of Western and Northern Europe."

"That still doesn't explain how it got there," the boy said, somewhat petulantly. "I mean, this so-called smog ends up in the atmosphere, this we already know, but how does it manage to get all the way to Northern and Western Europe? Does it hitch-hike a ride on a 777?"

A ripple of laughter ran through the class, and the acne-riddled young man grinned, proud of his quip.

Blake laughed with them. Although, it was moments like these when he wondered why he'd agreed to give up his time to be there once a week. He had enough work to do without having to drive over an hour cross-country to lecture this lot.

But the agency didn't see it that way. It believed that having a presence in educational establishments was key to spreading the word about the importance of safeguarding the environment.

"That's funny," Blake said. "But in answer to your question, no. You see, many different gasses combine in the Earth's atmosphere to produce a cocktail of damaging acid. The most dangerous of these being SO2, Sulphur Dioxide, and NOX, Nitrous Dioxide. These amalgamate with the moisture of clouds to form such things as rain, snow, fog, mist, clouds, and even flakes. *Acid air* is probably the best way to describe it. This *acid air* can then fall as precipitation – hundreds, sometimes even thousands of kilometres away."

"And that's where it gets its more commonly known name, acid rain," Clare added, knowingly.

Another hand went up.

This time, it was that of a scrawny-looking girl wearing black skinny jeans, scraggy brown hair, and a silver stud affixed to her right nostril.

"Yes?" Blake asked.

"How does acid rain affect humans? Earlier you said that thousands of people died, and many were, and even today, *are* still being hospitalised, but by what?"

"Well, there are a variety of symptoms. For example, mercury and lead attack the central nervous system, bringing on psychological disorders, whilst nickel and beryllium damage the lungs. Antimony can lead to heart disease, and cadmium causes liver damage.

"Yet, despite all this, we humans release in excess of 450,000 tonnes of these deadly metals into the atmosphere each year. Over half of them come from a single source – vehicle exhausts. And it's not just about what we breathe. Airborne particles settle on the foods we eat.

"You see, like acid rain, lead travels thousands of kilometres before descending to Earth. In fact, traces of lead and other pollutants have been found in the snows of the polar ice caps."

Blake paused as he noticed the looks of concentration on the sea of faces in front of him. In all the time he had lectured here, never before had he caught their attention as he appeared to have done right now.

"Don't get me wrong, I wouldn't give up my Range Rover for anyone," he said. "Where I live, and in some of the places I go to for work, I'd be lost without it."

There was laughter.

"Where do you live, Sir?" Clare asked.

"I live," he hesitated, and then added, with deliberate vagueness, "on the coast, near Bude.

"Banning the combustion engine isn't feasible. But what *is* feasible is innovating environmentally friendly alternatives. As you know, many car manufacturers are doing precisely that, but much more needs to be done by countries all around the globe. Countries like India, which has been reported to have the highest number of *dirty* cities in the world. That is, cities with the highest concentration of PM2.5 particles. 'PM' standing for particulate matter – airborne solid matter or liquid droplets that are one hundred times thinner than a human hair.

"Airborne toxins created by industry, cars, aerosols, burning forests and domestic fires are a controllable phenomenon.

"It's also theoretically possible to repair the damage caused by these pollutants. Ambitious experiments are being conducted every day to stem the acidification of Scandinavian and Canadian lakes. For example, liming the lakes with aluminium, calcium and other neutralising agents. Although, the results are far from satisfactory, since – in addition to the astronomical costs – there's the fact that these technical fixes don't actually solve the problem.

"Because the fact remains, as long as we keep pumping acid into the air, it will be necessary to keep liming the lakes, and there's a good chance that the agents we're using to counteract the effects of acid rain may themselves produce a new generation of environmental problems."

Now, conscious and inspired by the class's full attention, Blake was slowly pacing up and down in front of his desk.

"So, is it true, Sir?"

Blake had been interrupted by a rodent-looking young lad with spectacles, a small nose and big ears. He had noticed the student before, but rarely heard him speak up in class, or with anyone else for that matter.

Blake stopped pacing. "Is what true?"

"Are humans living on borrowed time? Will nature reclaim the land by wiping us from the face of the Earth?"

There was a collective groan, some laughter, and eye rolling from the rest of the class.

This continued for a few seconds as Blake arched his head to see around the other heads and to make eye contact with the teenager. He quieted the rest of the room by shaking his hands, and then asked, "Is that what you think is going to happen?"

"I asked what you thought," the boy said, expressionless.

Blake shrugged his shoulders and leaned back on his desk again. "Well, most doomsday preppers believe that it's not a matter of if, but when."

"No, no," the boy disagreed, seemingly irked by Blake's flippant response. "And you still haven't answered my question. I'm not talking about chemical warfare here, or some ridiculous zombie apocalypse. I'm talking about hurricanes, earthquakes, tsunamis, floods, sinkholes, famine. Isn't the world already in crisis?"

There were more groans from the students. Some booed.

"Well, I'm not an expert..."

"...Yet, there you stand, preaching to us about the fragility of the environment."

"I was about to say, I'm not an expert on the humanitarian crisis, but I do follow the news, and, occasionally, what's trending on social media. So, in answer to your question, when it comes to the environment, do I believe that nature's going to wipe us out in a series of biblical meteorological events? No, I don't. Do I believe that climate change is real, and a serious threat to the future of mankind? Absolutely," Blake said seriously, and then added, with a smile, "If I didn't, I'd be out of a job."

More laughter, but rat boy wasn't amused. Blake knew this by the way he wouldn't relinquish eye contact.

This continued for a few seconds, until Blake looked away and was about to continue, when he was interrupted once more, "There's going to be a reckoning, Mr. Hudson. A time when we'll all be held accountable for the rape and plunder of the planet."

The words were as ominous as the silence that momentarily followed them.

"Rape and plunder? Dude. What's with all the revelations shit?" said a burly black lad.

The boy didn't answer. He was still busy staring off against Blake, who was still searching for something to say when he was, quite literally, saved by the bell.

The entire class rose to its feet in a babbling, chair-scraping cacophony.

"Okay. See you all next week," Blake said to no one in particular. He pushed his tablet and assorted papers into his briefcase, then checked his device for messages. By the time he looked up, the class had already emptied of its occupants, including doomsday boy.

He turned to leave, and was startled to find Clare standing directly in front of him. "Clare! You startled me."

"I'm sorry, Sir. I didn't mean to." She flashed a smile at him.

Not unlike her creepy class companion, she just stood, drinking in all six foot something of him with her eyes whilst hugging a collection of books.

"Is there something I can help you with?" he offered.

"Oh yeah, I just wanted to tell you how much I enjoyed the lecture today."

He nodded. "Well, that's great. Thanks very much"

There followed an uncomfortable few moments, during which the girl did not move out of Blake's way, but nor did she offer anything further to the conversation.

"Well, if there's nothing else, then I'd best get going," he said, looking over her shoulder.

"Oh, sorry," she said, moving to one side.

"Thanks. I'll see you next week," he answered, slinging his

satchel over his shoulder.

"Yeah, I look forward to it, she said with that familiar sickly sweet smile.

Blake left the classroom and – although he didn't look back – he could still feel her eyes on him. He hurried down the corridor and was relieved to exit the building, and feel the sun on his face. He paused momentarily, breathing in the fresh air.

Then, he slipped on sunglasses and made his way to the football pitch at the rear of the college where, at the stalls, he sat next to a man in a blue tracksuit who was furiously blowing a whistle in between shouting abuse at the players on the pitch.

The rest of the benches were empty, except for a couple of academic spectators.

PE teacher Matt Allen was Blake's closest friend. He lived in Bude and looked nothing like a PE teacher. With short, dark wavy hair, a goatee, and an earring in his right ear, he looked more like a pop star than a teacher.

"How's it going?" Blake asked, taking a seat next to him.

"Could be better," he replied. Then, shouting to a player on the field, "Wakey, wakey, Dave! Try passing that bloody ball!" Then he said, without turning, "I tell you, I'd get a better game from a bunch of twelve year olds. So, how did it go with your little lot today?"

"Well, besides the creepy teen who's obviously O.D.'d on way too many episodes of Doomsday Preppers, and the girl who's itching to file a harassment case, it was a fantastic day," Blake said cheerfully, looking out at the players on the pitch.

"There you go, told you things would get better."

They exchanged glances. Matt smiled. "So, how is your number one fan?"

"The same," Blake replied indifferently.

"Maybe you should just give her one and have done with it."

"Thanks, Matt. Any other good advice on how to get myself fired, besides having an affair with one of my pupils?"

Matt grinned. "I didn't say have an affair with her, man."

He was obviously teasing, and this made Blake smile to himself as his friend proceeded to bark more instructions at his football team.

"Christ! Are they thick or what? I tell you, if United play

anything like this lot next week, we won't stand a fucking chance," Matt cursed, shaking his head in a hopeless gesture. Then, snapping back to his happy-go-lucky self, "Are we hitting the town tonight or what?"

"Sure, where do you fancy?"

"Anywhere we can get wrecked."

"That's understood."

"Plymouth it is, then." Then, shouting out to the field again, "I saw that, Jason! You do that once more and you're out... I mean it!"

"I'll leave you to it, then," Blake said, standing up.

"Cool, I'll see you tonight."

No sooner had Blake left than Matt was back to the football game in hand, shouting and gesturing at the players.

Blake walked back to his vehicle, climbed behind the steering wheel, and drove out, off the school grounds and into the busy Plymouth traffic, completely oblivious to the pair of green eyes that watched him until he was no longer in sight.

3

The atmosphere, 500 miles West of Heathrow Airport – England – 21:00 Local time.

The Boeing 747 lurched eastwards. It was on its way out of Orlando to London's Heathrow, with just over an hour left in its nine-hour journey. Ahead, the sky was a painting of reds and orange strokes, featuring flicks of white cloud. The northeast sky was an inky mass of darkness.

Adam hadn't been a qualified pilot for very long, and thus, as part of his induction, he had been assigned to the flight as 2nd Officer. This was his first transatlantic flight, and he was excited.

He noticed flashes of light up ahead and asked, "What was that,

Captain?"

"What was what?" Captain Richard Ormond replied, without turning around.

"I don't know – looked like flashes up ahead."

Peering out the glass, 1st Officer Geoff Harrison said, "I can't see anything."

"I'm sure I saw a light," Adam reasserted, frowning.

"Probably just a solar flare," Geoff suggested.

"No, it was more than… there!" Adam exclaimed, pointing to the horizon as another flicker manifested itself. "Did you see that?" Richard asked.

"Yeah," came Geoff's perturbed reply. "What do you think it is?"

"I'm not sure. We know there's a fairly large weather front to the northeast and—" he glanced at the instruments in front him, "radar confirms that, but the flight plan should take us safely around it."

Flicking a switch, Richard spoke into the microphone that hung in front of his mouth. "London approach, Endeavour 101."

There was a blare of static and then a metallic voice came through the cabin speaker.

"London approach; go ahead, Endeavour 101."

"London approach, we have eyes and radar confirms what appears to be some pretty choppy weather ahead. Our plan was supposed to take us around it but, now, we're not so sure. Could you tell us what you see?"

"Stand by, Endeavour 101"

"Do you think it's a tropical?" Geoff asked.

"I don't know what it is," Richard replied as another strobe of light ripped through the clouds. "Whatever it is, we best avoid flying straight into it."

The passenger cabin was quiet. But for the snoring of an elderly man in seat B42, most of the passengers were asleep. At the rear of the cabin, the flight attendants, Jane and Amanda, were busy talking in whispers.

In Seat C36, Tracy had had the misfortune of sitting next to a newlywed couple. They had spent most of the flight snogging. And when they weren't doing that, they were droning on about their honeymoon in Florida, and when they got bored with that, they insisted on laughing – loudly – at the seemingly endless selfies they'd snapped on their phones.

"This is us at Universal Studios..."

"This is us at the Epcot Centre..."

"This is us at..."

"...Shut the fuck up!"

At least, that's what Tracy wanted to say. Instead, she sat and smiled politely at their boundless enthusiasm.

It was no wonder that they both now sat with their heads lolling backward, forwards and sideways – with mouths wide open – as they slept. They had worn each other out!

Some people just don't have any manners, Tracy thought. Surely, they could have refrained from those noisy, slobbering kisses whilst a complete stranger sat in the seat next to them.

She sighed. Was it really the noisy kisses that irked her, or was it simply the fact that she was jealous? She had, after all, booked this trip to get away from the pain and the heartache she had felt, and was still feeling.

It should be me celebrating my honeymoon!

A tear slid down her pale cheek as, once again, she imagined the wedding, the dress, her family, friends, and the face of the man who should have been her husband.

She stared out of the window as the plane dipped its wings and began to bank left.

"Yes Sir, those new coordinates should see us avoid the worst of it," Adam said.

"I don't get why they didn't at least mention it to us earlier," the Captain grumbled.

"They said it was nowhere near us. The bloody thing shifted suddenly," the 1st Officer replied.

As the plane advanced, the storm grew closer. Now, the crew and the few passengers who were still awake could clearly see the huge mass of cumulonimbus clouds that had swallowed the amber glow of the sun in exchange for blackness.

Condensation was forming on the windscreen of the cockpit, and the flashing that had once been a small torchlight in the distance was now a menacing blanket of lightning.

"Should we warn the passengers?" Adam asked.

Richard pondered the question, and then confidently answered, "No. What's the point? Most of them are asleep anyway." Then, speaking into his mouthpiece again, he called, "London approach, this is Endeavour 101."

There was a pause, and more static, and then the familiar metallic voice once again, "Endeavour 101, London... a... ch... you have now.... tered..."

Another blast of static, and then nothing.

"London approach... Endeavour 101, London approach Endeavour 101."

Static...

"London approach, this is Endeavour 101 – please come in."

More static.

"What's happening?" Adam asked.

"It seems the storm's interfering with our radio," Geoff offered, dumfounded.

"It shouldn't do that, should it?" Adam continued.

Before Richard could answer, the plane dipped slightly, jolting the cockpit crew forward in their seats.

"What the hell was that?" Adam asked, looking around himself.

"Calm down, It's just turbulence."

The plane lurched forward again.

"Tighten your seatbelts," Richard instructed. Almost in unison, both pilots obeyed.

A bell chimed, the captain glanced at a monitor in front of him and then flipped a switch.

Seconds later, the cabin door opened and a pale-faced Amanda walked in. "What's going..." Her sentence was cut short as the plane dipped yet again.

"Wake the passengers. Tell them to fasten their seatbelts!" Richard ordered.

Without comment, Amanda left the cockpit, closing the door behind her.

Geoff flicked another switch on the panel above him, a bell sounded, and the "Fasten Seatbelts" light came on. Then, as Richard had before him, he attempted to establish radio contact with, at this stage, anyone who could hear them.

"Adam, I thought you'd plotted our course around the storm," Richard said.

"I didn't think I needed to," Adam panicked. "Look for yourself!" he added, pointing at the small monitor of the on-board weather radar, "there's a gap right through the cloud!"

Ignoring the young man's outburst, Richard glanced at the monitor, and then at his 1st Officer, who held his gaze and then shrugged. "I guess we don't have a choice. We're already committed – we're going to have to try and fly through it."

Outside, the condensation had turned into rain. It was now hammering on the windshield.

Inside, the once dormant passenger cabin was now a bustle of voices. Amanda and Jane were rushing up and down the aisle, responding to calls from apprehensive passengers whilst ensuring each and every one of them was seated with seatbelts securely fastened.

The old man in seat B42 had awoken from his slumber and was now swigging from a bottle of duty free scotch.

Tracy, in seat C36, glanced across at the newlyweds who had just moments before been snoring in a perfect symphony. She no longer envied them, as they huddled into each other, and instead, she wondered what their choice would be if they had to choose between life or each other.

Ha! Wanna' show me those pictures now?

"Excuse me… Miss? Miss?"

Tracy looked up to see a blonde flight attendant peering down at her.

"Yes?"

"Could you please fasten your seatbelt?"

"Of course." She complied, although she couldn't really give a shit about her seatbelt, for her mind was wandering once more.

She thought about Mark. What was he doing right now? Was he with *her*? She felt a surge of anger and watched as the weather outside sympathised by flashing, grumpily, and spitting rain at the window.

At the other end of the aircraft, Amanda joined Jane in the galley.

"Jesus! The whole bloody plane's in a panic, and that stupid cow was just sitting there, smiling out of the window."

"Probably frightened. Poor thing," Jane replied.

"Well, you seem pretty laid back... Shit!" Amanda cried as the plane suddenly lurched, hurtling her forward, but she managed to steady herself by grabbing onto one of the anchored trolleys.

"I've flown through loads of storms worse than this one," Jane carried on, ignoring her colleague's near mishap.

"Yeah, well, I haven't, and I'm starting to feel sick," Amanda retorted.

Inside the cockpit, the atmosphere had become tense. Adam's idea to fly through the weather front had proved an error of judgement.

Captain Richard Ormond had begun to sweat as he and his co-pilot clung to their controls in an attempt to level out the craft that was now bobbing and shaking as it was buffeted by turbulence.

"It feels like we're flying through a whole bloody bunch of storm cells!" Geoff declared.

Suddenly, all three men ducked, instinctively, as a rock struck and dented the windshield, leaving a mini crater in its wake.

"What the fuck was that?" Adam exclaimed.

"Hailstones," Geoff replied, ominously, "big ones."

Then, on cue, as if the co-pilot had just announced their arrival, an armada of the tennis-ball-sized boulders charged at the fuselage like a swarm of angry bees.

The plane sank once more.

"What happened to the gap?" Geoff questioned, incredulously.

Richard followed the co-pilot's gaze to the weather radar; the gap had closed in on them. They were now in the heart of the storm.

"Fuck..." Richard uttered, and then promptly jumped back in his seat as another crack appeared on the windshield. "We've got to get out of this!" He shouted over the din of the hammering storm, as he pulled back on the control column.

The engines laboured, loudly, as the plane began to climb and fork lightning stabbed one of the wings.

Fully aware of his mistake, Adam cowered – eyes wide with fear – his seat as the door chime sounded insistently.

Grunting under the strain, Richard began to say, "If we don't get out of this thing soon, we are going to…" His words were cut short as the plane began to shudder and one of the engines began to whine like whimpering animal.

Then, an alarm shrilled in the panel above their heads.

"Fire in engine one," Geoff said, quickly.

"Initiate shut down procedure!" Richard ordered.

Geoff complied.

Richard spoke into his headset, "This is Endeavour 101, declaring an emergency. We've sustained heavy damage and have lost one engine." The Captain's words were measured and eerily calm, given the situation and the fact that he was wrestling to retain control of his aircraft. "Repeat, this is Endeavour 101, declaring an emergency. We've sustained heavy damage and have lost one engine."

But there was no reply. Just static.

The cabin doorbell continued to chime insistently.

"Adam!" Richard yelled.

The young man finally jumped up from his seat, flipped a switch and the door burst open.

Amanda, her face creased into a mask of apprehension, burst in.

"Captain, are you aware that one of the engine's on fire?"

"Yes, we are." Geoff threw in, "I've just shut it down."

"You have?"

"Yes, Amanda, now, get out of here, can't you see we're in the middle of something?" Richard snapped.

"I don't understand," the Flight Attendant continued. "If you've shut it off then why is it still on and burning?"

The two pilots exchanged glances.

"Which engine are you talking about?" Geoff demanded.

"Two."

Now it was Geoff's turn to look perplexed. "Are you sure?"

"Yes I'm sure; the flames are licking at the bloody side of the plane! I've got passengers screaming!"

"But that can't be. The alarm said it was engine one…" Geoff trailed off here.

"Well, the alarm must be wrong," Amanda, insisted, "I know

what I saw. Come and see for yourself."

"Shut it down!" Richard ordered. "Adam, get back there and check."

However, as Adam moved to unbuckle himself, the aeroplane began to shudder, and then there was a thunderous whomph as something slammed into the side of them. The impact was so powerful it knocked Amanda off her feet and slammed her against the cockpit wall while conjuring a chaotic discord of alarms and buzzers that filled the cabin. Then, the aircraft slowly began banking right.

Richard reacted instantly by stepping on pedals and pulling at the control column, but it was having no effect. "What the hell is happening? Talk to me, Geoff!"

"Engines one and two are dead!" Geoff uttered, staring at his gauges in disbelief.

"That can't be….that's a whole side of the plane," Richard said through clenched teeth, as he battled to stall their gradual tilt and plunge to the right.

Geoff flicked several switches above him and waited anxiously for a reaction, but nothing happened. He flicked the switches on and off again, but still nothing.

"We've lost hydraulics," he declared, gravely.

The passenger cabin was now a dissonance of terrified screams as they fell, following the motion of the craft.

Jane were thrust onto the aisle floor as the old man in seat B42 lost his bottle and, in bizarre reaction to everything that was happening around him, groped on the floor in an attempt to apprehend it.

Tracy revelled in the terror of the couple next to her. She no longer cared for her life since life without Mark wasn't worth living anyway.

Looking out of the window, she marvelled at the colour of the lightning. It was unlike anything she had seen before. It blinked an eerie colour of green, or was it yellow? She couldn't quite make it out – it seemed different every time. Were these the colours of imminent death?

In the cockpit, Richard and Geoff battled against the will of the flying machine, but no matter they did, they were unable to regain control.

Behind them, eyes wide, white knuckles clinging to the control panel, Adam ignored his captain's cries for assistance. He was too petrified to move as he contemplated the watery grave that awaited him.

"Mayday! Mayday! Mayday! Endeavour 101!" Richard bellowed into his mouthpiece. "Can anybody hear us? We're in a dive! I repeat, we're in a dive!"

But the only response was the cacophony of the alarms and buzzers.

Whoop! Whoop! – Pull Up! Whoop! Whoop! – Pull Up! Whoop! Whoop! – Pull up! Too low! – Terrain! Too Low! – Terrain!

The weather continued to pummel Flight 101 with torrential rain, hailstones and gale force winds until it finally smashed into the icy waters of the Atlantic Ocean.

4

B road – 2 miles South of Bodmin Moor, England – 10:30 a.m.

Dr. Sky McPherson pushed off the car radio, putting Bob Dylan out of his misery. She'd unconsciously sung along with him for half the song, before she'd remembered she couldn't stand him, or any of that we-love-you-peace-man-music. In fact, she loathed it. Especially since, as always, Dylan had evoked thoughts of her parents, and she felt sad.

Sky had never truly felt that she had her parents' undivided attention, since she'd always had to share them with every good cause known to man. Something that had been immortalised in a black and white photograph of Sky, age two, sitting in a pushchair and holding a *PEACE FOR ALL - BAN THE BOMB* banner. The photograph had made the front page of the national press, and, by her parents' reaction, you would have thought they'd just discovered that their child could save the world.

Sky loved her parents, but she had made it her life's ambition not to be like them.

And it was this determination that had driven her to study hard, achieve her goals, and carve a career for herself. One that could afford all of the basic things she had been denied as a teenager, such as beauty products. Not that she needed them, for Sky was a natural beauty with long black hair, violet blue eyes and a fit body, honed by regular exercise and ritualistic yoga.

After living and working in London for five years, driving through the winding, narrow roads of Devon and Cornwall always made her feel as if she'd been liberated from some kind of metaphorical urban cage. And yes, she saw the irony. She'd worked so hard to forge her career, and yet she enjoyed her escape from the very city that had enabled her to succeed. Yet, her relatively new job as a forensic pathologist with the Cornwall Coroner may well have proved demanding and often stressful, but she loved it. She had become a fully-fledged forensic pathologist eight months back, and joining the Cornish Coroner in a senior post whilst also lending support to The Coroner for Exeter and Great Devon District was a major professional fulfilment.

The BMW passed a sign for Trevan, a picturesque village just off Bodmin Moor, that also told her to *please drive carefully*.

Five minutes later, she was piloting the car off the main road, and up bumpy dirt track.

There was a police car parked in front of the weather-beaten farmhouse. Next to it, a uniformed police officer talked to a nervous-looking postman. The pale-faced young man chattered while the officer took notes.

Sky stopped the car next to a Royal Mail van. As she left the vehicle, she noticed a heavy-set, middle-aged man with a moustache, dressed in a rumpled dogtooth suit, emerging from the house. She was opening the boot to the BMW and taking out her briefcase when he asked, "Doctor McPherson?"

"Yes," she replied, pressing the close button on the hatch.

"I'm Detective Inspector Morrison," he said in a cultured Cornish accent.

"It's nice to meet you," Sky said, shaking his hand.

"Likewise. You found it okay, then?"

"Sat Nav."

"Right. Sorry to trouble you on your day off. The usual doc is on a call and wouldn't be able to get to us for some time. This shouldn't take long."

"It's no problem. What do you have?"

They started toward the front door.

"Elderly woman. He found her," Morrison said, nodding at the postman, "when he tried to deliver a parcel this morning."

They stepped inside the house. A strong musty odour hung in the air. Faded wallpaper dissolved into the gloom of the place. They walked through a very short corridor, passing various paintings in cheap gold frames, and one large sepia photograph of a smiling young couple. Sky stopped and looked at the picture.

"I think that's her husband," Morrison offered.

"Where's he now?" she asked.

"Dead. A long time ago."

Sky nodded. "What about children?"

"A son – in Australia, I think."

Sky nodded whilst wondering how long it had been since he had last seen his mother.

"She's through here," Morrison said, interrupting Sky's thoughts and waving her into the nearby doorway.

The kitchen curtains were still drawn. A single beam of sunlight shone through them, casting an eerie spotlight over the dead body. The old woman was slumped over the kitchen table with her arms folded in front of her. Her grey hair was in plaits and it gleamed under the invading sun.

"We think she passed away in her sleep," Morrison said as Sky pulled on a pair of surgical gloves.

Sky nodded. "So, what's a detective inspector doing out here?" she asked casually as she opened her briefcase and took out a dictaphone.

Morrison smiled. "I was in the area. Not much happens around here so we tend to muck in wherever we can."

"I see," Sky replied. Then, moving over to the body, she began her preliminary examination.

She bent over and closely examined the old woman's face. Her eyes were sunken and her mouth was open, as if she'd frozen in that state after gasping for her last breath.

Sky spoke into the dictaphone, "Elderly lady, mid-eighties. Well nourished." She touched the old woman's face, delicately. "Probably been dead for, um... No apparent cause of distress."

She tried to push the body up in order to examine the woman's front, but grunted when it resisted.

Morrison came over and helped her move the corpse into a sitting position.

Sky examined the old woman's hands, the rest of her body and her neck. Then, speaking into the dictaphone again, "Preliminary examination suggests death by natural causes. The time is now…" She looked at her watch, and noted, "8:33 a.m."

"It was her birthday last week," Morrison said.

"Really?" Sky replied, looking up at him. "How old?"

"Eighty-four. That's why the postman was 'ere. He was delivering a parcel."

"From her son?"

"Looked like it."

"Any other relatives?" Sky asked, moving over to him and pulling off her gloves.

"I don't think so."

"Poor woman," she said, looking over the body. "She probably never even had the pleasure of seeing her grandchildren."

They emerged from the house, squinting into the sunshine. Morrison gestured at the police officer, who was still talking to the young postman; she nodded in acknowledgement, and spoke into her radio.

"We'll get her moved from here, then, if you could…."

"I'll get a report to you later on this morning," Sky anticipated.

"Thank you. So, how long are you going to be with us?"

"Well, I've agreed to a trial period of six months."

"Where are you staying?"

"Parkview, Exeter."

Morrison's eyes widened. "Nice," he said, appreciatively.

"Yes, it is," Sky agreed.

"Think you will miss the hustle and bustle of London?"

"I don't know. Maybe," she said thoughtfully. Then, looking around at the green rolling hills that surrounded them, she added,

"This morning, driving through Bodmin Moor, I realised that I've already developed a particular fondness for this county."

"And you fell in love with it."

Sky smiled.

"Happens all the time, you're smitten. You won't be able to leave us now," Morrison said.

Sky laughed, slipped into the driver's seat of her car, and added, "We'll see. It was good to meet you, Detective."

"Likewise."

She pulled the door shut, started the engine, and drove off.

Morrison watched the black BMW leave the dirt track and join the main road.

That was when a shadow smothered the surrounding countryside. He looked up; a giant black cloud had swallowed the sun.

5

Sea Emperor fishing trawler – 20 Miles Northwest of Newquay, England – 12:00 p.m.

The sun was hot as Arthur McElvoy stood on the deck of the forty-five-foot fishing trawler. Shading his eyes with his hands, he looked across the waters to the black clouds on the horizon. They did not look good.

We really should be heading back, he thought as a fresh breeze blew up around him, bringing with it the smell of rain. Thunder rumbled in the distance. It had been doing so for the past hour, and it seemed to be getting closer with every moan.

Arthur moved aft and joined the other three crewmembers who were busy deploying fishing nets with the help of a large hydraulic arm.

"I think we should head on back home," he said seriously,

scratching his beard.

"Why?" asked one of the heavier men. "We've only just got here."

"Because that storm's getting closer, Bill, and it ain't looking too good."

"You worry too much, old man." This time it was Glen, a skinny young man with a pasty complexion.

The sun hid, momentarily, behind a cloud.

"I thought you said we were going to miss the storm," said an overweight man in his fifties named Trevor.

"We were, but now the wind's gone and changed, 'asn't it? I'm telling you, they wouldn't have issued warning if it weren't serious."

Arthur was feeling nervous now. Not only was the storm getting closer, but the gale preceding it was growing stronger, and was now violently rocking the vessel.

"Look," Bill spoke again, but paused as more thunder cracked nearby. "I ain't leaving all these fish to those Spanish bastards. As it is, the fucking government's cut our fishing allowance. I've got a family to feed."

"Bill's right, Arthur," Trevor agreed.

"I vote we stay. I need the money," said Glen.

"We just need four more hours," Trevor began. Then, in a more coaxing tone, he added, "come on, Arthur, mate, we've been through much worse."

Arthur sighed, "We're not even supposed to be 'ere. It ain't right."

"It ain't right!" Bill echoed, losing his patience. "How can it not be right? We were born 'ere. My dad went fishing with your dad. These are our waters. We should have first catch, not some garlic-smelling Spaniard who's ruined the crop in his fucking waters and has come over 'ere to nick ours."

The others mumbled their approval as thunder cracked overhead, announcing the arrival of heavy, black rainclouds. They drifted ominously over the fishing trawler.

"It's the law, Trevor," Arthur stated, calmly.

"Fuck the law!" Glen spat.

"I don't get it. Don't you care about what's happening to our stocks?" Bill asked.

"Of course I do, just…" Arthur began.

"…I don't think you do, mate" Bill interrupted. "The stocks 'ere are getting less and less each year. There isn't enough for us, never mind a bunch of foreigners!"

"Yeah," Glen piped up again, "Why should we let those government wankers decide where, when and who should fish 'ere. It's our country. Just because they've gone Euro-fucking-mad, it doesn't mean the rest of us have!"

Arthur answered, but his voice was drowned in a massive thunderclap. The sky was now a blanket of billowing blackness, and the atmosphere was charged with electricity. Lightning flashed as the men contemplated both the weather and what had just been said.

"Look, at the end of the day, you're the skipper, if you say we 'ed on 'ome then that's what we'll do," Trevor reasoned, "but I can tell you, it ain't right, mate. It ain't."

Arthur thought about this. As much as he didn't like it, the boys were right. He looked at the sky and then at the ocean. It was relatively calm, and they had been through worse, much worse. Eventually, he said, "Okay…go get the kettle on. Let's have a brew."

"Yes!" Glen punched the air and scampered off.

"What about you, mate?" Trevor asked.

"I'm just going to make sure the nets are secured, so we can ride out this weather."

"I'll help ya'."

"Nah, you're alright. You go on ahead. I'll be there in a few."

"You sure?"

"Yeah, I'm sure," Arthur confirmed, staring out to sea.

"Don't take too long, it's going to chuck it down any second," Trevor said, patting his friend on the shoulder.

The rain was nearly upon them. Arthur could see it approaching as a distant mist. Just minutes before, the sun had been shining in a clear blue sky, and now; day had turned into night.

Arthur McElvoy watched as the wall of rain sped across the ocean towards him.

He was drenched in seconds.

6

Environment Agency HQ – Bristol – 15:00.

The Environment Agency had over 10,000 staff, working out of offices across England. All with one purpose – *'create better places for people and wildlife, and support sustainable development'*.

It was a 'non-departmental' public body, which meant that while it wasn't run by British Parliament, it was nonetheless accountable to it, via its ministers. Furthermore, the agency's board was under appointment by the Secretary for Environment, Food and Rural Affairs.

This was something that amused Blake, since he'd lost count of the times he'd heard his boss crow about the fact that the agency was an 'independent body', when there was no doubt in his mind that, ultimately, all roads led back to London.

Riding the elevator to the fifth floor, Blake wondered how long the meeting would last today.

His didn't enjoy staff meetings. He'd much rather be out doing his job than sitting in a room and talking about doing it. Worse, he knew that once Hamilton started talking, there was no stopping him. The man did love the sound of his own voice.

The bell sounded and the elevator doors opened. Blake made his way down the corridor decorated with an assortment of posters. One featured blue and white text on a black background that read, *"The Ocean Doesn't need a Facelift. Say NO to plastic!"* Another showed a beautifully blue image of planet Earth, as seen from space, with the tagline, *"There is no planet B."* Another featured the photograph of a solitary black refuse bag abandoned on the side of a road. The caption read, *fly tipping is a crime.*

The posters continued until Blake rounded a corner and

stopped in front of a reception desk. Behind it, a blonde girl in her twenties was keying information into a computer.

"Hello, Melissa," Blake said, smiling. "Is he in there?"

The girl looked up and returned the smile, "Hello, Blake. They're all in there, and you, naughty boy, are late!" She made a show of biting her lip.

"I know, I know. Traffic," he said, walking across the hall to a set of double doors.

Without knocking, he pushed the doors open. Inside the spacious room was a large, oval boardroom table surrounded by fifteen chairs. All were taken but one.

"You're late," said a spindly man with spectacles. He was sitting at the far end of the table. He was Hamilton, and he was Blake's boss.

"Sorry, traffic," Blake apologised, shrugging, and slipping into the free chair. He nodded at various people as they smiled at him.

"Right," Hamilton said, decisively. "Let's, finally, get this meeting underway." He glanced at some papers on the table in front of him. "The Prime Minister has a bee in his bonnet about this power station in Derbyshire. As you may have noticed, Number 10 is still getting a lot of flak from the press about it. And now, to make things worse, some bloody action group has published what it believes is" – he made quotations with his fingers – "'*compelling proof*' that the place is making people sick. Now, what the hell is going on, David?"

Hamilton was looking very expectantly at a blonde thirty-year-old man, three seats down on his right. "Have the six months you've spent investigating this place been a waste of time?"

"No, of course not," David replied.

"Is there any truth to these rumours? Do you even have the foggiest yet?"

"No. There's no truth. We've completed tests and the place is safe. Those are just the fabrication of a bunch of activists with nothing better to do with their time. They've failed to submit any actual, tangible evidence."

"Well, the PM doesn't seem to think so, and nor does the bloody media."

"I'm telling you, it's old news," David said, waving his hand apathetically.

"Hey!" Hamilton snapped, leaning forward in his chair, his eyes narrowing menacingly. "It obviously not old news, because if it were, I wouldn't be mentioning it to you today, would I?"

An awkward silence fell over the room.

"Would I, David?" Hamilton prompted.

"No," David acknowledged in the tone of a small boy who had just been spanked for misbehaviour.

"Maybe we should re-open the investigation," suggested a statuesque brunette, named Jackie.

"And risk looking incompetent in the eyes of the press?" answered an older man next to her.

"It's no worse than those doctors forcing the issue and bringing the whole mess out in the open again. Right now, the focus is, surprisingly, still on the issue. If we don't act, we'd be feeding them a new angle; we failed the original investigation and we failed to act even when new supposed evidence was published."

Hamilton smiled proudly.

"I agree with Jackie." It was David speaking up. He straightened in his chair as if to encourage himself to speak. "It's my investigation. I would like to re-open it," he said, knowing that this was exactly what Hamilton wanted; the man just expected him to say it, thereby acknowledging that he had not done his job properly in the first place.

"Good," Hamilton replied, smiling wryly. "I want a preliminary report by the end of next week."

David nodded in agreement.

Then, flipping to a cheerful mood again, Hamilton continued, "So, what's next?" He looked around the table. To his left, first seat down, sat Terry, a burly thirty-year-old man with curly black hair. He was holding up his hand.

"Oh yes, Terry," Hamilton nodded, knowingly. "You wanted to discuss something."

"Yes, it's referencing a call I received from one of my contacts at the Met Office. He told me about this mass of cloud..."

He produced two sheets of paper from a folder, and slid them across the desk. One sheet was a black and white satellite photograph of a swirling cloud. The other a printout containing meteorological information.

Hamilton studied both sheets whilst Terry continued, "You'll see from the printout that this cloud contains an unusually high content of Nitrous Dioxide, lead, and a high level of an, as of yet, unidentified toxin."

Hamilton nodded.

"Well, my contact has been tracking it and he says that it originates from somewhere in Northern Europe."

Hamilton finally looked up, and shrugged his shoulders. "And?"

"Well, I thought it might be a good idea to continue monitoring it for precipitation and, if necessary, obtain some samples and have the lab run tests."

"What for?"

"Well, for content. If those figures are accurate, the rain from this cloud could be extremely toxic."

"Killer rain?" Hamilton asked, eyebrows lifting inquisitively.

"Possibly. Paul, my contact, said that this cumulous nimbus could well have formed over Iceland…"

"…Yes, thank you, Terry," Hamilton interrupted.

"…If so, that recent explosion at the chemical plant could have…"

"I said, thank you. That will be all, Terry," Hamilton said, firmly. Then, smiling sweetly, he added, "We really do need to press on. Can we discuss this in more detail after the meeting?"

"Of course," Terry agreed.

"Good. So, what's next?" Hamilton asked, consulting his notes, "Ah, yes, Jackie, Fibredome, and the river pollution."

For the next two and a half hours, the team discussed various environmental issues relating to their assigned territory, as well as collaborative investigations with other offices in different regions of the country. Subjects ranged from fishing quotas through to flooding, as well as waste management and conservation.

It was with tired and bleary eyes that Blake finally glanced at his watch. It was five-thirty, and Hamilton was still droning on in the background.

Suddenly, the noise stopped.

"Are we keeping you, Blake?" Hamilton asked.

"Sorry? What was that?" Blake asked, snapping out of his daze.

"Never mind," the man replied. "I think that'll be all for today. Terry, don't forget that analysis report. I need it by the end of the week. Oh, and by the way…." He stood up, gesturing for Terry to follow him to the other side of the room.

Blake stood up from his swivel chair and grabbed his suit jacket from the backrest.

The room was a medley of chatter, shuffling papers and ringtones as agents reactivated the sounds on their phones before making their way towards the exit. Blake looked across at Hamilton, who was now standing in the corner of the room with Terry.

"See you later," he called out to them.

But neither of them replied, for they were both deep in conversation. Whatever Hamilton was saying, it was making Terry frown.

The drive home was hot and humid. There was a tailback on the motorway, due to a jack-knifed lorry. The police, and what seemed to be all of the emergency services, were at the scene. A grim-faced officer wearing a fluorescent jacket ushered the Range Rover slowly along. Blake spotted the mangled tin can that was the Ford Fiesta.

On the road, ten yards away, lay the body of the driver; ambulance men were huddled around it. Further on, he could see two bundles on the tarmac, both covered with black plastic black sheets.

Blake switched on the radio and inhaled with relief as he, eventually, was able to pick up speed and put some distance between himself and the scene. He was suddenly very eager to get home.

"…The Cornish Coast Guard has started the search for a missing fishing trawler. The Sea Emperor lost radio contact some time late this afternoon. Stephen Norton has the details…"

7

Coast Guard speed cruiser – Sixty miles south of the Cornish coast – 21:00.

The speed cruiser moved slowly through the eerily calm waters of the Atlantic Ocean.

The searchlight on the bow probed the darkness as both men, subconsciously, leant forward from their position in the cabin. As if by doing so they would be able to see further into the night.

"Where the hell is she?" Gary, the heavier of the two men asked, breaking the ten-minute silence.

Mike, his colleague, glanced at the radar screen in front of him. It was lifeless.

"God knows. According to the coordinates, we should be right on top of her."

"At least the bloody weather's calmed down," said Gary.

"Yeah, one minute a storm and the next..." Mike left the sentence unfinished, but he was referring to the ocean's calm.

Something about it unsettled him.

"Do you think they've gone under?" Gary asked in a whisper.

"I don't know," Mike answered as the radar suddenly beeped to life, startling them both.

Mike smiled. "At last."

"Hold your horses. It might not be them."

"Of course it's them," Mike stated, grinning at his colleague. "How much do you wanna' bet?"

"Let's just wait and see."

Gary pushed the throttle and the boat leapt forth, speeding toward the unidentified dot on the radar screen.

Five minutes later, the white fishing trawler appeared like a phantom in the night.

"Told you!" Mike said happily, as they drew closer to the boat and the words *Sea Emperor*, hand-painted onto the bow, revealed themselves under the searchlight.

Something about Mike's complacency irritated Gary.

"Shall I radio base and tell them that we've found her?"

"No, not yet," came Gary's swift reply. "Let's have a look on board first."

"You're the boss," Mike complied, still grinning as if the whole affair was one of his practical jokes.

Gary killed the engine. Both men fell silent as the cruiser drifted toward the ghostly vessel. The only sound was the rippling and sloshing of water.

The cruiser's powerful searchlight scanned the fishing trawler, illuminating a boat that didn't appear to have sustained any superficial damage.

So why did Gary feel so damn uneasy?

Mary Celeste.

He shivered.

Years of early morning fishing expeditions on the Atlantic Ocean had taken their toll on the Sea Emperor. The white paint that covered most of the ship had been diluted to faded grey, and the once bright red trim was now a tired orange. A small cabin with re-enforced, salt-stained glass windows sat in the middle of the vessel, like a mini lighthouse.

Only, the cabin was shrouded in darkness. There was no sign of life.

"Hello, on board!" Mike shouted, breaking the silence and obviously startling Gary, much to his amusement. He grinned his childish grin.

No reply.

"Probably all stoned," he added, throwing a rope over to the craft.

"Hello, Sea Emperor. It's the Coast Guard!"

Just the sound of water sloshing against the bow.

As Gary fastened the rope, joining the two boats, Mike disappeared into the cruiser's cabin and reappeared moments later, carrying two flashlights. He handed one to Gary and then, with a deep sigh, he climbed off the rescue boat and onto the trawler.

Nothing appeared to be out of order. In fact, everything seemed very much in its place, right up to the gleaming surfaces of the deck.

"Hello?"

The deathly silence continued to cocoon them both and the nervousness that taunted Gary had now spread over to Mike. "Enough to give you the creeps, innit?" he asked, wiping the beam of his flashlight over the deck.

"You're not kidding. Hello!" He called out. His voice was devoured by the expanse that surrounded them, but it gave nothing in return.

"What about inside the cabin?" Mike suggested as the beam of his flashlight revealed the door cavity.

Both men entered as their lights scared back the darkness.

"Doesn't look like much has been going on here," Mike said.

"Nah," Gary replied, distracted.

Where the hell is everybody? Could they have fallen overboard during the storm? All of them?

"Is there anybody on board?" He shouted into the gloom.

"Let's take a look down there," Gary said, shining light over the wooden steps that led into the bowels of the vessel.

The compartment was relatively small; twin bunk beds, a couple of battered lockers, and a screwed-down table, surrounded by benches.

In the corner stood a gas stove, normally used to boil water and reheat the occasional stew that had been lovingly prepared by one of the fishermen's wives.

Everything looked fine. As if the vessel had simply navigated itself here, without its crew.

"Looks like they just decided to abandon ship," Mike said.

"Yeah, but they thought they'd leave the place nice and clean for when we got here," Gary replied, scanning the rest of the claustrophobic space.

"What do you mean?"

"Didn't you notice the deck? It was practically polished."

Mike's eyebrows lifted. "What are you saying? That they decided to clean up, before diving overboard?"

"I'm not say anything specific. I'm just saying that everything looks too damn…"

The words escaped him.

"Let's just tow her back to shore. Let the police handle it," Mike said, starting back up the wooden steps, but he stopped when Gary suddenly grabbed his arm, making him jump.

"What the…" He didn't finish his sentence, for he had turned around to see his partner shining the light of his torch to his face, spotlighting a hushing finger over his lips. That same finger moved, and pointed across the room, at one of the lockers.

Gary had heard something. He wasn't quite sure what, but the noise was definitely coming from within one of the lockers.

Mike descended the two steps, quietly.

Then, as if guided by telepathic communication, the two men moved in synchronisation. Neither of them knew what exactly they were going to find in the locker, but both made their approach a cautious one. As they drew near, they could see that the metal actually rattled at regular intervals.

Slowly, flashlights aimed like weapons in front of them, they took up positions on either side of the cabinet.

Gary held up five fingers, and mouthed the numbers in ascending order as he closed each one.

Five…

Mike glanced at him nervously, then at the locker again.

Four…

Rattle.

Three…

The boat groaned and began to sway as a gale blew up outside.

Two…

Hearts pounding. Breaths held.

Rattle!

One!

Gary yanked the locker door open and gaped, open-mouthed, at the naked man crouched inside.

What was left of the old man's balding grey hair was matted to his head. His knees were drawn up close to his face and his hands were clasped tightly together on top of them.

He was shivering. His lips blue, his face pale. He did not react when the locker door was opened. He just sat, motionless, eyes wide but unseeing.

"Jesus Christ…" Mike whispered as he released his breath.

"Get a blanket from one of those bunk beds," Gary ordered.

He knelt down next to the man who he estimated must have been in his late sixties.

"It's all right. We're not gonna' hurt you," Gary said reassuringly. "What's your name, mate? Can you tell me your name?"

No reply was forthcoming, but he wasn't surprised. The man seemed to be in shock.

Mike returned with the blanket. Gary took it off of him and draped it, the best he could, over the shivering, fragile frame of the old man.

"Can you tell us what happened here, mate?" Mike asked in a raised voice, as if the man were deaf.

"He's in shock. We better get him to the boat," Gary said.

"Good idea."

They half-coaxed, half-pulled the man out of the closet.

He offered no resistance, but made his rescuers jump out of their skin when he let a metal fishhook slip from his hands and clatter, loudly, to the deck.

The two men exchanged glances, but said nothing. Instead, they hurried up the wooden steps.

The gale whipped around the trio as soon as they emerged from the cabin. It tugged at the hessian blanket and slapped it across the old man's bare legs as they carefully crossed over to the cruiser.

On board, Mike, immediately disappeared into the cabin, and returned with what looked like a large sheet of tin foil. He wrapped it around the old man, who remained expressionless throughout.

"There you go, mate. This should keep you warm." Then, to Gary, he asked, "what are we gonna' do?"

"We're gonna' have to get him back to shore."

"What about the others?"

"We'll radio back coordinates. Get search and rescue out here. Hopefully, they'll be able to get more sense from him back at base."

"What about the boat?"

"We'll tow it back with us now."

"Okay."

Mike moved aft of the cruiser and pulled hard on a towing line. The cable whizzed loudly as it unravelled from the cog. Once he had pulled enough slack to reach the Sea Emperor, he climbed back on board and fastened it.

"Okay!" he shouted.

"Good. Let's get going."

Mike had started to climb back onto the cruiser when he noticed that the fishing nets were still deployed. "The nets are still out!"

Gary was helping the man into the cruiser's cabin. "Bring them in, but make it snappy," he shouted back without looking around.

"Roger that," Mike complied.

He moved to the back of the trawler, and was relieved to find that the nets were retracted electronically. He pulled the lever, and a powerful searchlight, mounted on the top of the cabin, sprang to life, illuminating a patch of ocean. Then, there was a whirring and cranking sound as the giant metal arm that hung out of the back of the boat started upward.

Mike watched, impatiently, as the net slowly emerged from the water.

They had obviously caught a lot of fish, since the sound of the motor began to shift, pitch and whine as it laboured under the strain.

Mike stared at the surface of the water as he waited for whatever was weighing down the net to appear. He half-expected it to be a shark, and the last thing he wanted was one of those things thrashing and gnashing its teeth at him in the semi-darkness.

And that's when he spotted it. He squinted as he tried to decipher the blur beneath the surface of the water, but there was no mistaking the large pale blob.

It is a shark!

He peered closer as the ghostly apparition began to materialise before him, and then quickly jumped backward; it wasn't a shark he was seeing, but something worse.

Something much worse.

The net slowly emerged from the ocean with its hideous cargo that dripped water like icicles in the white of the floodlight.

Mike opened his mouth to scream, but no sound emerged. He moved to leave, but his feet were frozen to the deck, such was the horror of what he was seeing.

Then, the motor stopped whirring. The net hung, heavily for a few seconds, before, suddenly, swivelling inward, towards the very spot Mike now occupied.

He finally found his feet and turned to run, but slipped on the wet surface and, with arms flailing, fell heavily onto his back. He lay there, eyes shut, as a painful spasm shot up his spine and into his skull. Then, he opened his eyes, just in time to see the net split open and spew its contents onto him, pinning him to the deck.

The weight squeezed the breath from his body as he lay there, frozen with terror as the smell of fish and dead flesh flooded his nostrils. He could barely see, for his face was covered with seaweed and crawling with sea urchins. Only his right eye remained partially uncovered, and its eyeball swivelled, frantically as it searched for any sign of Gary. Mike opened his mouth to scream, but gagged as one of the creatures from the net scrambled inside. He coughed and spluttered, tasting salt water and involuntarily crunching down on the unwelcome guest. A ball of bile rose in the back of his throat as he started to gag.

Then, suddenly, the weight eased on his body. Gary was standing over him with an incredulous expression on his face. He was saying something, but Mike's terror-stricken brain refused to translate it.

What was happening? What was the weight on top of him? It could not be what he thought it was; that wasn't possible. That would be just too hideous. Too incompressible...

Gary yanked his colleague to his feet.

"Mike! Mike! Are you all right? Mike?"

But Mike just stumbled away, coughing out the sushi from his mouth and spattering the gleaming deck with vomit.

It took several seconds for Gary to comprehend the scene before him.

It was a mound of death.

The naked corpses of what remained of the Sea Emperor's crew lay with their legs and arms entwined around each other, like a macabre sexual orgy. It was a grotesque catch of human suffering; gaping neck wounds, hacked limbs, genital mutilation, and mouths that had been pulled wide by metal fishhooks. The grey eyes gazed at him with lifeless terror, as if crying, imploring him for mercy on a horror bestowed upon them erstwhile.

It started to spit rain again as Gary stood on the deck of the Sea Emperor and wept.

8

Newquay Police Station. 23:51.

When Detective Inspector Morrison entered the interview room, he winced; the smell of seaweed and a medley of other odours hung heavily in the air.

Now dressed in a grey jump suit, and draped in the same silver tin foil, the old man sat behind a battered wooden desk in the centre of the stark grey interview room.

His eyes remained sunken and expressionless, just as they'd been when he'd arrived.

Morrison glanced at the wall mirror, almost as if seeking reassurance from it, but he didn't know why.

He sat in a chair opposite the old man, who continued to ignore his visitor, and seemed to have adopted an obsessive interest in the invisible patterns on the table.

The room was silent, but for the shallow breathing of the detainee.

"Hello," Morrison said, tentatively.

No reply.

"I'm Detective Inspector Morrison. What's your name?"

Nothing.

At fifty years of age, and having been in the force for almost thirty of those, Morrison knew that a suspect as quiet as this one was not to be trusted. "Arthur, we've contacted your wife. She's on her way over here. She's very worried about you."

Silence. The man's eyes didn't even blink at the mention of his wife.

"The doctor's checked you over, mate. He says there isn't anything physically wrong with you, apart from mild hyperthermia and dehydration. So, why aren't you talking to me, Arthur, huh?"

Still no movement or reaction of any kind.

From behind the two-way mirror, PC Baxter, a twenty-two-year-old ginger-haired man, known as "Ginger" to his friends and colleagues, watched Morrison trying to coax the bearded man into talking to him. Twenty minutes or more ticked by, and no matter what Morrison said, the old man didn't so much as even glance at him. He just stared at the table.

Then, Ginger was mid-yawn when the old man's head suddenly snapped up.

Morrison was taken aback as he found himself staring directly into the old man's cold, black, dead eyes.

Shark eyes!

Only these sat deep in their sockets, scrutinising him with expressionless curiosity that sent a chill scuttling down the veteran's spine.

Oh shit!

Morrison moved to leave his seat, but he was too late.

Through the two-way mirror, Ginger watched as the ineffectual old man leapt over the desk with the speed and agility of a striking panther. He crashed into Morrison, toppling the man backwards in his chair. They both fell, sprawling to the floor, where he clamped his bony fingers around the detective's throat and proceeded to choke the life out of him.

"Fuck!" Ginger exclaimed.

Before long, Morrison's head started pounding in a silent scream for oxygen as he kicked and clawed, but to no avail.

His assailant's attack was frenzied, relentless.

The police officers stormed into the interview room, where the once mute man was now gargling and screaming a stream of incomprehensible words as he squeezed his hands with homicidal intent.

Seconds were like minutes, and voices were like echoes as Morrison's mind clouded, and a parade of thoughts drifted to the fore: his childhood, wife, children, life, and death.

The neon light above his head darkened. Raised, hollow voices cried out as Ginger and his two colleagues attempted to pry the vice-like fingers away and wrench the rabid creature from him.

Somewhere, someone triggered the alarm. It sounded loudly, as two more officers piled into the small room.

All four men attempted to detach the old man from their commanding officer, but all appeared to be powerless against his super-human strength.

"Get him off him! Get him off!" Ginger garbled through gritted teeth and spittle as they pulled the demented man upward from the floor in a medley of grunts, groans, strains and swearing.

Yet, still, the thin, bony fingers remained coiled around the D.I's throat until, suddenly, they relinquished their hold, and metamorphosed into a fist that swung at Ginger, hitting him squarely in the cheek and sending him reeling backwards, over the table and to the floor.

It took the young officer a few seconds to recover. "You bastard," he seethed. He picked himself up and lunged back into the fray.

The room was a conglomeration of shouting from the police officers and wailing from the old man as they struggled to restrain him.

Meanwhile, Morrison was on his knees, coughing, spluttering, and gasping for air.

That's when, with one last inhuman shrug, the old man literally flung all four officers off of him and to the four corners of the room as he started toward the door, only to stop, abruptly, as his legs buckled beneath him.

He collapsed to the floor, where he began to thrash, spasmodically, around, like a malfunctioning humanoid, as his eyes rolled up into their sockets, until just the whites could be seen. Then, he arched his back, as if someone had just zapped a high voltage through him, until he froze that way.

"Get a doctor!" Ginger yelled through gasps.

One of his colleagues promptly scurried out of the room, careful not to tread on the *thing* on the floor.

Then, as unexpectedly as it had all started, it ended.

No more thrashing or screaming, just silence as the old man lay there, motionless, the whites of his eyes blindly stared at the ceiling as everyone else simply stood around him, panting and wheezing in total astonishment.

9

Plymouth College, England.

The smell of trainers, disinfectant and a medley of other inimitable school odours grabbed Sky, and dragged her back to her academic years that, whilst not altogether unpleasant, were nonetheless a time she'd prefer to keep firmly in the past.

Her footsteps clicked loudly and she made her way down the main corridor, passing photographs of sporting events, framed diplomas, and a conglomeration of printed and hand-written posters of all sizes, each vying for the attention of everyone and anyone who cared. She passed a group of students loitering near the staircase to the next floor. One of them wolf-whistled her.

She turned and smiled at the trio of young lads, dressed in jeans, T-shirts and branded footwear. When she looked back at where she was going, she collided with a longhaired young man. The impact knocked the bag off her shoulder and sent his phone clattering to the floor.

He retrieved the device, gave her a dirty look, and then resumed his journey.

"Oi!" Somebody shouted from further down the corridor.

The boy stopped instantly.

"What the hell do you think you're doing?" Matt Allen asked, walking up to them. "Andrew, how many times have I got to tell you not to text and walk in the corridor?"

"There's no damage done, honestly," Sky interjected, retrieving her bag.

"No, this isn't the first time and he's got to realise that…" …he stopped in mid-sentence as he noticed her stunning blue eyes.

"Um, you didn't even apologise," Matt muttered, without taking his eyes off her.

"There's really no need," Sky smiled awkwardly.

Matt ignored her, turned to the boy, and asked, "Well, what have you got to say for yourself?"

"I'm sorry," the boy mumbled.

"I'm sorry," Matt mimicked. "Oh, go on, get out of here," he added, jerking a thumb down the corridor.

The boy scuttled off and resumed texting.

"I can still see you, you know!" Matt shouted after him. Then, maintaining eye contact with Sky, he thrust out a hand and smiled, warmly, "Hello, I'm Matthew Allen, P.E. instructor."

"Never have guessed," Sky said knowingly.

"Oh, right," Matt smiled, looking himself up and down; he was wearing a tracksuit.

"I'm Sky, Sky McPherson," she said, shaking his hand.

"Sky... what a great name."

"Thank you."

"So, are you a new teacher here?"

She laughed.

"Please tell me you are," Matt said in mock imploration.

"No, I'm afraid not. But, I am looking for the principal's office."

"Well, you're on course," he said, pointing to the end of the corridor. "It's just down there – turn left and carry on until the end. Actually, I'm going that way. I'll walk with you."

"Are you sure that's no trouble?"

"It would be my pleasure."

"Okay."

They started down the corridor.

"So, are you from around here?" Matt asked.

"Well, I am now. I'm on a six-month placement here."

"So you are a teacher," Matt said excitedly.

"No. I'm a forensic pathologist."

"A pathologist?" Matt echoed.

"Yes, I know, not very glamorous," she said.

"I would never have guessed."

They walked a few more steps in silence, and then he asked, "So, what brings you to our school?"

"I need to talk to one of the girls here. There was an incident involving her uncle yesterday evening."

"Oh, right. That would be Clare."

"You know who that is?"

Matt nodded.

"I dropped by her house. Her aunt told me that she'd come into class today."

"Yeah, I know. It's amazing, although to see her, you wouldn't think anything was wrong."

"Why do you say that?"

"Well, after her uncle's death, I'd have expected her to be in bits, but instead she's strutting around college like without a care in the world."

"Well, people deal with grief in different ways. Maybe she wasn't as close to her uncle as you think," Sky suggested.

"Maybe. Although, he and his wife did pretty much raise her after her parents died," Matt said thoughtfully, and then added in a hushed tone, "Hey, do you know what happened to him? The radio said that he died in police custody. Is that true?"

They stopped outside a door marked *Administration – Please Knock.*

Sky pulled a face and shrugged.

"Oh, you can't discuss it. Right?"

She nodded.

"Okay, well, we're here."

"Thank you. I appreciate the escort, Matt."

"Oh, you're welcome. Please, get lost again soon."

They laughed.

He was cute, but she was running late. "I'd better get in there," she said.

"Right, okay…well, nice meeting you."

"And you," she offered, then turned and knocked on the door.

***

The sky shone brightly in a clear blue sky, and a spring breeze rustled through nearby trees. On the football pitch, the blue and white teams were running around, tackling each other as they vied for control of the football.

As Blake watched them through the window of the empty classroom, he wondered what exactly so many people found addictive about the game. He didn't like football very much; he preferred rugby, but he was looking forward to the final next week.

It was when the white team scored a goal that Blake felt the presence. Someone had entered the classroom, and was standing behind him.

He turned around to see Clare McElvoy, watching.

"Clare…." he said, surprised.

"Hello, Mr. Hudson," she said, clutching the ubiquitous bundle of books to her chest.

"We weren't expecting to see you here today," he said, staring at the books.

The girl shrugged, "Why not? I am a student here, right?"

She followed that with one of her sweet smiles. There was something about that smile, today of all days, that unsettled Blake.

"Well, you've suffered a great loss…" He let the words hang, deliberately, so he could gauge her reaction.

When the girl's eyebrows lifted, he felt that he had to justify himself. "Didn't the police come to see you?"

"Yes. But they've gone now," she said casually. "They came around in the early hours. I think it was about 04:00." She shook her head, "It took me ages to get back to sleep." Her eyes widened. "I was nearly late for class!" Then, her smile faded and she cocked her head to one side, like an inquisitive bird. "What are you doing here? It's Tuesday. You don't have class until Friday."

The girl's question was so unexpected that Blake actually found himself replying. "I've just dropped by to pick Mr. Allen up. His car's in the garage."

Why was he explaining himself to this girl? She was the one who shouldn't been here. The one that should have been at home, grieving the death of her uncle.

In what was an instinctive response, he stepped forward and held both of the girl's arms, lightly. Then, in a soothing voice, he said, "Clare, I don't think you should be here."

The girl said nothing. Instead, she just closed her eyes, breathed deeply, and said, breathlessly, "I've been waiting for this for a long time."

And, before Blake even had the chance to absorb the words, he felt himself being tugged forward and kissed, full on the lips.

Her embrace was strong and demanding.

Blake's refusal was equally so.

He pushed her away, "What the hell do you think you're doing?" He wiped his mouth with the back of his hand, as if by doing so he could erase what had just happened.

"I was kissing you," she replied casually.

His brain froze. He did not know what to do or say to this girl. Her uncle had died last night and today she appeared totally indifferent.

Worse.

She just kissed me!

He started forward. "I think we should get you home," he said, walking past her.

"Great," she squealed with delight. "Are you taking me?"

He stopped. Turned around and said firmly, "No. I'll get the staff nurse to take you."

"Don't bother," she said, losing her smile. "I've got a lecture to go to."

"Clare," he began, and then, searching for the words, he said, "You can't stay here."

"Why not?"

His mind was reeling. What if someone had witnessed what had just happened?

"Because it isn't healthy," he blurted out.

"Who says so?"

"I say so."

"Why?"

"Because it isn't."

"Why isn't it?"

"It just isn't, okay?" he said, angrily. He took a few seconds to compose himself. The girl was unsettling him, and it was showing. "I'd better get to Mr. Allen or he's going to think I've forgotten about him," he said, moving to leave. He was eager to get out of the room and away from her. He would visit Administration on his way out.

"I saw you," she said, stopping him in his tracks.

"I'm sorry?" he asked.

"I saw you at The Pit with Mr. Allen."

Blake turned to face her. Her eyes had that mischievous sparkle in them again.

"You were there with those two girls," she continued in a reprimanding tone.

This conversation was insane.

"I don't know what you're talking about," Blake said.

Although, he remembered Friday night very clearly. He could not remember exactly how many drinks he and Matt had knocked back, but he did remember picking up Leticia and Marie, and ending up at the nightclub famously known as *The Pit*.

Clare continued, as if reading his thoughts, "I know them; they're a right pair of sluts."

Her statement was expressionless.

"Really?" came Blake's feeble response.

"You really shouldn't hang around with girls like that. You'll be getting a reputation."

"Well, thank you, Clare. I'll be sure to bear that in mind, next time I'm out, socialising."

He had tired of this conversation.

"You should meet up with Tracy and me. We go to The Pit every Friday night. Will you be there this week?"

"No, I don't think so," he said, firmly.

"Why not?"

"It's just not my scene."

"It looked like it was your scene last week."

"Well, we were just checking the place out."

"You didn't seem to be paying much attention to the establishment."

"Where were you? I didn't see you," he said, changing the line of conversation.

"Oh, we were there," she said, as another faint smile parted her lips.

A few seconds ticked by. He just stared at her. Eventually, he said, "I need to get going," and walked away.

"Matt," she said after him.

Blake stopped once more. "What?"

"His name's Matt, isn't it?"

"That's right, Clare. His name is Matt," he said impatiently, and added, "but to you or any other student in this college, his name is Mr. Allen."

"That isn't what he asked me to call him the other night."

"I'm sorry?" Blake asked, irritated.

"That's right. He told me not to call him Mr. Allen the night he took me for a drive in his car."

"What are you saying?" he asked, tentatively, for he was afraid of the answer.

The girl didn't reply immediately. She deliberately kept him in suspense for a few seconds, and then she blurted out, "I'm saying that Mr. Allen showed me a good time."

"You mean he took you out."

She laughed, "I mean he showed me a good time. Come on, you must know what I'm talking about, Mr. Hudson. Or can I call you Blake?"

"It's Mr. Hudson," he retorted.

Clare just smirked off his coldness. "He took me out to this isolated beach he knows."

Blake's heart skipped a beat. He did know of a place Matt boasted he took all of his so-called dates.

Matt. Really? No way. The words stuck in his throat, but he had to ask, "Clare… are you implying that you and Mr. Allen…"

"…Oh, no, I am not *implying* anything," she said, and paused.

Blake exhaled. "I don't believe you."

"Why don't you ask him?" she suggested, nodding toward the door.

"Ask me what?"

Blake spun around. Matt was standing in the doorway.

"Matt…" Blake murmured.

"Ask me what?" He repeated.

Blake turned to Clare.

She stood, defiantly. She wanted this. She wanted Blake to question Matt in front of her.

"Ask you if… if…" he glanced at her, and then back at his friend.

"What, man? Spit it out," Matt said.

"…ask you if you were bloody ready. I've been waiting ages," Blake finally said.

Clare's shoulders slumped.

"Sorry. You know what that lot are like. A bunch of tarts, crying over scraped knees."

"They ought to try playing a real man's game, like rugby," Blake said with a grin.

He turned to look at Clare. That twinkle had disappeared from her eyes, and now it was Blake's turn to smile, smugly.

Matt followed Blake's gaze. "Did I interrupt something?"

"Oh no, Mr. Allen." Clare sparked to life once more. "Mr. Hudson and I have made our arrangements," she said cheerfully.

Then, almost breaking into a skip, she made for the door, but paused on the threshold and turned, "I'll see you Friday, Blake," she said, flashing another smile.

Then, she was gone, whistling down the corridor as she went.

"Uh hum, that's a bit familiar, don't you think?" Matt asked, walking up to his friend.

Blake was still processing the exchange.

"You need to stay away from her," he said suddenly.

"Um, shouldn't I be telling you that? You two were looking particularly cosy when I walked in."

"Not a chance. The girl's mental."

Matt noticed the look on his friend's face. "You all right? Hey, there isn't really something going on between you…"

"…Don't even joke about it," Blake said, sighing heavily. "Did you know she was at The Pit the other night?"

"Is that right? I didn't see her there," Matt said, sitting on a desk.

"Nor did I."

"She probably followed us there."

"Yeah, well it wouldn't surprise me." There was tension in Blake's voice.

"Steady on, mate. I was only joking. What's got into you?"

"I'm telling you. Something's not quite right with that girl."

Matt laughed. "There's nothing wrong with her. She's just has

61

a crush on her teacher. She's not the first, and she certainly won't be the last. As you'd expect, I get it all the time," Matt grinned. "What's she doing here today anyway?"

"Good question."

"Have you heard any more about her uncle?"

"No. Have you?"

"Well..." Matt began excitedly.

"What?"

"Oh, man," he shook his head, incredulously, as he replayed images in his mind. "I met the sexiest piece of skirt in the corridor. She was wearing this black trouser suit... and get this, I thought she was one of the subs, but it turns out, she's a bloody doctor! And I'm not talking general practitioner, but a bloody pathologist! Can you believe it?"

"Hello again," said a familiar female voice.

Matt recognised it instantly, and turned to see that Sky McPherson was standing in the doorway. He shook his head. "Okay, so, I suppose this is the part where the ground opens up and swallows me, right?" Matt's cheeks had flushed red.

"Sky?" Blake said.

"Blake," She uttered, suddenly feeling queasy. "Oh my God, I don't believe it!"

Blake laughed, "No way!"

Matt gawked at them both when, suddenly, the gorgeous woman from the corridor threw herself into his best friend's arms.

"What are you doing here?" It was Sky asking the question as she emerged from the embrace.

"I work here," he explained with a big smile. "Well, kind of."

"You do?"

"Yes."

"But the last I heard, you'd become some kind of environmentalist."

He laughed. "Well, not in the sense of someone who dons sandals and holds placards. I'm more of a conservationist. I work for the Environment Agency."

"So what are you doing here?"

"I lecture here once a week."

"You're joking. Seriously?"

"Yes, seriously."

"Blake Hudson, a lecturer," Sky said slowly, as if the impossible had just happened.

The sound of Matt deliberately clearing his throat caught their attention and Blake tore his eyes away from the woman to see his friend staring at him, expectantly.

"Oh, of course. This is my best mate..."

"... Matt, um... Allen, isn't it?" she interrupted.

"The very same. I met Doctor McPherson earlier, in the corridor."

"Doctor McPherson?" Blake asked.

Sky nodded, beaming.

"I can't believe it, you made it!" he said.

Sky smiled. He was impressed. She liked that.

"Didn't you know?" asked Matt, as if this were old news. "Doctor McPherson is a forensic pathologist."

"Good for you," Blake said as memories flooded his mind. "So, what brings you here?" he asked.

"I'm looking for a pupil of yours."

"Really?" Blake asked, smiling. He still couldn't believe that Sky McPherson was actually standing before him. "And who might that be?"

"Um, Clare McElvoy?"

Blake lost his smile and the room fell silent.

10

The Lookout Pub – Plymouth, England.

Half an hour later, they were sitting at a window table of a pub, overlooking Plymouth Harbour.

They had invited Matt to join them, but he'd tactfully declined, saying he was late for an appointment.

It was late afternoon and the pub was empty, but for a young couple sitting at a table across from them. The waiter, who couldn't have been much older than seventeen, casually strode over, carrying a tray with their order of scones and tea.

Sky thanked him. The boy mumbled something, and then disappeared back into the kitchen.

"So," Blake began again, but then started chuckling as he shook his head.

"What?" she asked, smiling with him.

"I'm sorry. I just can't get used to the fact that you are *Doctor* McPherson now."

"Why?" she asked, still smiling.

"Well...." He struggled to find the right words. "No particular reason – it's just, well, the last time I saw you, you were only dreaming of a being a doctor. Now, ten years later, you're a pathologist. It takes some getting used to."

"It just goes to show; dreams can come true," she said lightly.

"Why pathology anyway? Of all things, cutting up dead bodies?" He pulled a face. "I'm sorry."

"No, it's okay. Most people have that reaction. But what they don't see is the bigger picture.

"Pathology isn't just about cutting up dead bodies. It's about the discovery. The investigation. The search into someone's past. Unravelling the mystery of why and how someone died can reveal so much about how that person *lived*. Eating habits, lifestyle, fitness, are all crucial pieces of a much bigger puzzle. One that, when finished, often leads to the dispensation of justice for some and peace for others."

"Wow, since you put it that way…" He grinned.

Sky shook her head, then sipped her tea. "You can tease all you want, but I love my work. It's rarely the same and always fascinating. Anyway, what about you? Ten years ago, you were very anti-establishment, denouncing anything to do with politics and government. You were hell-bent on breaking your father's heart; now, look at you. Public servant."

"Well, not exactly," Blake said, buttering his scone.

"What do you mean, not exactly? You work for the E.A., don't you?"

"Well, yeah."

"They're a government body, aren't they?"

"Um, not quite. Anyway, I wasn't anti-establishment. My father was a politician and, at the time, I was going through my rebellion phase, but I never said I was…"

"You fibber!" Sky cried, smearing blackcurrant jam over her scone. "You used to hate politics and politicians. And, if my memory serves me well, that was the very reason why my parents bloody adored you."

Blake laughed, defeated. Sky was right.

"Okay, okay, you got me. Speaking of your parents, how are they? Still fighting the good fight?"

Sky lost her smile.

"What?" he asked, concerned.

She spoke, but her eyes were fixed on the miniature jam jar on the table in front of her. "They're dead," she said flatly.

"What? No," Blake breathed with incredulity.

"Passed away. Four years ago. Plane crash, over Brazil."

"Oh my God, Sky." Blake was shocked. "I'm so sorry."

He reached over and touched her hand. It was an instinctive gesture that, once complete, made his heart somersault. This surprised him.

Sky looked up, eyes brimming with sorrow. She slowly pulled her hand away, took another sip from her cup, and forced a smile. "They didn't even get to see me graduate medical school."

Blake groped for words and then rushed, "I don't know what to say. I am so sorry. I didn't know."

"It's okay. It's been a while now. Ultimately, they died for their cause. And, if I could talk to her now, I'm sure Mum would tell me, that's exactly the way she wanted it to be. Kind of poetic."

Blake hesitated. He wasn't quite sure how to respond to that. Partly because his mind was still busy trying to decipher her reaction to his touch.

She swallowed hard then, shifting to a brighter tone, asked, "Anyway, how about yours? How's life treating them?"

Sensing she wanted to change the subject, he nodded and said, "They're good. Thanks. You know, still the same."

"Do they still live in that big house in Cambridgeshire?"

The question sounded pointed, but he answered casually, "Oh no, they've moved from there. Retired to the Cotswolds."

"Nice," she said, raising her eyebrows.

The wealth contrariety between the two families had been, and Sky thought always would be, a contentious issue. She'd often wondered if this was due, at least in in part, to the fact that deep down, in some dark recess of her mind, she was jealous of Blake. Jealous that he'd had both the financial and emotional support to be whatever he wanted to be as an adult. She'd enjoyed no such privilege. Her parents would have been much happier if she had chosen to join Greenpeace rather than go into medicine.

Rarely did a week go by where she didn't wonder what exactly her parents would have made of her professional achievements. Her mother never had understood why she chose to 'carve up dead bodies' for a living. Ironically, her reaction hadn't been so dissimilar from that of the man in front of her.

Blake Hudson, son of Giles Hudson, the politician, and her, Sky McPherson, daughter of Alan McPherson, a new age traveller, had studied at Cambridge together. Five years, during which the pair had been inseparable. Blake's looks made him the most eligible man, and Sky, the most envied girl on campus. He'd been hooked on her beauty and intelligence. She'd been hooked on his wit and charisma.

However, their ambitions differed. Blake wanted to marry and have children. Sky wanted to become a doctor and then travel. He believed they could have both. She believed they could not. This, coupled with the ever-present social divide between them, had led to a breakdown in their relationship that culminated with Sky telling Blake that she had made plans for the future and that they no longer included him. For the first time in his life, Blake had suffered a broken heart.

Sky vowed never to return to Cambridge.

Blake vowed never to love again.

"Sky?"

He was calling to her. She was staring past him.

"Oh, I'm sorry," she said, smiling apologetically. "I was just remembering college."

"All the good times, I hope."

"Of course," she said, putting on a big smile.

"You were telling me about Mr. McElvoy," Blake reminded her.

"Was I?"

"Earlier. I asked if you knew what exactly had happened to him."

"Yes, and I remember us changing the conversation. Because I'm not supposed to discuss cases with you."

"Oh, go on, what's the point of being friends with a beautiful doctor if she can't give me an inside exclusive?"

The words had just fallen out of his mouth. He could have kicked himself.

Beautiful? Really? Shut up, Blake!

If Sky registered the compliment, she didn't show it. "No," she said.

"What do you mean, 'no'?"

"I mean no. It's more than my job's worth to discuss details with you."

Blake pulled a sad puppy face. One she remembered well.

"Oh no, seriously? Does that face still work on people?"

"I don't know – is it?"

She shook her head.

"Oh go on, Sky. Please. I really need to know."

"Need?" She looked at him curiously.

"Well, as you know... His niece comes to my class and, between you and me, I think she might have a screw loose."

Sky cocked her head and leaned forward, "Why do you say that?"

"I don't know. I can't explain it. Her behaviour's just a bit... off. I mean, the fact that she even showed up for class today. Don't you think that's weird?"

"Weird, but not unheard of. I told Matt the same thing. People deal with grief in different ways."

"Wait? Hang on... you spoke to Matt about this, but you won't tell me?"

"I spoke to Matt about Clare. Not about her uncle, or the details of his death."

Blake pulled the puppy face again.

"Didn't we just establish that that doesn't work?"

Surprisingly, it was, but she wasn't going to tell him that. Seconds ticked by. Blake was still looking very sad, and damn handsome with it.

"Really?" she asked. Then, leaning forward once more, she added in a conspiratorial whisper, "Okay. But, this is completely off the record. You cannot discuss it with anyone, and I mean no one."

Blake made a show of crossing his fingers and then his heart.

Sky rolled her eyes. "Off the record, it seems that he suffered some kind of aneurysm."

"And you think something brought it on, but you don't know what yet, right?"

Sky was surprised. "What makes you ask that?" She wondered if Blake knew something.

"Well, the police haven't released any details yet. They must suspect something."

"Well, they have to weigh all the evidence. Most of the evidence, in a case like this, is supplied by the post mortem, and I'm still waiting for the lab results."

"But what's your prognosis?"

Sky shifted in her seat. "Are you sure you're an environment officer and not a lawyer? Or a journalist, for that matter?" she asked.

"I'm sure," he laughed. "It's just, well, not much really happens around here."

"So I've heard. Blake, seriously, this is my job."

"I get it. Besides, you can just say I was helping you with your enquiry.

"Yes, well, there's a big difference between necessary and voluntary disclosure."

"Sky, it's me," he said reassuringly.

He had lost his cheeky smile and was looking directly into her eyes.

She took a few moments. Enjoying the intimacy of the act, and then glanced around the room.

It was empty.

She proceeded in a lowered tone, nonetheless, "There's a suspicion that McElvoy may have mutilated and then murdered all of his crew members."

She leaned back in her chair again.

Blake's eyes widened. "Oh my God. Why?" he asked, his voice a whisper.

Sky shrugged. "Well, that's what we're trying to find out. It could well have been a symptom of the embolism. You know what an embolism is, right?"

"Yes, a blood clot."

"That's right. A blood clot that forms somewhere at the back of the brain. Normally, these blood clots are caused by a ruptured artery, fragments of a diseased organ, or even a small mass of bacteria carried through the blood stream. Eventually, the fragments," Sky began to gesticulate, "plug a major artery, and that's when the problems start."

It was then that Blake really noticed her eyes. In the fading daylight, they were like fireflies, burning in the darkness. He wanted to kiss her. He didn't know why, but he just felt compelled to lean across the table and...

"...When I did the post-mortem," she continued, "I noticed that there was a large haematoma at the back of McElvoy's brain. That was, obviously, what killed him. The convulsions he suffered prior to seizure could also explain his strength," Sky said, as if thinking aloud.

"His strength?" Blake had that same inquisitive look on his face.

"When McElvoy was brought in, the police struggled to restrain him. Apparently, he manifested *inhuman* strength. To the point where a total of four officers struggled to contain him.

Remember, we're talking about a sixty-something-year-old man. As it turns out, it wasn't they who ultimately ended the struggle, but it was the embolism. He collapsed and died, shortly after. But I'll know more when I get the results."

Blake was staring at her.

She gave him a few seconds and then asked, "Are you alright?"

"Yeah," he breathed. "It's just that…"

"…I know it's terrible…"

"…No, I was going to say, I don't know which part of that I found more shocking; the detail, or the masterful way in which you delivered it."

Sky's eyes narrowed. "Blake," she complained.

He grinned. "I'm sorry, but I'm pretty turned on by that. Not the whole aneurysm thing – that's just gross."

"Stop it! You're making fun."

"I'm not, Sky. You're amazing," he said, through an incredulous laugh, still maintaining keen eye contact. The line was delivered far too earnestly, and the moment rapidly turned awkward.

Sky recovered it. "Anyway, enough of that. I've already told you more than I should have. How about I ask you some questions now?"

"Shoot," he said casually as he leant back in his chair.

"This girl, the niece…"

"Clare."

"Yes. Clare. Did you ever meet her uncle?"

"No, I had no reason to."

"And Clare's never mentioned anything about him to you? You know, habits, vices, things like that."

"No. Then again, why would she?"

"Well, you never know, people talk. Maybe he'd been acting strange lately."

"No. What did she tell you?"

"Nothing. I haven't managed to speak to her yet."

"I thought you said you came to the college to talk to her?"

"I did, but she said she was in a hurry. Had to meet a teacher for lunch or something."

"A teacher?" Blake's eyes widened, but he said nothing.

"What?"

"Are you sure she said she was meeting a teacher?"

"I'm positive. Why?"

"Oh, no reason," Blake replied thoughtfully.

"Oh, come on, Hudson. Are you really going to play it like that after what I've just told you?"

Blake was looking at her again, and there was something about that gaze that really unsettled her, as if he was reading her mind or something.

"What?" She asked, looking at herself, wondering if she had spilt something.

"It's just…" He broke off in mid-sentence as the waiter walked by.

Then, he spoke, quietly, as if the pub were rigged with invisible microphones, "This is strictly confidential."

She threw him a look.

"Right. Sorry."

He spent the next fifteen minutes telling her all about Clare McElvoy, her behaviour, and what she had said about Matt. He included everything, and felt much better for it.

Sky had listened to everything without interrupting once. Blake concluded that she hadn't changed one bit. She was still the same beautiful, patient, intelligent, and articulate girl he had known all those years ago.

The same girl he'd thought about marrying. Not that she knew, of course. She had ended their relationship before it got that far, and he was surprised to find that the memory still hurt. Somewhere, deep in his stomach, he still felt sadness, and he hadn't even realised he still felt that way, until that very moment.

Sky's gaze had turned to the harbour and beyond. The sun had disappeared behind a blanket of black clouds. The rolling emissaries were announcing rain.

"What are you going to do?" She asked, turning her attention to him once more.

"I don't know what to do, for the best. If I go to Truman, the college principle, I'm going to find myself in the middle of a bloody enquiry. If I don't, then God only knows what rumours she's going to spread."

"What about Matt? Do you think he is having a relationship

71

with this girl?"

Blake hesitated, and then said, "I don't really know. There's no doubt that Matt's a bit of a lad, but this... I'm not sure."

"Maybe you should tell Truman. You know, cover yourself."

"What, tell him about Matt?"

"No, I mean tell him about the way this teenager has been behaving around *you*. But, now that you've mentioned it, maybe you should tell him about Matt, too."

"Tell him what exactly? I don't even know if what Clare said is true. I mean, look at the way she's been behaving around me. It could all just be a figment of her imagination."

"What if it isn't?"

Blake paused.

She could tell he was struggling. "Look, first things first. Sleep on it. Then, have an honest chat with Matt about it. Then, see how you feel after that," she offered.

Blake nodded, "Thanks"

"What for?"

"For listening to me. We haven't been together for more than a couple of hours, after literally years, and I'm already telling you my problems."

"No, don't be silly. I actually enjoyed listening to you. Everybody enjoys a bit of a scandal, and I don't get much of that where I work. My clients are very tight-lipped," she smiled.

"I can imagine," Blake agreed.

A rumble of thunder intruded on their conversation. It came from deep within the clouds that were approaching rapidly.

"Looks like rain," Sky said, staring out of the window.

"Yes, thank God," he said, following her gaze. "We need rainfall, if we're going to get through the summer without a serious water shortage."

Sky glanced at her watch. "I better get going," she said. She reached into her bag and pulled out a small wallet.

"Oh no," Blake said as soon as he spotted the leather purse. "I'm getting this."

"I don't think so," Sky said. "I suggested tea, remember?"

There was determination in her face, and he knew better than to argue.

"Okay. My shout next time."

"Sure," she smiled.

They made their way to the till, just as the freckle-faced boy emerged from the kitchen.

Unlike in their previous encounter, he seemed to notice her this time, and made a point of looking her up and down.

When she eventually received her change, and her receipt, they made for the exit.

Outside, the air was close and humid. They were silent as they crossed the busy street and walked toward their cars, until Blake said, "So, when are we having dinner?"

"Sorry?"

"Dinner. My shout, remember, for coffee."

"Blake, it was just coffee."

"And this is just dinner. Go on, for old time's sake."

She hesitated a few seconds, and Blake half-expected her to say no, but instead she said, "okay."

"Cool."

"Where are you taking me?"

"I'll surprise you," he said.

11

Greentree Farm – 20 miles Southeast of Plymouth – 18:31.

They drifted over the hill like giant UFOs, slowly and ominously smothering the remaining daylight as they neared the small coastal farmhouse.

"Ouch!" Joyce cried as thunder cracked overhead. It sounded as if it was coming from inside the loft.

She shook her finger, sucked the tip of it, and then sat, staring at the small puncture wound. "Bloody weather," she cursed.

Thunder had made her nervous ever since she had been stuck in a panoramic lift with Su Shin Yang, an Asian businessman determined to convince her to head up the Hong Kong branch of his company. That night, there had been 60-mile-an-hour winds shaking the panoramic lift while sheet lightning lit the city periodically.

She hated lightning, and that stormy night had only served to make things worse.

The calling started again, hurtling down the stairs with the insistence of a hungry baby. It brought her crashing back from the memory of an evening that had closed one chapter, and opened another very important one in her life. She looked out of the window; the rain was close. A few droplets had already spat at the glass as darkness enveloped the surrounding countryside.

"Joyce! Joyce!" The rattling, throaty voiced continued.

"All right!" She yelled back at the ceiling. "I'm coming! I'm coming!"

She looked down at her masterpiece. The earless embroidery of a black and white cat stared back. She so desperately wanted to get a black and white cat. Especially now that they no longer lived in the city, but her mother was allergic.

"Joyce!"

Sticking the needle into an eye of her embroidered creation, she set it aside. Then, she heaved her bulk out of the armchair and shuffled to the window, where she peered out into the darkness.

Lightning flashed. As it did so, it illuminated Joyce's reflection in the glass, giving her a snapshot of herself; white bloated cheeks with straggly brown hair that fell over broad shoulders.

She wanted to cry. She felt ugly. What had she become?

It was then that she saw them, flying around the yard like white phantasms.

Her eyes widened.

"Oh no!" she cried and hurried to the door, where she grabbed an anorak from the nearby coat stand, slipped into it and, ignoring more calls from the old woman upstairs, launched herself into the dark.

The wind tore at her coat as drops of rain spat at her.

She frantically searched the yard, but it was difficult to locate the clothes in the gloom. Eventually, she managed to locate a white shirt as it flapped about on the gravelled drive.

Clutching the lapels of her anorak, and battling against the wind, she chased the runaway garment and grunted with frustration when, each and every time she lunged for the thing, it blew away from her.

Thunder boomed overhead like an angry god and she couldn't decide what to do first – apprehend the now mud-spattered clothing or shield her ears from the sound. Then the rain came. Suddenly, and in such a torrent that she was drenched almost instantly.

The water seeped into her clothing, into her hair, through her scalp, and into her blood stream, and, as it did so, it made her smile.

More thunder.

However, suddenly, she was no longer afraid. It was as if the rain had brought with it a sedative. A drug more powerful than anything else she had ever experienced before.

She could feel it inside her. Throbbing at her temples, rushing through her bloodstream and probing at the deep, dark recesses of her mind. It searched, yearned, begged to become acquainted – not with the person she was now, but the person she'd used to be... strong, smart, successful, ruthless, and, most importantly, in charge.

As the rain fell, Joyce Masters wept. She was free. No more fetching and serving, cleaning and wiping. Like a supreme being, the rain had come to take her away. And, as if it were a supreme being, if not God himself, Joyce fell to her knees, thrust her arms to the heavens, and allowed the water to baptise her as her friend, the thunder, roared, and her companion, the lightning, struck the farm, killing all the lights inside.

Joyce stared at the upstairs bedroom window and sniggered.

Things are going to change around here. Tonight. Now.

In the bedroom, the old woman shivered under the covers.

To her, it felt as if she had been calling to her daughter for hours, but without reply. Now, her throat was sore and, once again, she was lying in her own urine, and, to make things worse, all the lights had gone out. She felt alone. Afraid. And where was her daughter when she needed her?

On cue, in a scene worthy of a Hammer House horror,

lightning flashed, thunder roared, and the bedroom door swung open.

Dolores squinted through the gloom, but she didn't recognise the outline of the person who was standing, motionless, in the doorway.

"Joyce?" she called in rasping voice.

No reply.

"Joyce, is that you?"

Still nothing.

"Joyce, the lights have gone out. And, it's happened again; I'm sorry, but you took so long. I called for you, but you didn't respond. What was I supposed to do? You know I can't get out of bed on my own. You really should spend more time up here, with me. It makes sense, rather than you going up and down those stairs."

The old women's voice rattled on in the darkness, but still no reply was forthcoming.

More lightning. More thunder.

Now Dolores could see. It was her daughter standing in the doorway. It was Joyce. She could tell by that heavy frame of hers.

Relieved, the old woman continued, "Why didn't you answer me? I've been calling you for a very long time. Where have you been? Joyce... Joyce?"

Nothing. Seconds washed by.

"Joyce!" The old women whined in a frustrated guttural drone. "Why won't you answer me?"

The room was silent but for the drumming of the rain on the roof and the loud gurgling of the drains. Then, once again, the strobe flicker of lightning lit the room with an odd verdant hue. The effect lasted long enough for Dolores to see that her daughter had moved from her position in the doorway and was now standing at her bedside. She was holding something in her hand, and it glinted.

12

Stony Point – 19:05.

Outside, the rain fell, heavily.

Inside, the dulcet tones of Sade's "No Ordinary Love" filtered down from the first floor as Sky admired the photographic prints that adorned the walls of the living room.

Her attention, however, was drawn to a charcoal sketch on the far side of the room. It depicted two children, their faces blurred, and emphasising pitiful black eyes.

"La Petite Morte."

She looked up from the picture.

Blake, now dressed in jeans and a black shirt, had entered the room. His short hair was still shower wet and his eyes seemed to sparkle to compliment the smile on his face. Sky's stomach rolled. Just like it had when she'd first seen him at the college.

He looked good.

"Sorry?" she uttered.

"That's the name of the painting," he said casually.

"Oh, right."

"It means…"

"…The small dead," she interrupted.

Blake smiled. "Yes, it does. It was a gift from my mother."

Figures.

Blake noticed the look on her face. "I know. That was my reaction, too."

Thunder grumbled, loudly.

"See, even the weather has an opinion," Blake joked.

"My God, is it ever going to let up?" she asked, looking out the window.

"Apparently, there are going to be dry spells later," Blake announced as if he were a seasoned television presenter. "Would you like a drink?" he added, moving over to a tiny alcove carved into the wall, which had been skilfully converted into a drinks cabinet, complete with glass door and recessed lighting.

"Actually, I'm on call, but coffee would be nice."

"I see. No rest for the wicked. Does this mean there's a good chance you're going to bail on me, mid-dinner?"

"I'm afraid so. Sorry. But, don't worry. As I'm constantly being told, nothing much happens around here," she said, raising her voice, as Blake had disappeared into the kitchen.

"Yes, that's what I like about the place," came his muffled reply.

There was a short interlude. The only sound was the rain tapping on the window, and the occasional tinkle of stainless steel against cup.

Sky admired the room once more. Blake had done well for himself, although, she couldn't help but wonder if the interior design was all his taste, or if Mummy had had a say in it.

Sky knew Alicia Hudson enjoyed controlling her son's life. It wouldn't have surprised her to hear that Blake had moved to the Southwest just to escape her controlling clutches.

And so the floodgates opened. Memories that, somewhat surprisingly, still stung after all these years.

"I didn't bother with sugar," Blake said as he entered the room, carrying a small tray. "I assumed you were sweet enough." He set the tray down on the coffee table and sat on a nearby armchair.

Accepting his waved invitation, Sky joined him. "Am I that transparent?" she asked.

"Well... not transparent, as such. More like..."

"Predictable?"

"No, not at all, I..."

"...One," she interrupted.

"Sorry?"

"I take one sugar in my coffee."

"Oh, right," he said. "I'll just go and get some."

She laughed. "I'm kidding. Blake, this will be fine, thanks. You've got a lovely place here."

"You think so?"

"Yes. I really like it," she said earnestly.

"Thanks," he said with a smile. "I quite like it, too."

They drank in silence.

It seemed that now that they had each other's undivided

attention, away from everything and everyone, they were both suddenly unable to articulate.

"I think you were right. The rain seems to have calmed down a bit," Sky said, breaking the quiet.

Really? The weather. You're going to talk about the weather?

"Yes, it has."

"I guess, next, you'll be telling me that predicting the weather is one of your favourite pastimes."

"Nothing so imaginative, I'm afraid. I do have a computer upstairs, though, that gives me all of that detail."

"Really? There's an app for that, though, isn't there?"

"Funny. No, this is a bit more sophisticated. For work, of course."

"Oh, of course," she said, nodding.

"What?" he asked.

He knew she was teasing him.

"Well, you know what they say about boys with toys."

"It's not a toy, I'm telling you. Would you like to see it in action?"

"Sure," she said, humouring him.

"Follow me."

They climbed the stairs to the sound of Sky's heels clicking loudly on the metal steps.

"What's through there?" she asked as they reached a door on the first floor.

"That's my bedroom."

"Oh…" She said, nodding. "Aren't you going to show me around?"

"Absolutely. I'm going to give you a special tour later," he said, glancing back at her.

Even in the dim lighting of the stairwell, Sky could have sworn she saw him grinning.

The rain's drumming was much louder on the second floor and a gale screamed around the building, as if begging for shelter from the precipitation.

Blake flipped on a light, illuminating the circular room.

Sky walked over to the balcony doors and stared at her reflection in the glass. "Wow, you must have the most spectacular views from here," she said, unconsciously fixing her hair and noticing that, behind her, Blake had sat at his desk.

"It's breathtaking. When I was first shown this place, it was the view from this room that sold it to me. Of course, it looked a little different then."

The computer's large flat-screen was projecting a screensaver of a star simulation. It disappeared with one swipe of Blake's finger to reveal a spinning world globe. Sky joined him by the desk and stood behind him, looking over his shoulders. She could smell his aftershave. It was a rich, wooden aroma, and smelt delicious.

She surreptitiously breathed it in.

Blake touched the screen again. The globe stopped spinning and a flashing rectangular frame appeared in its centre.

"Where would you like to go?" he asked brightly.

"Oh, I don't know. Where can I go?" she asked, laying her hands on his shoulders.

He was pleasantly surprised by her touch, but didn't show it.

"You can go anywhere in the world."

"Really? Oh, well…" She pondered, like a game show contestant unable to decide on which prize envelope to choose. "England, I suppose," she said, finally.

"England it is," he complied cheerfully.

Blake touched the image of the globe and spun it, as one would a physical object, until a magnifying glass appeared. He double-tapped and, almost instantly, a map of the United Kingdom presented itself.

"The pictures you are about to see are coming live from the Met Office's central computer."

"Are these satellite pictures?"

"Aha," Blake confirmed, nodding his head.

Then he touched the screen once more, and the small rectangular shape hovered over the south of England. A few double-taps of his finger revealed London and the surrounding area. The map was very similar to that shown on a weather report, but parts of London seemed obscured by a grey haze.

"What's that?" Sky asked, pointing to the grey blur on the screen.

"That's cloud."

"Cloud?"

"Yes... you see here," he said, pointing to the digital map. "Most of the picture is clear. That means that there is hardly any cloud in the troposphere, which means good weather. And you see here," he said, pointing to hazy London, "that means cloud."

"Rain?"

"No, not necessarily, it's probably just smog. You know that kind of blanket grey cloud you can get on some days?" he asked, turning his head slightly around.

"Yes."

"Well, that's most probably what that is."

"My God, you can tell all that from here?" she asked, incredulous.

"Yes, I can tell all sorts things from here. Air quality, cloud density, pressure readings, you name it."

"Wow, that's amazing," she said, moving from behind him to lean on the desk, where she could get a closer view.

"Yep, those good old satellites are useful for many things, beyond communication and navigation."

"What about Southwest? Let's look at Cornwall!" she said excitedly.

"Okay." Blake touched the screen again, and the picture of London and the Southeast metamorphosed into a map of England.

Several taps later, the Southwest of England was displayed on the screen. The image was a complete contrast to the one they had seen earlier. This time, a black and white haze blotched out most of the area, leaving only a few clear spots. Directly over the Stony Point region, there was a chequered image of black and clear skies.

"Wow, is that what's looming over us right now?" Sky asked, her face green from the glow of the screen.

"Yep."

"How far can you zoom in with this thing?" she asked.

"As far as you like, really. Look."

Blake tapped the screen over Stony Point and the area was magnified. Then he pinched the area with two fingers, and they were zooming through the black layer and peering down on what looked like the ground from inside an airborne plane.

A few pinches later, Sky's mouth dropped open. The image was a fluorescent green, similar to that seen through night vision lenses. It was a picture of Sky's car, parked outside of Blake's house.

"Oh… wow," she whispered incredulously. "I can't believe it. Is this live?"

"Actually, this is a photo. They're taken at intervals, as the satellite passes overhead, and the image is updated each time. This kind of technology is still very expensive and only a few agencies are allowed access to live pictures."

"It's amazing. How come you have access to this?"

"Well, officially, I don't. But because I work for the EA, and I have connections at the Met Office, I can log straight into their portal to get the latest data."

"I am really impressed."

"Yeah, told you it wasn't a toy," he said with a grin.

Sky smiled. "I suppose it won't be long before this kind of thing will become standard for everyone with a mobile device."

"Well, it kind of already is. Many weather apps already contain the data. It's just the imagery that isn't available."

"I must admit, I'm not a technophobe, but all of this surveillance stuff really does give me the creeps. I mean, phone hacking, web cam hijacking. It's enough to make you paranoid."

"Why? It's technology. It's the future."

She eyed him, seriously. "You sound like an advert."

He chuckled.

"So, what kind of weather can we expect for the game on Friday?" she asked, looking back at the monitor.

"I thought you didn't like football," he commented, touching the screen.

"I didn't. But I fell out of love with rugby a long time ago."

Blake looked at her. However, either she was hypnotised by the image on the screen or she was deliberately avoiding eye contact.

After a few taps on the screen, the globe re-drew itself, revealing a map of the United Kingdom. One more tap placed a white grid over it and invoked a small black window containing alphanumeric data.

"What's that?" she asked.

"It's the Atlantic Ocean," Blake replied as he tapped more commands. Almost instantly, a chequered quilt of black and grey blotches covered the grid. "Okay. You see down here?" he asked, pointing at the data at the foot of the screen.

"Yes."

"Well, this is the wind's direction and, underneath here, these characters tell us whether we have high or low pressure. This picture is telling us that there's low pressure sweeping across the Atlantic, and with it, it's bringing this," he said, pointing at grey and black blotches.

"So that means that we can expect more rain, right?"

"Yes, although these blotches aren't really much to worry about. In fact, there's a good chance they'll just fizzle out before they even reach us. No, there's something else much bigger and much scarier than that." He turned to Sky and looked her in the eyes. "You know the showers we've had today?"

"Yes," she said, forcing a laugh. "But I'd hardly call them showers."

"Oh yes, they were," he said in a melodramatic voice as he turned his attention back to the glowing monitor. "Compared to this…" He double-tapped, "they are."

For the second time that evening, Sky McPherson's mouth dropped open. In a vision reminiscent of the many television documentaries she'd watched about hurricanes and tornadoes, the image on the screen was that of a giant black and grey swirl, as seen from space. As she stared at the screen, the picture flickered, giving the impression that the gargantuan mass was moving.

"What the hell is that?" she gasped.

"That's Mummy," Blake replied, excited.

"It looks like a tornado."

"It does, but it isn't," he reassured her.

They exchanged glances.

Then, regaining the weatherman voice he had mastered so well, he said, "That's what meteorologists often refer to as a low pressure system."

"Low pressure!" Sky echoed.

"It's basically a rain storm."

"A hurricane?"

"No, not quite. We don't tend to get those in Britain. I think the last *great storm* we had was back in the eighties. Although, as you know, the global climate has changed. It's one of the reasons we're actually starting to spot the odd tornado."

"So, are you saying that that thing, whatever it is, is actually heading for us?"

"Afraid so. Unless that wind shifts, dramatically, that mother is heading straight for us."

"So, does that mean that the worst is yet to come?"

"Oh yes."

"When?"

"I'm not sure, exactly. But judging by wind speed, I'd say there's a good chance of it reaching us by Friday."

The room fell silent, but for the hum of the computer's fan, the moaning wind, and the distant rumble of the surf lapping on the shingled shore.

"You're impressed, aren't you?" Blake asked with a smirk.

"No, I'm just wondering whether or not they'll cancel the match on Friday and, if not, what to wear."

Blake's smile disappeared. "So, you weren't joking then."

"About what?"

"About liking football."

"No, of course I wasn't. What makes you think that I was joking?"

"I don't know," he said, getting up from his seat. Then he added, as casually as he could, "Of course, you could come with us. I'm sure Matt won't mind you tagging along... That's if you haven't made plans with anybody else, of course."

"Well, that's odd, because I didn't think *you* liked football either."

"I don't. But Matt's team's playing, and, well, he's a bit fanatical, and has been hassling me about it."

There was a long pause before she finally said, "I'll think about it."

Blake nodded. "Good." Then, looking at his watch, he said, "We'd better get going or we're going to be late."

They left Blake's office and made their way down the

stairwell.

"Well, I hate to see this," Sky said as she opened the door to a still night. "But you were right. It looks like the rain's stopped."

Thunder rumbled in the distance, as if to remind her that the respite was only temporary. The scent of the ocean and wet grass hung heavily in the air. It prompted Sky to take in a deep breath, and it was in that moment that she felt she truly understood what had lured the handsome conservationist here.

"Your car or mine?" Blake asked, appearing at the door.

"Well, I'm on call, so it would make sense if I drove."

"Okay, sounds good to me."

A subtle alert tone sounded like a megaphone in the still of the moment.

"Oh no. What's that?" Blake asked warily, even though he already knew the answer.

Sky plucked the device from her coat pocket and read the message. Her shoulders slumped. "I'm so sorry."

Blake sighed, and leaned heavily against the doorframe.

13

B Road – 21:07.

The BMW's headlights pushed back the blanket of darkness as Sky McPherson cursed Detective Inspector Morrison for messaging her at such an inopportune moment.

She had been enjoying herself. *But what are you expecting? Just pick up where you left off? You dumped him, remember? You don't even know if he's seeing someone... No, but imagine the look on his mother's face if you showed up in her son's life once more?*

Priceless!

The thought made her smile, but the moment didn't last long before memories barged their way to the fore and, once again to her surprise, so did the hurt. Never, in her entire life, had Sky McPherson felt as worthless as she had on that hot summer's day, ten years earlier.

The invite had been a long time coming. It had seemed that the Hudsons found every opportunity to avoid meeting her. Blake's father, the politician, was away at a conference, they had an official function to attend, they were on holiday, or they already had other guests staying for the weekend. It was excuse after excuse, or, as Mrs. Hudson would have her son believe, reason after reason why it was not convenient that they visit, as a couple.

And this had saddened Sky. Not for her, but for Blake. She'd known how much his parents meant to him, and the fact that there might be something about her that displeased them broke her heart.

Now, finally, that was going to change. She had already resolved that she was going to kill them both with kindness. She'd even ditched her trademark jeans and T-shirt in favour of a traditional, flowery summer dress and sensible flat shoes.

"Wow, you look, um, different," Blake had said when she climbed into the passenger seat of his car.

"Really? Is it that bad?"

"No, when I say different, I mean you look beautiful, Sky. Just different, too."

"Really? You're not just saying that?"

"Well, the cardigan might be a bit over the top."

"You think so? I was going for traditional fifties chic."

He turned to her, "Sky, I'm kidding. Babe, come on," he took her hands. "They're going to love you, I promise."

"It's not *them* I'm worried about. I've met your father, remember? He's lovely. It's your mother I'm worried about."

"She's going to love you, too, silly. How couldn't she? You're gorgeous. Besides, even if they don't, who cares? I'm the only one you need to impress, and I think you're well-fit. Well, you're alright." He winked at her.

She play-thumped him in the arm.

He chuckled.

Then, seriously, he said, "It's going to fine. Really." He looked straight into her eyes, in that inimitable way of his that made her feel giddy, like she was the only girl in the world. He followed that up with, "I love you. Please don't work yourself into a state over this."

"I just want to make a good impression…"

"…for me, I know."

"I know how much your parents mean to you."

"Not as much as you," he said, caressing her arm. "I mean it," he said earnestly. "Now, come on or we'll be late. And that simply won't do, for either of us," he added, mimicking his mother's voice and then rolling his eyes in an overly girly way.

Sky laughed.

They did make it on time, and arrived to find that Alicia Hudson had set the table so that they could take brunch *al fresco*, on the patio that overlooked the sprawling expanse of manicured lawn that they called the back garden.

Then, it was a grand tour of the mansion the Hudsons called their *humble* home.

Afterward, they enjoyed homemade lemonade while Alicia interrogated Sky about her past, her hopes, and her aspirations. The inquisition included background information on her parents and their origins, as well as what they hoped to achieve by campaigning against the capitalism that, ultimately, at least in Alicia's opinion, was what made the world go round.

Giles Hudson, ever the gentlemen, rescued Sky by changing the subject, and told his wife that she was oversimplifying what was essentially a complex subject.

Then Blake joined in, and before anybody knew it, the gathering was talking politics, which inevitably led to the usual debate between father and son about the environment, and what steps, beyond rhetoric, the government was actually taking to combat global warming and safeguard the health of the planet for future generations.

Afternoon came and went, and Alicia Hudson ended the debate by announcing that they did not have any coal for the BBQ.

"Mum, burning fossils fuels. Really? Why can't you use gas like everybody else?"

"Cook by gas? Blake, stop being silly. Barbequed meat, by gas? Whatever next? Now, would you please do as I ask?"

"Come on, son. You know she's going to get her way anyway.

We may as well capitulate now," Giles Hudson chimed in, placing an arm on his son's shoulder.

Cue awkward moment, where a young Sky was unsure what to do next – go with the men or stay with Mrs. Hudson.

Mrs. Hudson made the decision for her.

"Sky's going to stay behind and help me with the salad. It'll also give us girls the opportunity to have a chat without you two hanging on our every word."

Blake glanced at Sky, who smiled and nodded reluctantly.

"Okay, see you in a bit," Blake said, pecking her on the cheek.

"Come on, son, you're going to the DIY store, not to war," his father teased.

Then, they were gone.

No sooner had they left the building, and Sky was already feeling nervous. Alicia was tall, elegant, and rich. Sky was tall, but the similarity ended there.

"Okay, so, where do we start?" she asked cheerfully.

Alicia looked her up and down in such a way that made Sky wonder if she had a stain on her clothing. "Do you always dress like that?" Alicia asked, casually, as she retrieved salad ingredients from the fridge.

"I'm sorry?"

"Do you always wear that kind of dress?"

"Well, actually, no…"

"…It doesn't suit you."

The clipped words were delivered somewhat matter-of-factly, as if Alicia had just told the silly girl that the sky was blue, not green.

"You see... to pull off that kind of look, one needs a modicum of poise. I'm afraid you've managed to simply look uncomfortable for most of the day."

Several seconds of absolute silence passed as Alicia lined up all of her ingredients on the counter. Then, and only then, did she glance at Sky, who was unconsciously gawping at the woman as she tried to process what she had just said.

"Oh, my dear girl," she said delicately, "I do hope I haven't offended you. Just thought you might appreciate the feedback. You know, one lady to another."

Sky didn't know what to say, but heard herself squeak, "Thank you." Then, she watched as the woman proceeded to shred the salad and chop onions, all with the efficiency of a sous chef. After a minute or so of salad prepping activity, during which Sky could only watch, for she had lost all ability to speak, the woman said, once again, without so much as a glance.

"What exactly are your intentions toward my son?"

Her schoolteacher tone was clipped, her delivery expressionless and, once again, she did not dignify her guest with eye contact, preferring instead to focus on the job in hand.

Sky's tongue felt thick, paralysed, as if it had been injected with anaesthetic, as she struggled with a torrent of thoughts. What to do? What to say? So, she just stared; transfixed by how Mrs. Hudson's fiery red hair shone in the sunlight that was streaming in through large arched windows.

Why is this woman being so mean to me? What did I do wrong?

Finally, she garbled, "Well, we haven't really discussed…"

"…Because he's not interested in getting serious right now. You know that, don't you?"

"We weren't really planning on…"

"…but then, nor are you for that matter, right? That's what you said earlier today, wasn't it? You said, you wanted to carve a career for yourself, and that you didn't plan to join *the cause,* as you put it. Well, my son is also planning a career. God willing, he'll be happy to follow his father's footsteps into politics, and, well, he could really do without the distraction. It's this very reason why he never became serious with all the other girls he dated. So, as you see, this *thing* you believe you have between you. It really isn't going to work. You both come from completely different backgrounds."

Now Mrs. Hudson stopped slicing tomatoes, and juice dripped from the knife as she finally gave Sky her cold blue eyes.

A lump formed in Sky's throat and she could feel the early onset of tears. She felt hurt and angry at herself for being incapable of managing the situation, but this was Blake's mother, so what exactly could she say to her that wouldn't be twisted in the eyes of her beloved son, the man she happened to love, also?

"Mrs. Hudson, I love your son…"

"…Don't be ridiculous!" the woman snapped. You don't even

know him."

"I've known him long enough to know that I am in love with him."

Eyes burning with resentment, Alicia Hudson stepped forward. The act was enough to make Sky want to step back. Better, turn and run from the building, never to return.

"You still don't get it, do you?" she asked, mildly amused. "He doesn't love you. He is just having a bit of fun. Just like he has with all the other girls that fall for his charm. Do you honestly believe that you are the one? Come on, Sky, you're a bright girl. You were of no fixed abode until you moved into student accommodation. What could you both possibly have in common? Think about it."

Try as she did, there was no holding back the tears. They burst through the dam of her violet eyes and were then streaming down her face. It would be easy to have thought that the reason for Sky's tears was Mrs. Hudson's mean-spirited and unprovoked attack. But Sky's tears were for more than that. She was crying because she knew that, when push came to shove, the woman's words didn't stray far from the truth. Her life was no fairy tale. It was a true story of hard graft, economic uncertainty and student loans.

Blake was popular, especially with other girls, and he had had several relationships before her. Why would she even think she was the one?

When Mrs. Hudson noticed how distressed Sky had become, she was sure to turn on the charm, insisting that she had only been so candid because she knew that a strong and intelligent girl like her would appreciate it. Then, she urged Sky to freshen up before dinner and, by the time the others returned, there was no sign of her heart-wrenching tears.

The rest of the evening went by as if their conversation had never taken place. However, Blake had noticed that something was off and, as soon as they left the Hudson home, he questioned her.

Her response was to burst into tears, which she explained were a result of an emotionally charged visit, and she told him that she would be fine after a good night's sleep.

Reluctantly, Blake accepted this.

Sky couldn't tell him what his mother had said. She tried, but she simply could not. She knew how much his mother meant to him. Telling him about that would undoubtedly cause them to fall out, and she didn't want to be responsible for that.

Besides, the woman's words were still rattling around in her mind the following day.

Think about it.

She did. Repeatedly.

Their relationship had never been the same again, until one day something happened that ended things for good.

A few months after that visit, she won a scholarship and left Cambridge for London, where she threw herself into her studies and enjoying the life. She rarely visited her parents. Not because she didn't care about them, because she did. She just couldn't handle how being around them reminded her of all of the things that used to be wrong about her life – school bullying, life as a nomad, no prospects beyond *the cause*, and him.

When Sky McPherson left Cambridge, she made a vow; nobody would ever make her feel the way Alicia Hudson had that day, ever again.

It was gone eight-thirty when she turned the BMW onto the gravelled drive that led to Greentree Farm. An ambulance was parked outside the house, flanked by two patrol cars with their full beams shining towards the front door. The yard was a hive of police activity, and she wondered what could have possibly happened to warrant so much police presence.

She pulled up alongside the Ford Mondeo she recognised as belonging to Morrison. She retrieved a sterile white jumpsuit from the boot of the car, slipped into it, grabbed her hard case, and made for the entrance. Sky passed the ambulance; the back doors were open and she saw a spindly, middle-aged woman with wispy white hair, sitting on the back step. She looked shaken. A paramedic was fussing around her as she chattered agitatedly to two police officers.

Inside, the house was dark. Flashlights of the investigating officers danced around the house like an army of fireflies. The stairs were directly in front of her, and she instinctively held up a hand to fend off the glare from a flashlight that someone was shining in her face.

"I'm looking for D.I. Morrison," she snapped.

The beam of light left her, and pointed up the stairs. "Thank you." She said irritably as smudges of light floated in front of her eyes.

"Dr. McPherson!" a voice called.

Sky looked up. Morrison was leaning over the banister, clutching a flashlight in his right hand.

"Detective Inspector?" she asked, unable to make him out in the dim light.

"Yes! Up here!" he called, illuminating her flight up the stairs.

"Sorry to drag you out 'ere at this hour," he said as she reached the landing.

"I would say it's no problem, Detective, but you do seem to be making a habit of it," Sky said lightly, but her smile was lost in the darkness. "What happened to the lights?" she asked.

"Storm knocked the power out. We've been onto the electricity people, but power's out in the whole area. In the meantime, we should be getting some mobile floodlights out here shortly. Well, when I say 'shortly', I use the term loosely," he grumbled.

"So, what have we got?"

"Well," Morrison began, training his beam on a door across the landing, "Unfortunately, what appears to be a homicide."

"Really? I thought you said not much happened around here, Detective?"

"Well, it appears I may have been wrong," Morrison replied pensively.

With that, he snatched a flashlight out of the hand of a passing officer and handed it to Sky.

"After you," he said.

The blackness was diluted as they entered, and shadows peeked out from behind the scantily furnished bedroom. The room smelt damp, but this aroma was masked by one that was much more repugnant. At least, it clearly was to Morrison who, periodically, placed his arm over his nose.

"We're getting some light up here now," Morrison reiterated with an impatient sigh, glancing back down the stairs.

"Thanks," she replied, not looking at him, but advancing into the room.

"She's on the bed," Morrison said glumly.

Sky aimed her torch to reveal a mound of blankets. Then, she found a nearby chair, balanced her case on its arms, and retrieved a pair of gloves.

"Coming through!" a voice shouted.

"Bloody 'ell, 'arris, I asked for that light, bloody half an hour ago," Morrison barked.

"Sorry, Sir, I had to…" the young officer began.

"…Don't bother with explanations. Just get the bloody thing over there!" Morrison illuminated a path to the bed.

"Yes, Sir."

The young officer moved forward carrying the floodlight and trailing a long electrical lead behind him. Then, after fumbling about for a minute or so, he finally managed to plug it in and switch it on. The powerful halogen bulb transformed night into day, revealing a large, grubby-looking room with sloping wooden beams.

A metal-framed double bed sat to one side of the room. It was unmade and discoloured pink bedding spilled to the floor like the entrails from a slashed stomach. Sky moved over to it, dictaphone in hand, to a tableaux she had never witnessed before.

The old woman was lying on the bed. Her glazed eyes were lifelessly staring at the ceiling. She was naked, but for a light blue nighty that Sky noticed was at least two sizes too big. She had soiled herself, and the stench grew stronger as Sky approached. Her arms had been placed across her chest, as if she been laid to rest in a suitable posture that would allow the forensic team to pay their respects. Her wrinkled skin was no longer translucent pink, but a yellow, waxy hue, and her lips…

Oh God, what they have done to her lips?

They were sewn together in a crude cross-stich fashion, like a macabre roast.

"Is this exactly how you found her?" Sky asked.

"Of course," Morrison replied, joining her by the bed and visibly cringing as the toxic stench of human faeces smothered him.

A police officer, with paparazzi enthusiasm, entered the room and began snapping photos of the scene. Each flash of the camera was like lightning to Sky, searing images of the dead woman onto her brain. She made a conscious effort to ignore the happy snapper, and speaking as professionally as she could into her dictaphone, she began her preliminary examination.

"Elderly female, in her seventies, visibly malnourished." She paused a few seconds, and then said, "The victim appears to have been placed, or, more specifically, arranged here, with her hands crossed over her chest. Her lips have been crudely stitched together by what resembles tapestry thread. This has resulted in massive loss of blood, which has pooled around the body and has been absorbed into the victim's nightwear. This would indicate that she was still alive when the sewing took place. There's bruising to the temple…"

She gently prodded the discolouration with a gloved finger. "…It is likely that she was struck by a blunt object, probably in order to subdue her and to facilitate the stitching."

Sky broke off there as her imagination projected images of the events that had most likely taken place there. She felt a sudden urge to run, screaming, from the house, but she fought it back.

However, Morrison must have noticed the look on her face, for he asked, "Are you alright, Doc?"

Sky didn't reply. Instead, she spoke into her dictaphone, continuing, "There is no sign of rigor, indicating that death could not have occurred much longer than six hours ago… I need to turn her over," she said to no one in particular.

Reluctantly, Morrison and the young police officer moved in to help her. "After three," Morrison said. "Two…three…"

They turned the old woman onto her side. The task was easy, for she couldn't have weighed more than eight stone.

The nightdress had moved up, revealing part of the woman's left buttock. The flesh was blue, grey, and covered in what looked like burst boils.

The young officer baulked.

Sky continued her dictation. "There are pressure sores present in the region of the buttocks, indicating that the victim may have been bedridden." She pulled the flimsy cloth down, as if to protect the dead woman's dignity. Then, she delicately unbuttoned the back of the nightdress, and looked up.

She didn't have to ask; Morrison flicked on his flashlight and handed it to her.

She shone it over the corpse's back, highlighting a series of dark discolorations, the approximate sizes of a five pence coin. She examined the marks closely, and when she was satisfied, she handed the flashlight back to its owner and continued, "There are dark blotches to the back, suggesting lack of, or bad blood circulation. These coupled with the absence of rigor mortis would suggest that death occurred over three, but no longer than six hours ago. Therefore, the time of death would have been approximately," she looked at her watch, "7:00 p.m."

At this point, the young officer, known as Harris, fled the room. In complete contrast, the photographer seemed to be showing an unhealthy interest in the corpse, and squeezed off four more photographs in quick succession.

Morrison felt obliged to say something, "He's not used to this kind of stuff."

"Based on what I've heard, I would have thought most of your men aren't, Detective," Sky said matter-of-factly.

Morrison shrugged his shoulders and stood up straight, as if he was going to deny the presumption, but he thought better of it. She was right.

Sky rebuttoned the gown and, as if aided by telepathy, Morrison helped her roll the woman onto her back once more.

Sky stood up straight and removed her gloves.

"So, what's the prognosis, Doc? What do you think killed her?" Morrison asked.

"It's hard to say, really. It could be anything from the blow to the head to heart failure."

"Heart failure?"

"Yes." Sky met the inspector's gaze. "Detective, whoever did this did so out of pure cruelty. This woman was still alive when they sutured her lips. Can you imagine how terrifying and excruciatingly painful that must have been?"

She didn't wait for a reply. Instead, she returned the dictaphone to her case, and snapped it shut. Then, with one final look at the inspector, she said, "I'll know more after the post mortem."

Blinking as the camera flashed more pictures, she hurriedly left the room.

Morrison joined her as she was descending the stairs. He aimed the beam of his flashlight on the steps in front of them. "You mentioned that she'd probably been bedridden. You deduced that just from the marks on her back?" he asked, trying to keep up with her.

"She was also under-nourished, which would suggest that she had some kind of illness that stopped her gaining weight. I doubt if anyone as emaciated would have been able to walk around, at least not unaided, and there was no walker or any other aid in the room. Then, there was the ammonia."

"Ammonia?" Morrison echoed with a sneer.

"Beyond the relatively fresh smell of faeces, Detective, there was a notable smell of stale urine, which would suggest frequent bedpan use, although that isn't necessarily conclusive, nor did I see the presence of said bed pan. This would suggest that she was most likely incontinent, but whoever was supposed to be taking care of her wasn't doing a particularly good job."

"Right," Morrison said, lifting his eyebrows. "So, what do you think was wrong with her?"

"It's hard to say, really. It could have been any number of debilitating diseases."

Sky stopped as they reached the foot of the stairs and met his gaze... "But then, you already know that, don't you, Detective?" she asked with a faint smile.

A few seconds went by. He returned the smile.

Sky walked away from him, toward the front door. Raising her voice, she threw back, "Not just a pretty face, eh, Detective?" she asked, stepping out into the night once more.

Morrison chuckled, and then followed her out.

Outside, Sky sucked in the fresh evening air. It was such a relief to be out of that bedroom. "Did she live alone?" She asked as they reached her car and she began to wriggle out of the white jumpsuit.

"No. According to the neighbour," Morrison nodded toward the ambulance, where the woman with the wispy white hair was still chattering on, "She lived with her daughter."

"Where's she?"

"We don't know. She seems to have disappeared."

"Do you think she did this?"

"It's hard to say… According to the neighbour, the daughter hardly ever left the house since moving back. They had all their groceries delivered. The neighbour stopped by after the power cut out to ask if they needed anything, and that's when she found the body. By the way, you were right about her. She has been bedridden for over two years now. That's why the daughter moved out here to live with her. Apparently, she used to be some bigshot at a Japanese electronics firm."

"Detective!" someone shouted.

"What?" Morrison barked back in the direction of a bobbing flashlight that had appeared out of the darkness.

"I think we've found something," the voice said.

"What is it?"

"Another body, Sir. On the beeeeeaach!"

The voice trailed off as the officer slipped over. All that could be seen was the beam of the flashlight flailing back and forth, followed by a loud thud and the word "SHIT!"

"For the love of God, man," Morrison grumbled. He turned to Sky, who was suppressing a smile. "Thanks again, Doc."

Then, he was off, walking in the direction of the fallen officer.

Sky looked on, still smiling until her mind replayed the snapshots of what she had witnessed inside that bedroom, and now, more than ever, she longed for her mother's embrace.

The officer had found a body on the beach, wedged between two rocks. It turned out to be that of Joyce Masters, the forty-year-old daughter of Judith Masters.

Joyce Masters had drowned. There were no signs indicating that she had been forced into the water by anything or anyone. The preliminary conclusion was that the woman had deliberately walked into the ocean and drowned herself.

14

The drive back to Stony Point was long.

Sky felt drained, and the image of the old woman continued to haunt her in the dark of the car, to the point where she half expected to look in the rear view mirror and see those filmy white eyes staring back at her.

The only effective distraction was Blake. She didn't know why, but she found the thought of seeing him comforting, and the sight of the majestic lighthouse reassuring. She pulled up outside and switched off the engine. Then, she sat for a few moments, clutching the steering wheel as she collected her thoughts, and her composure.

She touched her chest, as if to verify what she already knew; her heart was pounding. Something was off. She couldn't quite explain it, but something was unsettling her. It felt as if there was some big, black woe, tugging at the fringes of her mind, like potentially hideous bad news. It could not be what she had seen at the farm, although it had undoubtedly been the catalyst, for she had obviously examined plenty of cadavers in the past five years, many of which had been the result of violent homicides.

Maybe it was the fact that this was her first major placement since her London residency. But why? She wasn't exactly afraid of hard work, nor did she ever shy away from being a team leader. She welcomed it. She welcomed the responsibility. That was because she was both confident and competent in her work, as well as meticulous, hardworking and thorough. All words that featured regularly in her appraisals.

So, what's your problem? Why are you suddenly feeling so vulnerable?

There it was!

Vulnerable.

The thought alone irritated her. So, she gave herself a mental talking to, gathered her emotions, and stepped into the night. The air was fresh, heavily impregnated with the scent of rain. Nearby, the odd rumble of thunder reminded her that it wasn't done.

She knocked on the front door and listened to the sound of the ocean as she waited, before it was replaced by muffled footsteps on stone floor.

The door opened, and it was in that moment, as she watched him standing before her, that she understood her feelings. Blake looked dishevelled, but every bit as handsome. His normally gelled hair was flat, and his dark brown eyes looked glazed and sleepy.

"Hey," he said in a soft tone, smiling warmly. "All sorted?"

It took Sky a few seconds to reply, "Yeah. Yes, thanks." Regaining her composure, she added, "I'm so sorry about this evening, Blake."

"It's okay."

"We can do it some other time. That's, of course, if you still want to now, as you're probably going to wonder if this is going to happen every time…"

"It's okay. Really."

"I really am sorry, but it's work."

"Have you quite finished apologising?"

"I'm sorry…" She laughed.

There was an awkward moment.

"Look, are you coming in or are you going to stand there all night?" he asked.

"I, well, really, I should be getting back."

"What? Drive home? Now? Don't be silly. It's like an hour or more to yours. You may as well stay the night."

"Oh no. I couldn't."

"Of course you can. Besides, I've made dinner."

"What?"

"Don't get excited. It's just pasta. The water's on and I've already made the sauce, straight from the jar," he added proudly.

"Wow. I didn't know you cooked."

"I don't."

She laughed.

"So?" Blake stood, expectantly, with his hand still resting on the door. "It's all right, you know. I won't molest you in the middle of the night. Or, at least I'll try not to," he added, grinning.

"You always were a spoil sport," she said in mock disappointment as she stepped inside.

"Here, let me take that," he said, gesturing to her coat as she tried to shake it off.

"Thanks."

He hooked the coat over the door and ushered her through to the living room. "So, would you like a drink now?" he asked, moving over to the cabinet.

She thought about it. Technically, she was still on call.

"Just a small one."

She felt like she needed something.

"What would you like?"

"Actually, I think I could use a Brandy."

"Blimey. Brandy. To warm you up, or steady your nerves?"

"Both. So, bring the bottle," she laughed.

He eyed her seriously.

"I'm kidding," she added.

One hour, and a plate of pasta later, they were both sitting in the lounge, sipping coffee.

"You still haven't told me anything about this emergency that took you away from our dinner date, or can't you talk about it?" Blake was sitting opposite her in an armchair.

"You're right. I can't discuss it with you, but suffice to say that there are some really sick people out there."

"Yeah, I know. We vote for them all the time," He said with a wink. He didn't know what Sky had witnessed, but he could tell that she had been somehow affected. "So, do you want to sleep in my bed tonight?" he asked, changing the subject.

"Oh no, the sofa will be fine, thanks," she said, patting the cushion next to her.

"No, I insist."

"Blake, really… I don't want to put you out."

"You won't be putting me out, at all."

"So, where will you sleep?"

"Well, same place as you."

Sky smiled broadly. "I don't think so."

"Why not?"

"Well, because.... I," she fumbled, but the words wouldn't come to her, and she felt her face blushing.

He laughed, "Hey relax, I'm kidding. I pulled a spare toothbrush out; it's by the sink."

Sky's eyebrows lifted.

"Well, you never know when good old friends are going to stop by," he said.

The rain came back during the night and the sound of tapping on the window woke Sky from a restless slumber.

She slipped out of the bed.

Blake's shirt, that she had borrowed to use as a nightdress, flapped loosely across her bare thighs as she crossed the round room and quietly descended the cold, but mercifully quiet, metal steps.

The living room door was open and Sky's heart started pounding as she approached it. Blake was in there, and by the sound of his deep and rhythmic breathing, he was fast asleep. A knot formed in her throat, she felt giddy, and her palms began to sweat.

Get a grip!

But, she could not help herself. Blake could be lying naked beyond that door, and there was no point denying how she was feeling. The symptoms were obvious; she had just been repressing them. Blaming everything else other than accepting what was perfectly clear, that she still wanted this man. Even after all of these years, she still wanted and maybe even loved him.

She paused by the doorway.

The kitchen light was on, and the overspill was shining an amber spotlight on the quilt that was lying in a heap on the floor while Blake lay sprawled on the sofa, wearing nothing but his boxer shorts. She drank in his long, powerful legs and muscular body as her heart rapped at her rib cage like a precocious child.

She was not yearning for Blake at all. She had given up on him and anything to do with him many years before, and she did not intend to go back to that, she had no intention of feeling that vulnerable in the hands of another human being, ever again. No, there was some other perfectly rational reason why she was now tiptoeing across the room, towards the sofa with just one thought in mind – to touch him, even if it was only for a few seconds.

She was within touching distance now. All she had to do was reach out, but she couldn't. Instead, she stood, motionless, fixed to the spot as her throat dried to dust and blood thumped so loudy behind her ears, she wondered if he might actually be able to hear it. Then, in that moment, his right hand moved. It travelled from his chest to his stomach.

However, Sky had not seen this, for, at the first sign of movement, she had darted into the safe haven that was the kitchen. There, like some love-stricken teenager, she leaned heavily against the wall, her breath fast and shallow.

She turned to the sink, filled a glass with water, and drank with a desperate thirst.

The sound of the rain pelting the kitchen window drew her attention to the open blinds. She watched her reflection and then allowed her mind to drift through the glass to the blackness beyond. There, she saw the image of Judith Masters, and she was instantly reminded of the evils of man. With that, she fled the kitchen, climbed the stairs two at a time, and dove under the safety of the covers, where she replayed images of Blake over and over in her mind.

These were her last thoughts as she drifted off into a deep sleep, completely oblivious to the dark skies that were gathering overhead.

15

Morning came too soon, with the sound of Blake's voice calling to her, many times, before Sky actually awoke from a blissful sleep.

He entered the room, carrying a tray of hot coffee and warm croissants. "Fresh from the bakery," he announced proudly, depositing the tray on the bedside table whilst Sky, conscious of what her hair must look like first thing in the morning, sat up, frantically tucking the loose strands behind her ears.

"Did you sleep okay?" he asked.

"Great, thanks," she replied, still composing herself.

"Well, you'll be pleased to know that it's going to be sunny today, but we can expect more of those stormy showers tonight."

"Have you been consulting your computer again?" she asked, discreetly admiring the black suit he was wearing.

"No, I watched the weather forecast this morning," he replied. There was a pause as he looked at her, and then he said, "I've got to go now, but I'll leave the key in the door. Just push it back through the letterbox when you leave."

"Are you sure? I mean, I can get dressed…"

"… Don't be silly. Take your time. I'll see you later?"

Sky had no idea what that meant exactly, but she found herself saying, "Okay."

With that, Blake disappeared out the door.

A few minutes later, she heard the Range Rover's engine start, and then fade into the distance.

She stretched; the bed was comfortable, and her toes felt particularly warm, so she looked up to discover the early morning sunshine, streaming in through the large window and casting a hazy golden glow over the bed.

Reluctantly, she slipped out from under the quilt, padded across the room and caught her breath; the view was stunning. White, foamy peaks rode aquamarine waves as they rolled, lazily, to the shore of a coastline that stretched for at least a mile, while seagulls glided lazily in a pale blue sky.

The shrill of the phone brought her back to the present, where she found herself sitting in her small office in the coroner's building.

She hastily answered it, "Doctor McPherson."

"Sky?"

"Yes, who is this?"

"It's Blake."

"Oh, hi, hello." A smile spread across her face, although her voice remained cool and casual.

"I was just ringing to see if you got into the office okay."

"Oh, yes, fine, no problem. Thanks. "

"I know what the traffic can be like from my place first thing in the morning."

"Oh yeah, you're right. It was hell. I came across a twack of ducks, and a man on his bike, and several seagulls."

Blake laughed. "You were lucky, then. Wait, did you say a *twack* of ducks?"

"That's what they're called, aren't they?"

Blake continued laughing.

"What?"

The laughter at the end of the line continued until she joined in.

Then, there was a pause.

Sky wanted desperately to find something else to say, to sustain the conversation, but, suddenly, her mind went blank. "You were right," she stuttered, "the views from your place are incredible."

Really? How pathetic are you? I'm desperate!

"Yes. They're pretty awesome," he agreed.

More silence.

"You must be pretty busy today," he offered.

He was referring to the early morning news bulletins, reporting on several incidents of random acts of violence that had taken place the night before. Three people had died and more had been injured in what were seemingly unprovoked attacks.

"We did take delivery of a few clients this morning, yes. I'm due to start work on them shortly." She glanced at the pile of manila folders on her desk. One of them caught her attention.

"Any idea what's going on?" He asked.

"No idea," she said distractedly as she plucked the file from the stack, "at least not until after the post mortems."

The label affixed to the folder read: *McElvoy, Arthur.* She opened it.

"So, when are you going to make it up to me?"

"Make what up to you?" she asked, thumbing through the sheets inside the folder.

"Dinner."

"Dinner? We ate last night."

"You know what I mean; dinner, that isn't from a jar, and doesn't feature uncooked pasta."

"Oh, well, oh my God!"

"Alright, it wasn't that bad...."

Silence.

"Sky? Are you still there?"

"Yes, I'm here. Sorry, that wasn't aimed at you. I'm looking at Arthur McElvoy's lab results."

"Arthur...?" It took Blake a few seconds to register the name. "McElvoy. What about him?"

"They found an unknown substance in his blood."

"Unknown substance," Blake echoed. "Like what?"

"I don't know. But whatever this thing is, it must have attacked his system with the ferocity of a virus."

"Is it something he ingested?" Blake asked.

"I don't know. I'll know more after the autopsy." She bit her lip, and then said, reluctantly, "Blake, I need to go."

"Yes, of course. No problem." He was about to disconnect, but thought he heard her say something. "What was that?" he asked.

"I said, I'll see you tonight, then."

Blake smiled, "See you then." He pressed the disconnect button on his mobile phone and slipped it back into his coat pocket. He squinted into the sun that was bright in the Eastern sky, in complete contrast to the bubbling black mounds that were slowly advancing from the West. Around him, the Cornish countryside was a canvas of lush green trees and sprawling fields.

Slowly, his gaze drifted back, like a director's camera, panning over the distant hills, the surrounding valley, and then the quarry, where a crater roughly the size of a small football pitch had been carved out of the earth and filled with water.

"Looks like more rain," the farmer said.

Blake followed the elderly man's gaze and, right on cue, deep guttural thunder rumbled in the distance. "I think you're right," Blake said, pausing on the approaching gloom. Then, "So, when did you discover them?" He asked, stepping cautiously down the embankment toward the pool.

"This morning. Cows won't drink anywhere else."

"What time this morning?"

The old man pondered for a few seconds and then said, "Oh, round about six-thirty."

"And they definitely weren't here yesterday?"

"Nope. As I say, they won't drink anywhere else, and as soon as I let them out, they come trotting 'ere. Must be somethin' in the water somethin'."

They were at the water's edge now, and Blake could see them; hundreds, maybe thousands of dead fish were floating on the surface.

He scanned the immediate area around the pit, looking for tyre marks or anything else that would indicate any human interference with the quarry, but found nothing. He made a mental note to check the surrounding area.

"And you haven't seen anyone around here? No trucks or vans?" Blake asked.

"No, nothing."

"What about people? Any anglers?"

"Nah, nobody ever bothers to come down here. A lot of people don't even know the place exists."

"How about smells? Have you noticed any unusual smells lately?"

"Smells?" The old man frowned. "No, no smells."

"So, nothing out of the ordinary?"

"No."

"But you can't see this place from your farm, is that right?"

"That's right."

"So, it is possible that someone could have come here, and dumped something in the water without you seeing them?"

"I only live a few miles down the road."

"But you aren't here all the time?"

"Not all the time, no, but they come here every day," the farmer said, nodding at the black and white cows grazing nearby. "And where they go, I go."

"Okay." Blake produced a black, numbered notebook from the inside pocket of his jacket, and wrote in it. "Sorry, and your full name, again is?"

"Trevor, Trevor Wilson."

"And where do you live, Mr, Wilson? Just in case I need to contact you."

"Trevassy Farm. As I said, it's just a few miles down the road."

"And Mr. Wilson, you wouldn't happen to know who this quarry belongs to, would you?"

Farmer Wilson moved closer and said in a hushed tone, "Well, I heard it belonged to the M.O.D."

"The Ministry of Defence?"

"Yeah."

"How do you know that?"

"It's just what I heard."

"What about the fish? Do you know how long the fish have been in this quarry?

"I think it's a couple of years now."

"And you've never seen anything like this before?"

"No, but there's no knowing what that lot have left behind. They could've carried out all kinds of experiments in 'ere."

"Is that just what you think, or do you actually know something?"

"I don't know anything. You're from the government, aren't you? You probably know more than I do."

"Actually, the Environment Agency's is pretty much an independent body."

"What, they privatising you, as well, now?"

Blake smiled, "You could say that."

"I've gotta' get me a pair of those," the farmer remarked, eyeing Blake's green waders. "Come in handy in the dipping season."

"You dip cows?"

"No. I would have a bit of a job doin' that," the farmer

chuckled. "Nah, dipping sheep."

"You have sheep on your farm as well as cows?"

"No, I don't, but my mate Vince does."

"Right," Blake smiled, crouching down, picking up a deflated life jacket, and slipping it over his head.

"Planning on doing some swimming?"

"Regulation."

"More rules. I don't know how you people know whether you're coming or going. Every day, they bring out different rules."

Blake flipped the locks on the hard case he had brought with him. He removed what looked like a small milk bottle and then, slowly and cautiously, stepped into the water.

"You wanna' be careful where you put your feet. It's deep in there," the farmer offered.

Blake slipped a rubber glove onto his right hand, and then collected a water sample. Once the bottle was full, he screwed on the lid, shook it, and then held it up to the sun.

"See anything in there?" the farmer asked, squinting at the bottle as if it were some kind of a crystal ball.

The water had a verdant tinge, but that wasn't anything unusual. Blake dated and noted the location on a sticky back label, and then affixed it to the bottle.

"Nothing obvious," he said, "but the lab will tell us more."

A strong breeze blew at them.

"You can smell it," the farmer said, sniffing the air.

"Smell what?" Blake asked.

"The rain. Oh yeah, this is gonna' be some storm."

"How do you know?"

"The cows," he said, looking down the valley. "They're headin' back in. Always do when it's bad weather."

"Right." Blake nodded, following Wilson's gaze.

Sure enough, the herd was trotting off in a disciplined single file line.

"Probably just had enough grass for one day," Blake said, but the farmer wasn't looking at him; he seemed much more interested in the gathering gloom.

"Would you mind?" Blake asked, gesturing to a fishing net he had left on the embankment.

Wilson hurried over to the net and passed it across.

Blake used the net to fish out one of the corpses, which he studied carefully. The fish's dead eyes stared back. Its gills were open, indicating that it had mostly likely been struggling to breathe moments before its death.

"What do you think caused this then?"

"I don't know," Blake shrugged, looking across the water. "It's unlikely to be a disease of any kind."

"Why's that?"

"Well, if you're sure that the dead fish weren't here yesterday, then it's highly unlikely that it was a disease. Diseases in fish are normally slow-acting and tend to affect a particular species. Here, all of the fish have been killed, indiscriminately. Which means that, whatever it was, it was potent."

"Like what?"

"Well, it could be anything, really. From a rise in water temperature to a pollutant in the water, which, at this moment in time, seems most likely."

"Could it have the same effect on my girls?" Wilson asked worriedly.

Blake looked at him.

"Me cows," Wilson explained.

"Well, that's it, we don't know. My advice would be to keep them well away from here until we've established exactly what happened. Do you know if this quarry has an outlet of any kind, like a stream or something?"

"Not that I know of. Have you ever seen anything like this before?"

Blake shook his head, "A few times, but not on this scale."

"I 'aven't neither," Wilson said, leaning forward in order to get a better look at the dead fish, but immediately snapped his head away. "Phew... what's that smell?" he complained.

"Well this is it," Blake pondered, staring at the fish as if his gaze would revive it. "I thought the smell was decomposition, but they haven't been here long enough for that. Could be B.O.D, yet there's no real discolouration in the water."

"Come again? B.O. what?" the farmer asked, still wiping his nose.

The stink was like rotten eggs.

"Biochemical Oxygen Demand," Blake explained. "Lack of oxygen can kill fish, and cause the water to smell."

"You mean stink!"

Blake smiled.

"So, what would suddenly cause this lack of oxygen?"

"Again, in such short a period of time, I don't know," he replied distractedly as he surveyed the surrounding area.

Then, he shook the dead fish into a plastic sample bag, sealed it, and placed it into his hard case. From there, he retrieved a small electronic device, about the size of a large remote control, with an LCD display, and a flexible probe protruding from one end.

"What…" Wilson began.

"..It's a D.O. metre," Blake anticipated. "It's used to measure the dissolved oxygen in the water. It's what the fish need to breathe."

Blake immersed the probe into the water, and watched as the LCD screen returned the data; it was normal.

He deposited the D.O. metre back into the case and pulled out another specimen bag.

Treading carefully, he began turning over stones until he found a small grub. He picked it up, examined it, concluded it was dead, and placed it in the specimen bag.

Lightning flashed in the distance, closely followed by a rumble of thunder.

"Just to reiterate what I said earlier. I would keep your cows away from here. Just as a precaution."

"Right," the old man said, eyeing him suspiciously.

Then, with Wilson's help, Blake gathered his equipment and made his way back to the Range Rover. There, he removed his waders and dumped them in the boot.

"So, what now?" the old man asked.

"Well, as I said, we'll run a mass scan on that sample and keep you informed." Blake paused for a few seconds, and then said, "Just one more thing. Do you know how the water in here is replenished?"

"Well, it's mostly rainfall, I would have thought."

"Just rainfall?"

"As far as I know. Why?"

"Just wondering," Blake said pensively as he climbed behind the wheel of his car.

The dark skies moaned as Blake drove away.

16

Trevassy Farm – Cornwall – 19:30

The rain hammered down on the old farm, flooding the yard and bubbling over the clogged-up guttering. It was as if it was searching the whole structure of the building, seeking an entrance, a hole, a crack in the wall, somewhere it could gain access to reach the old man inside.

Farmer Wilson was preparing his dinner when one long drop of water fell onto his loaf of bread and was absorbed into the yeast compound.

"Blast!" he cussed. "Damn rain!"

The house was steeped in gloom, and it seemed that the 60-watt bulb was on its way out, as it kept flickering while that ever-mournful gale had been resurrected, and was now howling around the building, rattling the glass in the peeling window frames. This drew Wilson's attention, and that was when he noticed them.

"What the hell…"

He screwed his face up as he peered through the rivulets of water streaming down the glass. All fifteen of his cows were in the yard. They stood, unmoving, facing the house, as rain scurried down their coats and dripped off their ears. They watched Wilson with unblinking black eyes as he peered out of the watery blur.

All right. How did you girls manage to get out, then?

He clearly remembered herding them into their pen and locking the gate. However, now, as real as his leaky roof, the cows were bundled together, filling up the yard with a mass of steaming bodies.

"I tell ya'. You girls got a bloody mind all of your own," he muttered.

Thunder boomed overhead, and it made him jump. The roof creaked under the torrential onslaught, composing a low drone like a swarm of angry insects. It was unlike anything he had heard before.

The drip over the table was now a steady stream, and Wilson hurried over to the sink, fetched a saucepan, and placed it under the infiltrator, instantly creating a tinkling symphony. He slowly looked up at the roof, as if there was somebody up there, somebody whose weight was going to bring the whole thing crashing down on top of him.

IT, the rain, was here and it was hunting him; streaming over the roof, seeping into the walls, and trickling under the door.

Then they began. In unison, the whole herd began mooing.

"Serves you bleedin' right; that'll teach ya' to leave your pen and go out walkin'. Now you can stay out there, for all I care."

Wilson may have spoken the words, but he was thinking something completely different. One of the region's best and most expensive pedigree bull had successfully inseminated the majority of those cows. If they stayed out in the rain and caught cold, there was a good chance some might well lose their calves.

He couldn't take the risk.

There was only one thing for it – he would have to go out there and get them back into their pen.

He cursed as he pulled his raincoat off the stand, and then cursed again when he heard his boots slosh in the pool of rainwater that had seeped under the door.

The liquid enveloped the soles of his boots, but failed to penetrate the rubber tread.

"Bloody hell!" He looked down to see that the water was oozing, like a poisonous snake, toward the table.

More thunder cracked overhead.

He pulled his coat on as the synchronised mooing continued.

However, Wilson was going to sort them out. He would take a stick to them, if he had to.

"Yeah, you girls are in a whole load of trouble." He snatched the door open and launched himself into the rain. It pelted his face as the gale tugged at his coat and yanked off his hood.

Lightning flashed.

Green lightning?

The rain stung his eyes, hissing and spluttering as it drenched his balding head, driving into his skin and infiltrating his pores.

More mooing.

More thunder.

Wilson struggled to keep the coat around him as he battled forward.

Lightning flashed.

"Come on!" he shouted over the din. "Get back in there!"

The cows did not move. They simply watched.

"Go on! Get in there, I said!" he shouted, waving his hands around.

The action loosened his coat collar. The rain was relentless. It washed over his neck, dribbled down his chest, seeped into his vest, and soaked his skin. "Go on, I said! Get back in, before I use the bleedin' stick on the lot of ya'!"

"NOW!" He screamed in frustration.

Nothing. The cows would not budge, but they did stop mooing.

That was when Wilson noticed her. Betty, his black and white Holstein pride and joy, was standing at the front of the herd.

"Go on, Betty, love. Go on!" he said in a calmer voice, pushing the cow's head around.

However, the cow was anchored in place, and instead of moving, she swung her head back, butting Wilson in the chest. The impact sent him stumbling backward and, as much as he tried to retain his balance, the old man slipped in the mud and fell, heavily, into a pool of water. It engulfed him, seeping into his eyes and ears.

It took him a while to recover from the shock of the impact, the cold of the water, and the dirt in his eyes. He emerged, spluttering and swearing, and was about to scream something at the cow, but stopped.

Suddenly, he felt queasy.

It was an odd sensation, unlike anything he had experienced before. It felt like an alcoholic buzz, something he was very familiar with – only, this was different. He could actually feel it, gradually spreading through his system. It started in his toes, travelled up his legs, through his groin, into the pit of his stomach, and up his spine, until it reached his brain, where warm tentacles probed and prodded the darkest corners of his mind.

Meanwhile, Betty and her friends had moved forward, towards his fallen body.

He looked up, squinting into the precipitation as the cow's large bulk loomed over him. He watched as the reflection of him, sitting in a puddle of muddy water, appeared in her black eyes.

"That's it… That's my girl…. Come and help me up… Come on."

With that, the cow threw her head up to the sky and mooed once more. In unison, the other cows joined in. The cacophony was loud and frightening.

Wilson wanted to block his ears. Instead, he tried to scramble to his feet, but the movement was too fast, causing him to slip and fall onto his back once more.

Suddenly, Betty jumped forward and tossed her head in the air, mooing like a newborn calf.

Wilson tried to roll out of her path but he was too late. The whole of the fifteen-hundred-pound cow stomped onto his groin in the form of a hoof.

Wilson wanted to scream, but all of the air was sucked out of his lungs as pain engulfed the lower part of his body. Such was the agony of the first blow that he hardly noticed the second stamp on his chest that crushed his breastbone. Hyperventilating and coughing blood, he crawled onto his side as the warm tingle inside his skull did its best to mute the excruciating pain. Slowly, he dragged his body through the muddy water in an attempt to escape the deranged bovine, but progress was minimal – the attempt to escape the lethal hooves, futile.

Thunder roared and lightning flashed as the cows watched Wilson's puny attempt to slither away, but only for a short while.

Betty danced forward and trampled over her owner, smashing one hoof into his back, another into his skull, and another onto his outstretched hand.

The rest of the herd followed suit, jumping and kicking the stricken human until his body was nothing more than a mangled mess of blood and bone.

17

Stony Point - 20:45.

Blake glanced up at the window; the rain was still falling heavily, and had been for the past hour.

He wondered where Sky was, and if she was okay. The news had talked of several accidents in the region, due to bad weather. There had also been reports of localised flooding, mudslides, and several bizarre incidents of reckless driving.

Where is she?

He realised that he was no longer miffed by the fact that he was being stood up again, but worried that something might have happened to her since all of his calls had been instantly diverted to voicemail.

Lightning flashed outside.

He was sitting at his computer now, looking up plans for the quarry he had visited early that day.

Wilson was right; there was no other water source. Which meant that the lake was in fact replenished by rainfall alone. However, if that was true, and if everything Wilson had told him was right, then it would suggest that whatever had poisoned the fish had originated from the rain.

As if to confirm this, an eerie green flash of lightning illuminated the room, but Blake was too busy scanning low-pressure trajectories to notice it.

Could there be a link between the rain and the dead fish?

Of course there could. He lectured about this very thing in college every week – acid rain.

Yes, but toxic enough to kill thousands of fish? And why would it affect just them? Or has it?

He argued with himself. The theory was absurd. Of course, there had been many cases of acid rain affecting both animals and vegetation, but the symptoms and the effects were gradual – they didn't happen overnight.

Despite this, Blake's fingers worked the keyboard and, before long, the spinning globe filled his computer screen.

He pinched to zoom into a map of England.

Gradually, patches of black and grey appeared, smothering most of the Southwest. The data at the foot of the screen told him that there were light winds, which meant that the rain was here to stay.

He zoomed out. The screen refreshed, revealing a map of the United Kingdom and then the cloud layer.

He tapped a key on his keyboard. A rash of white squiggles appeared, along with numerical data – wind speed and trajectory.

He pinched to zoom out. The map of the United Kingdom dissolved into that of Europe. Now, the white squiggles streaked north, from Cornwall to the Hebrides, and beyond. He paused as his brain, like the hard drive of his machine, processed the information.

The sound of the doorknocker echoed, loudly, up the stairwell.

Sky!

Within seconds, he had left his study and was descending the stairs two at a time. He snatched the front door open, just as she was about to knock again.

"Late again," she said cheerfully as she stood there, holding her handbag over her head.

Blake stood aside, ushered her in, and closed the door behind her.

"I tried to call you," she said, shaking the rain from her handbag, but, would you believe it, my phone died, of all nights. I tell you, this weather is really starting to get to me."

Blake noticed a nervousness to her chatter, and that she was avoiding making eye contact with him.

"I left work and it was fine, and then, suddenly, I felt like I was caught in the middle of a bloody monsoon! I'm surprised I got here at all. Did you hear about all those accidents? My God, it was bad! I couldn't see three feet in front of me, and then," she swallowed, "then, this bloody maniac in a bloody lorry nearly ran me off the road! I had to pull onto the grass verge, but then I got stuck in the bloody mud. So, I did first gear, second gear, to try and get out. I could really have used your four-by-four. Luckily, eventually, and just seconds after I had a major meltdown, I realised that my car isn't permanent four-wheel drive, and that I needed to switch the damn thing on. You know, it would really help if they bloody pointed this stuff out to you when you buy these things! Anyway, I'm here… finally, but, as you can see, late again…."

"…Sky…"

"What's the time? Right, it's late, but I'm sure we could find somewhere, that's if you want to brave the bloody hurricane out there…."

"…Sky…"

"…I really am sorry…"

"…Sky!" Blake said, forcefully.

She flinched at his raised voice, but finally stopped chattering. He noticed she was shaking.

"Oh my God, Sky. Are you okay?" He asked, anxiously, as he helped her unwind from her coat.

She looked at him as tears welled in her eyes. "I nearly died tonight," she said, flatly. "That maniac came out of nowhere. He missed my car by inches and then ploughed into someone else."

Her voice was an incredulous tremble.

"Hey," he cooed, pulling her to him. "It's alright. You're alright." His voice was warm and comforting, his embrace strong and reassuring, and the scent of his aftershave soothing.

She melted into him and allowed the tears to come, for she was a shipwreck of emotions, and he her island. For several minutes, the sound of her heart-wrenching sobs upstaged the storm outside.

Eventually, she emerged from her nest in his sweater and their eyes met for several seconds before he gently leaned forward and kissed the runaway tears on her cheek. The heat of his closeness was electrifying, the softness of his lips intoxicating.

She turned her face so that their lips were closer as his stubble

117

brushed against her, the sensation abrasive yet seductive as it sparked and reignited a love that had been buried deep within her breast.

Thunder rumbled loudly overhead as the rain battered the lighthouse. It was searching for a way inside. A hole in the roof, the crack of an open window, or even the slit under a door – any way it could find an entrance and be absorbed into a host. As the green lightning flashed furiously at the watertight building, their mouths met in a desperate and passionate kiss. Blake's masculine aroma fuelled Sky's need as the scent from her damp hair instantly aroused him. Their mouths remained adhered, neither of them wishing to let go as they fumbled with each other's clothing.

He expertly unbuttoned her blouse while she unbuckled his belt. He unbuttoned her trousers as she pushed off his sweater. She explored his chest with her hands, as if discovering it for the first time, as he kissed the mounds of flesh imprisoned in her bra.

Then, she kicked off her shoes and stepped out of her trousers, seconds before he pushed them backwards until they slammed, loudly, against the door.

Almost as if it had sensed the human presence, the rain washed onto the front step and merged into a swelling puddle. It rapidly gathered form, and then slowly trickled under the door, towards Blake's shoes and Sky's naked feet.

She was delicately nipping his neck, but her urge was to bite it for her senses were on fire, and a collection of emotions battled for manifestation – love, lust, anger, sorrow and desire were just some of the complex feelings she was experiencing, but there were only a few she was willing to express right now.

Slowly, the rain sluiced into the house, engulfing Blake's shoes and leaking, hungrily, forward to Sky's beckoning toes.

Closer…

…Sky unbuttoned and unzipped Blake's jeans as he finally freed her breasts from their prison.

…Closer…

…He teased and nipped her nipples with his teeth and tongue, causing her to squirm and moan with pleasure…

…And just inches away…

…She searched his back, his torso, his hair with her fingers as their mouths kissed, hungrily, desperately, while she clutched his hands, guiding one over her thigh and then down between her legs.

He wanted her. She needed him. Their hunger for each other was matched only by their desire...

…the rain finally touched her heels and rapidly moved to engulf the rest of her naked feet …

…his fingers slid deep between her legs, and began to probe gently, making her gasp loudly in breathless anticipation.

…the rain began to infiltrate her pores, and soon it would be absorbed into her blood stream, and then into her brain…

…he tugged at her delicate underwear; it ripped easily, fuelling both of their desires.

Then, he scooped her into muscular arms, pausing only to allow her to free him from the confines of his jeans, before slamming her, passionately, against the door where, shoes squelching loudly in the pool of water, he thrust deep into her, causing her to cry out in a concoction of pain and ecstasy.

They kissed hungrily, noisily, and eagerly – each deliriously excited to have their desires finally fulfilled.

Outside, the rain spat viciously and the thunder roared angrily, drowning out the sound of thumping on the door as the scene was, intermittently, filtered green.

18

Exeter, Devonshire – 21:00.

"You can't light that up in here," the taxi driver barked at the boys in the backseat of the cab. They had been in his car for no more than seven minutes, and were already getting on his nerves.

Alan had been happily listening to the news on the radio when this lot had flagged him down, and he had thought twice about stopping, especially when one of them actually staggered into the path of his taxi. They had obviously had a skin-full already, and were going to finish themselves off at the club they were going to. He had heard all kinds of stories about that place.

None of them good.

"Why not?" asked the skinnier of the lads who couldn't have been far out of his teens.

"Because I say so," Alan replied, watching them in the rear view mirror. He heard the sound of sniggering, but chose to ignore it.

As his passengers set about planning their 'pulling' strategy for the evening, Alan couldn't help but wonder what was wrong with the youth of today. Humans had never had life this easy. Yet, earlier today, he'd heard a news bulletin about a bunch of teenagers who had raped and then doused an old woman with petrol, and set her on fire.

The world's gone mad!

He stopped the taxi at a red traffic light.

The streets were empty. Most likely the result of the police warning, issued earlier in the evening. It encouraged the public to be vigilant in the wake of a series of random acts of violence in the city.

The few who had ventured out into the night were either standing, like zombies, under the falling rain with their hands thrust to the skies as if at worship, or chasing each other through the streets in a nerve-jangling siren of screams.

Peering through the windscreen, Alan caught sight of a threesome on the opposite side of the junction, two males and a female. They were weakly spot-lit by a jaundiced streetlamp, which meant that most of what they were doing was in shadow, but what he could just about discern made his face crease with incredulous disgust.

The female had her back against the lamppost. One of the males appeared to be embracing her from behind while holding her arms above her head, while the other was searching under her skirt as she threw her head back, revealing a deranged look of ecstasy.

Whatever they were doing, she was enjoying it. Right there, in the middle of the street, under the pouring rain.

The lights changed green, and Alan was relieved to be moving once again, and grateful that his passengers had not noticed the *ménage a trios* across the road.

"How long to the club?" Luke asked.

He appeared to be the older and the best looking of the three. He wore his blonde hair neat and short in back and on the sides, had a healthy complexion, and Alan estimated he was most likely in his early twenties. "Shouldn't be long now," he replied. "Providing we get there in one piece."

They were driving down a long, rain-drenched road.

In the streetlights, a bunch of youths shoved a rubbish bin through the window of a jeweller, setting off the alarm and an orange flashing light. Then they jumped about, roaring with laughter and congratulating each other on their deed. Suddenly, as if they had just beamed down, a team of police officers pounced on the hooligans, grappling to overpower them.

Luke craned his neck in an effort to see as much as he could of the incident.

"Fucking hell, man, did you see that?" his skinny companion cried excitedly as he buzzed down the window, stuck his head out, and cheered at the scuffle.

"Yeah," Luke replied, perplexed. He had never seen such blatant vandalism in the town before. In fact, he was quite perturbed by the whole scene. He'd witnessed a few of these episodes this evening, and it was making him feel uneasy.

"We'll have less of that, if you don't mind," Alan said in a raised voice, so that the youth could hear him.

Tristan reeled his head back in, shaking the raindrops that clung to it over his two friends, who both squealed dramatically.

"The problem is that the majority of them can't handle their drink, and then they get out of control. It's the police I feel sorry for," Alan offered, deliberately loading his words as he watched his passengers in the rear view mirror.

"You're 'aving a laugh," was the third lad's contribution. The stocky guy with a crew cut had been busy for most of the ride, surreptitiously rolling a joint. "If you ask me. I reckon that most of those cops ought'a get nicked for abuse of power, mate."

"And what exactly are you basing that opinion on?" Alan

asked.

"Well…" the youth struggled to find the words. "I see videos about it every day in my stream."

"Oh well, if you've read about on Facebook then it must be true," Alan replied dismissively.

"Oi! What's that supposed to mean?" Jason leant forward.

Luke pushed him back.

"Nothing. I was just agreeing with you." Alan's reply was indifferent. This youth was obviously drunk and looking for trouble.

Luke opened his mouth to join in the discussion, but decided against it. His head was feeling giddy, and the motion of the taxi was making him want to puke. He knew he shouldn't have mixed his drinks, despite his friends' insistence.

"Here we are," Alan said as he drove into a pool of blue light and onto a thumping baseline that vibrated through the car.

Jason and Tristan sprang out, leaving the door ajar, and instantly joined a queue of people who seemed oblivious to the falling rain.

"Oi, you two!" Luke called.

Neither of them answered, both busy eyeing the girl in front of them. She was wearing tight leather trousers and a jacket pushed open by a well-filled bra.

As if by some extrasensory perception, the girl turned and smiled at them both, running her fingers through her rain-drenched hair and then licking them. Both lads looked at each other, unable to comprehend their luck.

Meanwhile, Luke was handing over cash to the taxi driver.

"Do you come here often?" Alan asked as he took the money and then rummaged around in a small plastic container.

"Don't worry about the change," Luke said quickly, holding up a dismissive hand. "No, I don't. What's it like?" he asked, trying to suppress a grin, for he knew perfectly well that this would be the last place the old man would frequent.

"It depends."

"On what?"

"On what kind of person you are."

Both men looked up as two police cars, sirens wailing, sped

past.

"They seem pretty busy tonight, don't they?" Luke asked.

"Too busy," Alan replied without taking his eyes off of the flashing blue lights of the vehicles.

"Oh well, best get in there," Luke said, with one leg already hanging out the car door.

"Yeah," Alan nodded. "You be careful."

With that, Luke stepped out into the rain, and the taxi slowly drove away.

He looked up and squinted. The building looked like a giant warehouse. It was built of red brick, and was quite handsome, but for the need of a lick of paint around the edges. From the centre, a large protruding balcony overlooked the street and bore the large blue neon lettering that welcomed revellers to '*The Pit.*'

"Come on!" Jason shouted from his place in the queue.

Luke ran over, but instead of standing with his friends at the mercy of the pouring rain, he took shelter under the balcony.

"These clothes cost me a fortune," he joked, but the real reason was that he felt as if he was going to heave at any moment.

Meanwhile, his friends queued patiently as the precipitation fell heavily, soaking them all.

19

Mrs. Tennyson waved her hand in the air, trying to attract the attention of passing waiters, but they seemed oblivious to her as they buzzed to and from other tables. Eventually, she caught the attention of a tall, suited, middle-aged man.

"Yes, madam?" he asked.

"Another one of these, please," she said, holding up her empty tumbler.

"And what would that be, madam?" the man asked, collecting two more empty tumblers from the table.

"Scotch, double. Oh, and could you bring the wine list, too?"

"Of course." The man smiled courteously and left.

Barbara Tennyson glanced at her watch. It was nine-fifteen and still no sign of him.

So, what else is new?

She wondered what he would have to say if she was late arriving at one of his precious dinners. *See how that would impress his fucking clients! Well, I am going to show him. I have played the fool long enough, but not anymore.*

That was why she had asked him to meet her there tonight. It would be their chance to talk. Somewhere away from the office, the clients, their friends, and everything else Jeff put before her.

Including that harlot, that bitch you keep taking away on so-called business trips.

She looked around the room – it was late, but the restaurant was still very busy.

The Seasons was Barbara Tennyson's favourite restaurant. It was one of a rash of designer eateries opening in the city, specialising solely in vegetarian dishes. She concluded that this was probably why her husband was late again. He had groaned, audibly, when she'd told him she had made reservations at the Michelin-starred restaurant.

Jeffrey Tennyson was a carnivore, one of the noisiest meat eaters Barbara had ever met. She sneered inwardly as she replayed a mental image of him, sitting at the dinner table, slobbering over the roasted flesh of a dead cow. Sometimes, he was so busy wolfing down the meat that he failed to pause for air, thus exacerbating that nasal whistling sound she hated so.

The suited man arrived with her Scotch refill.

"Thank you," she said, taking the glass off the tray and downing its contents, wincing as it burned her throat.

"And the wine list, Madam," the man said casually, handing her the card. "Would Madam care to see the menu?"

"No, thank you. I'm still waiting for someone."

The volume on the city suddenly increased as the front door opened.

A reptilian smile spread across Barbara Tennyson's face as she watched her husband enter the restaurant and scan the room for her. "He's here," she said, smirking.

"Does that mean that Madam would like to see the menu now?"

"About time."

The waiter looked down at the woman, confused. However, following her gaze, he realised that she was not talking to him, and he stood aside as the overweight man with short grey and a matching goatee took his seat at the table.

He did not bother with a greeting, but instead launched straight into an exasperated, "Why you wanted to have dinner here is beyond me."

Then, he proceeded to shake off his coat, revealing the overstretched waistcoat of his designer suit.

"Because I like it here."

"I gathered that," her husband replied, looking around the room, and then at the man in the suit who was hovering nearby.

"Martini, dry, and hold the bloody olive."

"Straight away, Sir. Would you care to see the menu, Sir? Madam?"

"So what was it this time, dear?" Barbara asked, "Entertaining clients, call from abroad, last minute crisis?"

"Jesus, Barbara, we haven't even had dinner yet, and you're already drunk."

"I haven't even started drinking yet. Look," she said, holding up her glass, "my glass is empty." Then, looking up and sideways, she added, "and you haven't brought me my Scotch yet, have you? What's your name?"

"Anthony, M..."

"... or should I just call you Mister Waiter?" she chuckled. "I like that, Mister Waiter."

The man smiled with her. "Actually, it's Anthony," he repeated, "Madam, and I'm the manager."

"Anthony, I'm Jeffrey Tennyson and this is my drunken wife."

With a smile, Barbara retorted, "Oh, seeing that we are introducing ourselves, I'm Barbara Tennyson, and this is my cheating husband."

Anthony smiled, uncomfortably, and just wished they would make their minds up about the menu so he could be on his way.

"Are you still here?" Jeffrey Tennyson barked. "How long does it take to get a drink in this vegetable parlour, for Christ sake?"

"I was just wondering if…"

"And bring me that Scotch, Anthony, there's a good boy. Oh, and, while you're at it, you may as well bring us a bottle of Dom Pérignon, as well?"

"I don't want Dom Pérignon," Jeffrey Tennyson said in a hushed voice.

"Who said it was for you?" Barbara replied in an equally hushed tone.

Anthony, no longer caring whether the couple ate or not, headed for the kitchen. He had enough of his own problems tonight, and the last thing he needed was to get involved in a marital row.

As soon as he entered the kitchen, two young men in white overalls, Mark and Robert, intercepted him. Mark, the skinner of the two, asked agitatedly, "Anthony, what the hell are we going to do?"

"I told you, Mark, I have tried to call Chef, but he's not answering the phone."

"Well, where the fuck is he?" cried Robert, Mark's much heavier colleague.

"I don't bloody know, "Anthony answered, controlling his tone, well aware of the rest of the kitchen staff. "Look, I've got to get this drinks order to the bar. As soon as I've done that, I'll make some phone calls to see if I can find someone."

Robert sneered, "What if you don't?"

"Then you're just going to have to manage."

"What?" they both squealed, in unison.

"I have got a full house out there tonight. I haven't got time for this." Anthony's voice was low but assertive, and, after staring intensely at the two men, he turned and made for the swing doors.

Robert shifted his weight from one leg to the other, as if building himself up to something.

He turned to Mark, who spoke up, "Look, Anthony, we're not paid to take on this responsibility, you know."

"No we're not, "Robert echoed.

The manager was just about to push the doors open, but stopped and turned around. "What are you saying? That you…"

Suddenly, the swing doors burst open. The impact launched Anthony into the arms of the two young men.

A waiter popped his head around the door and bellowed, "I'm still waiting on my order for table 10. Am I getting it tonight or should I order veggie burgers from McDonalds?"

"See what I mean?" Mark asked, nodding his head at the doors.

"Look," Anthony began, re-composing himself and straightening his tie. "I'm just as pissed off about Chef's no-show as you are, but I've got a restaurant full of people, all waiting for their food. I'm relying on you two to pull through." Then, holding up a finger, he added, "and, I don't want to hear another word about it."

The apprentices looked at each, and then turned to say something, but all they found was swinging kitchen doors.

Back at the Tennyson table, Jeffrey snapped, "I don't know what the hell possessed you to make a reservation at this place. You know I hate this vegetarian crap."

"You know how much I hate meat, but it doesn't stop you," Barbara Tennyson retorted.

"Why should I suffer just because you've discovered the latest fad?"

"It isn't a fad, Jeffrey. I have been a vegetarian since we met, or have you conveniently forgotten ten years of marriage?"

"How could I possibly forget?" Jeffrey mumbled.

There was a long pause as both of them looked around the room, feigning interest in what everyone else was doing and saying. There was a couple in the corner, a young girl with an older man. Jeffrey wondered: father or lover?

"I called you at the hotel," Barbara interrupted.

"Did you?" he asked, disinterested.

"You weren't there. You'd only just finished telling me that you had tons of work to plough through before your next meeting."

"Did I?"

"Yes, you did!" Barbara shrieked, thumping her fist on the table in order to get her husband's attention.

It worked. He turned to her, eyes bulging with incredulous anger, "Get a grip of yourself, woman. You're making a scene," he said through clenched teeth as he smiled at those people who had looked up from their meals.

"Ha!" Barbara released a short cackle. "If you think this is a scene, you haven't seen anything yet."

The venom in his wife's eyes took Jeffrey aback. Something was wrong. Something was very wrong. She obviously knew more than she was letting on. Had she found out about his assistant?

A flicker of fear crossed his eyes. He wanted rid of Barbara, but not like this. After all, she was the one with the money. She was the one who owned the business. If she divorced him now, citing adultery, it would have serious consequences on his financial future.

"For Christ sake, Barbara. You are like this every time I get back from a business trip." He shook his head and then lit up a cigarette.

"There's no smoking in here," she hissed, "It's a public place."

"So what? He's taking his time with my drink and I need something to occupy me whilst I indulge you in your neurotic episode."

"So, you think I'm just having an episode, do you?"

"Yes, I do. And before you start on Emma, you should know that she' nothing but a pillar of strength. Without her, I would never have won this new account. Because, you see, Barbara, business isn't just about selling a good product, it's also about offering a good service."

"Have you quite finished talking down to me, you condescending prick?" she snapped. "If it wasn't for my money, you wouldn't have a business."

Barbara was a drunk, but she was not stupid, and Jeffrey realised that he had to calm her down before she said something that he would regret.

"I just want to know one thing, Jeffrey…"

Anthony arrived at the table, carrying a small tray with their drinks.

"…How much more of a better fuck is she?"

Anthony blushed, and his instincts screamed at him to turn on his heels, but he couldn't.

Aware of the man's presence, Jeffrey said nothing.

Barbara smiled, enjoying his discomfort. "Well, come on, on a scale from one to ten. How much better is she?"

"I'm not having this conversation with you," Jeffrey said petulantly.

"Oh, why not?" she slurred. Then, looking up, she added, "What do you think, Mister Waiter? Don't you think this would be the perfect opportunity for us to have a decent, open, and honest discussion about the flexibilities of Jeff's assistant?"

"Well, I..."

"...What in Christ's name are you waiting for, man? Leave the drinks and go!" Jeffrey bellowed.

For the second time that evening, the people at a nearby table stopped chatting and turned.

"You can't take him anywhere," Barbara said to them with a giggle.

Anthony hastily placed the Martini in front of Jeffrey, deposited the bottle in front of Barbara and, in his mind, cursed Chef and having ever gotten up that morning.

"Would Madam care to...?"

"No, she wouldn't! Get lost!" Jeffrey hissed.

Anthony left the table, feeling a strong sense of empathy for the waiters he employed.

"What's the matter, darling? Your Martini not dry enough?"

She was toying with him. That was exactly what she was doing. She knew about his affair with Emma, but she was not going to come out with it. She was going to torture him with hints and innuendo.

"You didn't answer my question."

"What was your question?" he asked, absent-minded as his brain processed a myriad of 'what ifs.'

"I asked you how good she is in bed, since I'm wondering if she's good enough to lose your business." Barbara Tennyson smiled; she was enjoying herself.

Jeffrey Tennyson downed his Martini in one go; it was going to be a long night.

Nobody noticed the short, tubby man enter the kitchen and exchange his rain-soaked jacket for a dry white smock.

However, as Chef slipped his hat on, and moved over to the giant oven in the corner of the kitchen, his two young apprentices scuttled over to him like a pair of anxious children.

"Where the hell have you been, Chef?" asked Robert.

Chef said nothing. Instead, he dialled the oven to gas mark 9 and began peeling a head of garlic.

"Chef!" It was Mark now. "We've been rushed off our feet, Anthony is out of his pram, and it's all because you didn't bother letting us know you were going to be late."

Still no answer. The peeling continued.

With a huff, Robert set off to find Anthony whilst Mark continued his reprimand. "It's not fair on us, you know," he said, trying to lock eyes with his mentor.

However, Chef was busy; he had a meal to prepare and he was already running late. Ever since that maniac had rammed him at the traffic lights and moulded his car around a lamppost, Chef had thought about nothing else but the kitchen.

At first, he had been worried about how late the ordeal was going to make him, but then, as he stood in the pouring rain, his concern had turned into a pleasant urgency. That same urgency that was on his mind right now. The guests in the dining room were waiting for their meal and, tonight, Chef had something very special on the menu.

Something very special, indeed.

Anthony stormed through the swing doors and watched as the young lad followed his boss around the kitchen.

"What on Earth is going on here?" Anthony demanded.

"He won't talk to me!" Mark whined.

"Chef?" Anthony demanded.

He received no reply, just the machine-gun chopping of vegetables. Anthony walked up to the tubby man and repeated in a stern voice, "Chef? I'm talking to you."

This time, the man stopped what he was doing. Then, after a nail-bitingly long pause, gave his manager his cold black eyes, and smiled. The smile was cold, empty, as if generated by a robot, and it chilled Anthony, to the point where the restaurant manager knew better than to pursue his attempt to solicit an explanation right now.

After several seconds, Chef turned his gaze back to the job in hand and resumed chopping a green pepper.

Anthony straightened his tie, his composure, and then made his way to the swing doors, closely followed by the two puppies.

"Well?" Mark demanded.

"Well, what?" Anthony asked, conscious of the other three kitchen staff who had stopped working, and who were trying to listen in.

"Is that it?"

"Is what it?" Anthony asked in his favourite hushed tone. "He's here now and that's all that counts. I shall talk to him later." He straightened his tie again, and then glanced at the others who were watching, open-mouthed. "Haven't you got any work to do?" he snapped.

The trio instantly went about their duties.

"And I suggest you do the same," Anthony added to the two boys.

With that, he left the kitchen.

It was getting late, and most of the diners had paid for their meals and left the building. Only a few lingered, including the couple who still had not ordered anything to eat, but who were busy shaking accusatory fingers at each other whilst talking in tense, hushed tones.

Anthony watched them from across the room, and wondered whether he should bother going over and asking if they intended to order tonight or if they were just going to use his restaurant as a domestic battlefield.

Then, as if they had read his thoughts, Mrs. Tennyson beckoned him over. Taking a deep breath, Anthony walked up to the table and smiled politely.

"Yes, Madam?"

"Could I have another bottle of this, please?" she asked, holding up the half-empty bottle of champagne.

"Of course, Madam."

"Don't you think you've had enough?" Jeffrey Tennyson asked.

"No, I don't," she replied, somewhat ironically in a slurred tone.

"Take no notice of her; she's too pissed to know what she's saying. In fact, bring us the bill, we're leaving," Mr. Tennyson added, searching the inside of his suit jacket for his wallet.

"I am not ready to leave. I haven't had dinner yet," his wife said defiantly.

"Barbara, darling, your memory is failing you; you haven't eaten a solid dinner since the seventies. Your diet consists of a bottle of gin in the morning followed by a bottle of Scotch in the afternoon."

Barbara cackled, holding up a wavy finger. "Oh yes, very droll," she said. Then she looked up at Anthony and continued, "I didn't tell you, did I, what's your name?"

"Anthony."

"Anthony. I didn't tell you that my husband lost his true vocation in life: comedian."

"The bill, please," Jeffrey seethed.

"I told you I haven't finished yet," Barbara retorted, eyes wide.

"You've had more than enough, Barbara. It is time to go."

Anthony turned to fetch their bill. The sooner he saw the backs of these two, the better he was going to feel, customers or no customers.

"Anthony! Don't forget that bottle, will you!" Barbara shouted after him.

The manager turned to Mr. Tennyson, who shook his head in disagreement.

Barbara noticed the exchange. "Don't ask him for permission! I have my own mind. I make my own fucking decisions!" Barbara's voice was loud. Shrill.

Now, one of the remaining couples hurried over to the cashier's desk and, after speedily entering their credit card pin number, left the building.

"Oops," Barbara giggled, holding a hand to her mouth.

"Have you quite finished making a spectacle of yourself?" Jeffrey Tennyson asked, his voice indignant.

"What's the matter, darling, can't handle the competition? You'd know all about making a spectacle of yourself, wouldn't you?"

She poured more from the bottle. However, as she did so, her husband attempted to steal the bottle away from her; Barbara was having none of it. A grapple for the bottle ensued.

Anthony watched from across the room. The sight would have been comical, had it not been so tragic. This was getting out of hand. Clasping the Tennyson's receipt, Anthony hurried across the room to the battling duo just as she lashed out at her husband, scratching his face with red painted nails.

"You bitch!" he shrieked.

Barbara cackled maniacally, "Serves you right."

"What is wrong with you?" Jeffrey asked incredulously as he examined spots of blood on his fingers, and then rapidly placed a napkin to his face, as if she had nicked an artery.

Barbara simply smirked, then took a swig from the bottle.

Anthony, appalled by the couple's behaviour, concluded that he *wanted* them to leave.

"Maybe if you'd spent just a little more time at home with me, instead of jet setting across the world with that bean pole, half your age, you'd know what's wrong with me," she said, tears welling in her eyes.

"Madam," Anthony began tentatively, "Perhaps it would be beneficial to both of you, if you took this discussion home."

"I gave you the best years of my life, and how do you repay me?" Tears and mascara dribbled down Barbara Tennyson's face. "You pass me over for that whore!"

Jeffrey Tennyson's suspicions were accurate. His wife did know about him and his assistant and, at that moment, all he wanted to do was hide behind the napkin he was still holding to his face. He willed himself to say something, but the words would not come to him.

"You thought I'd never find out, didn't you?" she hissed through tears. "But I know, I've known for ages, but I just hoped that she was just a fad, that you were having some kind of midlife crisis!" She sobbed, heavily, loudly, and then, as if to console herself, took yet another swig from the bottle.

Anthony was about to say something, but was upstaged by a blood-curdling scream, this was accompanied by a loud crashing sound.

As he turned, the kitchen's swing doors flew open, and out of them spewed most of the staff, screaming and waving their hands in the air as they fled out of the building and into the rain.

"Dear Lord, what now?" Without thinking, Anthony raced toward the kitchen and pushed through the swinging doors. The scene that greeted him was like something out of his worst nightmare.

The normally bleached white floor was awash in a tide of red fluid, from which, bloody footprints and skid marks led, via a series of erratic squiggled patterns, in all directions. The normally pristine worktops were a mess of chopped vegetables, pots, pans and blood spatters.

Anthony's paralysed mind could do nothing but gawk at the spectacle before him, before it finally tuned into a thumping sound, originating from behind one of the counters.

Heart hammering, eyes bulging, he slowly inched his way through the gooey substance, toward the sound. Eventually, as beads of perspiration appeared on his forehead, and his throat thickened into a nauseating knot, he neared the corner of the unit and, cautiously, peered around it.

On the floor, in a pool of blood, lay a skinny, headless corpse; it was Mark, and his legs were still twitching and kicking against the unit.

Anthony choked on the bile slithering up his throat and turned to flee from this nightmare, but slipped on the bloody slick of the floor and fell, smacking his face against the cold tiles. He retched as he lay amidst the coppery smell of blood and his own vomit.

A minute or so oozed by as he lay, motionless, while his mind, numb with shock, attempted to process the images in his head. However, it was not long before he registered approaching footsteps, and, instinctively, he flipped onto his back just as the giant shadow loomed over him.

Barbara and Jeffrey Tennyson were too busy squabbling to notice Chef trudge up to them. They only paused to look at the podgy, diminutive man when he dumped the large silver serving cloche on their table. It jangled, loudly, startling both of them.

"What the fuck...." Jeffrey Tennyson exclaimed, but retreated in his chair when he looked up, into the fixed and dilated pupils of what appeared to be a mad man, with wild hair and blood spatters over his face and all down his whites.

Both of the Tennysons watched in stunned silence as Chef grinned, excitedly, and then removed the lid from the platter and announced, "Dinner is served!"

20

Stony Point – 23:05.

The intruder light had come on, and the overspill was shining into the circular bedroom. The rain had slowed, but it had not stopped.

Blake and Sky lay naked. They had made love again since their encounter at the door. Only this time, the urge to climax had been tempered, and they had taken the time to enjoy each other's bodies. Neither of them spoke for a while, as they processed a conglomeration of thoughts.

"Sky?" Blake's voice was an alarm bell in the still of the bedroom.

She swallowed in an effort to moisten parched vocal cords. "Yes?" she croaked

"Are you awake?"

He heard a giggle as he realised that the question was redundant.

"Do you feel like talking?" he asked.

"What about?"

"I don't know, just talking."

"It was good, wasn't it?" she asked casually.

He grinned. "Yes, it was."

Although she could not see his face, Sky knew that Blake had enjoyed her again. It had been clear in his kisses, his embrace, his passion, and the way his beautiful brown eyes would never leave hers, but instead reached deep inside of her and reignited a passion that she had never experienced with any other man.

She had forgotten this about him.

His method, his confidence, his *need* to watch and to ensure that she was deriving as much pleasure as he from the act, and it excited her. He excited her. With his clean smell, his muscular embrace, his passion and his tenderness. His signature methods aroused feelings in her that she'd thought had been buried a long time ago, but they hadn't. They had just been dormant, waiting for the moment, the opportunity, for now.

"So now what?" Blake asked, as if reading her thoughts.

There was a long pause.

She smiled, excited, "Now we rebuild our energy reserves for the next round."

Blake laughed. "You always did have the best ideas," he said fondly, looking across at her. He admired the outline of her naked shoulders and felt compelled to roll over and kiss them, but he refrained from doing so.

They listened to the rain tap against the window for several seconds, until Blake suddenly rolled over and leant on one arm. "Sky?"

"Yes?"

"About tonight..."

"What about it?" she asked, facing him.

He wished she had not done that, because now he felt all his strength draining. "Well... Err..." he began. "I was... well, I..." Damn, he could not get the words out.

Sky smiled encouragingly.

The smile helped. "I think we should talk."

"It's all right, Blake. I know you'll still respect me in the morning," she joked, but her heart was thumping.

It was as if nothing had changed. Her feelings for him appeared to be as powerful now as they had all those years before, and this both delighted and scared her, with equal measure.

He smiled. "No, Sky. There are other things..."

"...Not tonight," she interrupted. Her voice was soft and seductive. Then, she leant over and kissed him full on the mouth. "Not tonight," she repeated, since she had no idea where this conversation was going, and she did not want to spoil the moment. This delicious moment of them warm and snuggled in bed together while the weather stormed outside.

Blake, much to his own amazement, felt himself blushing, although he had no idea why, but he was nonetheless grateful that the room was steeped in shadows. He so desperately wanted to talk to her, to explain, but Sky was right – they should not talk tonight, but soon.

"So, any ideas on how long this rain is going to last?" She was lying back, against her pillow once more. Her black hair fanned out behind her, as if arranged by a makeup artist.

Blake noticed her breasts peeking out from underneath the sheet, and the thought of her complete nakedness aroused him once more. However, he repressed the urge and lay back with her. "Well, it seems…" He began an impersonation of a weather presenter, moving his hands in the air in front of them, as if there were an invisible map "…that this low-pressure front that has swept in from the Atlantic Ocean is going to be with us for quite a while. We can expect heavy downpours overnight, here and here, and they may well last until the early hours of Saturday morning. So, expect the odd rumble of thunder…"

"….Odd rumble of thunder. That's an understatement."

They laughed.

"Are you hungry?" he asked, suddenly.

"Thirsty, and yeah, I could eat."

"Good."

He left the bed, pulled on his shorts, and spoke to the room, "Music on."

A hip-hop track Sky didn't recognise filled the room as Blake attempted to mime the words and perform a dance routine, all while pointing at her. Although, from the bad miming, it was clear that he didn't know the track either. She launched a pillow at him. He ducked, shrugged, and danced out of the room.

Sky laughed and then stretched in the warm bed.

Nothing has changed.

She was happy. It felt as if she had reacquired part of a memory that had eluded her all these years, reminding her how to feel happy again. It was an odd feeling, since she'd believed she was already happy with her life. Her career was going well, she enjoyed time with her friends, and even her few select relationships had been fulfilling. Nothing serious, but they had

137

suited her. They had made her happy.

But not like this. Not like now. This was a different brand of happy, one that she'd forgotten about, and had never experienced again, ever since she'd broken up with Blake, many years before.

Blake hummed as he descended the steps, but stopped and yelped when he reached the front door.

He looked down to see that he had stepped into a pool of freezing water, and that the door was open. He frowned, shivered, pushed the door shut, and resumed humming as he made his way to the kitchen.

21

The Pit Nightclub – Exeter

The Pit's entrance lobby was small, the walls decorated with red graffiti and illuminated by ultraviolet light.

Two bouncers, built like American football players, stood guard in front of double doors. One of them pointed to the reception desk. A slim girl with long, greasy hair and heavy makeup took Luke's money and handed him a ticket. Then, as one, the bouncers pulled open the double doors and the pounding percussion of a euphoric dance track smacked Luke with force.

He descended several steps to find himself on a balcony overlooking a circular dance floor. It was dark, but for the occasional strobe of coloured lights and lasers that illuminated a sea of undulating bodies that ebbed and flowed to the massive tune that sent shock vibrations through his extremities.

He smiled.

The atmosphere crackled with sexual tension. It invigorated him.

"Come on, Luke!" Jason yelled as he descended more stairs and disappeared into the crowd.

Luke followed through the throng until they reached the bar, where he ordered a lager and then turned to scan the masses for his two friends, but they seemed to have disappeared.

He took long drafts from his drink as he surveyed the area. The place was teaming with sexual encounters. To his right, a couple shared a barstool. Their silhouettes appeared to be that of a man and woman, but as the laser beam zapped them, he could see that it was actually two girls. Directly in front of him, a man slid his hand under his partner's skirt. The girl, who was busy nipping the man's ears, stopped abruptly and squealed as her partner's fingers probed deeper, into her crotch.

Luke chuckled.

Everything about this place was intoxicating: the flashing lights, the sexual encounters, the shroud of fog drifting out from the dance floor, and the anonymity that the shadows provided. Then he saw her, intermittently, through the heaving bodies and the pulsating strobe. She was on the opposite side of the dance floor. Her hair was jet-black and iron straight. She was wearing leather trousers and a white bra that shone purple under the ultraviolet glow.

Then, the room slipped into slow motion, or at least it seemed that way. The lights flashed, the bodies moved, but none of them like her. Her dance was ethereal, yet animal, wicked, yet innocent.

Their eyes met.

Without thinking, Luke pushed forward, into the crowd, descending the few steps to the dance floor.

She was wild. An untamed animal as she swung her head from side to side while humping the loud, pulsating rhythm that was the very air around them. Now, her hands were moving, searching her breasts, her thighs, and then between her legs as she watched him through the curtain of hair that hung in front of her face.

Luke was closer now. No more than ten feet away. He was aroused at the thought of her, oblivious to the masses surrounding him. He was the hunter after its quarry, and nothing and no one would stop him from capturing his prey.

That's when they stepped in front of him, blocking his view and donning maniacal grins. It was Jason and Tristan. They winked at him and then joined the girl. Jason pressed his six-foot, muscular frame against her rear, slid his hands down to her thighs, and then tugged her tightly to him as he began rubbing himself against her while licking his lips.

Luke watched through the swaying crowd as Tristan sniggered and fell to his knees beside the rocking couple. He wondered what game his friends were playing. In all the time he had known these two lads, he had never seen them behave like this – at least not in a nightclub.

He smiled, disarmingly. However, neither of his friends responded. Instead, Jason began a thrusting motion with the girl, who bent over, sticking her tongue out at Tristan, who mimicked her performance. Both of them laughed as Jason's thrusting motion kept pushing them to and from each other.

Watching two young men indulge in sexual enticement, especially when those two men happened to be his friends, wouldn't normally have been something that would turn Luke on, but tonight... Tonight, things were different, and the tightness in his jeans made him realise that he found watching the threesome, the thrusting, the music, and the darkness of the club sexually stimulating. His friend's antics had actually turned him on, and he wanted more.

And that's exactly what he got.

The girl, never taking her eyes off him, rubbed her breasts and then slowly offered them to Tristan, teasing him by bringing her encased nipples within inches of his face, and then drawing back again. His torment continued for a few minutes as Jason continued to grind against her.

Luke glanced around the room, conscious of the other people there, but nobody seemed to care. They were all too busy dancing or engaging in their own brand of sexual stimulation.

It was like a dream.

Luke looked down into the golden depths of the pint in his hands and wondered, for a moment, if somebody had spiked it. Then, he drank greedily, blinked, and looked around once more.

Nothing had changed.

The music still throbbed, the lights still flashed, and the bodies still heaved. He was not dreaming – this was all happening for real, and it was happening now.

He approached the trio, climbing the few steps off the dance floor. He wanted to join in but, despite his arousal, he found himself wishing that his friends would leave her to him.

They smiled and pouted at him. He shook his head incredulously. He was still finding it difficult to believe that his friends, both seemingly in happy relationships, were behaving like this, and so publicly.

None of it mattered now.

From the floor, a tittering Tristan searched between Luke's legs, feeling for his erection. Then, he promptly began to unbuckle his belt, but Luke slapped his hand away, smiling. Watching his friends was one thing, but having them undress him was another.

Suddenly, Jason stopped dry humping the girl and pushed her towards Luke in an offering gesture. The girl, who was still caressing her encased breasts, willed Luke to touch them. After hesitating a few moments, and snatching one last look at the madhouse around him, Luke sank his face into the girl's soft mounds. She smelt and felt good.

He kissed and licked her exposed flesh. Then, spurred on by the chanting of his friends and the ecstatic moaning of the girl, he ripped off her bra and paused to suckle for a few seconds. Then, he emptied the last of his lager over her breasts, tossed the glass aside, and licked at the excess.

Tristan joined him, and they growled at each other like dogs fighting over a rump of meat. There was another tug at his belt and, for a moment, Luke thought it was one of the lads, but when he looked down, he was pleased to discover that it was actually the girl. He was on such a high now, and grunted with pleasure as her fingers travelled into his boxers and began to handle him.

He closed his eyes, enjoying her touch.

Jason unbuttoned and unzipped the girl's trousers, and then he caught Luke's hand and thrust it towards her navel. Luke complied, determined to give her as much pleasure as she was giving him. His fingers slipped into her panties and he began to probe her with a hungry lust.

Tristan had stopped suckling now, and his mouth had moved over the girl's shoulder, seeking and finding Jason's mouth.

They kissed, eagerly.

Luke forced a smile, assuming his friends were caught up in the heat of the moment, but he soon learned that it was more than that as their arms entwined and their tongues united.

Jason had fully released the girl now, and was devoting his full attention to searching under Tristan's shirt and trousers.

The girl pulled Luke's jeans down, slightly, just enough so he was hanging out of his boxers, fully erect and ready for her. Then, with hands low on his rear, she pulled him to her, making it obvious that she wanted him, and was ready. Luke allowed himself to be handled but, through the corner of his eye, he could see that Tristan had unzipped Jason and was now slipping to his knees once more.

The girl threw her head back and allowed Luke to bite her neck.

Tristan's hands were inside Jason's boxer shorts.

The girl had backed up against a column, and Luke slid her leather trousers down, and, without hesitation, lifted her leg over his arm and entered her, grunting as he did so.

His two friends had disappeared into the shadows, but as the lights flashed, they illuminated an incredible scene: Tristan, back in his kneeling position, was fondling Jason and his mouth was wide open. Luke spotted them, and sudden revulsion swelled in the pit of his stomach. Sweat poured down his face as he worked between the girl's legs. His heart pounded, the music throbbed, and the girl wailed with delirious pleasure. Normally, such vocal appreciation of his performance would have spurred him on, amplified his pleasure, but this time, it did not. This time he could not concentrate. Something was off.

In a series of strobe snapshots, Luke watched as Tristan took Jason in his mouth.

He rammed the girl. Harder. Harder.

Jason caressed Tristan's head as it travelled the length of him.

Luke continued pumping, but stopped kissing and biting the girl. He was going through the motions, but could still catch glimpses of his companions, and it was disturbing him.

Meanwhile Jason was laughing, deliriously. The sensation was sublime, and the warm tentacles that pricked beyond his psyche were tripling, amplifying the pleasure of Tristan's warm mouth around him. The act was something he had never experienced before, and he relished it as his temples throbbed, his heart pumped, and the music hammered. Then, he helped Tristan to his feet; they both exchanged glances and then giggled with excited anticipation.

Luke, drenched in sweat, was still thrusting deep inside the girl who was screaming with pleasure, urging to keep going, telling him not to stop, never to stop, but, suddenly, he did. He withdrew, so she pulled him back. He tried to free himself, but vice-like hands, low on his back, forced him to stay inside her.

"No!" he said through clenched teeth and unclamped himself from her grip.

The girl eyed him, angrily, but said nothing.

Dragging his jeans up, Luke gulped in the foggy air, trying to recover his breath. He looked across at his friends. He could almost hear Jason laughing above the music as the flickering lights highlighted the sickening scene.

Gay sex was something Luke could not stomach. Two men, one bending over whilst the other... He shuddered as the image of his two friends played, like a broken film reel, repeatedly in his mind. He wanted to retch. Where had this come from? He had known them both for years. They had prowled for girls together. They were both in relationships, with girls!

What the fuck's this all about?

The thought was incomprehensible to him, and it actually made him angry, as if his friends had personally betrayed him in some way, after all this time. In that moment, the girl hissed at him and, for the first time, Luke noticed the dark cavities that were her sunken eyes.

She's on something!

He watched her, dumfounded, as the hissing continued loudly. Then, she held up a bony finger and pointed at him, as if he were an intruder in the cult's den.

What the fuck's she on?

Had she enticed him into having sex with her just to accuse him of rape? He had heard about this before, and the thought made his stomach turn. Panicked, he looked around. The crowds were still oblivious to what was happening. Only now, the sexual enticement had turned into the act itself. Could he hear, above the pounding music, terrified screams for help? Or was that his own voice inside his head?

He watched, aghast. The whole place was a mass of heaving bodies. Minutes before, the place had just been like any other club, but now it had metamorphosed into a sick, sexual orgy. People were on the dance floor, up against walls, masturbating or engaged in a frenzy of heterosexual and homosexual intercourse.

He had to be dreaming. This could not be happening.

But it was.

He looked across at his friends. Tristan was standing now, and Jason had pulled up his trousers. They were both fixing him with icy glares. Luke shook his head in disgust and, buttoning his jeans, moved to leave. The sooner he got out of this hellhole, the better. However, as he passed her, the girl grabbed him by the hair and yanked him back. Luke cried out in pain and, taking advantage of the momentum, swung around and punched her.

He saw the girl's mouth open, but the music drowned her scream as she fell, sprawling, backwards. The thought of whether or not he should stay and check if she was okay did cross Luke's mind, but he decided against it. He would deal with the consequences later. Right now, he just wanted out of the place.

He elbowed his way through the crowd, heedless of the sexual spectacle that was taking place around him.

He was halfway across the dance floor when the music changed to a slow, pulsating rhythm that prompted a series of static red lights to fade up and out, making it difficult for him to pick his way through the writhing bodies. Then, he misjudged the step that led off the dance floor and tripped, but a pair of hands broke his fall, and when the lights faded up, he saw that it was Jason.

Luke shrugged his friend's hands off and continued on his journey. He climbed both steps in one go and hurried to the next flight of stairs.

Jason's hands gripped him again, pulling him back.

As he tried to shake him off, another pair of hands appeared out of the smoky gloom and grabbed his arm. It was Tristan.

"Get off me, man!" Luke warned.

Fingers reached for his crotch, but he slapped them away. More hands tugged at him as he pulled and then stumbled forward, momentarily releasing the hold on him as he scrambled up the stairs. However, it was not long before more hands surrounded him, and, like a forest of branches, they clawed at his face and clothes.

"No! Get off me!" he yelled. "Get off me!"

He kicked and punched all around him. Some hands relented as others anchored themselves. They tugged, and he crashed to the floor, smacking his face on the steps as they dragged him back down, into the darkness.

"No! No!" he screamed, and wriggled to free himself, but it was to no avail. For every hand he shook off, another five took hold, ripping his T-shirt and pulling at his jeans.

Within minutes, Luke was naked, and knots of fingers searched every inch of his body. They grabbed, scratched, caressed, and tugged at his chest and his groin. They probed, groped, and licked him.

"No!" he cried in terror as they carried him a few feet and then dropped him, violently, onto the floor once more, where the air was forced out of his lungs by a huge weight pressing on his back.

Boots, heels, arms and bodies pinned his face to the carpet, where he breathed in the stagnant stench of booze, mould and leather. Vicious hands pulled his arms and legs apart and a searing pain shot up his back as someone entered him from behind.

"H....e.....l....p!" He garbled, and opened his mouth to scream, but gagged instead as something hard and fleshy was pushed inside it.

Then, the weight was on him again, causing him to, involuntarily, bite down on the foreign object, filling his mouth with blood and asphyxiating him.

The music continued to play, and Luke could just about discern the manic cries of his aggressors over the rhythm as his mind rapidly began to drift into a whirlpool of images. Within the swirl, he saw his parents, himself as a child, and a multitude of ghosts he could not recognise. Then, slowly, all of the sounds began to fade and the world turned black.

22

The music had ended, replaced once more by the sound of the elements outside. Sky stretched under the warmth of the covers as she waited for Blake's return. She was content. She had absolutely no idea where things would go from here, but right now, in this moment, she felt happy, and she planned to make the most of it. She smiled at the thought of Blake and rolled over, rubbing her face on his pillow where there were still traces of his aftershave.

She breathed in.

Clutching the blade in its hand, the presence crept up the stairs and paused by the bedroom door. It took in the balcony, the furniture, and the bare shoulders of the naked body in the bed. It had wanted this person. It had yearned for a moment with her, and that moment was now.

Blake whistled as he rinsed out the two champagne flutes and placed them on a tray with the bottle of Prosecco, a moving-in gift from Matt Allen that he had not quite managed to open, until now. He also sliced a couple of mangos and arranged them, decoratively, on a plate. Then, he rummaged in the cupboard for the savoury snacks and some chocolate.

Sky smiled when she felt a presence in the doorway, and rolled over only to find a hand over her mouth, and the cold blade of a knife prodding at her throat.

The shadow hovered above her, like the grim reaper himself, but said nothing as Sky's eyes darted to the safety of the open door and back again.

The silhouette was that of a slim figure with shoulder-length hair.

A woman?

Sky desperately sucked air through her nose as her heart raced while she struggled to process what was happening to her.

What do you want? Who are you?

Suddenly, the blade eased its presence and a hand yanked her, by her hair, out of the bed until she fell heavily onto the wood floor. Then, before she could gather her senses, the presence knelt beside her, pulled her head back by her hair, and was prodding the blade to her throat once more.

From their new position on the floor, the overspill of the stairwell light highlighted part of the intruder's face. Sky could just about distinguish the small jaw and the straggly brown hair. She had seen this profile before. She knew this person.

"Don't say a fucking word!" The voice hissed.

"What… what do you want?" Sky gulped.

"I want you," the voice replied in a gleeful, whispered tone.

"Who… who are you?"

"Have you forgotten me already, Doctor?"

In her panicked state, Sky searched her memory, but she couldn't place the voice. She recognised it, but couldn't associate it with anyone.

"But then, you've had other things on your mind, haven't you?" The intruder paused as thunder rumbled overhead. "What was he like?"

"What… what was who like?" Sky asked, although she felt as if she knew exactly who *he* was.

A slap cracked across her face, exploding white flashes in front of her eyes. "Don't fuck with me, Doctor," the voice snarled through gritted teeth.

Blinking rapidly, Sky stuttered, "You mean, you mean Blake?"

"Mr. Hudson," the voice corrected. "He doesn't like strangers calling him by his first name. Only close friends are allowed to do that."

It was then that Sky realised who it was.

"And, are you one of those friends, Clare?"

"Of course I am," the girl sniggered; seemingly embarrassed by the fact that Sky had identified her.

Sky licked her lips and tasted blood. She didn't know whether it was from the blow to her face or the impact from falling to the floor, but her nose was bleeding.

"Blake will be up soon," Sky said quickly.

"I know," the girl replied confidently. "But you'll be gone by then, so it won't make any difference."

The words renewed the current of fear already running through Sky's body. *Stay calm. Try to reason with her until Blake gets here. What is he doing anyway? Oh God!*

She was shivering now, both from the cold and out of sheer terror

"Now I know why," Clare said.

Sky followed her gaze and noticed that the girl was admiring her breasts, and it repulsed her.

"He likes them big," the girl smiled.

"Clare, I don't know what I'm supposed to have done, but if you…"

Another blinding slap silenced her.

"Shut up!" The girl hissed. "You fucking whore! With your flash car and your expensive suits. You think you can take him from me. But you can't!" She yanked Sky's hair back, as if to prove her dominance. "You can't! He's mine!" Then, much more calmly, she added, "You didn't answer my question, Doctor?"

Trembling, Sky asked, "Wh… what was your question?"

"You didn't tell me what he was like."

Thunder rumbled.

Blake? Where are you?

"Answer me, whore!" the girl demanded through clenched teeth.

"You tell me, you've had him a lot more times than I have, haven't you?" Sky replied defiantly, half expecting another slap.

However, the girl seemed to take this as a compliment, and began to giggle. Then, she pointed a knowing finger. "You're testing me, aren't you?" she asked, nodding her head. "You want me to tell you what it was like so you can compare, and see if I'm telling the truth. Well, here's one for you, Doctor." She leant forward and whispered in Sky's ear, "How do you think I got in here tonight, if he hadn't given me a key? He told me to let myself in whenever I needed. Or, more specifically, whenever *he* needed me to." She let out a short, suppressed cackle.

These last words stung Sky more than the blows to her face,

more than the blade that was etching into her neck. Was Blake really having a relationship with this girl? Had everything he'd told her that day in the pub been a lie?

Suddenly, she felt angry. Angry and dirty, as well as an overwhelming desire to kick the bitch away from her, drag on some clothes, and escape from the building, never to return.

However, Sky knew that she would not stand a chance. The slightest movement from her, and that blade would cut her. Her only chance was to stall. Try to reason with the psycho and hope that Blake would hurry back up the stairs.

Blake, be okay. Please be okay.

"So, what was he like?" Sky asked.

"The best I've ever had. Nothing like those skinny idiots I used to hang around with," Clare sneered, and then added, appreciatively, "Blake's got it, and he knows what to do with it, all right."

If there was any smile on the girl's face, it disappeared instantly when she spat, venomously, "But then, you'd know that, wouldn't you?"

Suddenly, in an astonishing move, the girl left Sky cowering on the floor and crawled up, onto the bed, with the agility of an arachnid. There, she breathed in the scent of the sheets. "Hmmm... I can smell his cum," she said enthusiastically.

Sky was too shocked to be disgusted.

"Hmmm, yes... I can smell him... yes."

Clare was lying on the bed now. Knife glinting in her right hand, she began to rub herself on the sheets.

It was time.

Sky McPherson summoned all her strength and, with the speed of a wildcat, pounced up from the floor, and launched her way to the door.

However, Clare had anticipated this move and, with mirrored speed, the teenager jumped up from the bed and was standing in her path.

Sky opened her mouth to scream, but the sound never left her lips. The blow to her face was so powerful and unexpected that it launched her backwards, slamming her head against the opposite wall and crumpling her to the floor. She lay there, dazed, but conscious enough to see Clare McElvoy lunging at her, bread knife raised to strike. Sky screamed, and shot hands out to defend herself, temporarily blocking the path of the menacing knife, but the girl seemed blessed with inhuman strength and, aided by gravity, she bore down on Sky.

Lightning flashed, snapshotting the deranged look on teenager's face.

The blade was inches away. Clare was sniggering. It was clear that she possessed enough strength to break Sky's weak defences, but she was toying with her, enjoying the creases of terror in her face. The tears of horror in her eyes.

Sky's arm was aching, her muscles buckling, her heart pounding, and her adrenaline coursing under the strain. She knew she wouldn't be able to hold out much longer. She had to do something, and she did. With all the strength she could muster, she lodged a knee in the girl's crotch, causing her to cry out and her grip to slacken, temporarily, long enough for Sky to deliver a right hand uppercut to the girl's jaw, propelling her backward.

Sky wasted no time in scrambling forward toward the door, but Clare was up in hot pursuit, slashing at the air and chopping the floor behind her. Then, just as Sky reached the door, she felt fingers close around her bare ankles and she fell, crashing to the floor once more.

"No!"

She scrambled to free herself, and kicked, viciously, but the hands wouldn't let go. "Blake! Heeeeeeelp!" she screamed with abject terror, her nails scraping on the wood floor as she was dragged backward.

Suddenly, the grip was relinquished and, as Sky turned, she saw the blade plunge straight for her right leg. She snatched it away and the lethal metal sank into the wood.

Lightning flashed and, in a scene out of one of the worst horror flicks she'd seen, she saw Clare McElvoy cackle with glee whilst stabbing at the floor around her feet.

Sky was in a sitting position now, kicking and scrambling her way to do the door, but her reserves of strength were fast dissolving. She knew she was no match for this killing machine and, as she watched the girl jump to her feet and tower over her with that same evil leer on her face, she knew there was nothing she could do to stop the inevitable.

That's when thunder clapped and lightning flashed, and Clare froze.

Sky did not turn around. She did not need to. The surprised look on the girl's face said it all.

The tray clattered loudly to the floor in a cacophony of smashing glass, crockery and fizzing alcohol.

"What the fuck…" was all Blake could breathe out at the spectacle before him: Clare towering over Sky's cowering, naked body, clutching a bread knife.

For an almost comical few seconds, all three people just gawped at each other, with the only sound being that of rasping breaths, fizzing wine, and pelting rain against glass.

Then, the killing machine resumed its mission and, in one swift movement, raised the blade to strike.

Sky screamed.

Blake, automatically, hurled himself forward, roaring, "NOOOO!"

He crashed into the demented girl, grabbed her thrashing wrist, and careened her backward, propelling her through the balcony doors.

Sky ducked instinctively as the room exploded into a dissonance of shattering glass, crashing surf, crackling rain, and a howling wind that swept angrily around the room, as if looking for someone to blame.

Blake panted loudly as he stared in disbelief at Clare's body, sprawled against the balcony railing as blood dribbled from a gash in her head.

Sky's murmuring brought him back. She was snivelling and shivering.

He snatched the quilt from the bed, knelt down to her, and wrapped it around her.

"Are you okay?" he asked, raising his voice over the din.

Sky did not reply. Instead, her head remained bowed against the elements.

"Sky?" Blake repeated, tucking the cover around her.

Finally, she looked up, eyes wide and full of tears, but she didn't say anything. Overwhelmed, he pulled her to his chest and caressed her hair. "It's over now, darling. It's all over," he repeated soothingly as the rain invaded the house, gliding on the carrier wind, desperately searching for a new host, but in such a small spray it was powerless.

A few minutes went by while Sky sobbed in Blake's arms, and then, suddenly, she looked up at him. Their eyes met, but neither spoke. Instead, she pulled herself from his embrace and gingerly stood up.

She was cold, wet, and still incredulous as to what had just taken place here. None of this could be true. It was all just a nightmare. She was having a nightmare and, any second now, she was going to wake up. She had to wake up because it was impossible for her to comprehend that this hideousness could really have happened. That one of Blake's students had actually broken into his home. No, not broken in – she'd had a key. He'd given her a key to walk into his house and try to kill her.

With a fucking breadknife!

Dazed, she searched through the debris for her clothes, not remembering that they had undressed downstairs, earlier in the evening.

"Sky?" Blake stood also, his hair damp from the mist that was whizzing around the room.

She looked across at him, eyes wide and wild, and then at the twisted body of Clare McElvoy. She pulled the quilt around her and then, inexplicably, began to laugh aloud.

Blake realised that she was in shock. He needed to get her out of this room and downstairs, where he would fix her a strong drink and call the police.

Sky moved to leave but, suddenly, yelped and hopped about, only to lose her balance and fall against the door, slamming it shut. She allowed herself to slither to the floor, and grimaced with pain as she inspected the shard of broken glass that had incised a nasty slit in her foot.

"Fuck!" The blood oozed to the tips of her toes, where it dripped onto the floor, joining the cocktail of rain and wine.

"Who left that glass there?" she joked.

"Come on," Blake said, moving toward her. "Let's get you downstairs."

"Don't touch me!" she said, holding up both her hands.

"What's the matter with you?"

"Just stay away."

"Sky…"

"…Just get away from me!"

The tone in her voice told Blake to back off, and he did. "Look, Sky, you are in…."

She held up her hands to silence him. Then, she slid back up the door, clutching the quilt and trying not to put pressure on her injured foot.

"Okay," he said. "Let's just get out of here, okay?" His tone was low, conciliatory.

She said nothing. Instead, she turned the handle and pulled the door open. Instantly, a stream of turbulence rushed through the room, tugging it shut again.

Blake moved to assist, and that was when they heard the piercing scream.

He turned just in time to see Clare, with a blood-smeared face and rain-drenched hair, hurtling towards him, blade raised, screeching like a wild animal.

"Blake!" Sky screamed.

He intercepted the girl's outstretched hand, momentarily controlling her slashing arm, but the momentum knocked him backward until he was pinned against the door. They fought for control of the knife, but Clare was terrifyingly strong and Blake had no other option but to head-butt her, hard.

The shock of the impact caused the maniacal creature to relinquish her clasp and stagger backward. Blake seized the opportunity and launched a karate kick to the girl's stomach, which forced her to double over, inviting him to deliver a powerful uppercut. His fist smashed into and shattered cartilage in the girl's nose, and sent her reeling backwards. She fell, heavily, on her backside, and slid on the wet floor.

Yet, with the agility of an acrobat, and the terrifying imagery of a demented jack-in-the-box, she sprang up again and, screaming, she charged at Blake with the knife once more.

She slashed his arm. He yelped.

He delivered a right-hand blow to her jaw. She went back.

She slashed at him.

He delivered a left hook. She jumped back.

Another kick, another right hook. Finally, she fell back out, against the railing once more. Seconds whirled by, and then, to their utter disbelief, they watched the girl rise, slowly, to her feet all over again.

Lightning flashed.

Dripping blood and rainwater, Clare McElvoy stood, wearing that same maniacal grin.

This was just too much for Sky. Something snapped inside her head, and before she knew it, she felt her legs rushing her forward and, arms outstretched, screaming with rage, she collided with the girl and propelled her over the railing.

Blake raced to the balcony and looked over.

Clare McElvoy was lying, back broken, on the rocks one hundred feet below. She gazed, lifelessly, up at him, until the tide eventually rolled over and then claimed her body.

23

An hour had gone by since the episode in Blake's bedroom, and neither of them had spoken a word during that time. Blake had nursed Sky's wounds and bandaged her foot. She'd not moved or spoken throughout, which worried him.

He kissed her forehead and whispered, "It's going to be okay." He did not know why he said it or even if Sky could hear him, but it didn't matter; all that mattered was that they get through this, together. He sat her on the sofa, nestled a glass of Brandy in her hands, and wrapped her in the quilt once more.

He needed to think. He made coffee whilst trying to process exactly what had happened to them that night.

The bottom line was that Clare McElvoy, his student, armed with inhuman strength and his own bread knife, had tried to kill them, but had failed because Sky had pushed her over the balcony.

His balcony!

He rubbed his temples. It had just gone past 02:00 a.m.

Mercifully, the rain that had otherwise not desisted since yesterday afternoon had taken a break, bringing a surreal quiet to the land. Although, even in the dark, Blake could still make out large shapes scurrying across the sky like a group of stealth assassins readying themselves for the next assault. He sat at the breakfast table and sipped, as fast as he could, strong black coffee. He needed to think, and he was finding it difficult through the overwhelming sense of fatigue that was settling into his limbs and causing a dull ache behind his eyes.

She was acting as if she was possessed. Yes, but by what?

The ache had now metamorphosed into a headache. He knew it was most likely a by-product of everything that had happened, and he had already swallowed two pills in an attempt to stave off the symptoms, but they didn't seem to be having any effect.

"Blake?"

He jumped up from his seat, spilling coffee over his hand and whirling around.

Sky was standing in the kitchen doorway. She was dressed now. Her once immaculately groomed hair was in matted strands around her face, though. Her eyes had dark rings around them and there was a vicious red welt on her throat, where Clare had prodded her with the knife.

"Sorry," she said flatly. "I didn't mean to startle you."

"No, it's fine," he said as he rinsed his hand with cold water. He was pleased to see that some life had returned to her eyes and that she was actually talking. "How are you feeling?" he asked, drying his hand with a tea towel.

She nodded. "Okay, considering I've just killed someone."

Blake didn't know how to respond to that. He simply gave her an encouraging smile, since he could only imagine how she was feeling right now. If he was having hideous flashbacks, then there was no doubt that she was also. Somewhat clumsily, he walked over and put his around her. She didn't respond to the embrace, and he felt it. It reminded him of how she had reacted earlier, in the room.

Does she blame me for what happened?

He pulled away from her. "Sky, I'm worried about you."

She moved past him to the breakfast bar and drank from his coffee cup.

There was a long pause.

"Sky, I know this is hard for you, but we need to talk about it."

"Why?"

He didn't actually know why. He just knew that she or, most likely he, would feel better if they at least talked about what had happened. "I just don't think that bottling everything up is going to do you any good."

She let out a short laugh. "Really? So, now you think you're a therapist."

"I just think we need to talk about what happened," he said softly.

She said nothing. She simply drank some more from his cup. Sky knew that her silence was hurting him, and there was nothing she wanted to do more than to run up to him and throw herself into his arms, and insist that he tell her that all of this, everything but for the beautiful time they had spent together, was just one horrifying nightmare. But she knew it wasn't that easy. She suspected that he might even try to make her think it was, but it wasn't.

She had killed someone, another human being, and there'd be no amount of cuddling, talking, or consoling that would ever change that.

"We are not responsible for what happened up there tonight," Blake said seriously, as if he had read her mind.

"Do you really believe that?" she asked, peering into the depths of the cup.

"Absolutely. Of course I do. You must do, too. Right?"

"Then why haven't you called the police?" She was looking at him now. Watching him, expectantly.

He didn't respond.

Eventually, she shook her head knowingly, "Well, that just proves…"

"…It isn't that."

"What then?"

"I tried."

"And?"

"There was no answer."

"What?" She laughed. "No answer from the police?"

"Something strange is happening."

"Strange? You mean like pushing that girl off the balcony? Yeah, I'd say that's pretty strange."

"No, I mean something really strange is going on," he said pensively.

"Blake, what the hell are you talking about?"

"Well, not being able to get through to the police is one of them, but I'm not just talking about that. I'm talking about Clare and Arthur McElvoy."

Sky screwed up her face, and then looked at him questioningly.

"I've been going over this in my head. There has to be some kind of connection here. Don't you think?" he asked.

"A connection? You mean, other than the fact that they were related?"

"What does that tell you?"

She shrugged her shoulders. "Blake," she sighed... Whilst curious, she was also tired, and not in the mood to play twenty questions.

"Do you remember telling me about Arthur McElvoy at the pub that day?"

She shook her head. "Don't remind me."

"What did the police say was so unusual about him before he died?"

"You mean besides him reeking of seaweed?"

"Seriously, Sky."

"I am being serious. I just don't know where you're..."

She stopped mid-sentence. It *was* clear to her now. "Oh my God," she breathed. "Are you thinking that it might be hereditary?"

Blake cocked his head. "Something like that."

"But there's no history of mental illness."

"So, what does that prove?"

"Not much really. But I would have expected to see something in his medical file."

"Maybe there was. You just missed it."

She threw him a look. She was very thorough in her work, and she would have noticed something that obvious.

"Even if your theory is correct, what does it prove?" she asked.

"Well, it proves that both of them were loopy, and that what happened tonight was just another consequence of that. Christ, the police witnessed Arthur's outburst first-hand."

"We've still got to prove that both of them were mentally ill, Blake."

"Well, the autopsy will reveal that, won't it? Didn't you tell me on the phone that day that they found something in his blood?"

"Yes, there was something, and I asked for further tests, but I haven't seen those results yet. If there isn't any physical evidence, we have nothing. It's not as if we can submit them both for psychoanalysis."

"Except the fact that the police witnessed first-hand what that old man was capable of, and what he did to the rest of his crew." Suddenly, his headache appeared to ease. He might actually be onto something. He could feel it.

"That still hasn't been proven," Sky said in an attempt to keep his optimism anchored to the ground.

"Maybe. But, come on, Sky, what are the chances of someone boarding that boat, doing that, and leaving again?"

"Yes, I'm hearing your theory, but things tend to work differently in court."

He walked over to her and said, optimistically, "Can't you see it, Sky? If we can prove that Clare was a few sandwiches short of a picnic, just like her uncle, then what happened up there was just self-defence. Christ! It *was* self-defence!"

Blake was pacing around the small kitchen now. He felt invigorated. Hopeful. "I've spent most of the past hour worrying about what the hell we were going to do when the police got here. You know, feeling guilty, feeling like a fucking criminal! What for? I haven't done anything. WE haven't done anything wrong, Sky!" He was feeling much more positive now. "That psycho broke into my home, and she attacked us…"

"Blake…"

"…Okay, we'll have to get through all the questions and…"

"…Blake…"

"…All the…"

"Blake!"

"What?"

"Aren't you forgetting something?"

He looked at her, perplexed. She was still very serious. For some obscure reason, she wasn't sharing his newfound optimism.

"What's wrong?"

"Clare didn't break in here."

"What do you mean?"

"What do you think I mean?" she replied, raising her voice. "There's no sign of forced entry. That would indicate that Clare did not break in, but that she let herself in." Sky let him absorb the words, and then added, "With a key. The one you gave her."

"What?" His smile melted.

"She told me, Blake."

"Told you what?"

"That you were having a relationship with her, and that you gave her a key." She leant back against the breakfast bar, as if to steady herself.

"And you believed her?"

"Why wouldn't I?"

He frowned. "Thanks very much."

"Well, what am I supposed to believe, Blake?" She stood up straight and held a hand to the red welt on her neck. "The girl was holding a knife to my throat! Why the hell would she lie?"

"I thought that was obvious by now. The girl was fucking loopy!"

"That's your theory. Do you want to know what the police's theory is going to be? Clare McElvoy, your student, was having a sexual relationship with you. Then you decide to have a fling with an old flame. Clare, obviously unstable for whatever reason, comes here, and lets herself in with *your* key. An argument ensues. We ambush the poor cow and knock her over the fucking balcony!"

Sky's eyes welled with tears. Blake moved to go to her, but she waved him away.

"I didn't give her a key, Sky," he said seriously.

"Then how did she get in?"

"I don't know. We must have left the door open – after you got here, remember?"

She remembered, but she couldn't think straight. Her mind was a racing track of blurred thoughts. She said nothing. Instead, she stared into his hazel brown eyes as if searching for the truth in there.

Blake spoke calmly and clearly, "I told you about her. You know what she was like. She had a crush on me and I did not encourage her in any way."

"But you didn't report this crush, though, did you, Blake?"

"No. You know I didn't."

"Why not?"

"I told you. I didn't think I needed to. Look, Sky, I'm not a cradle snatcher, no matter what you may think of me."

"You don't know what I think of you."

"Then why the fuck don't you tell me?" he yelled, frustrated, turning from her and rubbing his skull.

There was silence, but for the faint gurgling of drainpipes outside.

Then, he added, "Sky, ever since we met again, I've been trying to understand how you feel, but you just keep playing it cool."

"Well, now you know what it feels like, don't you?" she said petulantly, and could have kicked herself.

"What's that supposed to mean?" he asked, turning to her once more. "Christ, Sky, is that was this is all about? Getting even about something that happened years ago?"

She swallowed hard and wanted to say something. Preferably something that didn't make her sound like a love-stricken brat, but she was unable to articulate anything at all, leaving his words hanging heavily in the air.

After a long pause, he sighed and said, pragmatically, "Look, it's probably best we try and stay focused on the problem in hand."

"Fine by me," she said. "So, let's start with why you didn't call the police."

"I did."

"And?"

"I couldn't get through."

"What do you mean, you couldn't get through?"

"Exactly that. I dialled 999 for the best part of an hour, but I just kept getting some message about demand for the number being high, to hold or try again later."

She observed him.

He snatched his mobile phone from the table and handed it to her.

She looked at the phone and then at him, and then back at the phone again. She grabbed it from him and dialled 999. There was ringing on the line, and then a short tone, followed by a tinny female voice, *"Sorry, we're experiencing a particularly high volume of calls at this time. Please hold, or try your call again later."*

Sky disconnected, and then redialled two more times.

Same recording.

"My God," she whispered. "There must be a fault."

"There isn't. I called the operator and she confirmed the lines are genuinely busy."

"But how's that possible?"

"That's what I asked her, and even she was baffled."

"What's going on?"

"I wish I knew. Things must have got worse out there since last night."

"So, now what?"

"So, now we don't really have a choice. We go down to the police station and tell them everything in person."

"What if they don't believe us?" Sky asked, her eyes wide, as if she had only just realised what telling the police would entail.

"They will," Blake said, decisively. Then, "Come on, we can tune into the news on the way."

24

"...this special bulletin, once again. A hundred people have died, and many more have been injured in a spate of random acts of violence in the region. Over a thousand police officers, from around the country, have been drafted in the drive to restore order. Steven Scofield is on the line, once again, live from Exeter Police Station. Steven, what's the latest?"

"Jackie, I cannot describe to you just how chaotic things are down here. You would have to see it to believe it. I don't know if you can hear them, but behind me, there is literally a mob of about a thousand, maybe more, people here, who are literally fighting and jostling their way to the now closed gates of the police station. Many of them are frightened for their lives. Most claim to have witnessed some truly horrendous things tonight. Terrible things that include, but are not limited to, rape, mutilation and torture. Worse, these seemingly random acts of violence aren't necessarily being committed by strangers on strangers, but by family members against their own. I've even heard some extraordinary unconfirmed reports, and I should stress that these reports are unconfirmed, that even some members of the police may have been involved in some of tonight's incidents. Some truly bizarre and horrifying stories. As I said, in my entire career, I have never witnessed anything like this..."

"...Gosh, Steven, where exactly are you? Are you somewhere safe right now?"

"Well, Jackie, we're actually holed up in a locked van, in a car park overlooking the police complex, and, yet, the sound of the crowd is deafening, even from here."

"Steven, can you tell us, are the authorities any closer to understanding what exactly is causing these riots?"

"No, not really. Although, earlier, I did manage to snatch a brief comment from one of the senior detectives here. He speculated that the violence is most likely the result of drug and

alcohol binges, but I can tell you, many here do not share that opinion. In fact, the people I spoke to insist that what they saw had absolutely nothing to do with drugs or alcohol."

"Are the authorities clutching at straws, do you think?"

"Well, that certainly appears to be the case, yes."

"And, do we have any clue about the extent of these riots? For example, have there been any other reports of similar instances from other parts of the UK?"

"Not as far as we know, Jackie. The only area currently affected appears to be the Southwest. In fact, this very thing is baffling the authorities. Nothing like this, nothing as senseless or as random, at least not on this scale, has been reported anywhere else."

"Steven, most people, some would say luckily, are in bed, asleep, and most likely completely oblivious to what's going on out there. But for those who aren't, and are perhaps worried for their safety and that of their loved ones, what's the general advice?"

"Please remain calm. Remember, these are isolated incidents. As you reported earlier, the police have drafted reinforcements into the region. Teams are being deployed, as we speak, at various so-called hotspots in the area and, we're told, are already making a difference; order is slowly being restored. However, the police are asking that people not put themselves at risk. Stay home. Stay calm, and do not venture out unless absolutely necessary."

"Steven Scofield, thank you so very much. Please stay safe."

"Thank you."

"We will be bringing you further updates on the riots as they come in.

"And, of course, it's not just these riots that are stretching the emergency services to a breaking point, but it's also the weather. Torrential rain and gale force winds have not only hampered police operations, but have left hundreds of homes without power and under water. There are multiple red warnings in effect, as severe flooding, mudslides, and even sinkholes have been triggering some large-scale evacuations. Kevin Smith has the details. Kevin."

Sky switched the radio off.

They were driving down a narrow, windy road that led away from Stony Point towards the main road, and Exeter. To their left was a muddy, vertical wall, from which the road had been carved many years before. To their right, a sloping grassy embankment led to a large lake. The rain had stopped and the moon made the occasional appearance from behind the giant black silhouettes that still dominated the sky.

Thunder rumbled in the distance, confirming that the deluge was far from over.

"What are we going to do?" Sky asked, realising just how silent the Ranger Rover had become without the news babble.

"I'm not sure," Blake replied pensively.

"I could try ringing Morrison again," Sky suggested.

"And tell him what?"

"What do you think?"

"You've been trying him ever since we left the house. The man obviously has more important things to worry about. I don't know why we're even bothering to go down there," he said, squinting as a pair of headlamps appeared in the rear view mirror, dazzling him.

"What do you mean?" she asked, pulling at her seatbelt that suddenly felt as if it had etched a groove in her chest.

"Why are we bothering to go down to the station? We won't even be able to get into the place. You heard what that reporter just said."

"Well, shouldn't we at least try?"

"What for?"

"Because I have killed someone, that's what for!"

"It was self-defence, and it was either her or us, and, quite frankly, I'm glad it was bloody her," he replied, adjusting the rear view mirror.

Blake was annoyed. Not only had the unresolved business with Sky created a palpable tension between them, but the idiot in the car behind them was driving with his full beams on. "Dip your fucking lights!" he yelled at the mirror. Then, eyes back on the road ahead, he said, "Do you think the police are even going to be interested in what you have to say, given everything that's going on tonight?"

"Um, correct me if I'm wrong, but weren't you the one who suggested we drive down there?"

"Yeah, well, it was a shitty idea. I've changed my mind. I think we should turn around and go home. Wait it out until daylight."

"What are you suddenly afraid of?" she asked, looking across at him.

"I'm not afraid of anything. I just don't think there's any point in…"

The jolt cut Blake's sentence short and propelled them both forward against their restraints.

"What the fuck…?"

In unison, they turned to see that a white van was tailing them.

"Slow down, Blake. Let him go round us!" Sky cried.

"Slow down? What about my car?" He retorted incredulously.

"Just let him pass," Sky repeated.

She was reminded of the madness on the radio, and her altercation with the truck was still fresh in her mind.

"I have slowed down," Blake snapped as he monitored the van in his wing mirror. He slowed the car to forty. The van hesitated, and then, without indicating, began to overtake them.

As the vehicle drew level with the Range Rover, Blake turned to yell at the driver, but was unable to see to do so – the cabin was in complete darkness, front windows tinted.

"Fucking maniac!" Blake shouted.

In that moment, there was an engine roar and then a high-pitched crunching sound as the van veered into the side of the Range Rover.

Sky screamed as the impact sent them, tyres screeching, toward the edge of the road. They fishtailed a few times before Blake managed to straighten up, but the van was coming in for more. Instinctively, Blake stomped on the accelerator; the SUV growled and lunged forward, narrowly missing another scrape as they rounded a bend.

The van drew level once more.

"Blake…" Sky murmured as she shrank back into her seat.

"I know," he replied, decelerating, but the van mirrored the move.

Another bend.

The van's lights flashed and its horn blared tauntingly before…

Smash!

It slammed into their side once more. This time, Blake was ready for the attack. "Hold on!" he shouted over the din of the engines, and steered to compensate. However, despite his counter-attack, the van managed to push them further towards the edge and off the road, in a screech of tyres and grinding metal.

"You bastard," Blake seethed through clenched teeth as he fought to retain control.

Sky screamed again as they bumped on and off the tarmac, and the moonlit lake winked at her, menacingly. The vehicles flanked each other as they stormed down the narrow road, swerved around another bend, and then smashed into each other again as they battled to retain their positions on the road.

Blake turned hard left and the van veered into the muddy wall, snapping its wing mirror and dredging down a cloud of mud and rock. The driver recovered, and came back at Blake at full throttle, shunting the Range Rover onto the grass verge, closer to the edge.

Sky screamed.

Slam!

Again...

And again...

Blake felt the steering wheel lock and battled to regain control, but to no avail. The van swerved away again, preparing for another attack. It was as if the demented driver knew of the SUV's predicament, and was preparing to strike the killer blow.

The seatbelt that had been irritating Sky moments before was now a major comfort.

The van came back, slamming into the side of their vehicle, shunting them to the edge and sandwiching them between it and the metal parapet, illuminating their predicament with a fountain of sparks.

This was the most dangerous part of the road, hence the metal railing. Without it, Sky could now see a very steep embankment that led directly into the lake.

She squeezed her eyes shut, horrified by the inevitable.

Suddenly, Blake's window shattered into hundreds of pieces, showering them both with glass. The fresh scent of rain and the deafening sound of the two angry engines flooded the cabin.

It took a few seconds but, when Blake recovered, he yanked left angrily on the steering wheel. To his surprise, and seemingly that of the van driver, it responded, sending the SUV sideways, smashing into the van, and sending it back into the rock face where it dragged down another landslide of debris that hammered loudly onto both vehicles.

It was then that the car appeared from around the bend in front of them. It flashed its lights and honked its horn in protestation.

Sky opened her eyes as the world slipped into slow motion. The scene played out under the glare of flashing headlamps, the soundtrack of blasting horns, and labouring engines.

The Range Rover's steering wheel locked once again, and, this time, no matter what Blake did, it would not budge as they sped forward, on a collision course with the oncoming vehicle.

"Oh my…" Sky breathed as Blake slammed on the brakes, but the momentum had seized control and was dragging them forth.

Five feet…

Blake threw himself over Sky as the van struck, shoving them sideways, through the metal parapet and down the embankment, toward the foreboding inkiness of the lake.

Behind them, the crash was loud as the van clipped the bumper of the oncoming car, swerved sideways, and then somersaulted several times down the road until it slammed into the grassy verge.

Meanwhile, the Range Rover bounced down the hill until it jumped over a boulder and dove, nose-first, into the lake.

It took only moments for the freezing water to invade the vehicle through the shattered driver's window.

Blake reacted immediately and unbuckled his seatbelt.

"Oh….G…o….d!" Sky stuttered, as the icy water washed over her.

"Stay calm, Sky, unbuckle your belt." Blake said calmly, although he knew the car was sinking fast. The bonnet was already under water. They needed to get out, and fast. Sky fumbled to release her belt, but she couldn't disengage the lock.

"I can't do it! Blake! It's stuck! It's stuck!"

"Okay, let me try," he said, maintaining his composure, as if he had trained for this kind of eventuality.

The car was filling rapidly; the cold water was at their waists and constricting the breath in their lungs.

Blake, his footing on the brake's pedal, was finding it hard to keep his balance as he tugged at Sky's restraint.

"Blake…" she whimpered, reading the frustration on his face.

"Don't worry."

She was hyperventilating now, her eyes wide with terror as she watched the water rise rapidly to their chests.

"Get me out of here! Get me out of here!" she screamed, tugging at the seatbelt.

"Sky!"

"Get me out!"

"Sky!" He cupped her head in his hands. "Baby," he cooed, locking eyes with her. "That isn't helping. I'll get you out of here. I promise," he said earnestly.

Tears of frustration welled in her eyes.

He smiled at her, reassuringly, kissed her quickly, and said, in his best Arnold Schwarzenegger impression, "I'll be back."

With that, and to her utter disbelief, he left her and began to climb upward, into the rear of the vehicle.

"What? Blake! Blake!"

She strained to look after him, but she couldn't. The car was on a vertical dive and she was dangling forward, strapped in like an astronaut as her body began to shiver violently.

The water was at shoulder level now.

"Oh… my Go…d… Bla… ke…" She coughed as bitter lake water made her gag.

Choking and spluttering, she cranked her head as high as she could above the rising tide. Then, suddenly, and with a loud grown, the SUV slipped beneath the surface. Sky managed to snatch one last breath, seconds before the water rose over her head, and then promptly expended it by tugging and clawing at her restraint.

The act was futile.

Now, as she sank towards her watery grave, as the freeze seized the mobility of her limbs and the world dimmed to blackness, but for the pallid blur of the moon overhead, Sky McPherson felt loneliness press against her, stronger than the body of water that was drowning her.

She longed for her parents' embrace and prayed that they'd forgive her for betraying their love by rejecting them in favour of some idealised view of the person she should be.

Her body began to spasm as her brain protested against the lack of oxygen, and then, suddenly, a peculiar calm washed over her. She no longer feared death, but smiled at it as images of Blake's face appeared before her like a developing Polaroid.

Blake. I'm sorry. I'm sorry, Blake.

She was crying inside, her mind racked with sorrow. Remorse. Deep remorse, that she had not been a stronger person all of those years before. Strong enough to embrace not only who she was, but reconcile this with her heritage, as well as who she'd aspired to be. Strong enough to fight for the one person who, beyond her parents, made her feel safe. Loved. Instead, she had tarnished everything with her self-loathing and used that skewed projection to escape the one thing to which she had lost all control – love.

She watched, painfully, how, in her mind's eye, the man whose body had once been a paragon of health, whose smile had been as bright as the sun itself, slowly began to wither and twist into a shrivelled corpse.

NO!

She reached for him.

No!

He reached for her.

Then, she was floating, free amidst a whirlpool of snapshot images of her parents, her childhood, her life, and him.

Seconds seemed like hours as she drifted higher and higher towards heaven until she broke the surface of the water to a symphony of coughs, splutters, and gasps as the same air that had abandoned her moments before was now forcing its way back into her lungs, oxygenating her blood and feeding her starving brain.

As she drifted back to consciousness, she became aware of a strong arm supporting her waist, and of a kicking motion that was slowly propelling her back to shore. She felt herself hauled out of the water, onto the grassy verge, where she lay in recovery for a few minutes.

The smell of rain hung heavily in the air but, thankfully, there was no precipitation. She was shivering. Yet, the air felt surprisingly warm when contrasted to the freeze of the lake water.

Thunder groaned, as if protesting against her salvation.

"Blake! Blake!" she cried, turning to the lake.

"I'm here!"

"Blake!"

"I'm here, Sky. I'm here."

She looked up. Blake was crouched next to her, breathing heavily, water dripping from his wet body.

She sighed deeply as relief washed over her like a warm shower. "Thank God," she breathed, "Thank God."

Blake had used the Stanley knife from the case in his boot to cut Sky's seatbelt. He had rescued her.

"Blake…" She started crying.

He put his familiar strong arms around her once more and pulled her to him. "It's okay. We're okay," he said, chest heaving against hers.

And that's when it happened. Right in that moment, as she felt his breath on her face, the warmth of his body, the security of his embrace... It felt as if someone, somewhere, had opened a massive floodgate, and, finally, after all of these years of repressing, and pretending that she was over this man, Sky McPherson realised that nothing could be further from the truth.

She loved him more than she ever had or ever could love another. She looked up into his face and he looked down at her.

"Are you okay? We need to get you back. You're shivering."

"So are you," she said through shudders while looking into his eyes.

"Then, I'd better get back, too," he said, smiling. He moved, but she stiffened. "What's wrong?"

She grabbed his head with clumsy cold hands and kissed him – deeply, fully. The move was unexpected, and it took him a few seconds to reciprocate.

Eventually, when she finally let go, he said, "Blimey, what did I do to deserve that?"

Thunder boomed overhead and they looked up.

"Great. Do you think it's going to throw it down with rain as too?" She asked.

"Well, look on the bright side," he said, standing up and forcing as smile, "at least we're out of the lake." He helped her to her feet.

They started back up the embankment, where they climbed the slippery, grassy slope until they reached the road once more. At the top, they both looked at the smoking, mangled remains of the van and the wreckage of the car.

"I better go and see if there are any survivors," she said, starting forward.

Blake caught her arm, "No!"

"Blake," she protested, looking at his hand on her arm.

"We need to get back to the house," he said flatly.

"Blake, they may need our help."

"It's more than our help that they need," he said.

She hesitated.

"Sky. Come on. We need to get back," he insisted.

Reluctantly, she followed him as he led her away from the road, up the hill, and back towards Stony Point, pausing only to ensure that nobody was following them.

25

They had been walking for over thirty minutes. The shortcuts they had taken through fields and over brooks had led them to a road overlooking the tiny village of Tresea. It was perched on a cliff-top location, rising above the ocean. The place looked deserted. Uninviting. There were no lights burning behind windows. No activity outside.

Nothing could be heard, but for the roaring of the nearby stream that had now swelled into a small river that had burst its banks and was washing over the tarmacked road and rushing down the embankment, towards the village, like a slithering black menace.

"Where is everyone?" Sky asked through rasping breaths.

"I don't know," Blake replied, looking around them. He felt uneasy. It was still the early hours, but there was something unsettling about the quiet. "They may have already been evacuated, due to flooding," he said, nodding.

Sky followed his gaze over the scurrying water and towards the village, where the occasional moonlit glint suggested that it was at least ankle-high.

"Come on, let's go," he said, breaking into a run.

"Hang on, Blake. Where to?" she asked, not following.

He stopped, looked back at her, and said nervously, "I don't know, but we can't stay on this road – it's too dangerous."

They were on a small, arched bridge. The recently formed river had burst its banks and was sloshing anywhere gravity would take it. In front and behind them, the drowned road sparkled under the moonlight like one massive sheet of glass.

"Blake, as much as it grieves me to say it, I need a rest." Her voice was loud in the emptiness of the night.

"We might be able to catch a lift with someone from there." He pointed at the village.

"I thought you said they'd been evacuated."

"They may have, but it's worth a…" Blake stopped talking when he heard a rumble in the distance. Only, it wasn't thunder – it was the sound of an approaching vehicle. Its guttural drone was loud and unmistakable. It was a truck of some kind, and it was approaching fast, from behind the ridge in the road.

"Oh, great. We can ask him for a lift out of here," Sky said happily.

Blake said nothing.

"Can't we, Blake?" she asked, looking at him and losing her smile.

The headlights were a glowing haze behind the ridge.

"Blake? What's wrong?"

"Let's wait and see," he replied, not taking his eyes off the oncoming glare.

The sound of the truck's engine grew rapidly until, suddenly, it appeared over the crest of the road. The horn blared loudly, echoing around the valley.

"Get off the road!" Blake yelled. He snatched her hand and tugged her off the road, and down the embankment, where they slid on the wet grass and fell into a heap on the ground.

"Blake!" Sky said angrily as she recomposed herself.

The lorry sped by where they had been standing just seconds before, blasting its horn once more.

"Well, I think we can safely count him out for a lift," Blake replied, staggering to his feet and then extending a hand to Sky. He looked towards the village. "Let's head down there. See if we can get help. Maybe find a car."

After taking a few steps, he realised that Sky was not following. "Sky?"

She said nothing.

"Sky?"

She was looking up the embankment to where she noticed that the lorry had skidded to a halt, approximately ten yards down the road, and it was idling.

"Come on!" Sky squeaked excitedly.

Before Blake could say a word, she was off, scrambling back up the embankment.

"No, wait!" He shouted after her as the truck driver gunned the engine.

He started up the slope in pursuit. "Sky! Stop!"

In that moment, the truck began to reverse up the road.

Now, Blake knew. He could not explain how, but he just knew. "SKY! WAIT!"

However, she was back on the road already, smiling and panting.

She turned to look down at him, put her hands on her hips, and frowned. "What's your problem?" she asked as the truck roared loudly towards her.

"Get out of the road!" Blake shouted.

"What? Why?" she asked, not comprehending the hysteria in his voice.

The lorry was ten feet away, approaching rapidly. It was not going to stop.

Sky turned to it. "Oh my…" The jolt snatched the rest of the words from her mouth as Blake, in a move worthy of a trapdoor spider, grabbed her, and dragged her back down the embankment once more.

The eight-wheeler garbage truck missed her by seconds, and then screeched to a halt in a fetid cloud of carbon monoxide and decay.

"What the hell's going on?" She complained, picking herself up from the wet grass once more.

Blake did not reply. Instead, he caught her hand and, before she knew it, they were both running, sliding and sloshing through the bog, towards the nest of houses.

Behind them, the lorry trumpeted angrily, veered off the main road, and plunged down the bank in pursuit.

The hamlet remained lifeless. The windows black. There were no curtains twitching, nobody curious about the commotion. Darkness reigned, but for a few weak street lamps.

The lorry's growl grew louder.

"Through there!" Blake shouted, avoiding the main road through the houses and opting instead for a tiny alleyway that sliced between two cottages.

The truck was thirty feet back, picking up speed.

Behind the steering wheel, the driver fixed his quarry with wild eyes and a gleeful leer. He wanted them. He wanted to squish them, just as he had his colleagues earlier that day. He had particularly derived much pleasure from mowing down his supervisor. The moron had stood in front of his truck, thinking that that was going to stop him from abandoning his shift. The skinny runt's body had snapped like a matchstick when it had connected with the truck's bonnet, but that hadn't stopped the driver from reversing back over him and the rest of his workmates when they'd nosily chosen to abandon the safety of the canteen to investigate.

There had been quite a few other pedestrians since, including an elderly couple who had broken down by the side of the road. The old man had tried to flag him down, but driver must have snapped his arm when he'd driven straight at it. The best part was when his wife had crouched in the middle of the road, wailing over the old fart. He'd reversed over top of her.

Now, he had come across these two – and to think he would have missed them, but for the fact that he had spotted the attractive little morsel in the rear view mirror. He could not wait to hear the sound her delicate little body made under his wheels. He blasted his horn again, upping the terror a few notches, as they glanced back from time to time to watch his *beast* gain on them. And, aided by gravity, it was gaining fast.

They had reached the alleyway now. Blake's first instinct was to hide in one of the houses, but he knew better than that. It would take more than a thin layer of bricks to stop a truck at that speed.

They entered the alley. Up ahead, a streetlight shone brightly, spawning the silhouettes of two men. Blake and Sky slowed instinctively. The two strangers were blocking their exit.

"Blake!"

They observed the stance of the two men.

The trundle, slosh, grind and growl of the dump truck reminded them that it was not stopping for anything. They had no choice, but forward.

"Don't stop! Keep running!" Blake yelled over the din.

The two men, faces obscured by the gloom, stood bolted to the ground. They were waiting for them.

"Blake..."

He tightened his grip on her hand, "Keeping running, as fast as you can! Don't let go. We're going to have to ram them!"

"What?" she cried.

Blake still couldn't see their faces, but he wasn't prepared to take any chances.

Attack now! Ask questions later. "When I say jump, jump and kick!" he shouted as they stormed towards the strangers.

"Jump!"

In unison, they leapt into the air, legs outstretched.

There was a grunt and a wheeze from one man as Blake's boot connected with his stomach, and a squeal of pain from the other, when Sky's outstretched foot snapped into his knee. All four people splashed into a heap in the water.

Behind them, the lorry struck the cottages with the force of a meteorite. Metal screeched, glass shattered, wood splintered, and bricks crumbled, spraying dust into the air.

Yet, the metal beast did not stop.

Now, with a mangled, blood-spattered facia, a fuming radiator, and with one eerily blinking headlamp, it relentlessly – albeit at half the speed – continued to bulldoze its way towards them, spewing a cloud of rubble in its wake.

It didn't take long for Sky to regain her composure.

She slapped, punched, and kicked until she was back on her feet, and splashing for her life once more. That was until she noticed that Blake was not running with her. She turned to see that he was still wrestling in the flood with one of the men whilst her opponent continued to writhe nearby. Unsure whether to nurse his knee or the bloody nose she had gifted him.

Behind them, she watched the evil eye of the metal monster wink as it continued on its destructive path towards the trio. It was gaining. No more than twenty feet away.

Blake was, once again, face to face with the madness of the rain. His assailant's manic grin and dilated pupils were as terrifying as the spittle dripping from the man's mouth was repulsive. The man, the stranger, his hands clamped around Blake's throat, was hell-bent on snuffing the life from him, and there would be no amount of clawing, kneeing, or kicking that would deter him from his murderous intent. it felt no pain. No emotion. It was a robot, sent by the rain with just one mission, and nothing could stop it, except...

The decorative white rock that made a sickening, squelching sound as it smashed into the back of the man's skull. Instantly, the grip slackened, the man's body went limp, and he fell heavily onto Blake, forcing what little air was left in his lungs, out with a wheeze.

"Come on!" Sky screamed, "There's no time to kiss and make up!" She dragged Blake to his feet as he gasped for air.

The truck was no more than ten feet away. So close that they were momentarily enveloped by the debris that preceded it.

The wounded man barely had time to look up before he was showered by falling cement, this was closely followed by a tidal wave of water, and then the full weight of the truck's tyres crushed bones and squelched him into an omelette of flesh and blood.

They emerged from the alley and paused. Ahead of them was an enormous grassland that sloped, steeply, into darkness.

Beyond that, the moon flickered periodically off a calm ocean. It was no more than half a mile away. They could even hear the sound of the surf.

They exchanged looks.

"We'll never make it," she said, answering his telepathic question.

"We... have... no choice," he breathed.

The screeching, crashing, growling sound of the truck's destruction signalled that it was gaining, and was seconds away.

"I guess it's worth a try!" Sky yelled sarcastically, grabbing Blake's hand and breaking into a run.

Five seconds later, the lorry emerged from the alley in an explosion of dust and debris, making matchsticks out of what was left of the cottages. It trumpeted loudly in celebration of its freedom. No more restraints. The driver was going to crush them.

The wetland they were traversing was deep and obscured, making their progress difficult and perilous. They each, in turn, slipped and threatened to tumble into the wash but for the other's support as they sloshed into the gloom, toward the sound of the ocean.

More trumpeting! The driver was delirious with excitement as he watched his quarry slip in and out of view of the truck's eye.

"Blake... it's gaining!" Sky panted as the engine sound grew louder. She was struggling. Although they were going downhill, she was expending most of her energy in trying not to slip over.

"Keep.... going!"

The lorry was almost upon them, so close they could feel the heat of the radiator on their backs.

"Faster!" Blake yelled over the sound of the engine.

"I aaaaaaaaam!" she screamed, losing her footing, but Blake held her upright.

Then, as a new day flirted with the horizon, the clouds parted and, to their horror, realisation dawned. Their mutual, albeit wrong, assumption had been that they were running towards some kind of beach, where they could wade out to sea and away from the reach of the heavy truck, but this had been their biggest mistake.

The tiny hamlet of Tresea was set on a cliff-top location, and the drop was no more than thirty feet in front of them. They could only imagine just how far down the plunge was from there.

They were speeding forth. Both afraid that the momentum they had built up was going to run them straight over the precipice.

25 feet….

…"Blake!"

20 feet…

…"Get ready! I'm going to push you!" he shouted.

15 feet…

…"What?"

There was no time to reply. Blake shoved Sky, as hard as he could, to the right with the back of his arm. The impact was sudden, and Sky lost her balance. She slipped and fell with a loud splash, slamming a rib against a protruding stone. The shock of the impact twisted up her gut and into her brain, causing her to abandon all sense of control, and, instead of steadying her fall, she allowed herself to tumble forward with the flow of water, towards and then over the cliff's edge.

Before the driver realised what was happening, it was too late. Both of his prey had rolled out of his path. He screamed with rage, slapped his steering wheel, and stomped on his brakes. The wheels locked and slowed, but the momentum was too much. The lorry sailed, somewhat gracefully, in the water – towards the beckoning cliff edge.

In a desperate bid to cheat an icy death at the bottom of the Atlantic Ocean, the driver swerved hard; the metal beast groaned under the strain of having its head pointing in one direction while gravity dragged it in the other. It howled as the front left wheel lifted into the air, followed shortly by the next, and the next. Then, there was a deafening crash as the metal beast slammed onto its side and slid – wheels spinning, engine roaring, and glass shattering – helplessly toward and then over the edge. The machine's carcass smashed onto the protruding rocks with an almighty boom of twisted metal. It hissed and groaned as the ocean bathed and then slowly pulled it into its Cimmerian world.

It took a few seconds for Blake to digest what had actually happened to them, and it was then that he noticed that Sky was nowhere in sight. He hauled himself to his feet, but was unable to think straight. His brain was suddenly paralysed by a blind panic. He searched, frantically, nearby and then called out desperately. "Sky! Sky!"

The only response was that of the surf, the gale that was whipping around his wet and shivering body, and the occasional mournful cry of the sinking metal monster.

As much as Blake Hudson did not want to accept it, there was only one answer; he looked toward the cliff, and then half-ran, half-walked, and half-slipped his way to the edge.

No! This can't be happening. This can't be happening. Please, God. No! No!

Tears welled in his eyes. "Sky!" he screamed blindly into the darkness. "Sky!"

But there was no response.

26

At first, Blake thought he had hallucinated them, but he had not. Like fireflies, the flashlights were bobbing toward him through a gloomy dawn. There were two of them, and they were approaching fast.

Where can I go? Where can I hide? What about Sky?

He resolved that he was not going to run. He was not going to leave her here.

Thunder clapped directly overhead, and he ducked instinctively. Then, glancing at the nearing flashlights, he fell to his knees and groped in the water for a stone or anything that could be used as a weapon; if they took him down, it would not be without a fight.

Lightning flashed and he could just about discern two men.

They were coming to get him.

He looked around the open field. There was nowhere to go. No place to hide.

Where the fuck is everybody anyway? How the hell can a lorry plough its way through a whole village and nobody notice?

The lights homed in on him and he shielded his eyes to fend off the glare. He felt pathetic, kneeling in a stream of water, shivering and cowering like a wounded animal.

The men were ten feet from him.

That was when he heard the sirens in the distance. He looked up. Sure enough, he could see the reassuringly blue flashing lights of two vehicles.

He wondered if they were rushing to some other emergency, but hoped they were coming to save him, and, sure enough, to his utter relief, he watched them pull up on the main road beyond the village.

Meanwhile, the two men were advancing on him. All he had to do was hold out until the police got there. He emerged from the stream of water, revealing a small rock in his right hand whilst using his other to fend off the glare of flashlights.

"No, you don't wanna' be doing that, son," a gravelly voice said with a strong Cornish accent.

"Get away from me!" Blake growled, waving the rock around, menacingly.

The men stopped in their tracks.

"I said, get away!" Blake screamed, sounding almost as demented as all of the other freaks he had encountered on this most bizarre of nights.

He was not acting. His heart was racing. The adrenaline was still pumping. He was terrified for Sky, and so traumatised by everything that had happened that he was more than ready to bash in both their skulls.

Another Cornish voice suggested, "Put the rock down, mate."

Blake glanced behind them. He could see more flashlights approaching in the distance. This gave him courage. "Don't come any closer or I'll smash your fucking heads in!" He growled.

"You're not going to do anything," one of the voices said, moving forward.

This startled him, and he promptly lifted the rock to strike, but the sudden movement caused him to slip on the boggy grass and, no matter how much he tried, he lost his balance and fell, arms flailing, with a loud slosh. He emerged from the stream of water choking and spluttering. He had also lost his weapon, and was now at the mercy of these maniacs.

Lightning flashed as the duo peered down at him, training the beams of their torches at his eyes.

"What the hell's goin' on?" one of them asked. "The whole bloody place has gone fuckin' mad."

"Poor bastard," the other commented.

"Shall we cuff him?"

"I think we better 'ad. Don't want a repeat performance of what happened to Perkins."

"You're right. I can't believe he bit his ear clean off like that."

As they bore down on him, Blake threw his hands up in defence.

"It's all right, we're not gonna' hurt ya'."

"Wait. You're police?" Blake asked incredulously.

"That's right. We're police, and you can either come quietly or by force. The choice is yours, mate. But I'm warning ya', with the night we've had, we're not gonna' be taking any shit from you."

They hauled Blake to his feet.

One of the officers, known as Ginger, spoke into his radio while the other attempted to snap a pair of handcuffs onto Blake's wrists.

"This is Baxter. Confirming, one suspect in custody, over."

"Two! Sky's down there!" Blake snapped, pulling away from the officer who was trying to cuff him.

"Oi! I'd calm down if I were you."

"Who's Sky?" asked Ginger.

"She's the lady that's with me. She's down there," Blake struggled, nodding towards the cliff.

"Okay, mate. For your own safety, let my colleague put the cuffs on you."

"No! Not until you find Sky!"

"If you want us to help your friend, you need to cooperate with us. Now, either you let the officer put the cuffs on you, willingly, or we'll have to do it by force."

"The fuck you will! She could be dying down there for all we know, and all you're worried about is cuffing me!"

"It's for your own protection. Now, I'm not gonna' tell you

again."

"No!" Blake's nerves were a mess. He struggled to get away. He had to get away. Their priorities were all wrong. They were wasting time with him rather than looking for Sky.

The officer spoke into the radio.

"This is Baxter. We've got another one of 'em 'ere. We're gonna' need back-up."

A tinny, crackly reply said, "Roger, Baxter, we're on our way down to you right now."

Ginger turned to look at the approaching flashlights, as if to confirm what he had just heard.

Blake noticed this, and said very quickly, "You don't understand, I'm not one of them!"

"Then why won't you let us cuff you, mate?"

"I will! But you two morons aren't listening to what I'm saying."

"No, we can hear what you're saying, mate, but what you don't realise is we're the ones in charge here, not you. Now, either you let us cuff ya' now, or we'll do it by force, and then nick ya' for resisting arrest, too."

"Why don't you…"

Blake's sentence was cut short by a low chopping sound. His eyes darted all around, but he couldn't work out its origin. Then, suddenly, the helicopter sprang up from behind the cliff face, drenching the trio in a pool of fluorescent light.

Taking advantage of the distraction, the second officer tripped Blake up and pushed him, face-down, into the water once more, smacking his head against the rock he had been holding just minutes before. The police officer proceeded to cuff his gargling prisoner, as quickly as possible, before yanking him up from the water again.

"No…" Blake murmured, dripping, spitting out water and sucking in air. "No, Please…"

Ginger spoke into his radio again as the police helicopter circled overhead, "Thanks, Eagle 1. Any survivors down there?"

"That's affirmative," came the crackly, tinny reply. "One female, no obvious injury. Search and rescue have been advised, E.T.A. 30 minutes, over."

Blake could barely hear what was being said. His mind was drifting. He couldn't process whether he had actually heard the words *female* and *survivor* or if it was just what his fuzzy mind wanted to hear.

More officers arrived on scene, speaking in loud tones over the whirring blades of the hovering helicopter. Then, everything went black.

27

23 Parkview – Exeter, England – 15:03.

The subdued babble of the TV brought Blake out of an exhausted sleep. He was lying in a double bed, in a spacious, tastefully furnished room that he didn't recognise. Opposite him, glass balcony doors mounted a picture of grey clouds drifting across a blue sky.

His head hurt, so he instinctively touched his forehead, and felt gauze and plaster. Then, he hauled himself up and grimaced at the stiffness in his joints.

A flat screen television, at the foot of the bed, was beaming a picture of a grim-faced reporter in front of a muddy torrent of water. Behind her, somewhat bizarrely, a floral-patterned armchair was floating lazily down the middle of a row of houses. After a few minutes of gawping at the news report of flooded houses and grainy night-vision footage of daring helicopter rooftop rescue missions, he took in the rest of the room in an effort to identify where he was.

The wallpaper was a warm rusty colour with subtle triangular patterns. The carpet was cream, with a bed quilt to match. There was a large pine wardrobe, and a dresser carrying a large cylindrical vase, this hosted a trio of sunflowers.

The door opened and Sky walked in. She was dressed in jeans and a blue sweater. Her hair was in a ponytail, her face was scrubbed of makeup, her arm was in a sling and, other than a few cuts and bruises, she, much to his relief, looked okay. Sky glanced at the TV and then at the patient in her bed, and smiled.

"Welcome back."

Blake straightened up and promptly winced as a twinge of pain shot up his chest. Then, he glanced underneath the covers and groaned when he spotted a large bruise on his abdomen. He also realised that he was naked.

"You only had to ask," he said with a smile, although the comment was flat and contained none of the cheekiness that she found so attractive about him.

Sky returned the smile. "We had to get you out of your wet clothes.

"What happened?" he asked.

"You lost consciousness. They had to airlift you out."

"You're joking."

"You've been drifting in and out for hours. You hit your head," she nodded at the gauze on his forehead. "Do you remember anything?"

"Not much. Just fragments."

"Do you feel sick? Dizzy in any way?"

"No, I don't think so. Just have a splitting headache."

"Well, that's it. We need to be sure you're not concussed in any way. We were taken to hospital, but it was like a zoo down there. So I asked the paramedic to patch us up as best he could, and reassured them that I'd keep an eye on you."

"Are you okay? What happened?" He looked at her arm.

She followed his eyes. "Don't worry. It's nothing serious. Just a light sprain. I was really lucky."

"Where were you?"

"Well, after you shoved me – thanks for that, by the way – I actually rolled over the edge of the cliff…"

Blake's eyes widened, "What…?"

"…Luckily, it wasn't a sheer drop. I fell onto a ledge a few feet down."

"Oh my God…Sky. I could have kill…."

"...You actually saved my life. If you hadn't pushed me, I wouldn't have made it."

Blake said nothing.

"I mean it," she insisted. "You saved my life."

He smiled, weakly. "And you've been watching over me all this time?"

"Like your fairy godmother."

"But what about you? Are you really okay?"

"I'm fine. If you don't count being slashed at by some psycho, being rammed off the road by a deranged van driver, almost drowning, being chased down a field by an equally deranged truck driver... oh, and falling off a cliff."

"Is that all?" he asked.

"I think so," she smiled.

"Fuck," he uttered, "I really *do* know how to show a girl a good time."

She laughed. "Yes, and all I got was this lousy sling."

"Yeah, well, you're lucky. I came out of the ordeal with nothing. Not even my underwear."

"Yeah, well, try not to be jealous. At least you were out of it for most of the time. You missed all the commotion down at the hospital. I've never seen anything like it. There were patients not lying in trolleys, but literally sitting on floors in hallways."

"I feel like such a dick," Blake said sheepishly.

"Don't be silly. Head injuries are actually quite serious. Besides, you were amusing, most of the time. In fact, you actually came round at the hospital, starting babbling on about how we were all doomed and how you thought the rain was to blame for everything that had happened. Then, you vomited on the nurse's feet, which, may I add, is not a good sign with head injuries. Under normal circumstances, they wouldn't have released you, but, well, last night was everything but normal, and they were happy to release you into my care."

"Great, I feel much better now that I know I made a complete tit of myself."

"I'm just glad we're home."

"Oh, so that's where you've brought me."

"Yes. I've even washed and dried your clothes. I didn't think any of my stuff would look good on you."

There was a pause as they both, vacantly, watched an aerial view of what looked like a lake with a clump of houses sprouting from it.

Sky narrated. "There's been massive flooding. Thousands of homes are without power. Schools shut. Roads closed. Rail lines submerged, and even hospital services cancelled. It's really bad. The army's been called in to help. It's like some kind of apocalypse. There are whole villages underwater."

They watched the images in silence for a while.

"Oh, and I managed to speak to my contact D.I. Morrison. I told him everything that happened at yours. They're going to need to take a statement from you, too."

"What exactly did you tell him?"

"The truth. That she came around with a knife and tried to kill me. You know, he didn't even seem particularly surprised by what I told him, other than the fact that it featured me, of course. I asked him about that. He told me that they've been responding to worse. Although, I can't imagine how much worse anything could be after last night. Bottom line; some girl with a history of mental illness is the last thing on his mind."

"Clare had a history?"

"Yes; she started seeing a psychologist at the age of thirteen."

"Why?"

"I don't know all of the details, but it was something to do with the death of her father."

"So…"

"…Yes, your theory was right."

"Bloody hell, can I get that on record?"

"Anyway, her prints will be on the knife and your injuries will be consistent with the blade."

Sky paused to watch more of the televised news report, and then added absentmindedly, "They're comparing what happened last night to the London riots of 2011. MPs have been debating what to do about it."

"Do they really think last night was all about a bunch of pubescent anarchists?"

"That's what she's been saying." Sky nodded at the TV.

"And you believe her?"

She turned to him, and asked curiously, "Why shouldn't I?"

"I don't think last night was all about a bunch of bored, anti-capitalists hell-bent on destruction. I think it was more than that. You said it yourself. The police have been inundated with all sorts of cruel and unusual crimes. To the point where this guy, this detective you mentioned, wasn't at all surprised by what happened at my place."

"Right? So, what are you saying?"

He hesitated, and then, blurted, "At the hospital, last night. I wasn't rambling. I meant what I was saying."

"What, about your mother being upset that you'd gotten mud all over your clothes?"

Blake gave her a sideways glance. "No, I mean what I said about the rain."

Sky frowned.

He shifted, carefully. "Look, I know it may sound stupid, but I think there's a link between the rain and what went on last night. I mean, I'd have to get the water analysed, but I really believe that there's something in the precipitation, some kind of chemical or something."

Sky's eyebrows lifted.

"Yes, I know it sounds mad, but I'm telling you, it is possible that this particular band of rain is carrying in it a concentrated strain of something. Some kind of pollutant, something we've never seen before – but I'd need to see the lab results from the samples I took at that quarry to know for sure. Then, I could cross-reference those with the toxicological reports of Clare's uncle and, of course, her, and really anybody else who may have been exposed to…"

He stopped talking. Sky was staring at him.

He shook his head and forced a laugh, "Look, I know this sounds ridiculous, but…"

"I think I need to go call that doctor after all." She stood up.

"Wait, Sky…"

"No, Blake, I think I should. You know, just as a precaution." She pulled her phone up from the bedside table. She didn't really want to call anybody. She didn't even have anybody's number, but she needed to think.

There was a good chance that Blake was delirious, but something in the back of her mind was telling her that he may well be onto something. It was, ultimately, the first plausible theory she had heard. It certainly explained the randomness of the event.

Then, as if he had read her mind, Blake continued, "Come on, Sky," he said. "You told me that there was a foreign substance in McElvoy's blood. Now, which is easiest to believe; that an old man was experimenting with hallucinogenic drugs at the ripe old age of sixty-something, or that he somehow, unbeknownst to him, involuntarily ingested something?"

Sky hesitated for a few seconds, and then asked, "How exactly could this have happened?"

"I have absolutely no idea. I'm going to need to get back to the house. Track its origin."

He pushed the quilt back.

"You can't do that."

"Why not?"

"Because the place will be sealed off by now."

"So?"

"You'd be violating a crime scene."

"It's my home."

"You're a prime suspect, for God's sake."

"Sky, if I'm right, I think Her Majesty's Government is going to have more to worry about than whether or not I violated a crime scene."

"I know that. So you can dial down the condescension."

"I wasn't."

"You were."

"I wasn't."

"Whatever. Just do whatever you bloody want."

With that, she suddenly stood up and left the room.

Five minutes later, Blake emerged from the bedroom dressed in his clothes.

Sky was in the living room. She was standing with her back to him, staring out of the window.

"I've made tea," she said without turning around. "It's on the table."

Blake glanced at the tray and then at her.

A few seconds ticked by.

"Thanks for washing my clothes," he said.

"You're welcome," she replied flatly.

He took a few steps towards her. "Sky, help me out here. I really don't know what I said that…"

"…It's just never going to end, is it?" she interrupted.

"What isn't?"

"This. Christ, we could have died last night, three times! And, instead of thanking God, that we're still alive, you just can't wait to get back out there. There's always something with you, Blake. It's like nothing has changed. All hell is breaking loose and you, you're like some big kid. Acting like this whole thing is one big adventure."

There was a tremor in her voice.

"Sky, I am an environment officer. This is what I know. What would you have me do, hide out here and just hope it all goes away?"

She turned around. She was angry. He recognised the narrowing of the eyes, the wrinkling of her nose.

"No, I don't expect you to do that, but I do expect you, for once in your life, to…" She stopped in mid-sentence.

"What…?"

"Never mind."

"No, say it.

"I have nothing to say," she said obstinately.

There was another long silence, broken by Blake. "If you're talking about us, then I can finish that thought for you. I want us to discuss the future. Fuck, I don't know if I've thought about anything else, in between being slashed at and nearly run over," he smiled, "but I just don't think now is the time for that. I have some crazy theory to prove, and I need your help to do so, but you had better believe that, as soon as that's over, and you've proven that I may have banged my head harder than we both imagine, I want us to sit down and have a proper talk about things."

She looked away from him for two reasons; she suddenly felt completely foolish, perhaps even a tad immature, and a schoolgirl smile had appeared on her face, but she didn't want the hot school jock to see it.

"Sky. I can't do this alone," he said earnestly, angling his head so that she would look at him.

After a few seconds, she said, repressing a petulant tone, "What is it exactly that you need me to do?"

"I need those tox reports."

"You're insane."

"It's the only way. Those reports may be the only thing that will prove my theory."

"I've just finished telling them that I won't be in, despite them begging me to..."

"...We need that information, Sky," he said, seriously.

She hesitated, rolled her eyes, and then disappeared into the bedroom. As she slipped out of her sling and into her jacket, she noticed that the TV had stopped showing scenes of last night's riots and had cut to a reporter standing outside the gates of a football stadium.

"...officials have agreed that one of the most anticipated sporting events of the year will take place as planned.

"Tickets for the cup final between Cambridge and Plymouth Argyle sold out in hours, and, as you can see behind me, thousands of fans have already made their way to Home Park Stadium, here in Plymouth. This is in response to the introduction of additional security screening measures that were announced by police early this morning. Given recent events, the authorities are not taking any chances, and are advising fans to allow plenty of time for journeys and making it through security.

"And, from what I've seen so far, the only thing that police won't be able to manage is, as always, the weather."

28

Sky was, somewhat perversely, grateful that her colleagues were too busy doing their jobs to notice her slipping, surreptitiously into her office to grab a handful of manila folders from her desk and hurry back out of the building.

"Have you any idea how much trouble I'm going to be in if someone finds out that I removed these from the office?" she asked, handing Blake the folders and slipping behind the wheel of the BMW.

"I know, and I am eternally grateful."

"Yes, just remember that when I get sacked," she said as she started the engine and drove off at great speed, eager to put some distance between the coroner's office and herself.

It wasn't long before they were out the city and on the main road heading toward Stony Point.

"What exactly are you hoping to find in there?" she asked, glancing at Blake as he thumbed through the reports on his lap.

"I don't know; a connection," he replied pensively.

"Between what?"

"I told you – the rain and these deaths."

"Come on, Blake. You don't seriously think there's a link between them, do you?"

She'd been smiling, stopped when he glanced at her, and then rolled her eyes. "Next you'll be telling me that this is all the result of some government conspiracy."

"What if it is?"

"Blake…"

"…Did you know that, in the 60s, thousands of Americans, through no choice of their own, became human guinea pigs in an experiment conducted by the CIA? It dispersed a drug, as a gas, through the exhausts of cars…"

"…Yes, it's called carbon monoxide, and we're all guilty of that," she contributed.

"It wasn't carbon monoxide, Sky. They even admitted it."

"They didn't admit it, Blake."

"That's because they didn't need to. The evidence spoke for itself."

"So, you think that the British government is doing something like that to us now? Blake, you work for the government."

"I don't work for the government," he said distractedly, and then added, "Bloody hell, you may as well have asked me to read Egyptian. This doesn't mean anything to me."

"They're post-mortem reports, Blake. What did you expect?"

They drove in silence for a short while as Sky processed more thoughts. "Okay, let's say that you *are* right about the rain. That means that whoever gets wet is affected. Right?"

He nodded.

"So, if that's the case, why hasn't the whole country gone mad? And why is it that, with all of the rain, only a few have been exposed? You can't tell me that they're the only people who got wet."

"Maybe they were."

"So, you're suggesting that this band of cloud is discriminating. That it is actually choosing where and on whom to rain?" Sky laughed as she pictured a stereotypical cartoon of some wretched, depressed person with a squiggly cloud over her head.

Ignoring her mocking taunt, Blake said seriously, "I'm not suggesting that at all. I already told you that a cu-nimbus doesn't rain all the time. It can travel miles without precipitating anywhere."

"So, presumably, once someone has been infected, or rained on, or whichever way you would like me to put it, that's it – they're dead."

"I don't know. That's what I'm trying to find out," he said, waving the files at her.

"Well, I can tell you now, that isn't the case."

"How can you be so sure?"

"Because there are survivors. Admittedly, a lot of them can just about remember their own names, but there are survivors. Police have been picking up the so-called walking dead for most of the day. Many were found wandering the streets. A bit out of it, but seemingly okay."

Blake watched the road for several seconds as he took in the information, and then said, "It must have a symptomatic phase."

"What?"

"It wears off!" Blake looked at her. He was excited.

"Don't look at me, you're on a roll."

"It wears off, Sky. Which means, it isn't what the rain does, but it's what the people do while they're infected with it."

"Right, but it still begs the question, what exactly are they being infected with?"

"I don't know yet. But I am sure the answer is in these files and back at my place."

29

Stony Point – 16:20.

They were back at Stony Point within an hour. As expected, the door was sealed by yellow police tape with the words *'Crime Scene - Do not Cross'*.

Sky read the words as if she was seeing them for the first time. She knew that what they were about to do would most likely prejudice the case against them.

Blake, on the other hand, had no reservations in marching up to the front door, snapping the tape, and entering his home.

Sky shook her head, and then followed. "You do realise that the tape is there for a reason, right?"

It was cold inside the lighthouse. The place no longer felt welcoming to Sky. She paused in the hallway as a shiver scampered down her spine. It felt as if what had happened in Blake's room had happened a very long time ago. She had to remind herself that it had actually happened just hours before.

Blake was already climbing the steps when he realised that she wasn't following. "Are you okay?"

Images of Clare Hudson's blood-soaked face stared into her mind's eye.

"Sky?"

"I'm fine," she said, distracted.

"Are you sure?" There was concern in his voice.

She nodded.

He hesitated for a few seconds, and then disappeared up the spiral staircase. It was the police tape across his bedroom door that confronted Blake with flashbacks of what had happened in there, and suddenly, not unlike Sky, he no longer felt welcome in his own home.

The feeling annoyed him. It, not unlike its genesis, was an intruder in his home, he resented its presumption, and that it made him feel like he no longer belonged here.

He hurried upward.

In the study, he sat at his desk and touched the screen to wake up his computer. He launched the meteorological program. The spinning globe appeared, as did the map of the United Kingdom.

He touched the history menu, typed in a start date but left the end date blank, and then pressed 'OK'. The map redrew itself; most of the highlands and parts of Cornwall disappeared under a blanket of black cloud. He pinched to zoom into the Southwest region and, sure enough, parts of Devon and Cornwall remained under a shroud of blackness.

He accessed the date field once more, used the scroll buttons to cycle backward, and watched as the cloud regressed back out to the ocean. A smile spread across his face; so far, his theory had been correct.

Sky walked into the room.

Blake glanced up, "Come and look at this, quick!" he said excitedly.

"What am I seeing?" she asked, looking over his shoulder.

He pointed to black spots on the screen, "See these?"

"Yes."

"That's the rain."

"Right."

"Watch."

He pressed the scroll buttons, rapidly, causing the black clouds to move back and forth on the screen, toward and away from Exeter. "That's the rain."

"I don't think anybody's refuting it's been raining, Blake. What you're saying is that it has something to do with…" she stopped in mid-sentence.

"What?"

"Where is this?" She was pointing to a blue part of the screen.

Blake studied the monitor, "I'm not sure, exactly. Looks like the coast, just off Bude. Why?"

Sky didn't respond. Instead, she circled around Blake and

made for the post-mortem files that he had dumped on the desk.

"What? What are you thinking?" he asked eagerly.

"I'm not sure yet."

She was flicking through the files. Eventually, she stopped and pulled out a file marked 'McElvoy, A'. She scanned its contents.

"I don't believe it," she said, glancing at him.

"What?" he asked, frustrated.

She read from the report, "The trawler was found, adrift, 25 miles off the coast of Bude." She looked at him.

"Of course. The Sea Emperor," he breathed. "Arthur McElvoy was on that trawler. Do the dates match?" He pointed at the foot of the screen as Sky checked the date in the file.

"They do," she said. "Of course, this might just be coincidence."

"Of course it isn't. What else, Sky? Can you think of anyone else?"

"I don't know. It's hard, really. I don't recognise any of the area."

"What about the place you went to last night?" he asked.

"The old woman. She was found at her farm. It had a name, green..." she searched through the folders again, and then realised with disappointment why it wasn't there, "but the P.M. hasn't been performed yet. God, it was only last night; it seems like ages ago. But, Morrison text me the address and postcode..."

She picked up her phone and dictated while Blake punched the details into his computer.

"It's here!" He pointed to a location on the screen, just east of Bude. It was another incident in the path of the rain.

They exchanged glances.

"Another coincidence?" Sky asked.

"Do you really think so?"

She sighed. "You do realise, establishing that these people were exposed to the rain doesn't necessarily prove that it drove them to madness."

"No, but it makes a compelling case," he responded thoughtfully. "Who else? The quarry! The dead fish. that was... here." He pointed further East. "Still think it's a coincidence?" he asked seriously.

Sky said nothing.

"Next stop, Exeter, and I bet that if you look at those tox reports, you'll find that all of these people had an unidentified substance in their blood stream."

He watched her, expectantly, as she read the reports.

After what appeared to be an interminable few minutes, she breathed, "My God. This could be a photocopy of McElvoy's toxicological report."

Blake nodded, knowingly.

"What the hell is it, Blake?"

"I don't know. But whatever it is, you can bet your last penny that it came from that," he said, nodding at the dark mass on the monitor.

"Can you trace its origin with that?" she asked, nodding at the screen.

"To be honest, I have no idea how much history I can get access to from here. I would expect them to back up and clear the drives regularly, but there's no harm in looking." He cleared the date form the history field.

"How far back are you going?"

"Not sure. I'll just clear the date fields and see how far back we can go."

He pressed OK. The digital map redrew itself. He pressed the scroll buttons, and they watched as the black cloud retreated to the Atlantic Ocean.

"Wait, wait, wait," he murmured. He stopped scrolling. "Didn't that plane go down here, just South of Ireland?"

"Hold on," Sky said, holding up a hand. "You think this cloud was responsible for that, too?"

"Well, they did say that the pilot reported severe weather just before they went down," he offered. "That's weird, though."

"What is?"

"I'd have expected this cloud to have dissipated, at least from its current form, way before it reached the UK."

"Are you suggesting that this cloud isn't a cloud after all?"

"I don't know. I just know that I've never seen anything like this before. I wonder how far back this thing goes."

He continued scrolling until a blue box appeared – '*No further detail found!*'

"Is that as far back as it goes?" she asked.

"Yeah, it just ends here, over the Atlantic Ocean, somewhere Northwest of Ireland. There's no way of telling, at least not from here, where it originated from."

There was a long silence.

"So, what do we do now?" she asked.

"Well, I think the first thing we need to do is find out where this thing is heading now." He pinched the screen. The map redrew itself. He clicked buttons on the keyboard, and the date box disappeared, the current date and time appearing in its place.

"Okay, let's see, where are you heading now?"

"Will you be able to tell where exactly it's going to rain next?"

"Not exactly. I'm no meteorologist, but we should be able to at least get some idea of where this thing is heading, based on current wind trajectory."

"And once you know that?"

"I'm calling Hamilton, my boss, and telling him to put out a red warning."

"Will it be that easy?"

"No, but you know me, ever the optimist. Okay, here we go…" He pinched the screen once more. "Now, judging by the history, the cloud should be moving relatively slowly. We can use this to our advantage. We were lucky yesterday. It rained in the middle of the night, when most people were indoors or asleep."

"Lucky?" Sky questioned.

"Compared to what could have happened; we were extremely lucky." He refreshed the screen and the map redrew itself, but this time the sky above Exeter was clear.

"Where is it?" Sky asked, baffled.

"I don't know," Blake said. "Looks like it's disappeared.

30

"You have messages," Sky said, noticing the blinking number '2' on Blake's answering machine.

"Yeah, I've seen them; I'll play them later," he said, distracted as the green map redrew itself on the computer screen. He tapped keys, and a layer of squiggly lines appeared across the length of the map.

"Is that the wind direction?"

"Yes. It's blowing North-easterly." He touched the screen to zoom out. The map redrew itself, revealing a picture of the United Kingdom. He tapped the detail button, and the familiar black mass appeared forty or so miles Northwest of Plymouth.

Sky gasped, "I thought you said it was moving relatively slowly?"

"It is. Was." He zoomed in. The rain had crossed the county border, into Devonshire, and was just a few miles from the small village of Yeovin.

"My God, Blake. We've got to warn them!" She moved to snatch the phone from its cradle.

"No" Blake said, putting his hand over hers.

"Blake…"

Their eyes met.

"We can't say anything yet, Sky."

"Why not?" she asked incredulously.

"Because we don't have any proof."

"We've got all the proof we need in here," she replied, grabbing a handful of the folders from his desk.

"Come on, Sky. You've only just finished telling me that they don't prove a thing. We need to get that rain analysed."

"And what happens in the meantime?"

He thought about this, and then said, "Whatever happens in the meantime is beyond our control."

She stared at him. "I can't believe you're saying this." Then she pulled her hand away.

"Sky, trust me. The Environment Agency is not going to put out a public warning without concrete evidence. If I call Hamilton and tell him all of this over the phone, what do you think he's going to say?"

"Well, if he's got any sense, he'll praise you for the good work."

"Somehow, I don't think he's going to be that sensible. After all, you didn't believe me initially, did you?" He looked into her eyes.

There was a long pause.

"So, what are you going to do? Grab a receptacle and go stand out in it?"

"If I have to."

"Christ, this is insane."

She turned away from him and walked over to the window. There, she ran her hands through her unkempt black hair and took in a deep breath as a myriad of thoughts scurried across her mind, like the dark clouds outside.

She watched them, mesmerised, while Blake played his messages.

How's this all going to end? She wondered, as Cynthia Hudson's voice filled the room.

She reprimanded her son. She had left several messages on his mobile phone, but he had not returned any of them. Therefore, out of desperation, she was calling his house phone and leaving a message there, too.

Sky waited for the beep to signal the end of Mrs. Hudson's message before speaking. "You're wrong, Blake," she said, thoughtfully, her eyes still watching the spaceships drifting overhead.

"About what?"

"I believed you from the moment you told me your crazy theory."

"Then why…"

"…I'm a doctor. I need scientific evidence."

"Was that really it?" he asked as he walked up behind her.

She turned to him.

There was a pause.

"She's worried about you," Sky said flatly, nodding at the

answering machine.

"Then I'd better call her," he said, "but only after you've answered my question."

"What was your question again?"

"Come on, Sky, talk to me."

She sighed, and was about to reply when the second message started playing. A husky female voice filled the room.

"Blake, are you there? Please be there." A few seconds silence, then, *"I heard about the riots; CNN has been talking about nothing else all morning. I've sent texts and left messages on your mobile phone, but I haven't heard anything. I'm worried. Anyway, please call as soon as you get this. If I don't hear from you, I'll be catching the next direct flight to Heathrow. I miss you. Bye."*

The line went dead. There was a beeping sound, and then a robotic voice announced, *"No more messages."*

Seconds drifted into minutes.

They both remained unmoving, unspeaking, as if the air around them had suddenly turned into a delicate crystal.

Sky felt as if someone had just kicked her, repeatedly, in the stomach.

Oh God. Not again. He lied to me again.

Blake felt hot and cold prickles rise up the back of his neck and face.

Sky willed her legs to move, but they would not budge. She wanted to run. She needed to run out of this house, get into her car and never return here.

Quick! Get out! The walls are caving in.

RUN!

"Sky, I can…"

It was too late. Her feet finally kicked into gear. She ran out of the room and raced down the stairwell as the world began to spin like a director's camera, turning in a 360° dramatic scene. The stairwell encircled her; the walls closed in. She felt cheap, dirty and betrayed, and angry, very angry – just as she had all of those years before.

Blake had done it again. The thought was incomprehensible. The pain, unbearable. The tears had arrived by the time she reached the foot of the steps, as the faceless image of a woman embracing, laughing with, and kissing Blake, filled her head.

She yanked the door open and stepped out into the open, as if finally emerging from a cavern – a deep, dark black hole, devoid of oxygen and light. She sniffed and held her hand to her nose, as if doing so would stem the torrent of tears leaking from her eyes. She was devastated, but it was not all about the voice of that stranger, and more about the dreadful realisation that everything she had believed – the immunisation from pain, the indestructible armour she'd fabricated over the past decade – was all a lie... one ginormous, self-deluded lie.

She climbed behind the wheel of her BMW and swore when she realised that she didn't have the key.

"Sky!" Blake had appeared at the front door.

She looked up at him and then frantically frisked herself, until she noticed that he was carrying the key as he ran toward her.

"Sky! Please wait!"

She held up her hand, avoiding eye contact. "Could I have the key, please?"

"No, not until you've heard me out."

"Could I have the key please, Blake?" she repeated.

"You're being irrational, Sky. Let's talk about this."

She looked up with tear-soaked eyes and sprang out of the car. "I am being irrational?"

"Sky, I know how you must be feeling right now, and I am…"

"…You have no fucking idea how I'm feeling right now!" she screamed.

"I didn't want you to find out like this."

"…How exactly did you want me to find out? Would you have preferred I walk in on the two of you, like I did with Lisa, is that it?"

He swallowed, deeply, and spoke slowly, "Sky, I don't want to lose you again,"

"You should have thought about that before you lied to me, *again!* Now, give me my fucking key!" she growled, grappling with him, but he was much stronger.

"Sky, she's just someone I met…"

"…I don't want to hear this," she said, holding her hands over her ears like a child.

"Sky…"

"Fuck you!" She stormed away from the car, and ran down one of the winding footpaths that led to the beach.

Her mind was a thunderstorm of thoughts. Her stomach was a slithering knot of snakes, and her heart ached with such a fury that she could have died. Just throw herself to the ground and wait for the life to ebb from her eyes, just like the contentment that had already drained from her soul. Yet, with the agility of a football player, she ran down the coastal path, careful not to stumble over one of the main protruding rocks.

She needed the ocean. She needed to be alone, but, most of all, she needed this to be nothing but a wretched nightmare, a hideous ordeal from which she would wake and find herself in Blake's arms, languishing in the comforting scent of his cologne, basking in the honeyed glow of the sun.

However, the sound of boots racing and crunching on the pebbled shore behind her told her that this was not a nightmare, but real life. This was really happening and it was happening now.

"Leave me alone, Blake!" she yelled over her shoulder as she sprinted forward. However, the plashing sound continued as he continued to pursue her.

They were almost a quarter of a mile from the lighthouse before Blake managed to clasp Sky's arm and spin her around to face him. She shrugged him off while stumbling to a halt.

The surf exploded and their hearts pounded, as they stood, bent over, hands on knees, sucking in the ocean air. Minutes ticked by, where the only sound was that of their rasping breaths, and the roar and the fizz of the waves.

"Sky, I'm sorry," Blake breathed.

"She's the one you cheated on. You should be apologising to her, not me," Sky threw back.

"Sabrina knows the rules."

"What? The rules?"

"She knows I'm not looking for a relationship."

"I can't believe I'm hearing this."

"She wants her independence as much as I do."

"My God, you're an arrogant pig!"

"There's nothing arrogant about knowing what you want."

"And you always get what you want, don't you, Blake? Doesn't matter who you hurt in the process. Just fuck 'em and leave 'em, eh?"

"If I recall correctly, you were the one who did the leaving."

"Oh yeah, you made sure of that, didn't you?"

"What's that supposed to mean?"

"Everything, Blake! You humiliated me then, and you're doing it again now!"

He squinted at her. "I didn't humiliate you, Sky. You humiliated yourself. You went around interrogating all of our friends about me, and what I did when I wasn't with you. Who the hell does that?"

Sky panted a few seconds, before spitting, "Who? I'll tell you who. Someone you and your snotty-nosed mates made feel was unworthy."

"What are you talking about?" he asked.

"Do you think I was blind? Don't you think I noticed how we spent little if any time with your friends? Christ, it took over a year for you to introduce me to your parents."

Sky paused as, once again, she was drowned in a tidal wave of guilt – guilt for distancing herself from her own parents in her quest to appear more eligible, more worthy.

"I hate you!" she spat, through tears. "I hate you, your friends, and your family! You made me feel…" she faltered through tears, "You made me ashamed of my own parents, and I will never forgive you for that! Never!"

She was sobbing now, racked with grief, tormented with regret.

Blake simply stared at her. He was so stunned by what he'd just heard that he didn't even know how to process this, let alone formulate a response.

At least a couple of minutes had ebbed by before he was able to internalise everything Sky had said, and reconcile this to his own memories. The result surprised him, almost as much as it made him angry.

Very angry.

Not just because it, in his opinion, in no way reflected reality, but also because it meant that all of this time – all of these years that he'd spent dating different girls, none of which, for reasons unbeknownst even to him, seemed to measure up – had been wasted. They could have been together after all. If only Sky had had more faith in him, in their love.

The anger grew in intensity and, like the waves against the shore, it washed through his body and thundered against his brain. He wanted to rage. He wanted to start screaming at her, but instead, he said coolly, "Have you finished, or is there something else of particular importance that you'd like to add?"

She just watched him as she caught her breath.

"Well, who would have thought that inside such a brilliant mind were the fantasies of a petulant eighteen-year-old?"

She glowered.

"What's the matter? Am I not speaking the truth? That is what you want, isn't it, Sky, the truth? Okay, I have a few hard truths for you. I was never ashamed of you; you were ashamed of yourself. I was never embarrassed by your parents; you were! You, Sky, with your judgemental mightier-than-though attitude. I loved your parents because, unlike most people, including you, they stood for what they believed in, and they weren't embarrassed by it. I didn't avoid them by choice; I did it out of some warped sense of loyalty to you. As for my friends, you made no secret of the fact that you didn't like them, especially those without a dick, and I didn't want you to feel left out, or threatened – especially since you had absolutely no reason to. We also know that my father liked you very much. As for my mother, one of the reasons why I moved down here was to get away from her meddling ways. Especially after I found out how she treated you the day of our visit."

She looked at him.

"That's right, Sky. I'm not a complete moron. I knew something was off that day we drove home, but you were determined not to tell me about it, opting instead to do every fucking thing possible to break us up. Fuck!"

He was very angry now, and seethed, "All of the evils you lay at my feet are the rotten fruit of your own over-active imagination. You were so obsessed with being everyone other than yourself, that you rejected everything that meant something;

your life, your parents, me!"

"That's a lie!" she cried, sobbing uncontrollably.

"The only lie is the one you've been telling yourself all these years. And you've got the audacity to make me out to be the villain. You were so fucking distant towards the ends of our relationship that I actually thought it was me – I thought you didn't love *me*!"

He paused, simmering, as a lump formed in his throat. Then, "As for Lisa, you'd made it pretty clear we were done. You weren't returning any of my calls; you kept avoiding me at class. She was the result of a drunken stupor, brought on by you casually telling me you were leaving for London, which I interpreted as you not giving a shit about me anymore."

"You have no idea how I…"

"…Oh no, I think I have a pretty good idea of what a self-obsessed bitch you really are." He stepped towards her and said earnestly, as his eyes glistened with exasperated tears, "I loved you, Sky. I still do, but I love the woman, not the petulant brat. You just need to decide which one you really are, and while you're at it, you can stop living in the fucking past! Your parents are gone, Sky; they're gone, and you fucked up! You won't be the first or the last kid who didn't appreciate her parents, and it's shitty, I can't imagine how really shitty it must be, but you've got to let it go. You can't spend the rest of your life punishing yourself, believing you're unworthy, because you deserve to be happy – you really do."

He took a deep breath, and then said seriously, "We can't always right our wrongs, Sky, but we can learn from them, and in turn become better for it."

She frowned at him, and then spat, "Who the fuck do you think you are?"

"I'm Blake Hudson – who the hell are you?"

Sky's body was a mass of shudders. He had never seen her this distressed, but he resisted the urge to put his arms around her.

She needed this.

"Think about what I said. You know where to find me if you need me." With that, he turned to leave.

"Yeah, in bed, with *her*!" she yelled after him.

He paused for a few seconds, and then continued walking away from her.

As Blake Hudson moved closer to the lighthouse and further out of her life, Sky McPherson sank to her knees and, with her head in her hands, sobbed like a grief-stricken mourner.

31

As Blake climbed up the coastal path that led back to the lighthouse, a shadow fell over him. He looked up and, in a flat tone, asked, "What are you doing here?"

"Nice to see you, too," Matt said as Blake moved past him and headed for the front door.

"I thought you weren't here. Where's the beast?" Matt asked, following closely.

"Long story."

"Okay, I'm listening."

Blake stopped in his tracks and looked at his friend.

"Oh no, you've got that look," Matt said.

"What look?"

"That pissed off look you always get after someone's rattled your pram."

"No one's rattled my pram, Matt."

"So, what's wrong?"

Sighing, he said, "I told you, it's a long story."

"Then, tell me about it."

"Not now."

"Okay, you can tell me on the way."

"On the way? Where?" Blake's puzzled expression said it all.

"Oh no, oh no, no, no. Don't tell you me you've forgotten," Matt warned.

"What are you talking about?"

"The match, tonight – you know, the cup qualifier, Plymouth V. Cambridge…"

"…Oh shit, I forgot all about it."

"Oh man, you can't be serious. This was supposed to be our match. We even bet on it. Bloody hell, I wouldn't have thought even a sad Rugger like you could forget that! Have you any idea how hard it was to get tickets?"

"Sorry, mate. I've had a lot on my mind."

"Yeah, so you keep saying, but something tells me it was less about what you had on and more about what the doc had off," Matt grinned, knowingly.

Blake said nothing, and instead looked out to sea.

Matt grinned some more. "Bloody hell, you have, haven't ya? You dirty sod. So, I take it she doesn't know about Sabrina?"

Blake looked at him. "She knows."

"Uh oh, and I'm taking it, by the look on your face, that she wasn't impressed. Well, I did tell you that…"

"…Oh Shit."

"What?" Matt, asked, looking around.

"The football match."

"Yes, that's right. We're going to be late."

"They've got to call it off!" With this, Blake sprinted, toward the front door.

"Wait. What?" Matt rushed after his friend, but paused when he noticed the police tape around the doorframe. "What the…" he breathed. "Hey Blake, wait up!"

However, his friend had already disappeared up the stairwell, taking the steps two at a time.

Matt followed, but paused, once more, when he noticed more tape around the door to his friend's bedroom. He then hurried up the rest of the steps. When Matt entered the study, Blake was already sitting behind his computer screen.

"Um, Blake," Matt began casually, "call me nosy, but I think we need to talk about why the police have decorated all of your doors with crime scene tape."

Blake didn't reply.

"Hello?"

Matt joined his friend at the computer, and was about to continue when he saw what was on the monitor.

"What the hell's that?"

"It's the rain," Blake responded vacantly, "it's drifting towards

Plymouth."

"Right, and you're telling me that in a suspenseful movie line because…."

"They need to cancel the game!"

"Right," Matt nodded. "You've said that," he added casually and then, much more severely, asked, "Blake, what the fuck is going on? Why the hell is there crime scene tape all over your house, where's the doc, and, worse, why've you gone all Jack Bauer on me?"

"The rain is drifting towards Plymouth," Blake repeated ominously.

"Right, well, don't worry. They're not gonna' call the game off. They've sold something like fifteen thousand tickets; it's going to take more than a few showers for them to postpone."

"Does this look like a few showers to you?" Blake asked, pointing at the black mass on the screen.

Matt peered closely at the monitor. The huge black shroud did look rather ominous. "I don't have the foggiest, mate. I've no idea what I'm looking at."

"This isn't just a bit of rain, Matt. It's a storm."

"Okay, it's storm, but, for fuck's sake, mate, you're creeping me out. What's with the bloody weather report all of a sudden?"

"There's something in the rain."

"What, you mean, like water?" He grinned.

Blake rolled his eyes, "No, I mean like something toxic."

"Toxic. What, like radiation?"

"Something like that. There's a chemical in the rain. I don't know exactly what it is or how it works, but what I do know is that it can be absorbed through the skin, and that it's lethal."

"How lethal?" Matt asked seriously.

"Lethal enough to have caused all of the riots."

"What? Are you serious?"

Blake snatched the phone off the desk and dialled the number for the Environment Agency's head office in Bristol. After several rings, the phone was answered by a female voice Blake recognised as Melissa's. "Environment Agency, good afternoon."

"Melissa, hi. It's Blake. Is Hamilton there?"

"Oh hi, Blake. No, he's actually in a meeting."

"Put me through, will you?"

"I'm sorry, I can't. He's with the Deputy PM and I'm under strict instructions not to…"

"…Melissa, I need to speak with him right now," Blake said, suppressing the urge to raise his voice.

After taking a few seconds to consider Blake's tone, she replied, "Hold on…"

There was beeping on the line.

"Matt, what time's the match?"

"In just under two hours. Blake? What's going on? What's with the tape all over your doors, and where's the doc? Her car's outside. Where is she? Has something happened to her?"

"I can't explain right now."

"What do you mean?"

"Yes, Melissa?"

"Sorry, Blake. I spoke to him and he said he'll call you back."

"Christ, Melissa, I need to talk to him now!"

"I'm sorry, Blake. I tried, but I can't make him come to the phone. He already gave me a chewing out for disturbing him."

Blake sighed. "Okay. I'm sorry. Could you just, please, tell him that I need to talk him, *urgently*?"

"Of course. Is everything okay?"

"Wonderful. Just get him to call me, will you? In the meantime, tell him that I am going to issue a warning and stop the football game this afternoon. Did you get that?"

"You're going to what?" Matt chimed in.

"Melissa?"

"I got it. You're going to issue a warning to stop the game," she said as she wrote down the message.

Blake hung up.

"Blake…"

"…I just need to make this call, Matt, and I'll explain everything. I promise."

He was about to dial the number when he heard a faint clicking sound on the line, and then the dial tone disappeared.

"What the…."

Blake slammed the phone down and then picked it up again. The same; there was no dial tone. He tried a couple more times;

still nothing.

"What's happening?"

"Phone's just died. Can I borrow your mobile?"

"What?"

"Give me your mobile, Matt."

"Where's yours?"

Blake just stared at his friend.

Matt rolled his eyes and, reluctantly, fished his mobile phone out of his pocket.

"Mate, should I be worried about you?" Matt asked.

Blake was about to answer, but was startled by the ringing of his own phone.

He snatched it from its cradle. "Hudson."

"Blake?"

"Yes."

"It's Hamilton. What's the urgency?"

"Thank God." Blake was relieved. "We've got a major crisis on our hands"

"Go on."

"Well," Blake swallowed. Suddenly, he doubted his own theory. And the feeling grew worse the more he hesitated and listened to his boss' heavy, expectant, breathing at the end of the line. "I have reason to believe that a toxic substance has been released into the atmosphere, and, if we don't put out a red warning right now, thousands are going to be exposed to it."

Matt threw his hands to his head, as if he had just witnessed his favourite car smash.

"What kind of toxic substance?" Hamilton asked.

"I'm not sure yet."

"Well, is it a gas?"

"No, well, we don't know yet. It appears to be an unidentified strain of bacteria."

Blake avoided Matt's gaze. He could feel his friend's incredulous eyes on him.

"What kind of bacteria?" Hamilton asked.

"It's still unknown. We haven't managed to run any tests yet. What I do know is that it's lethal. So far, those exposed to the rain have become violent, even homicidal."

"What?"

Hamilton was doubtful. Blake could hear it in his tone, hell, even he could hear how ridiculous it sounded when he spoke the words aloud, but he closed his eyes and gripped the receiver; he was committed now.

"That's how it spreads, through precipitation," he said as casually as he could.

"Are you sure about this?"

"I'm positive," Blake said, confidently. "I've experienced its effects first-hand." He glanced at Matt, who was gawking at him with questioning eyes.

"You were affected by it?" Hamilton continued.

"No, but I have come into contact with somebody else who was exposed to it."

"It's contagious?"

"I don't know. I don't think so."

Blake allowed Hamilton a few moments to absorb the information and then continued, "Sir, there's a football match this afternoon; we need to stop it."

"On what evidence?"

Blake faltered, "Well, err, as I said, we need to run some tests, but I know this thing is bad."

"Come on, Hudson. I know my mother-in-law is bad, but that doesn't necessarily mean my wife would agree to me banning her from the house."

I'm losing him!

"If we don't stop this game today, there is no telling how many people are going to be exposed. Everything that has happened before now will be nothing in comparison."

"So, now you're saying that this rain is, was responsible for the riots, too, is that it?"

"I know it was," Blake said emphatically. More than he had intended.

Hamilton laughed aloud.

Blake paused, trying to remain calm, although he was starting to lose his patience.

"We need to call off that game," Blake continued.

"How can we? You've not offered one shred of proof, one piece of evidence to substantiate your claims. So far, I've heard nothing but theories and conjecture. I can't authorise a warning based on a hunch; the PM will have us both sacked before the day's out."

"It isn't just a hunch."

"Well, it certainly sounds like it."

"Did you even listen to a word I said?"

There was a tone to the question, and Hamilton noticed it. "Hudson, I know you think that...."

"... people are going to die!"

"Hudson..."

Blake removed the phone from his ear, then looked at his friend, who watched him with wide eyes, and then promptly mouthed the words, *"What the fuck are you doing?"*

Blake hesitated; he wanted to scream down the phone, but he knew that wouldn't help. Therefore, after taking another deep breath, he replaced the handset to his ear and continued, "Look, I know that I don't have any proof yet, but, I'm telling you, I can get all the evidence you need, but we have to call off that game. Please, for the sake of those people, put out a warning before it's too late."

He closed his eyes once more as he waited for the answer. There was a very long silence. "Mr Hamilton?"

"No."

Blake's eyes snapped open, "What?"

"Permission denied."

"After everything I've told you?"

"Blake, as you know, I'm not prone to dishing out pleasantries. In your case, I've seldom been dissatisfied with your work at the agency. But son, when you interrupt me in the middle of a meeting and start spouting off about a killer rain precipitating on people and turning them into homicidal maniacs without a scrap of proof, I have to question if you're spending way too much time in front of the Sci-fi Channel. I'm sorry."

"You will be when that rain hits Plymouth this afternoon." Blake's words were firm, and hissed out of gritted teeth.

"Whatever. In the meantime, I would like to discuss this incident in more detail with a view to launching an enquiry."

"Don't bother!" Blake snapped.

"What?"

"I'll call public health and get them to make the decision you find it so hard to even consider."

"Okay, so now you're actually starting to annoy me…"

"…Good, then maybe you'll stop talking shit and actually start listening to what I'm saying."

"Look, Hudson, I don't know what it is you think you know about the rain, but whatever it is, it has clouded your judgement. Now, I am not prepared to discuss this on the phone any longer. Come to my office in the morning and we will talk about it. We'll also have a chat about your insubordination while we're at it."

"Forget it."

"Hudson…"

Blake slammed the phone down. He remained there for a few seconds, hand still gripping the receiver.

"Well," Matt began brightly, "and this is just a guess, but I take it he won't be putting out that warning and calling the match off, after all."

"No," Blake replied pensively. "But I am."

"Uh oh."

Blake lifted the receiver and dialled for directory inquiries. "Yes, public health, please."

Matt scratched his head as Blake scribbled down the number.

"Blake, are you sure about this?"

"As sure as I'll ever be," he said with determination.

He dialled the number and waited for a reply. That was when the clicking sound returned.

"Public health, good afternoon…"

"Yes, hello, this is Blake Hudson of the Environment Agency… I need to…"

He stopped when there was a loud burst of static on the line.

"Hello? Hello?" The static continued until, suddenly, the line went dead.

"Shit!" He slammed the phone down and then picked it up again; still nothing.

"I don't believe this! The line's dead."

"Blake, maybe you should see this as a sign."

Matt's friend was not listening. Instead, he was holding out his hand, indicating that he wanted to borrow his mobile phone after all.

Matt, reluctantly, handed him the device. Blake dialled the number, and then looked at the display.

"Shit!"

"What?"

"There's no service," Blake replied, perturbed.

"Well, that's what you get for living on a rock at the end of the world."

"No, this place normally has great service. There's a mast just up the road." He touched the computer screen and a sad emoticon face appeared with the caption, "*No Internet Connection Detected.*"

"Fuck it…"

Blake left the desk and raced down the stairwell, but came to an abrupt stop at the front door.

"Shit! Where's my car?"

"That was my question, remember?" Matt said, following him down.

Blake threw his hands up when he remembered what had happened at the lake. "Fuck!" he yelled angrily.

"Right, that's it. Now, I'm officially worried," Matt declared. "First you let the police redecorate your home, then you go all creepy Mulder, then you piss away your job, and now you can't even remember where you left your car."

"If it rains on that football game today, I'm going to be the least of your worries," Blake said, climbing into the passenger seat of his friend's car. However, Matt wasn't moving. Instead, he stood in the driveway and folded his arms.

"Well, what are you waiting for?" Blake demanded.

"So you want a lift then?"

"Come on, Matt!" he shouted.

"I left the keys inside."

"Then go and get them," Blake sighed.

Matt turned to comply, but stopped and said, "Does this mean that we won't be going to the match after all?"

Blake just looked at him.

"I'll take that as a no, but I'm telling you now, I'm not going anywhere until you tell me what the fuck is going on."

"I'll tell you on the way. Now, hurry up!"

With that, Matt turned and went back into the house. Blake drummed his fingers on the dashboard. His mind was a twister of thoughts: the spectators, Sky, and last night's events. He wondered if he had been too harsh on her, but he decided that he had not. Okay, so she had found out about Sabrina. So what? It wasn't as if they had been dating for months and she had just discovered that he was seeing someone else. They had only met again just a few days ago. He simply had not had the chance to tell her, although he had tried, many times, but chickened out.

They'd been getting on so well, and telling her about his casual relationship with Sabrina wasn't as important as getting to know her all over again.

Are you a womanising bastard?

No, I am not.

Then why do you feel like one, Hudson?

I should go down there and make it up to her. Tell her that I didn't mean any of that stuff, and that I love her.

But you did mean it. Didn't you?

Christ!

All these nagging thoughts were driving him crazy, and time was ticking.

Where the hell are you, Matt?

Matt had decided to rush into the downstairs toilet. He had been desperate to relieve himself ever since he'd arrived but, with all the weirdness, he hadn't had the chance. As he stood over the ceramic vase, he replayed Blake's telephone conversation.

"There's something in the rain." What exactly? Some kind of chemical. How did it get there? How does Blake know about it? What happened to the doc?

He zipped himself up, and was about to leave when he heard it. It sounded as if a bulldozer was making its way up the coastal path, and then it transmuted into a beating sound that gradually drew closer and closer. He pressed his face to the glass of the small window, but couldn't see anything as the beating grew louder and seemed to move around the building.

He left the toilet and raced through the living room to a small sliver window near the front door.

Blake was still sitting in his car, looking skyward. Then, storm-like turbulence appeared out of nowhere, until it suddenly became obvious as the helicopter descended into view and landed in a clearing, several metres from Matt's car.

"What the…" he gasped, staring out the glass.

The helicopter was large, loud, and ominously black, with tinted windows and no insignias. It was a people carrier. By its length and windows, Matt estimated that it could carry at least twelve people. The whirring had barely slowed before the double doors slid open and four men, in black uniforms and matching caps, spewed out like ants from a mill.

They ran over to Matt's car, spoke to Blake through the passenger window for a few seconds, and then stood aside as one of them drew a gun from the holster on his thigh.

Matt jumped back from the window.

"Oh shit, oh fuck!" he whispered in a panic as he considered what he had just seen, before snatching another peek through the glass; Blake was leaving the vehicle, and was being escorted to the helicopter, where two of the men stood guard while another spoke, seemingly to himself.

Suddenly, in unison, two of his colleagues looked toward the lighthouse, causing Matt to snap back from the window once more.

"Shit! Oh Shit!"

They can't have seen you. It's too dark in here. What if they did?

He argued with himself, before summoning up all of his willpower to take another glimpse. The two men had drawn their weapons and were running towards the house.

"Fuck!" Matt breathed.

They've seen you.

Now, with widened eyes, he scanned the room for somewhere to hide, but found nowhere obvious. He looked up the steps and then, without thinking, he climbed them as quietly as he could, two at a time. He considered whether to try to hide in Blake's bedroom, but decided against it just as the front door clanged open.

He sprinted, as quietly as possible, up the rest of the stairwell and entered Blake's office, where his eyes frantically searched for a cubbyhole, or anything. However, there was nowhere to hide.

The sound of boots on metal clanged up the stairwell.

He scampered under the desk and found refuge against the modesty panel, the narrow strip of wood being the only thing separating him from the intruders. He listened carefully, over the muffled sound of the crashing surf and the idling chopper outside. They were ripping through the police tape and were rummaging in Blake's bedroom, one floor below.

They did see me, and now they're searching for me! Oh God, why? Who are they? What do they want? They're going to kill me!

Beads of perspiration pricked at his forehead as he heard footsteps in the stairwell once more.

No!

He drew his knees up, made a tight ball of his body, and pressed himself flat against the wood, as if he could be camouflaged by it.

The boots entered the room while Matt held his breath as a drop of sweat fell and exploded into his jeans.

The pair of boots walked over to the window.

Just one of them? Where's the other? Probably waiting by the door, making sure I don't run for it. Or, is he still searching downstairs? Oh God, I promise I'll make amends. Please!

He squeezed his eyes shut and swallowed on the dry sand dune that was his throat. After a few seconds, he reopened his eyes to see the shiny black boots walking towards the desk.

He subconsciously held his breath, causing his pulse to throb, his lungs to burn, and the tension to build in his skull, as his brain screamed for oxygen. Then, his body began to shake.

No, no, he might hear you! You might rattle the desk.

He squeezed his eyes shut again and willed the intruder to leave.

Then, as if someone had granted his wish, a radio crackled loudly and then a tinny voice echoed around the room.

"Collins, we need to get out of here."

"I'm on my way," an English accent replied.

The voice was so close that Matt refused to open his eyes because he had no doubt that whoever was wearing those boots had spotted him, and was now crouching down to face him, pointing a gun at his chest.

Yet, he had no choice. His whole body was shaking, violently now, as it protested against his refusal to breath, the physical compulsion to live overriding his mental decision to ignore reality.

He opened his eyes.

Yet, he was both surprised and relieved to find that he was alone under the desk. No man in black. No muzzle of a gun pointing at his face. Instead, the boots turned and left the room, clicking fast and loud down the stairwell. Then, there was a murmur of voices, shortly followed by the slam of the front door.

Matt erupted into a breathing frenzy as his body worked to recuperate.

A few seconds later, the whirring of the helicopter's engine increased as he peeked out, and then slowly emerged from the sanctuary of the desk.

He was alone.

Furtively and cautiously, he looked out the window just in time to see the last of the men enter the chopper and then slide the door shut.

Blake was nowhere to be seen.

Jesus! He must be inside. Where are you taking him?

The beating sound returned, the engine laboured, and then the helicopter slowly lifted once more. It ascended steadily until it drew level with the summit of the lighthouse, causing Matt to duck out of sight, before it banked right and swooped out toward the ocean.

Matt gawped out of the window once more, and watched the craft shrink into the distance, but oddly, the sound of the engine was growing louder and louder, the rumble nearer and nearer until…

"Fuck!" Matt yelled as another helicopter appeared from underneath the lighthouse.

He was temporarily confused, and then it occurred to him that it was a different helicopter – a twin of the first one.

It circled the lighthouse a few times and then dipped sideways, disappearing down the coastal path, heading toward the beach.

He watched as it landed a few feet away from someone down there. He couldn't identify whom, but could just about make out her long hair.

Sky?

She, not unlike his friend, was escorted to and compelled to board the flying machine.

A minute or so later, it, too, was heading away from Stony Point and disappearing into the horizon.

32

Somewhere in the Atlantic Ocean, West of the Cornish coast – 17:00 GMT.

The isolation chamber was fifteen square feet wide and hermetically sealed. It could be reached only by a small cubicle the size of a telephone box, called DETOX.

It was only after personnel were adequately suited and had submitted to the detox process – effectively, a microscopic acid mist for two minutes – that access to the chamber was granted. The process was fully automated, and controlled by a super computer and an array of carefully tuned sensors.

Inside his white space suit and with thick-gloved hands, Dr. Harket injected the green contents of the syringe into the test tube, snapped the plastic lid over it, and placed the phial inside a metal container, next to nine more.

"So, it is true, Doctor?" Peter, his young apprentice asked, holding the box steady.

"Is what true?"

"Is there enough toxin in that small test tube to poison a whole town?"

"Alex, have you been teasing our new recruit again?" the doctor reproached, without taking his eyes off the phial in front of him.

Peter looked up at a group of people who were watching the whole process from behind a wall of glass. At the centre was a gaunt-looking thirty-one-year-old man with grey eyes and a blonde ponytail, who suppressed a snigger and said, "Me, Doctor? You know I'd never do something like that."

Harket smiled, and mumbled, "No, of course not." Then he added, "You'll get used to him. Alex is our resident joker. Besides, he lied to you. There's enough toxin in one of these measures to infect a whole city, and then some."

The junior swallowed, hard.

Harket had noticed that his junior had already broken out in a sweat.

"Don't worry. You're perfectly safe inside that suit. Astronauts wear similar costumes to walk the surface of the moon. Now, could you put this," the doctor handed him a test tube containing newly transferred toxin, "into the decoder over there and start the analysis?"

The decoder was the size of a small photocopier and was used to analyse toxin samples and render resulting data directly to the central computer.

"Sure," Peter said brightly, although he was feeling somewhat unnerved, both by what the doctor had just told him and the fact that this was his first *walk* in the chamber, a moment for which he had received extensive training.

Nonetheless, the sweat was dribbling down his forehead, and he was frustrated by the fact that there was no way to mop up the tickling on his skin. Worse, his helmet felt particularly heavy and he was starting to feel claustrophobic.

Harket touched his arm, "It's alright, Peter, you're doing fine. Just relax, take deep breaths," he said, reassuringly.

Peter smiled, and had moved to leave when he felt himself being tugged backward, as if someone had grabbed his suit and was pulling at it. It was his air line – a flexible hose, connected to his suit and to runners in the ceiling that provided constant, breathable air.

Instead of rolling freely, the line was jammed.

Peter leaned forward in an effort to free himself, but the line would not yield, so he tugged at it in frustration.

"Hey," Harket tapped on his shoulder, "Steady with that thing. You'll breach your suit," he said, pulling gently on the hose to free it. "Alex, I thought you had the runners on these things checked."

"I did."

"Well, they obviously didn't do a good job. They keep sticking."

"Maybe he tugged too suddenly. They tend to lock like seat belts if you pull too hard."

"Whatever. Just get the damn things sorted, will you? Mine did the same thing earlier."

"Yes, Doctor," Alex complied, picking up the phone.

Harket pulled on the line a few more times, until it finally came free. Peter gave a thumbs-up, and then lumbered across the room with his line trailing behind him like a giant umbilical cord. He lifted the analyser's lid, slid the phial into the containment slot, and snapped the guards in place. Then, he dialled in the sequence on the keypad.

"Sample detected, Doctor Briem. Initiate sequence?" a sultry female voice asked through ceiling speakers.

"Confirmed, initiate sequence," Peter spoke confidently.

"Initiating sequence."

The analyser sprung to life, whirring loudly like a washing machine as it spun the sample to ensure that the final analysis would be that of the entire compound and not just one of its components. However, just seconds into the process, the monotonous drone shifted in pitch, then warbled to a stop.

"Acquisition error, Dr Briem. Sequencing interrupted," the computer announced.

Shit!

Several lights on the front panel of the decoder were blinking.

"What's the problem, Pete?" Doctor Harket asked without turning around.

"I'm not sure," he said sheepishly, "All the lights are flashing." He could have quite cheerfully slapped the sides of the damn thing, but reasoned that that probably wasn't a good idea, considering its deadly contents.

Dr Harket looked across at him. "Computer," he said, "Report."

"Acquisition error, Doctor Harket. Please reseat sample and try again."

Tittering was heard over the intercom.

Peter felt a burning sensation in his cheeks. The heat inside his helmet was already unbearable, and now he could taste the sweat on his lips. He so desperately wanted to mop his face.

"Hold on, I'll be right over," Harket said, snapping the lid down on another phial. He glanced up at the team behind the glass who, by the smirks on their faces, was finding the whole thing amusing. Harket smiled inwardly, sighed, and moved to leave, but, like Peter before him, was tugged back.

"Alex," he grumbled irritably.

"I've already called technical. We'll be looking at it as soon as you guys are done in there. Try moving forward, slowly."

"I was trying to move forward – that was the whole point!"

"Try again, gently, and it should come free," Alex offered.

The doctor rolled his eyes, but complied. It didn't work.

"Alex, I'm going to suspend this session, and bill all of the time wasted to your target until this thing has been properly fixed."

Alex instantly lost his smile. "Come on, Doc, that's not fair," he whined. Then, he barked, "Hey, Pete, since you can't get that thing to work, you may as well help the Doc free himself."

"It's okay. I think I have it," Harket said, leaning forward on the airline and doing exactly what he had warned Peter not to.

"Doctor, you probably shouldn't do that," Peter said, ironically echoing his boss's words as he moved to assist.

However, the doctor's patience was wearing thin. He awkwardly reached behind him, but his suit was too bulky, making the task impossible.

"Here," Peter said, clasping and tugging on the doctor's line, but the jam continued.

"Pass it here," Harket demanded impatiently.

Peter complied.

The doctor pulled on the line with restrained frustration.

Nothing.

"Hold on, let me check the runner," Peter offered, reaching up to the rail.

Like the wheels of a train on a track, the runner secured the air hose to a ceiling track. This enabled laboratory technicians to move freely without having to worry about tangles, or worse, tripping.

"I can see what the problem is," Peter said. "One of the fixings is loose, and it's pushed one of the wheels out of alignment. If you pull it gently while I apply pressure, it should realign itself."

"Okay," Harket said, irritated.

"Ready?"

"Ready."

Harket pulled gently on the line as Peter clamped the wheel onto the track with gloved fingers.

"Okay, give it a gentle tug," Peter said.

Nothing happened.

"A little bit more."

Still nothing.

"Just a little more."

"Jesus Christ!" Harket yanked at the line, and it slid forward a few inches.

"Yes, that nearly did it," Peter said excitedly. "Just one more tug should get it back on track, if you excuse the pun."

The doctor smiled and shook his head.

Alex rolled his eyes.

"Ready?"

"Ready."

Peter placed his fingers to the castors again.

"Okay."

Harket tugged hard, the line glided forward.

"Yay!"

"Well done, Peter," Harket said with a smile, and moved forward, but was instantly tugged back once more.

"God damn it!" He yelled, then turned and yanked on the line again.

"No, wait!" Peter yelled.

The line was actually free. The temporary restraint had been due to the wheels realigning. This meant that Harket's angry tug on the line met no resistance and, in turn, the momentum sent him, and his bulky suit, stumbling forward until he lost his balance and fell, smashing his visor against the corner of a bench and knocking over a collection of phials.

Glass from the shattered helmet stabbed at his face, turning his vision into blurred crimson.

"God damn it!" Harket seethed.

"Fuck!" Alex breathed, "Doctor, are you okay?"

"What does it look like, Alex?" Harket demanded from his position on the floor as he blinked blood from his eyes.

Peter had moved over to the stricken man, "Doctor, are you all right?"

"I think so," he replied, shaking his head, as he was suddenly feeling queasy.

"Doctor?" It was Alex again.

He and his colleagues were all leaning forward into the glass, trying to get a look at the man.

However, Harket had fallen behind a bench. All they could see was the back of his white space suit, and Peter, who was now standing over him.

Alex glanced at the black and white monitor, but its view was obscured also.

"You'd better decontaminate and get the hell out of there, Doctor. Your suit could be breached."

"You think?" Harket replied sarcastically.

"Here, let me help you to your feet," Peter said, extending a hand.

Harket, slowly and clumsily, hauled himself into a kneeling position with all of the dexterity of a pregnant woman.

"Hurry up, you moron!" Alex barked, "You need to get out of…"

Alex's words were interrupted by the computer.

"Warning – Contamination detected in isolation chamber. Initiate lockdown protocol?"

"Wait, what the fuck's she talking about?" Alex breathed, and then ordered, "That's a negative, Computer. Permission to initiate lockdown denied. Report."

"Pathogen detected in isolation chamber, Dr Wells. Initiate lockdown protocol?"

"NO!" Alex yelled. "That's a negative, Computer. Do not initiate lockdown protocol. Peter, what's going on in there? We can't see shit from here!"

Peter's eyes were already darting all over the chamber as he tried to work out what exactly the computer was referring to. As far as he could tell, all of the phials were accounted for.

Then, he spotted the overturned container on the floor. He quickly counted the phials. "Shit," he whispered.

"What?" Alex looked up. "What's going on, Pete?"

"It looks like a container was knocked over in the fall."

"Warning – Pathogen levels in isolation chamber now at ten percent. Initiate lockdown protocol?"

"NO, Computer, I've already denied your request. You will not initiate lockdown protocol! Acknowledge," Alex barked.

There was a pause.

"Computer, acknowledge!"

"I'm sorry, Doctor Wells. Containment protocols have been activated. If pathogen levels continue to rise, lockdown protocol will be inevitable."

"What the fuck is this?" Alex whispered incredulously as he tapped on the keyboard in front of him.

Meanwhile, Peter had counted nine phials out of ten in total; five were on the bench, four on the floor. All appeared to be undamaged.

"Thank God," he whispered as he hunted down the missing phial.

"Thanks Peter," Harket said, holding out his hand, but the apprentice simply brushed by him, muttering to himself while leaving giant bloody footprints on the pristine white floor. Harket watched, aghast, as the boy slowly lumbered past him and began searching under desks and behind disposal units.

"Peter! Help me," the doctor ordered as he struggled to get to his feet. Not only was the suit cumbersome, but he was feeling dizzy.

"Warning – Pathogen levels in isolation chamber now at thirty percent. Initiate lockdown protocol?"

Alex looked up from the monitor, where a flashing red banner was asking him the same thing.

"Denied! Computer, you are not to initiate lockdown protocol. Acknowledge!"

"I'm sorry, Doctor Wells. I am unable to acknowledge. If pathogen levels continue to rise, lockdown protocol will be

inevitable."

"Pete, you idiot! What the hell are you doing? Get the doctor out now!" Alex waited a few seconds, "Forget it, I'll fucking do it myself!" Then he added calmly, "It's okay, Doctor, I'm coming in."

"NO!"

All heads turned; it was Peter.

He was in the corner of the chamber, crouching down with his back to them. He was staring at something on the floor.

Doctor Harket had managed to turn around, and was now kneeling in a pool of his own blood, clutching the side of the table.

It was then that Alex noticed his shattered visor, "Jesus Christ. Doctor, are you alright?"

"I think so. Bit drowsy and hot," Harket replied, blowing air out of his mouth.

"Get him out of there!" Alex ordered.

"NO! You can't!" Peter cried, turning around.

His visor was steamed up; he was shaking and his face was wet with tears and perspiration. He watched as the doctor clumsily attempted to pull himself up from the floor.

Harket's face was burning, his hands and arms were itching, and he felt that if he did not get out of this suit, he was going to spontaneously combust. "Help me here, Peter," he said, forcing an embarrassed laugh and grunting with the effort of trying to get to his feet. "I feel like a beached whale!"

That was when the light inside the chamber flicked to a horrifying red, and a siren started wailing.

"Warning – Pathogen levels in isolation chamber now at fifty percent. Initiating lockdown protocol."

"NO!" Alex yelled. "Computer, you are not to initiate lockdown protocol. Acknowledge."

"Doctor Wells. Lockdown protocol is in effect."

As if to prove the point, there was the collective click and thud of multiple locking pistons firing.

"Denied. Computer, this is a cease and desist override order. Cancel lockdown protocol. Acknowledge!"

"I'm sorry, Doctor Wells. Override of lockdown protocol

requires level four access. You have not attained level four access."

All of the nearby computer monitors beeped and displayed a coloured graph, indicating the level of contamination in the chamber.

"Oh shit," Alex breathed, holding his hands helplessly over his keyboard like a witch doctor about to cast a spell. He looked at the black and white image on the monitor.

Doctor Harket, his mentor, the scientist he aspired to be, was still struggling to get up off the bloody floor, while Peter simply stood in the background – holding a broken phial.

Harket could feel it. The toxin was inside him, racing around his body, destroying and assimilating his antibodies, corroding his brilliant mind.

"Warning – Pathogen has reached critical levels. Initiating decontamination protocol."

Alex's instinct was to yell out an override command, but he knew it would be futile.

"Executing decontamination protocol in T minus twenty seconds, 19..."

"Oh my God, let him out! We've got to let him out!" Alex whined, "Computer, you're going to kill him!"

"We can't let him out, Alex, it's too late," one of his snivelling colleagues said gently. "He's been exposed. The room's full of it."

"These readings are off the scale!" Someone else gasped.

"18..."

"If we don't get them out of there, they're both going to die," someone else said.

"What about Peter? We've got to get Peter out!"

"He's safe in his suit!"

"10..."

"No, he isn't. It will eat through it. Prolonged exposure is corrosive. Exposure time in the chamber is double that of DETOX!"

"Don't tell me about my job! I know my job!"

"8..."

"We've got to get Peter out!"

The room was a dissonance of shrilling alarms, screaming, and sobbing, but all were powerless as the computer counted down to the inevitable.

"6..."

Peter looked at the broken phial in his hand.

There had to be a solution. He could survive this. In training, there had been a whole book full of safety procedures and fail-safes.

Where are they all now?

"5..."

Doctor Harket crashed to the floor once more. It felt as if his face were on fire, his lips shrivelled dry, and an army of fire ants marching under his skin.

"4...3...2..."

The world slowed, and all the voices came to him like the incantations of ancient demons. He could hear, over the sound of the alarm and the computer's countdown, Alex's voice, calling to him, but he could not understand what he was saying.

All he could think about was water; cool, crystal, sparkling water for his parched, chapped, shrivelled lips.

"1..."

The ceiling hissed. Instantly, a blanket of mist fell, enveloping him and filling the chamber.

At least three minutes had passed before Peter found his feet and, with astronaut footsteps, was able to walk forward, through the detoxifying fog. After what felt like a very long time to him, he finally reached the corpse on the floor.

His first impression was that he had made a mistake, and that, somehow, through the denseness of the fog, he had managed to stumble out of the chamber and into some hideous nightmare. This was the only way his brain could explain the grotesque mound before him.

"Detoxification protocol complete. All toxin in isolation chamber neutralised," the computer announced callously.

Vomit rose, deep from the pit of his stomach and, in a matter of seconds, was a large lump in his throat, and then a multi-coloured spatter on Peter's visor. He stood, motionless, over the thing on the floor. It was on its back, screaming in agony and clawing at the bloody, bubbling stump of its head.

Outside, behind the protection of the glass, the room sat in stunned silence, but for the weeping of one of the technicians.

"Initiating purification protocol in isolation chamber."

Instantly, there was a loud whirring sound, and the fog began to dissipate. Eventually, once the room was cleared of the mist, large shower heads sprayed water into the chamber, pelting Peter's helmet and bathing the bloody thing on the floor. Even then, as the solution rinsed the blood from the mound of melted flesh that was Doctor Harket's face, the space suit continued to twitch.

Peter stood, motionless for the next ten minutes, completely oblivious to the other spacemen who had joined him in the chamber.

33

It was almost dark before the helicopter's whirring shifted pitch, slowed, and then began to descend. There were no windows in the back of the craft, and thus Blake had no idea where he was. The journey had been silent, but for his barrage of questions that had gone unanswered.

Worse, each time he'd asked a question, his abductors would not even make eye contact with him – something that, after twenty or so minutes of flying time, had actually started to grate.

Who are you people? What do you want from me? What about Sky? Where is she? Is she okay?

There was a jolt as they touched down. Two of Blake's escorts stood up and waited for the red light above the door to turn green. When it did, the door swished open, dazzling them with the golden glow of the setting sun as a cold wind brought with it the sulphurous smell of crude oil.

The two escorts left the craft and flanked the door as Blake followed them out, ushered by two of the other mutes with black caps.

What he saw next literally made his mouth drop open. He was standing on a copper-coloured deck. It was covered in a network of pipes, pulleys and winches, and stretched as far as the eye could see, before blending into the horizon. The oil tanker was one of the largest of its kind. Blake estimated that the thing was probably as long as three football pitches, and it featured two helipads that were overlooked by a giant, white T-shaped control tower.

"Where are we?" he gasped as the gale snatched the words from his mouth.

If Blake was expecting a reply, none came. His escorts simply stood, legs astride, steadying themselves against the turbulence of the second helicopter as it touched down nearby. Shortly after, its doors opened, and a dazed and confused Sky stepped out, squinting into the wind.

"Sky!" Blake moved towards her, but two of his escorts blocked his path.

"Blake!" She shouted back, relieved to see his familiar face.

"Are you all right?" he asked as she joined him.

"I'm fine," she said sullenly, snatching her arm away from one of the escorts. "Where are we? What are we doing here?"

Blake shrugged. "No idea."

"This way, please," said one of the men suddenly.

"Oh, so you can speak then," Blake retorted.

"Where are we?" Sky demanded. "Why have you brought us here?"

"This way," the man repeated, taking her arm once more.

Blake boiled over, slapped the man's hand off her, and squared up for a confrontation as the other guards moved to intervene. They said nothing. Not that they needed to – their stances, and the fingers resting on weapons, told him everything he needed to know.

"Blake..." Sky said fretfully, tugging at his arm.

Eventually, he broke the stare off and looked at her. The wind was tossing strands of hair about her face, and her violet eyes were wide with trepidation.

He relaxed his own stance.

"This way, please," the guard repeated.

Sky threw him a look of contempt and stepped forward.

They were escorted from the helipads through a maze of pipes and across the ship, passing giant pulleys, thick chains, pipes, and a group of workers in immaculately clean blue overalls.

"Why do I get the feeling that these people aren't workmen?" she asked.

"Probably because they aren't," Blake replied loudly, hoping for a reaction, but none came.

They noticed that the ship was actually in a bad state of repair. Railings and winches were rusty. Paint was faded and peeling.

They walked to the base of the gargantuan white control tower. It stood at least eight stories above them, and ran the breadth of the vessel. From their perspective, they could just about make out the letters of 'S', 'M' and 'O' of a 'NO SMOKING' that was branded across it in giant red lettering.

They passed through a grey hatch and were presented with a staircase that led to the control tower, but they walked past this and through another hatch that led into a small, dingy compartment. Inside, one of the men pulled on a set of battered metal doors to reveal the egress to an elevator. He swiped a key card, punched in a number, and the doors swished open.

Blake and Sky exchanged glances as they were ushered inside the cabin, followed closely by their detail. Within seconds, the doors shut and the elevator began its descent, deep into the bowels of the ship.

The ride was short and, when the doors opened again, it was as if they had travelled into the future.

It was another world.

Gone was the decay, and in its place was what looked like the interior of a gleaming spaceship.

Waiting for them was a driverless six-seater people-carrier that, as soon as they had taken their seats, quietly whisked them down a long, clinically white corridor. The lighting was subtle, accentuated by low-level blue LED lights.

They travelled in silence but for the squeak of rubber wheels on the smooth floor, and the hum of the ship's engine.

Blake and Sky continued to exchange glances as if reassuring each other, both incredulous of their surroundings as they passed a series of hatched doors, each branded with an alphanumeric code.

After a minute or so, they came to an intersection where a hanging sign told them to continue straight for SECTION B, turn right for SECTION A1, or go left for SECTION A2.

The transporter continued forward until it reached SECTION F, where it stopped in front of a set of large double doors, these were guarded by another set of armed men in black.

They left their seats and Blake slipped a comforting arm around Sky's waist as one of their escorts flashed an ID at the guards and then at the camera above the doors. Instantly, the doors hummed open, unleashing a swarm of beeping sounds, ringing telephones and hushed voices.

They had reached the ship's control centre, at its bow. In keeping with the rest of the vessel, the lighting was subdued, contrasted by the glow of an array of flat screen monitors mounted onto desks and set into walls.

As the group walked into the centre of the room, the first thing Blake noticed, was the display wall. It was as least thirty feet square and, he imagined, had probably cost more than he made in a year.

Hell, probably more than I make in several years.

It was projecting a green pixelated map of the United Kingdom, not unlike Blake's meteorological program. It was surrounded by a series of smaller monitors, each displaying or scrolling data.

"This way," their escort prompted and indicated a short flight of stairs that led up, above the control room.

They followed, although Blake couldn't take his eyes off the map, since he believed he understood what he was seeing. It was a map of England, divided by county. It featured cloud formation and wind trajectory data as well as a trail of small red dots that led from the Atlantic Ocean into the mainland.

At the top of the stairs, they were ushered into a small office. The walls were padded grey, giving the impression that the place was soundproofed. Another large flat screen panel sat on a desk to one side of the room, opposite a tinted glass wall that overlooked the control room. By the window was a set of leather sofas. Seated on these were two men.

The first was a heavyset middle-aged man, bursting out of his military uniform. The other was much younger and thinner, with spectacles and a ponytail of blonde hair.

The military man glanced at the newcomers, scowled, and then looked up at the suited man standing nearby, who was busy watching the control room's large screen while talking on a mobile phone.

"Sir," one of the men in black announced as both he and his partner stood to attention.

The man in the tailored navy blue suit leisurely finished his conversation, and then turned around. He was short, yet slim. In his fifties, although he looked much younger, with short salt and pepper hair, and keen brown eyes that sat behind square spectacles. He smiled warmly, and then said, in a plummy voice, "Here you are. I was beginning to wonder."

He tapped the tip of his phone with manicured fingers, and then glanced at the two men in black, who instantly turned on their heels and left the room.

"Welcome aboard. I'm Williamson," the man said, extending a greeting hand.

On cue, the two men on the sofa rose from their seats, exchanged glances with Williamson, and then left the room without saying a word.

Williamson nodded after the two men, "Scientists and officers, geniuses at their craft, but seriously lacking in social skills. Oh, no offence, Doctor McPherson," he added quickly.

"Why are we here?" Sky demanded.

Williamson retained his smile and nodded, knowingly, "Straight to the point. I like that."

"You didn't answer the question," Blake contributed. "Who are you and why are we here?"

Williamson took his time. "You mean you haven't worked it out yet, Mr. Hudson?"

"Enlighten me," Blake said, making no effort to mask the irritation in his voice.

Williamson moved over to his desk and sat behind it. He gestured to the sofas, "Please, take a seat."

"We'd rather stand," Sky said. She already disliked this man. He had a certain smugness that made her want to slap his face. "And whilst we're standing, we'd appreciate an answer."

"You were about to make a mistake," the man said casually.

"What kind of mistake?"

"Mr. Hudson was about to cause unnecessary panic."

Blake and Sky glanced at each other and then back at Williamson, who took this as his cue to elaborate.

"Warning those people would only have created more chaos since, as you've already deduced, it's not the rain that kills, but those who are exposed it. Your initiative, whilst commendable, would have proved futile. Your goal, if you will excuse the pun, was to stop the game. However, you know, as well as I do, that the rain is not a living entity, but a meteorological phenomenon. It cannot decide where and on whom to precipitate. You may have succeeded in saving those spectators, but would have caused mass panic for millions of others..."

"Who exactly are you?" Sky cut in. "And, what gives you the right to decide who dies and who lives?"

"Who I am is of no importance, but my objective is."

"And what exactly is your objective?" She demanded.

"To ensure that this incident is cleared up quickly, and quietly."

"And how are you proposing to do that?"

"By waiting."

"For more people to die?" Blake snapped.

"For the cloud to disperse." Williamson stood up and walked over to the window "You know, as well as I do, Mr. Hudson, that this cloud will dissipate, eventually. It's only a matter of time."

"By then, countless of others will have died," Blake said anxiously.

Williamson continued, unaffected. "Yes, it has indeed proved somewhat..." he paused here to find the word, "resilient. We've been tracking it ever since the accident," he said, gazing at the green display on the control room wall. "It wasn't until it entered British air space that we discovered its power."

"What accident?" Blake asked.

Williamson did not reply.

Then it occurred to Blake, "You knew about this all along."

Williamson hesitated, then, "It was meant to be a revolutionary drug for the treatment of psychological disorders. A drug that would stir the dormant side of a disabled brain or heal a scarred one. Seven years in the making, hours of tests, millions on research and nothing, but then…"

Williamson paused, deliberately adding drama to the moment before turning around to reveal a new demeanour. His eyes were alight, his face brimming with excitement.

… "It all goes up in smoke. Never in my wildest dreams could I have imagined such a Godsend!"

"So, what went wrong?" Sky asked cynically.

Williamson shrugged. "Like most major scientific breakthroughs, it happened quite by accident. Totally unexpected. It appears that alone, this drug is a cure but, like many chemicals, when mixed, it is lethal. In this case, the drug was released into the atmosphere where it met with two of the world's most damaging pollutants, NO_2 and NOX. Then, somehow, the two amalgamated to produce an unprecedented and deadly toxin that incubates inside this remarkable delivery vessel, the cumulous nimbus cloud, and sporadically returns to Earth in the form of precipitation. It is then absorbed into the blood stream via the epidermis."

Williamson noticed the equivocal look on Sky's face, "You're sceptical, Dr. McPherson?"

"Bacteria that penetrates the skin without any visible inflammation or irritation?"

"Who said it was a bacterium?"

"The toxicological reports…"

"…With all due respect, Doctor, what you mistook for bacteria was just the remains of the victims' own antibodies..."

Williamson had that glint of excitement in his eyes once more. The same one that had made Sky want to slap him earlier.

"…as you know, the body's antigens produce antibodies as a defence against invading bacteria, such as the common cold, and, in most cases, it defeats the invading cells. But, every war has its casualties."

Sky suppressed a disbelieving laugh, "You're implying that the foreign cells we picked up were in fact normal antigens?"

"What else?" Williamson asked laconically.

"We couldn't identify them."

"Precisely. So, how could you possibly know whether or not they were just the remnants of the victims' own antibodies?"

"Because, we would have identified them as such."

"Not if they had metamorphosed."

"Into what?"

"Into a mutation of the drug."

Sky stared at him. "That's impossible."

Williamson just maintained her gaze as his thin lips creased into a faint smile.

"You just said this thing wasn't a bacterium."

"It isn't. It starts out as a chemical, a solution, conceived by the environment's corruption and our drug. When this is absorbed into the blood stream of a living animal, it triggers the defence system, the antigens create antibodies, and the battle begins. As the war rages around the host's body, the toxin rushes to the brain, hitching a ride on the blood stream. There, the drug element begins to stimulate areas of the brain. Only, now it is contaminated with something else. The result – violence, homicide. However, as I intimated earlier, given its diluted form, the toxin is weak, and thus eventually destroyed by the antibodies. Hence why most of the victims who are either isolated or restrained go on to make a full recovery."

"If you have all this information, why aren't you releasing it to the public?" Blake asked.

"Because this isn't a matter of public interest."

"No?"

"No," Williamson said firmly.

"Then whose interest is it?" It was Sky asking the question.

"Why, the government's, of course."

There was silence.

Blake was incredulous, "You're saying that the government has known about this thing all along?"

"Contrary to what you may think, Mr. Hudson, there are actually certain things that the public is better off not knowing."

"Such as whether or not there's something out there that can kill them?"

"Such as matters of national security," Williamson corrected.

Blake laughed.

"The subject of national security amuses you, Mr. Hudson?"

"No, but hypocrisy does. In one breath, you're talking about national security, which is ultimately about safeguarding the wellbeing of the country and its citizens, yet you withhold information about a toxin that could end up killing them. A toxin that you created!"

"If only. If only I could take credit for such a magnificent force. Admittedly, I did head the team that developed the original drug. Alas, none of them survived the explosion – a gargantuan setback. They were some of the best pharmaceutical brains in the world. It would have taken millions of pounds and several years to get anywhere close to where they were, so the project was cancelled, until now."

"You are...."

"...Mad? Don't you find that old cliché rather tedious? Every time someone expresses ardent ambition, a total dedication to something, they're labelled as 'mad'. Could it be that your average human being is actually intellectually incapable of comprehending the drive, the need, the thrill of discovery and accomplishment? Of appreciating the rush one gets from the realisation that something they discovered, something that they created, could actually change lives, maybe even the world."

"By turning us on each other?" Sky asked tightly.

"Of course not. But we haven't even begun to comprehend the magnitude of what we're dealing with... If we can learn to harness the power of the cumulous nimbus cloud..."

"...For what? Biological warfare?"

Williamson met Sky's gaze with eyes that flickered excitement.

Reality bit.

Sky uttered, "My God, you really are insane." She was incensed, but, controlling her emotions, she continued, "You talk about the thrill of discovery, yet you seem to have learned absolutely nothing. If there is one thing that history has taught us, it's that man is incapable of controlling nature."

Williamson did not respond immediately, instead, he looked out over the control room once more. "As much as the concept is abhorrent to you, from a scientific point of view, you must be able to appreciate its brilliance. It's stealth technology beyond anything anyone could possibly fathom."

"Yes, even you!" Blake exploded. "You're talking about a weapon that even *you* can't control!"

"Nature is indiscriminate, Mr. Hudson."

"All biological weapons are indiscriminate, and you want to build a new one. This flies right in the face of everything we have been fighting for – the total eradication of this kind of weapon."

"We?" Williamson turned to face them. "*We* didn't decide to fight for anything. It was decided by a bunch of weak-minded bureaucrats who believe peace can be achieved by rhetoric. What they failed to realise is that the best foundation for peace is the fear of war."

"You cannot be serious! Extremists have no fear beyond succeeding in achieving their own agenda. They can't be reasoned nor negotiated with."

"That is precisely my point," Williamson said.

"What *exactly* is your point?" Blake asked. "Instead of halting the proliferation of WMDs, we simply build alternatives? Sky was wrong. You aren't mad. You're a fucking idiot!"

Williamson didn't react to the insult, and instead continued, calmly. "Not bigger, Mr. Hudson, more efficient. Can't you see that something like this could be the solution to dealing with terrorists? An invisible force that infiltrates enemy lines and turns them on each other."

"But you have no control over it," Sky said in astonishment.

"With time, we will develop more control."

"You mean you still haven't learned your lesson with this disaster?"

"Let's not be naïve, Mr. Hudson. You know as well as I do, if we don't continue this research, our enemies will. Deterrents are the best…."

"… form of defence. You said," Sky interrupted. "Correct me if I'm wrong, but wasn't that the theory of the two so-called super powers a few decades ago? And what are we left with now? An ecological time bomb of catastrophic proportions, and that's just the nuclear debris that has been left to decay in hundreds of wastelands around the world…"

Sky found herself bristling with frustration. "…My God. Have we learned nothing? The world is sick, Mr. Williamson; no, not sick, it's dying, and it's dying because it was and is still being poisoned by us…"

"…but primarily by selfish, arrogant, short-sighted dickheads like you," Blake interrupted.

Sky glanced at him. "The fundamental issue that each and every fanatic is missing, be they religious, political or megalomaniacal, is that there won't be any land to declare your own, no borders to secure or property to acquire if we don't safeguard the one thing that we all have in common, our planet. Can't you see that?"

Suddenly, Sky was reminded of her parents, and she wondered what their reaction would be to this man's words, but then, this was exactly what they had spent their lives campaigning against, many years before.

And it was only now, only after surviving the extraordinary events that had led to this moment, to her standing before this man, that she understood. Her parents had not been misguided fools, nor lazy vagabonds, and they certainly hadn't been irresponsible parents who cared more about campaigning than they did their own child.

It was the opposite; they'd adopted these causes because they cared about their daughter and wanted her to inherit a different world…

"Sky?"

…One where her children and her children's children could live in peace, free from the fear of nuclear and biological Armageddon…

"Sky?"

…with clean, breathable air…

"Sky!"

They had wanted the world to stop and look at its mistakes so all could do better for the future.

"Sky!"

The mist cleared from her mind and she could see Blake now. He was standing in front of her, shaking her back into the room.

"Are you all right? You spaced out."

"Yes, I'm fine," she said, snapping out of her daze.

"Are you sure?"

"Yes," she said, forcing a faint smile. Then, turning to Williamson, she said, "The world has a right to know what you are doing here."

"Dr. McPherson, it would be naïve of you to assume that this was the only project of its kind. In fact, I could tell you stories about your everyday existence that would stop you from ever leaving your home and from eating anything you didn't farm there. For your own safety and sanity, this information is kept from you."

"What are you talking about?"

"I'm not talking about anything that you don't already know, but choose to ignore because it suits you to. By voting, you elect and thus charge your government with the burden of running the nation. They can only do this by making decisions that you may find unpalatable but, as leaders, feel are necessary."

"Like trying to weaponize a toxin?" Blake asked.

Williamson was about to reply, but stopped in mid-sentence when he noticed a presence in the doorway.

Peter Briem was standing there. His was looking an unhealthy pale and his eyes were wild, his hair mottled, and there was sweat dripping down his face.

Williamson did not react to the man's demeanour, and smiled, "Peter, good of you to join us. You know, we've been looking for you everywhere."

"I needed some time to think," Peter replied, his face expressionless. Then, glancing warily at the strangers in the room, he said, "I need to talk to you."

"Of course. I'll come over to see you as soon as I'm finished here."

"No, I need to speak with you now." Peter said forcefully, taking a step further into the room.

Williamson was calm. "Yes, as soon as I'm…"

"NOW! I need to see you now. Dr. Harket is dead!" He spat, his face creased with anguish.

Williamson smiled apologetically at his guests and moved to

the back of his desk. "Very well. Just let me grab some files."

Behind his desk, he triggered the silent alarm.

"I just need to take this down with me," he said, producing a white folder full of printed documents.

"I tried to save him, but I couldn't," Peter continued as Williamson made his way toward him.

"I know, Peter. And there was nothing you or anyone could have done to save him."

"But I was there. I was right next to him. I could have…" he broke off to wipe his forehead with the sleeve of his white jacket.

That was when Blake noticed the black rim around the young man's sunken eyes. It was then that Blake recognised the look. He had seen it before, in Clare's eyes, that stormy night at the lighthouse.

Oh God, Sky!

The pair of armed guards rushed Peter from behind, but he was ready for them. In one swift motion, he swung around with his right hand, snatched the gun off the first guard, and shoved him backward with the other. Guard number two stopped in his tracks as he saw the gun's muzzle train on him, and then his colleague, in turn.

Peter chuckled. "Pretty impressive, huh?" he said, moving slowly backward so that he commanded a clear arc of fire on the men, Williamson, and the strangers. The sweat continued to leak down the young man's face as his appearance appeared to worsen by the second.

Peter did not feel well. He did not feel well at all. He felt queasy, yet strong. Paranoid, yet energised. So energised he could run a marathon, or maybe even scale Everest. In fact, there wasn't anything he couldn't accomplish with his newfound strength. If only he could stop the burning under his skin, the throbbing behind his eyes, and the overwhelming need to punish someone.

"Put the gun down, Peter," Williamson coaxed.

"Why should I?" he asked, sweeping the weapon back and forth, enjoying its invisible power, its ability to make people cower without even touching them.

Suddenly, he stopped, as if he had just seen Sky for the first time, and asked, "What are you doing here?" as if he knew her.

Sky was startled, but found herself blurting, "Ask him." She nodded at Williamson.

"They are my guests," Williamson replied.

"Really? Are you going to carry out your experiments on them, too?" Peter asked.

Williamson said nothing.

"What, you have nothing to say?"

"Only that you should put down the weapon and let us treat you, Peter. You are unwell."

"Really?"

"Yes, you are."

The young doctor chortled, "If I am, then why do I feel so good? Hmm…" He moaned, appreciatively. "You want to know what it's like? I'll tell you, it's fucking awesome! It's like being on speed, but better. So much better that I could put a bullet through your head and not even flinch."

Blake glanced across at Sky. She was standing perfectly still as she listened to the young man's rant.

"Your toxin killed the one man who believed in me," Peter whined.

"I believe in you, Peter. The program believes in you. We need your help to carry on where Harket left off," Williamson cooed.

"Really?"

"Of course."

Peter laughed, then dabbed his forehead with his sleeve once more. "You must think I'm stupid," he hissed, thrusting the gun in Williamson's direction. "You don't need me. You've got Alex."

"Alex did not work as closely with Dr. Harket as you. He could never know as much as you do."

Peter liked that. He smiled.

"There'll be no more bullying, Peter. No more mocking. You will be in charge. You will be the one with the power."

Peter nodded, "Yeah."

"Exactly. So, come on now, put the gun down, and let us treat you before the toxin takes a hold?"

By this time, the whole control room had become aware of the commotion and had stopped what they were doing. Although, they could not see much, the control room glass was one-way, and thus obscured. The only thing they could see was the back of one of the guards, and the group that had collected at the foot of the stairs.

Peter was laughing now. A deep-bellied, guttural laugh that was on the verge of becoming infectious, until he stopped suddenly, looking at Williamson. "Do you want to know something, Doctor?"

"What is it, Peter?" Williamson asked with a smile.

"It already has."

With that, Peter casually shot guard number one in the head. The bullet pierced the man's skull through his forehead and emerged the other side, taking blood, brain matter, bone with it, and spraying the crowd below.

There were screams from the control room.

The guard went down as Peter squeezed off two more shots at guard number two. The first bullet hit him in the face, the second in his chest; the impact propelled him backward to join his colleague.

It was now or never. As Peter surveyed his deed with a maniacal grin on his face, Blake ran forward, slamming him against the wall and knocking the gun out of his hand.

Peter crumpled to the floor, temporarily dazed.

Blake grabbed Sky's hand and pulled her out of the office. They raced down the steps as two more guards climbed to meet them. Blake didn't hesitate. He used their momentum to kick the first guard in the face, sending the man reeling backward, toppling the rest of his colleagues like bowling pins.

They skilfully stepped over the knot of limbs and ran for the door.

Meanwhile, Williamson, still shaken by recent events, was back behind his desk, frantically pressing the intercom on his phone.

"Get some help in here, NOW!" Then, he reached inside one of the drawers, snatched a small pistol from its holster, and held it up with an outstretched arm, in his defence.

The room was empty.

He trained the gun on the open doorway as he heard footsteps on the stairs, but relaxed when he a group of puzzled guards appeared.

Williamson collapsed into his chair and smiled. He had come face to face with the madness of the rain, and its power was indeed awesome.

34

Matt stared vacantly out of his friend's office window. He had lost track of time, but it couldn't have been more than ten minutes since the helicopter and his friend had disappeared into the horizon.

He had spent most of this time gazing into space, trying to reconcile what he had just witnessed, and what to do next.

This can't be true. It can't. This spy crap is just the stuff of films, right? I have to call someone... Who? I don't know, the police. Can you trust them?

He moved over to the desk, picked up the phone, and put it to his ear.

The line was dead, just as Blake had said.

Yeah, but killed by what?

He listened hard, but the only sound was that of the rumbling surf outside. He quickly replaced the receiver as if, by holding it, he would be enabling whoever was listening to read his thoughts.

Whoever is listening?

He instinctively stepped away from the desk.

What do I do? What do you do when men in black, carrying guns, have abducted you friend and his girlfriend? Jesus!

He remembered the boots walking into this very office, and the debilitating terror that they'd invoked.

Who are they? What do they want? What would have happened if they'd found me?

He wanted to scream – so many questions without answers. He was alone, and there was nobody there to help him.

Call the police! And then what? Tell them what? They're going to think I've fucking lost it! Well, you won't know until you try...

He checked his mobile phone. Still no signal.

"Fuck!"

He was frustrated and scared. He took a few seconds and breathed deeply in an effort to calm the anxiety that, like a rising tide, was threatening to engulf him.

Come on, Matt. Sort it! Your friend is out there.

He descended the stairwell as stealthily as possible, half expecting a couple of the men in black to jump out at him. But he was ready. If they came at him from the steps, he would karate kick them in the teeth. He had the upper hand. He would send them sprawling down the steps where he would finish them with blows to the face.

Can you hear yourself?

I know.

Who the fuck am I kidding?

At the foot of the stairs, he poked his head around the door, but there was no one there; the entrance hall was empty. He opened the front door and peeked outside. Nobody out there either.

He then sat down in his car and took a few more seconds to gather his thoughts. He reasoned that the logical place to start had to be the nearest police station.

Let the experts deal with it. The police will know what to do.

He started the engine and, after checking, once again, that there was nobody hiding in the backseat, he drove away from Stony Point as fast as he could.

Night had descended prematurely, thanks to a series of ominous black clouds that drifted overhead like an armada of giant spaceships readying for an invasion. Thunder rumbled through them as if they were communicating with each other while the car creaked and rattled as it through the tight, winding road.

The sound unsettled Matt, so he switched on the radio.

"...Southwest will begin to feel the effects of the rainstorm that has swept back in from the Atlantic."

"So, bad news for the football match tonight then?"

"I'm afraid so. Unfortunately, it seems that this particular

storm is heading for Plymouth. Yet, authorities insist that the match will go ahead regardless. So, my advice is, if you're still thinking of braving the elements, then be sure to take suitable weatherproofs."

"Thanks, Gary; as always, you've made my evening."

"Sorry. But, as they say, I don't make the weather, I just report it."

"If only someone could. Thanks again, Gary. In the meantime, we are going into a commercial break, after which we'll be talking to the Prime Minister about the extra troops that are being drafted into the region to assist with the rescue effort, as well as the recently announced additional spend on flood defences. Don't go away."

Matt pushed the radio off. Listening to the match's impending doom wasn't making him feel any better, and it was suddenly so bloody warm in the car...

He buzzed down his window. Thunder rushed in. There was definitely the charge of a storm in the air. He could smell it. It was close, and he was scared.

"There's something in the rain. It's lethal. There's something in the rain."

Bake's words were echoing in his mind. He stomped on the brakes, bringing the car to a slippery halt. He was on the outskirts of a small village, and had spotted a red phone box conspicuously sited next to a bench overlooking the ocean.

He was about to leave the car when he noticed a convoy of two army jeeps and a police car slowly making their way up the hill towards him. Instinctively, he flashed his lights at the oncoming vehicles.

The army jeeps flashed back, but kept going until they rumbled passed him. The police car, however, came to a rolling stop in front of him.

Matt jumped out of the car as the two officers casually left their vehicle, pulling on their hats.

"Oh, thank God," Matt said quickly, clearly agitated.

"Everything alright, Sir?" one of the officers asked as they walked up to him.

"No, everything isn't alright. In fact, everything's pretty much shit," Matt said.

"What appears to be the problem, Sir?" the officer asked with trademark condescension. He was wary of this man with beads of perspiration on his forehead and his wild eyes. He was exhibiting much of the jitteriness of some of the other nutters they had met recently. The officer produced a notebook and began scribbling, "Well, why don't you tell me about it. You can start with telling me your full name and address."

"Is that necessary? Look, officers, we're running out of time. My friend has been abducted," Matt began anxiously, his emotions spewing forth.

"Abducted? By whom?"

"I don't know. They came in helicopters. They took him and the doctor away. They had guns!" He was shaking. "Do you have a cigarette?"

The officer shook his head.

Matt paused as he watched a Transit van trundle by.

"Okay, and what are their names? Sir?"

"What?"

"Your friends. What are their names? Sir?"

"Hudson. Blake. Blake Hudson," Matt said distractedly. He was finding it hard to focus. There were so many thoughts vying for attention.

"And you mentioned someone else?"

"I can't remember her surname. Sky's her first name. She's a doctor at the coroner's office. Are you going to start looking for them now?" Matt added eagerly.

"Most likely, Sir. But first I need some more details."

"Christ! What else do you need to know? These people have been abducted at gunpoint; what else do you need to fucking know?" Matt fumed.

The police officer, unaffected by the outburst, said calmly, "Maybe we should continue this conversation down at the station."

"Maybe we shouldn't," Matt said, shaking his head. Then, motioning to the jeep, "Maybe you should get your mate to call in that two people have been abducted by armed men."

"Okay, Sir, I'm going to need you to calm down."

"And I'm going to need you to do your fucking jobs!" Matt

retorted.

The police officers exchanged glances. Instantly, the other turned and talked quietly into his radio.

Matt looked at them. "What?"

"If you could just take a seat in the car please, Sir," the officer said.

"Have you even been listening to me?" Matt asked in bewilderment.

"Of course we have, Sir, but I'm going to need you to get into the car now so that we can finish this conversation at the station."

"Forget it!"

The other officer was facing them once more.

"Okay, so we can do this the easy way or the hard way, it's entirely up to you. If you want us to cuff you, then…"

"…Cuff me?" Matt spat. "Fuck you!"

With that, the two men lunged at Matt. One restrained him by grabbing him by his collar and the other by snatching one of his arms and bending it behind his back, then proceeding to snap on handcuffs.

"Get off me!" Matt protested. "Get off!"

"Think we've got another one?" the first officer asked casually. His voice was slightly wobbled by Matt's struggling.

"I don't know," the other one replied. "Let's get him back to the station. We'll let the sarge deal with it."

"No! No! You don't understand. No!"

"We understand, all right," the second officer humoured him, as his colleague opened the back door of their car.

"You've got to help them! Please, you've got to help them!"

"We are helping, Sir."

The second officer bundled Matt into the back seat of the patrol car while placing a protective hand on his head. Then, he slammed the door shut and joined his colleague in the front seat.

"Wait! Wait!" Matt cried as the officer indicated, and then pulled into the road.

"No! Blake! No!" Matt cried as lightning flashed and thunder attempted to upstage him.

"Looks like more bloody rain," the driver said, as the car slowly drove away.

35

They emerged from the control room still hand in hand. "Where to now?" Sky asked, breathlessly.

"I don't know," Blake replied, looking around.

There was no sign of the transport cart. To their right were two sealed doors, to their left, a long, dimly lit corridor led into darkness; straight ahead seemed to be their only option.

"This way!" he said, breaking into a run, but then, when he heard voices and footsteps approaching, he added, "Shit! Maybe not."

They skidded to a halt, turned on their heels, and ran down the dark corridor. After running for thirty seconds or so, they spotted a pair of double doors up ahead and another duo of armed guards. One of them was talking into his radio and looking towards them.

"Jesus, what is this place?" Blake mumbled under his breath as they slowed to a brisk pace.

Suddenly, both sentries started running towards them.

"What are we going to do?" Sky asked through clenched teeth, glancing toward the approaching men and then back up the corridor from whence they'd come. Blake weighed up the chances of overpowering them, but instantly dismissed the idea. Both were armed.

No, they would have to turn themselves in. Therefore, as the two men neared, he held up his hands in a peaceful gesture, and yet, much to his astonishment, the guards ran straight past them, disappearing down the corridor toward the control room.

"What…?"

"…They must have been called to Williamson's office."

"Oh my God, Blake, what happened back there? What are we going to do?" She was afraid, still rattled by what she had just witnessed.

Blake held her arms, looking around them for some kind of exit.

"We need to get topside," he said, moving forward.

"Blake?" Sky felt she needed to say something, but didn't

know exactly what. Her mind was numb.

They looked at each other for the longest time. He read the confusion on her face. "Look, if you're thinking about apologising for yelling at me earlier, then it can wait," he said seriously.

She frowned.

"No? That wasn't what you were going to say?"

"Um, if I recall correctly, you were the one who did the yelling."

"Now, you're just splitting hairs," he said with a smile, and then added, "Come on, we need to get out of here."

The green panel to the side of the now unguarded door suggested that it was unlocked.

Blake touched it; the doors hummed open to reveal another corridor of portal doors, each with its own glowing status panel – some green, others red. Most of the unlocked doors revealed nothing but storage.

"There must be a way out of here," he muttered, trying yet another door.

"Yes, Blake, but I think it's in the other direction. Also, any idea what we're going to do when we get there? We're on a ship!" Sky said through gasps.

"One thing at a time," Blake replied distractedly as he opened more doors.

"What exactly are you looking for?" she asked.

"I don't know. Maybe a way out of here, or even something useful like a bloody phone."

They had reached another set of double doors. This set was different; they looked more like fire doors, with circular windows of thick glass.

Blake had spotted similar ones in the main corridor when they'd arrived. Only, they'd been wide open. These were shut, transforming the corridor into what appeared to be train-like compartments.

The swipe panel glowed green, and Blake was about to pull it open when Sky caught his arm. "What are we doing?"

"Um, well," he began, glancing back down the corridor. "Last time I checked, we were running for our lives."

"Yes, but running where? It seems to me that we're just moving deeper and deeper into the ship."

"So, what's your prognosis, Doc?"

"Maybe we should turn back. At least we know where we came from."

"Right, so you much prefer our chances with Williamson's goons, or, maybe, if we're really lucky, we might run into trigger-happy Pete. He looked like he was game for a laugh. He certainly seemed to take a shine to you."

Sky sighed and rolled her eyes.

"Look, I'm sorry, but, you know, while I wouldn't want this to in any way to adversely affect your opinion of me or my masculinity, I've got to tell you, I was pretty freaked out by what happened back there, and I'm not in any particular hurry to witness a repeat performance."

Sky looked at him seriously, and then broke into a sudden smile, "No, it doesn't adversely affect my opinion of you. In fact, you were very Bond-like, especially the way you dragged me out of that room."

"Yeah?" Blake grinned.

"Yeah."

Blake moved in closer, "So, how about you…"

"…Really?" Sky scowled.

"No?"

"Bloody hell, even now, you think everything's a joke."

"Do I?"

Sky rolled her eyes again. "Come on," she said, tugging at the door.

"Wait, wait," Blake said seriously.

"What?" she replied, alarmed.

"Just tell me one thing."

She looked at him expectantly.

"How do you know we aren't walking straight into more trouble?"

"We don't."

"Okay, just checking."

"Come on," she pulled on the door.

He followed her through, into the next corridor.

This section was much smaller. At the far end was another

panelled door, and above it, a large white on black sign read, "RESTRICTED ACCESS – AUTHORISED PERSONNEL ONLY."

"What is this, *Journey to the Centre of the Earth*?" Blake remarked.

"What do you think's behind that door?" Sky asked.

"I don't know," he said, staring at the sign. "I supposed we could stare at the sign some more or we could just find out," he added, moving forward.

Sky caught his arm. "Blake?" She said.

Sensing her mood, he pointed on. "I'll make a deal with you. If there isn't any sign of a way out beyond that door, we'll turn back, okay?"

"Okay."

However, as they neared the door, they heard the sound of talking and approaching footsteps.

They were trapped.

36

The control room was a hive of activity. There were operators talking on phones, tapping keyboards, and chatting animatedly at desks while the two guards, gunned down by Peter and now zipped into black body bags, were hauled onto stretchers and unceremoniously carried away from the area.

Upstairs, in Williamson's office, a group of cleaners in yellow overalls were busy scrubbing and steaming away the blood from the walls and stairs.

Downstairs, Williamson was deep in conversation with a scowling heavyset man in a military uniform. He had not long left Williamson's office before all hell had broken loose. "I told you, bringing them here was a mistake," he growled in deep yet subtle American accent.

"What happened was not of their doing," Williamson said calmly.

"No, it was yours," the colonel threw back.

"I don't answer to you," Williamson snapped.

"No, you answer to the board, and they are not going to be pleased when they hear that you introduced two complete strangers to this facility."

"Would you rather I have allowed them to go to the local police?"

"No one would have believed them."

"Perhaps. But were you prepared to take that risk?" Williamson challenged.

The colonel didn't reply. Instead, he looked expectantly at the technician in front of him. The man was sitting in front of a bank of monitors, each one displaying a collection of video feeds from around the ship. The man worked fast, invoking a flicking slide show on both of the screens in front of him.

"Besides, wasn't it you who gave the order to have them brought in?" Williamson continued.

The colonel looked up and, seething, said, "Yes, I did. But I did not plan on bringing them back here."

"Right, and what exactly were you planning on doing with them?"

The colonel didn't respond.

"Oh, I see. Well, you may be a killer, Colonel, but I certainly am not. I am a scientist."

The colonel was about to reply, but was interrupted by the technician.

"..Sir."

"Have you found them?" he asked, looking over the man's shoulders.

"We've found Peter, Sir. But still no sign of the other two."

"Well, they can't have disappeared into thin air. Keep looking!" the colonel bellowed.

"Where is Peter?" Williamson asked, ignoring the colonel's outburst.

"Here, Sir." The man pointed to one of the monitors, which was in the process of projecting an image of Peter swiping his key card in front of a door, then disappearing through it and off the screen. "He's in sector Bravo 2, warehousing, near the engine room."

"Mirkoff!" the colonel barked at a nearby sentry. "Take those men and as many as you deem necessary. Bring him back, dead or alive. He's armed, so don't take any chances, and revoke his keycard!"

"Have you taken leave of your senses?" Williamson said. "The level of toxin in that chamber was off the scale. No human has ever been exposed to such a high dose. Statistically, he should have suffered an embolism or massive thrombosis by now. It is absolutely imperative that we examine him to learn more about how his body is coping."

"Fine, once my men have apprehended him, you can carry out all the experiments you like."

"No, you don't understand." Williamson grasped the colonel's arm. "I need him alive."

"And you will get him alive, just as long as he doesn't try anything stupid with my men. If he does, then they'll have to protect themselves."

The colonel glanced at Williamson's hand. Reluctantly, Williamson let go.

"You overreach, Colonel. This ship is under my control."

"It is, but my men and I are charged with the security of this vessel; your little pet killed two of my men and thus is now deemed a threat to this ship's security."

The colonel glanced back at the monitor; Peter was walking down a corridor, still carrying a gun in his hand.

A caption at the foot of the monitor read, *B2, SUPPLY ROOM.*

"And one other thing," the colonel continued, without taking his eyes off the screen in front of him, "Put your hand on me again or interfere with this operation in any way, and I'll have you removed and confined to quarters; are we clear?"

Williamson said nothing.

The colonel turned and brought to bear the extra foot or so he commanded in height by looking down on the shorter, thinner man. "Doctor?"

Williamson nodded, reluctantly.

Meanwhile, the nearby monitors were flipping through rooms,

corridors, and the deck as if the spaces were photographs in an album.

A few minutes flickered by.

"Where the hell could they have gone?" the colonel demanded.

"They could be inside one of the storage rooms, Sir."

"Well, screen all the rooms."

"I can't, Sir."

"Why not?"

"Because the cameras only come online if there's lighting in the room," Williamson interjected without taking his eyes off of the scrolling images, "and the lighting only comes on if the room senses a heat variation or movement."

"Another one of your ideas, Doctor?" The colonel asked.

"Indirectly, yes. It's part of the computer's power-saving directive. There isn't much point in monitoring a pitch black room, is there?" Williamson smirked.

"There is if you want to look at something that doesn't have a pulse."

"He's just about to move into A sector," the technician said to no one in particular.

"The deck?" Williamson asked.

"Yes, Sir, or the engine room."

"I thought I told you to revoke his key card," the colonel, snapped.

"I did," the technician responded sheepishly. "I don't understand what's happening."

"He must be using somebody else's key card," Williamson said casually. "Check all of the cards used in that section in the last…

Williamson didn't finish his words, as a realisation dawned….
"Seal that door, now!" he said quickly.

The technician typed on his keyboard until there was a beep and the words "*AREA CONTAINED*" appeared on screen.

"What was that all about?" the colonel asked.

"He's heading toward the engine room."

"So?"

"So, he's loaded with toxin, and therefore capable of anything."

The colonel sighed and snatched up a radio.

"Mirkoff… Cancel previous orders. Do not attempt to apprehend. Brien is armed and dangerous… shoot to kill… I repeat… shoot to kill."

Williamson was about to protest, but he was interrupted.

"..Sir? It's the engine room," the technician said, again, to nobody in particular.

"What about it?"

"Well, the guns…."

Williamson's eyes widened. "Yes, oh my God, you are right."

"What?" the colonel asked.

"Rescind your order, Colonel," Williamson said, rapidly.

"We've been through this…"

"…Rescind your order, Colonel, or we're all going to die!"

37

The footsteps were approaching fast.

Blake grabbed Sky's arm and pulled her through one of the doors. The room was dark, cold and smelt of chemicals, but at least they would be able to take refuge there.

Or so Blake thought. They'd barely closed the door behind them before the lights sprang to life and a voice said, "*Welcome, guests, to Pathology Suite 1.*"

The voice startled Blake who, like a rabbit in headlights, squinted, expecting a couple of guards to rush at them. Instead, before he even had a chance to take in the place, it was plunged into darkness once more.

Then, a tap on his shoulder made him whirl around, fists raised.

It was Sky.

After a few seconds, her face came into focus, partially illuminated by the glow of the light panel mounted on the wall. She was pointing at it and the speaker mounted above it. Then, she put the same finger to her lips and nodded at the door.

The footsteps had stopped just beyond the door, where two voices spoke in a foreign language that neither Blake nor Sky understood. Then, a third voice yelled something from further down the corridor.

The two men fell silent.

The voice, gruff and angry, drew closer and then spoke again.

"Yes, Sir," came the unified response.

"Now, get out of here!" the voice ordered, this time in perfect English.

Heels scuffed and footsteps retreated down the corridor once more.

Silence.

But, neither Blake nor Sky moved because they both knew, or, at least, they sensed, that someone was still out there. Seconds went by as they held their breaths, waiting for the sound of the third pair of shoes to walk away, but it didn't come.

Sky groped in the darkness until she felt Blake's arm underneath her fingers. It was taught with tension.

If whoever was out there opened the door, they would be discovered. He had no doubt about that, and there was absolutely nothing he could do about it, since he didn't have a weapon or anything. Nothing, but he his bare hands.

He was considering this when the door suddenly swung open, shoving them up against the wall.

The lights came on.

"Welcome, Sargent Khan, to Pathology Suite 1."

They stopped breathing. Their bodies protested. Sky squeezed her eyes shut as if, by doing so, she could wish away their predicament.

Blake, on the other hand, kept his eyes wide open. As far as he was concerned, he was in fight or flight mode. However, given their position behind the door, he doubted there would be much opportunity for flight. No, there was only one possible way they might get out of this, and that was if he managed to overpower the sergeant; he'd even kill him if he had to, although he had no idea how. Jason Bourne, he was not. Although, he had watched the films enough times to delude himself into thinking that he might be able to re-enact some of his moves.

Are you serious?

These thoughts and more were streaming through his mind when he noticed it. It was directly in front of him, like a sleeping ghost on an aluminium bed. It lay, motionless, as the presence continued to hover in the doorway.

What do you want? Piss off!

Perspiration had dampened his forehead, despite the chill in the room, as Sky's heart felt as if it was going to burst, Alien-style, from her chest.

It was so quiet in the room that they thought that they could actually hear whoever it was, breathing as he surveyed the room. His suspicion had obviously been aroused by the open door.

At least, that's what Blake concluded. When they had entered the room, he had carefully pushed the door back, rather than closing it, as he hadn't wanted the sound of the catch to draw attention. Ironically, his action had managed to yield precisely the opposite.

Sky's eyes were still tightly closed, and remained that way even after the door shut and the lights went out again.

Blake could have wept with relief when he finally heard the sweet sound of footsteps retreating, and then the swish of doors opening and then closing further down the corridor.

In the deathly silent darkness, they both let out noisy breaths and hungrily sucked in gelid air.

"That was close," Sky said through gasps, clutching her chest.

"I know," he said, still trying to rationalise whether what he had seen was real.

Are we really standing in the freezing dark with a corpse laid out on a metal gurney in front of us?

"I'm shaking," Sky said.

"You didn't see it, did you?" Blake asked.

"See what?"

Breathing in short, shallow breaths, Blake moved towards the glowing wall panel, but he didn't get far before the lights sprang to life, revealing a large rectangular room with fitted cupboards, an aluminium washbasin, and two gurneys – one empty, but the other, much to Blake's disappointment, was occupied.

"Welcome, guests, to Pathology Suite 1."

The words sank in this time.

It took Sky a few moments of squinting into the light before she spotted it. Then, way too eagerly for Blake's liking, she moved forward. He was about to say something, but then he remembered what she did for a living.

Slipping automatically into pathologist mode, she grabbed a pair of surgical gloves out of a nearby box and slipped them on. Then, without hesitation, she peeled the sheet back from the body of the cadaver. "My God," she breathed, looking down at the man. His jet-black hair was in stark contrast to his bleached white features. Then, she bent closer to get a better look at the man's face as Blake tentatively joined her.

"Um, Sky, if that computer knows we're here, then I'd say there's a pretty good chance that Williamson does too."

But Sky wasn't listening. She was much more interested in what she was seeing before her.

Most of the dead man's forehead was missing. In its place was a large pink and crimson crater. "This man has a massive laceration to the forehead and...." she trailed off, peering closely. Something was glinting from deep within the congealed wound, "There's something in there," she uttered.

She looked around the room and spotted the tray of surgical instruments. From it, she retrieved a pair of forceps and used them to pluck up one of the many minuscule fragments.

She held it up to the light. "Looks like glass." Then, turning her attention back to the corpse before her, Doctor McPherson was back at work, meticulously scrutinising the body for trace evidence of what may have put it in this terminal state.

"Sky?" Blake prompted, glancing at the door.

She probed the dark discoloration around the temple and nose with her fingers. "This level indentation here, and these fragments, would suggest that this wound was inflicted by a very heavy glass object."

Not because he wanted to know, but more because he felt compelled to share her enthusiasm, he asked, "Such as?"

"I don't know. It's hard to tell. Whatever it was, it was flat and hard. See how disjointed his nose is?" She pointed.

"What, like a window or something?"

"Could be. Maybe a glass door."

"Like the one outside?"

She looked at him and nodded, "Yes, like the one outside."

"Do you think someone did this to him?"

"It's hard to tell."

She took one of the corpse's hands and carefully studied its fingernails.

"What are you doing?" Blake asked, glancing around them.

"I'm looking at…"

"…Don't tell me. You're checking his fingernails to see if there's any evidence of an assault, because if he defended himself, there's a good chance that he would have cuts and or bruises, as well as potential trace evidence of his attacker under his fingernails, like skin or hair."

Sky looked up at him.

He shrugged. "C.S.I. Miami."

She turned back to the cadaver. "Actually, I was checking his manicured nails. Whatever this man did for a living, it wasn't hard labour." Then, glancing up at him, she added, "And yes, you're right. I can't see any obvious indication of a struggle. But what is this man doing here, Blake?"

"I don't know. However, you may want to turn that question on yourself, Doctor. We're supposed to be finding our way out of this place, not performing impromptu autopsies."

"You're right." She promptly pulled off the gloves and threw them into a nearby waste bin.

"Um, what, what was that? Did you just say I was right about something?"

She ignored the question and asked one of her own, "What do you think this is all about, Blake?"

"And that, as they say, is the million dollar question. Whatever it is, you can bet that Williamson and his cronies are responsible. Not just for him, but also for everything else that has happened as a direct result of the rain."

"But, why bring us here?"

"No Idea. Probably, exactly what he said. We know too much, and, had we gone to the police, there's a good chance they would have started asking questions."

"Maybe, but then again, you don't have any evidence." Blake went to speak, but Sky talked over him. "The only evidence we have is circumstantial."

"Why don't you say that a bit louder? I think the guards out there might have an opinion," he retorted sarcastically. "Jesus, Sky, after everything that has happened to us, you still doubt?"

"Of course not. I'm not doubting what happened, I'm just wondering what exactly we actually have to corroborate all of this."

"Um, hello, we're in a military installation masquerading as an oil tanker. Oh, and somebody tapped my bloody phone!"

"And you that how?"

"How else do you think they knew where we were and what we were planning to do? Besides, I heard them. At the time, I thought there was something wrong with my phone, but then the internet went down. You can ask Matt; he was there when…"

He broke off there. Then, "Shit! Matt!"

"What about him?"

"He was at the house."

"When they came for you?"

"Yes."

"What happened to him?"

"I don't know. They searched the house."

"Well, did they find him?"

"I don't know."

38

Exeter Police Station

"How many times do I have to go over the same thing?" Matt yelled, frustrated.

He was sitting in a small, cubicle-like interview room behind a scuffed brown desk. Overhead, a wall-mounted camera recorded every move, every word. They had been in the cubicle for nearly an hour, and they were still going over the same crap.

"Until you tell us exactly what you were doing at Blake Hudson's residence, now a crime scene. A murder crime scene, sealed off by the police and breached by you and your friends. What was your relationship with Clare McElvoy?" A police officer called Ginger asked.

"I told you, she was a pupil," Matt replied, running his hands through his hair in exasperation.

"And her relationship with Mr. Hudson?"

"He was her tutor, too. Look, if this is going to take much longer, not only do I want a cigarette, but I want a lawyer, too, and just so you know, I don't smoke!"

"You waived your right to counsel when you arrived."

"Well, I've changed my fucking mind. You think I can't tell where you're going with these stupid questions? Was Blake having a relationship with that girl? No. Did he kill her? I have no fucking clue – you're supposed to be the police. Did I have anything to do with it? The first I knew was when you told me, just now. Was my friend abducted by mean-looking bastards in equally mean-looking black helicopters? Yes, he fucking was, along with Sky. Could something be happening to them right now because you wankers can't pull your fingers out of your arses to do something? You fucking bet!"

Matt glared at Ginger, and the two men stayed locked in a stare-off until Matt finally broke away and looked at his watch. The match would be starting in less than an hour, unless he found a way to stop it. He took a few seconds and a deep breath, and then said, "Look, I really have told you everything I know. Please, could you talk to whoever's in charge and have them start a search for my friends?"

"We already have, Matt. Mostly because we're interested in hearing what he has to say about the death of one of his students, and why exactly he later returned to the scene of the crime. Look at it from our point of view, Matt. It's all a bit suspicious, don't you think?"

"Are you really telling me that, with all of the freak-show that's been going on around here lately, you're worried about some bloke returning to his own home?" Matt asked.

"No, we're more interested in why one of your mate's students was at his house and what subsequently happened there."

"Yeah, well, what happened there was that my mate and his girlfriend were abducted by secretive, military-style helicopters and, for all we know, could have been killed by now, yet you don't seem interested in them. Besides, I've already told you, Clare had been stalking Blake for some time. She most likely made her way there all on her own."

"Well, if she was, Matt, then why didn't he report it to anyone?"

"Probably because he didn't think it was serious. Although, you're probably best asking him... only, you'll have to find him first to do that."

"Must have been pretty serious for them to smash her face in and throw her over the balcony."

They locked eyes once more.

"Now, I am going to ask you one more time, Matt. What do you know about what happened there?"

Matt didn't respond. They were going round in circles, and he was sick of it.

"Matt?"

Silence.

"No problem. I can wait. I've got all the time in the world," Ginger said, folding his arms.

"As long as you find something to charge me with, as well as any evidence to support that charge," Matt threw back. "If you can do that, then I'd be more than happy to spend the night."

Now, it was Matt's turn to fold his arms.

"You violated a crime scene."

Matt nodded at the camera, "Check your footage. I think I distinctly heard you say that Blake violated the crime scene, not me. In fact, other than my telling you that I went there to pick up my friend and take him to the game, you have no evidence that even places me there."

"You really think that just because you've watched a few documentaries, you know the law?"

"Not the law, Ginger, but my rights."

There was a pause. Ginger was slightly taken aback by Matt's use of his nickname.

Matt had overheard it when they'd first arrived at the station.

"Now, either you call my lawyer, get your superior who obviously knows much more about my rights than you have explained to me, or let me the fuck out of here!" Matt yelled in frustration.

It took a few seconds, but Ginger finally spoke, to nobody in particular, "Interview suspended at eighteen–fifty-nine," and then he turned to his colleague, who had sat beside him, impassively taking notes throughout, and said, "Watch him. I'll be right back." Then he left the room, leaving Matt to drum his fingers, impatiently.

Outside the interview room, Ginger called to a man walking down the corridor. "Sir! Excuse me, Sir!"

Morrison stopped and turned to meet him. "Yes, Baxter?"

"Sir, just thought you might be interested... the suspect we brought in regarding the murder at that lighthouse. The one involving Doctor McPherson."

"Yeah, what about it?"

"Well, he appears to have information regarding Hudson."

"What kind of information?"

"I'm not sure exactly, but he seems to think that Hudson may have left the county, maybe even the country, Sir."

"Left? What do you mean? How?"

Ginger suppressed a smirk, "Well, he just told me some weird story about men in helicopters, possibly military, who abducted both Hudson and the doctor at gunpoint, and then disappeared out to sea."

"Are you having me on, Baxter?"

"No, Sir."

Morrison scrutinised the young man's face for a few seconds, as if checking that he wasn't playing some kind of practical joke, and then asked, "Any particular reason why he would say that?"

Ginger shrugged, "He claims he was there."

"He was there when it happened?"

Ginger nodded.

"When was this?"

"Earlier this evening."

"Okay, I'll have a word."

"There's more, Sir. About Doctor McPherson, he says that she was abducted, too."

Morrison's eyes widened.

"He says that he witnessed her being escorted aboard one of the helicopters."

"*One* of the helicopters?"

Ginger smiled. "Yeah. Apparently, there were two of 'em."

"I see."

Ginger lost his smile when he noticed that Morrison wasn't sharing his amusement.

"What else?"

"Well…" Ginger scoffed.

"Now please, Baxter," Morrison said impatiently.

"He said we should call off the match this evenin'."

"What match?" Morrison asked.

Ginger frowned, "The final. Cambridge V Plymouth Argyle. It's going to be a…"

"…Yes, yes, Baxter. You can spare me the details. Just tell me why he thinks we should stop the game." Ginger was about to scoff again when Morrison intervened, "and try explaining it to me without the schoolboy giggling, will you?"

The officer's smile vanished once more. "Well, he said there's something in the rain. Some kind of toxin. Apparently, it's deadly, and exposure to it can kill." Ginger suppressed a titter.

"And how does he know this?"

"Blake Hudson, Sir."

"The same man who…"

"…who was involved with the death of that girl, yes, Sir."

"I see." Morrison pondered.

"What do you think? Should we let 'im go with a warnin'?"

"Yes."

"Will do, Sir."

"But not until I have spoken to him. What's his name?"

"Matt, Matthew Allen."

"We're already looking for his mate, this Hudson bloke, right?"

"Yes, Sir, and the doctor."

"Any news?"

"No, nothing yet."

"Well, hop to it, Baxter. The man's a suspect after all, and

McPherson is a colleague."

"Yes, Sir."

With that, Ginger turned on his heels and moved to walk down the corridor.

"Oh, and Baxter!" Morrison called after him.

"Yes, Sir?"

"Did you say he saw them disappear out to sea?"

"Yeah."

"Don't forget to alert the Coast Guard."

"No, Sir."

Morrison mulled over what he had just heard for a while, before making his way down the corridor to *Interview Room 2*. He entered, closed the door behind him, and smiled, "I'm D.I. Morrison."

Matt nodded, "Cool, so, have you come here to help or are going to go over the same crap he did?" Matt asked flatly.

Morrison took Ginger's seat, next to the note-taking officer. "Well, Matt, as with any investigation, it's important for us to establish the facts before we go trailing off on some tangent."

"I've already given you the facts, but you appear to be selective about what you believe is and is not important."

"So, you don't think homicide is important, Matt?"

He was about to respond, impulsively, but then thought about it. "Of course I do, but, like I've already said, if Blake did push that girl over the balcony, it would have been self-defence. She was probably infected with this rain thing Blake was talking about. Not that she needed any help – she was already psycho."

"You think she was infected with the rain, Matt? You can hear what you're saying, right?"

"Yes, I can hear it," Matt retorted, sitting back in his chair, "and, I pretty much had the same reaction as you, but then I heard Blake on the phone; I heard what he said to his boss. For Blake to say that stuff, and piss away his job like that, well, there had to be something in it. Then, of course, when the choppers arrived... well, you can imagine, I was sold," he added sarcastically.

Morrison watched him for the longest time, before asking, "So, what exactly does Blake believe is in the rain?"

Matt shook his head. "I don't know. Whatever it is, he thinks that it's what has been causing all of these riots. He also believes that the same thing is going to happen at that football match, if you don't get them to call it off."

"You want us to call off the football match?"

"Yes."

"But we're the police, Matt, not the Football Association."

"You can call it off on grounds of public safety."

"Yes, as a precaution. But as a precaution against what? Infection?"

"Yes," Matt said excitedly. It seemed that someone was finally listening to him.

"But you can't tell me what kind of infection?"

There was a pause as Matt realised where the conversation was going; Morrison was the psychiatrist and Matt was the patient. He exploded, "The kind of infection that's going to get you and his boss sacked, because if Blake is right and something happens at that match tonight, and you two knew about it, then I'll make sure every national paper gets to know all about it."

"Two?"

"What?"

"Two. You said, you two. Who else knows about this?"

Matt thought about it. "His boss."

"Who's boss?"

"Blake's boss."

"The head of the Environment Agency?"

"Yes."

"He knows about this?"

"Yes, I told you, Blake called him, but his boss didn't want to know either. You do realise that if you spent more time looking for him, and less talking to me, that you could ask him about it yourself, right?"

"We are looking for them, Matt, and when we find them; there'll be a lot more that I'll want to discuss with Mr. Hudson. As for the football match, as it stands, I have neither the authority nor any plausible reason to request a postponement."

Matt shook his head, "You're making a big mistake."

"Perhaps. In the meantime, you're free to go, but only on the understanding that you remain available to police, pending the outcome of this investigation."

"Is that it? Is that all you're going to do?"

"I am sorry but there is nothing more I *can* do. We are already searching for your friend and the doctor, and, as I said, unless something major happens, for example," Morrison paused, looking Matt straight in the eyes, "a bomb scare, then my hands are tied. Now, I suggest you leave before I have you charged with wasting police time."

With that, Morrison stood up and left the room, leaving Matt with an overwhelming sense of inadequacy.

He had wasted all this time, yet had achieved absolutely nothing.

39

"So, who else knew?" Sky asked.

Blake thought about the question. "Nobody. Just you and me, obviously, and then Matt... oh shit," he added with a whisper as it suddenly occurred to him.

"What?" Sky asked.

"There was someone else."

"Who?"

"Hamilton," Blake spoke slowly.

"Your boss?"

"Yes."

"You think he's involved in some way?"

"I don't know. He did seem adamant that I do nothing until I spoke with him."

"Yeah, that's pretty damning; your boss wanting to talk to you about your job."

"No, it wasn't that. It was more the way he spoke on the phone. There was something about the way he dismissed something so potentially serious, out of hand."

"Maybe he just didn't believe you had a compelling case."

"Maybe, but then he was the same with Terry from the office."

"Same, how?"

"I don't know... defensive, anxious. A bit like how he was with me."

"Blake, you do realise what you're saying. If true, it would mean that things do go higher than we originally thought."

"Exactly," Blake agreed, moving over to the door. "That's why we've got to get out of here. Come on."

He opened the door and cautiously peeked out. The corridor was empty. "Okay, he said, stepping out.

Sky followed.

He looked up and down the hallway, back the way they'd come, or should they continue in the opposite direction, where an overhead sign warned them it was a *RESTRICTED AREA – LEVEL 4 ACCESS ONLY...*

Sky made the decision for him, and was already heading back to the compartment door, but she noticed that Blake wasn't following. "Blake!" she called in a loud whisper.

But, he didn't answer because he was too busy scurrying to the end of the hallway and peering through the glass panel in the door.

"Blake!" she called again, frustrated, while all the time checking the area around her.

"There's something in here," Blake said in a loud whisper as he pressed his nose against the glass. "I think this corridor ends here, and," he angled his head to get a better look, "I think there's something in here."

Unlike the other rooms, this one was lit by an ultraviolet glow that revealed the outline of what appeared to be rows of glass cubicles.

He turned his head left and right, but the view remained limited.

"Blake!" Sky whispered, angrily. "We've got to go, now!"

"I just want to see…" he pushed on the door, but it wouldn't open. He pulled it, and still nothing. Then he noticed the red wall panel – locked.

Sky wanted to scream at him, but suppressed the urge for fear that someone might hear her. Instead, she rushed down the corridor and tugged on his arm until he was facing her. "Are you insane?" she hissed.

"There's something in there, Sky."

"Who cares? Blake, we've got to go, now!"

"Whatever's in there could give us proof," he said desperately.

"How much more proof do you need?" she said through gritted teeth.

"We don't have any, Sky. You said it yourself. Whether or not Hamilton is involved, we have no evidence of any of this. Even if we manage to get off the ship, nobody's going to believe us."

Sky hesitated. Blake mistook this as her endorsement. He turned to the glass once more. "Now, if only there was a way to get in there... fuck!"

He ducked below the glass.

"What?" Sky asked, alarmed, while instinctively mirroring his crouching position.

"There's someone coming from the opposite side."

"What?" she whispered in a panic. "Back up there..."

"...No, wait!" Blake grabbed her arm, "If you stand up, he'll see you through the glass in the door. In there, quick!" he said, motioning to the door opposite them that was, mercifully, glowing green.

They darted inside, just as there was a beep and the sound of a lock disarming.

They were in a storage cupboard full of medical supplies. No sooner had they entered than the light came on, *"Welcome, guests, to B2 Alpha Storage."* The tinny voice sounded like a siren in the still of the closet. Blake slammed his hand onto the glowing wall panel and the light went out; then, he slid across, pressed his back against the door, and listened.

Thankfully, the footsteps walked by their door and faded into the distance.

This had barely happened before Blake, much to Sky's astonishment, was pulling the door open and peeking out, just in time to see the back of a man, wearing a white lab coat, disappear though the compartment portal at the opposite end of the corridor.

Then, he turned to see that the door to the restricted area was slowly being pulled shut by the closing piston. Blake left the threshold of the storage room with one giant leap, pushed on the door, and waited for the lock to engage.

It didn't. The panel glowed green. He had reached the door in time. He smiled and sighed, pressing his forehead against the cool of the glass.

Sky emerged from the storage room and punched his arm, startling him, "Have you completely lost your mind? Are you deliberately trying to get us caught?" she hissed, angrily.

"No, I've not completely lost my mind," he said with a smile, making an obvious display of pushing the door open.

She sighed apprehensively, glancing up the corridor "Blake…"

"I know. But we need this," he said seriously. "Besides, this place looks different. It may have a way out," he added hopefully, pushing on the door.

Sky was torn, but she knew she didn't really have a choice. She was hardly going to leave without him. Therefore, with one final look up the corridor, she reluctantly followed.

The room resembled another compartment. It was approximately thirty feet in length, twenty-five feet wide, and lit by ultraviolet recessed lighting, although this appeared to be dimmed, and thus barely pierced the gloom. From the glowing red panels, it was obvious that whatever lurked inside the cubicles was locked in there.

"What is this place?" Sky gasped. Her voice was a fire alarm in the stony quiet of the room.

"I don't know," came Blake's perturbed whisper.

Something about the space unnerved him, probably because it resembled the sets of some of the most disturbing science fiction movies he had seen.

They separated; Sky moved left and Blake to the right. Both were curious, yet apprehensive.

The darkness beyond the glass was thick and wrapped in a subtle haze that ebbed and flowed around silhouettes, like rising mist.

Sky stepped closer, cupping her hands around her face and then pressing it against the glass in an attempt to see beyond her reflection. However, she could see nothing but blackness and mist.

"Sky?" Blake called in a loud whisper.

She turned to notice that he too was peering into the glass in his attempt to identify what lurked beyond.

"I think I've found something," he said.

She was about to go to him when it came; the anguished moan, akin to the sound of a disgruntled cat, burrowed through Sky's nervous system like a dentist's drill. She yelped and instinctively jumped away from the cubicle as her heart attempted drill its way out of her chest.

The spectre emerged from the mist and slumped against the glass wall.

Sky backed away to the centre of the room, as did Blake, until they bumped against each other, just as another pained wail pierced the silence.

"Blake," she spoke, hyperventilating.

"I know," he looked to the exits on either side of the room. Both glowed red.

Still staring at the ghostly features behind the glass, Sky whispered, "What is it?"

"I don't know," Blake replied, following her gaze.

He could feel her trembling against him, and now he wished he had taken her advice and left when she'd asked him to. Now, his mind was unkindly projecting the memory of every horror flick that featured demons, monsters, and creatures nobody even knew existed, with the view of finding a potential match to whatever might be lurking inside the mist. Worst of all was the notion that, whatever it might be, the only thing that was keeping it from him and the woman he loved was a sheet of glass.

He scanned the room again. There had to be something. A light switch or something, and why the hell hadn't that computer thingy switched on the light and noisily welcomed them, as it had, most inconveniently, in every other room? The thought only made him feel worse because he concluded that there might be a reason for it not doing so. There might be a reason why the lights stayed off. Maybe, whatever it was that was now panting, like an overheated hound, was sensitive to light, and maybe he should not be making his way across the room, towards the other exit and the wall-mounted panel.

Maybe.

Yet, despite this, and in his usual pig-headed way, that he now realised perhaps wasn't one of his most redeeming qualities, and without taking his eyes off Sky, he tapped the touchscreen panel; there was a hiss and a click as the lock disengaged, and, to Blake's amazement, the panel turned green.

Then, it made sense to him; they could leave a room without a key card or biometric identification they just couldn't enter one without it. His first instinct was to grab Sky and run, as fast as their feet would carry them, but that was before he heard another anguished moan.

He turned; Sky was looking at him while biting her bottom lip. Something he had forgotten she was prone to when she was anxious.

He examined the door panel and spotted the lightbulb icon, sitting above the number 3. He touched the icon and changed the setting to number 8. Instantly, the lights came up, illuminating the room as well as the horror on both of their faces.

The old man leered at Sky from behind the glass of his cubicle. He was naked, with an emaciated body, large dark circles around his eyes, mottled grey hair and anaemic skin that shone translucent under the blue hue. He stood, with his face and one hand pressed against the glass, while the other disappeared between his legs. His pink tongue slithered across chapped lips as his breath came in short, shallow rasps, indicating the pleasure he was deriving from his public performance.

The cubicles that lined the walls were identical, and each contained a male or female occupant. Some were lying, asleep, curled up like animals. Others were sitting or standing in corners, vacantly staring into space.

Some were tethered by thick rubber straps.

Blake felt nauseous. "What is this place?" he breathed.

Sky shook her head. "Some kind of lab," she uttered in disbelief as she noticed an empty cubicle. The front window was missing, and she flinched inwardly as she pictured the image of the man in the morgue smashing his head into the glass wall, knocking himself into oblivion.

"So this is Williamson's idea of research for the benefit of mankind."

"He was developing a cure all right, against the toxin that he and his company created."

"My God. Let's get out of here," Sky began to say, but her words were interrupted by whimpering from the opposite cubicle, where a plump, middle-aged female, naked but for her underwear, was lying on a mattress on the floor. Her head lolled as her legs opened and closed, spasmodically, and she squinted against the harshness of the lights. Suddenly, she bolted upright, tugged violently against her restraints, and then fixed her intruders with an icy glare. Then, she spontaneously began panting until this was interrupted by a coughing fit that sent spittle flying and spattering against the glass of her cubicle.

As soon as she had recovered, she began a harrowed, incoherent howl that gradually metamorphosed into a guttural whisper, "H…E…. L… P   M…E… H…. E…L…P M…E…." Her eyes were wide open, pleading, imploring – begging the strangers to release her from the hellish turmoil of her mind, the searing hot tentacles that lashed her brain, and the army of mites that tunnelled under her skin. "P…l…. e…a…s…e," she continued, "H…e…l…p m…e."

"Christ…" Blake seethed. He couldn't bear it anymore.

He stepped forward, but Sky grabbed him. "What are you doing?"

"What do you think? I'm going to let her out."

"You can't!"

"Let go."

"Blake! You can't!"

"No, what I can't do is stand here and watch."

"Blake, these people are isolated for a reason. We've no idea what they have been exposed to, and if we breach…"

"…Fuck!"

"What?"

"Someone's out there!"

Sky followed his gaze and saw one of the security men, looking at them through the door window while swiping his card to open it.

The red light turned green.

"Quick! Through here!" Blake said, running to and slamming his hand against the glowing panel on the opposite side of the room. They scrambled through as fast as they could as a group of security men launched into the room in pursuit.

On the other side of the door, Blake kicked at the panel with all the strength he could muster.

"What are you doing?" Sky asked anxiously.

"I'm trying to disable the door."

"Does that really work?"

"I have no idea."

"Come on!" She screamed. She pulled at him, just as the panel disintegrated and fell to the floor in pieces as sparks spewed from the cavity it left behind.

They ran down the corridor and into what looked a mini warehouse with shelving full of various pieces of equipment. Behind them were two large white tanks, branded with the message, *"DANGER CORROSIVE CHEMICALS – "AUTHORISED PERSONNEL ONLY"*

At the end of the warehouse, Blake yanked open another hatch-like door and ushered Sky through while snatching a look behind them; they still had company. Although, their pursuers had slowed down, almost as if they were proceeding with caution.

Blake stepped through the opening and crashed into Sky. She was standing directly in front of him, staring in bewilderment.

"Welcome, guests, to the main laboratory."

The room was packed with glowing monitors, gauges and other scientific equipment.

At the far end of the room was a man in a white space suit. He had his back to them as he slowly ambled around the room, holding a beeping gadget in front of him like a weapon. There was a large control desk to their left, and behind that a glass window that looked onto a hexagonal isolation chamber, where more spacemen were busy taking readings.

They stopped what they were doing and looked up at their visitors.

"What the…?" Blake didn't finish his sentence.

"My God," Sky whispered. "This is a contaminated area."

"What?"

"The doctor is right, Mr. Hudson. You are in a sealed area and you have no protection." The voice was Williamson's, and it was booming out of the paging system, as if he were God himself.

Blake scanned the room for a way out.

"There is no way out, Mr. Hudson. We had to seal off the area."

Glancing behind them, Blake saw that the door they had just come through was now locked, and there was no sign of the guards.

He turned; the door at the opposite side of the room was locked also. However, that didn't deter him from clutching Sky's hand and running forward.

"Mr. Hudson, please," Williamson's voice continued.

At the door, Blake tapped the control panel, but the red light remained constant. He turned to the room once more; Sky was biting her lip while the spacemen had stopped what they were doing and were watching them, as if they were a pair of trapped animals.

That was precisely how they felt. Williamson was right. They were trapped in a contaminated zone, just as he had no doubt planned. There was no doubt that he had tracked and led them here to be exposed, like one of the wretched creatures they had seen in that room.

He pulled Sky to him with a strong arm. So, was this what the toxin was like? Invisible, odourless, tasteless? Did it just sneak up on you and, before you knew it, turned you into some kind of homicidal freak?

"I am concerned for your safety. You could be contaminated," Williamson said.

"Really?" Blake shouted at nowhere, sarcastically.

"Yes."

"As concerned for us as you are for the guinea pigs you have locked up back there?"

"Well, I tend to refer to them as patients, but yes."

"Do you always tie down your patients, Doctor?"

There was a pause. "Yes, I do, especially when they are a danger to themselves."

"You are carrying out experiments on these people," Sky shouted at the cameras she had located in the corners of the room.

"You are mistaken; we are trying to help them. They are infected with the rain. We brought them here for treatment and we are learning. However, we don't have time to discuss this right now. Please, for your own safety, you must leave the laboratory.

"And go where?"

"Return to the room you were just in and enter one of the isolation compartments."

Blake laughed. "Oh yeah, let me think about that for a second – um, fuck you!" he yelled.

"The compartments are state of the art. They can scan your whole anatomy for the toxin. Once we've established how much you have been infected, we can start the treatment."

"Well, you won't be insulted if we stay here and take our chances."

"Don't be foolish, Mr. Hudson. The more time you spend in that room, the more you are being exposed to the toxin and the less chance we will have of treating you. If you want to live, you must enter one of those chambers now, before it's too late."

Blake and Sky looked at each other, and the room fell silent.

40

A395 Road – Eastbound, toward Plymouth.

Matt hadn't been driving on the dual carriageway for long, and it would be at least another hour before he reached Plymouth. That was if they would allow him to make the journey without hindrance, for they were following, watching, as they drifted angrily yet lazily above, spitting and taunting him with the threat of unleashing more chaos on the unsuspecting world once more.

It wasn't raining, but the sheen on the road and the spray in the air told Matt that it had not long finished.

Kick-off was in five minutes.

Matt knew that he wasn't going to make it on time, as much as he had absolutely no idea what he was even going to do when he got there.

I'm hardly going to rock up, nab the first policeman I can find, and say, "Hey, what's up? I'm Matt. You haven't got the foggiest who I am, but I'm pretty sure that in a few minutes you're going to think I'm a nutter, oh, and by the way, did you know that this rain that we're getting soaked by is actually toxic, and we're all going to go fucking loopy soon and start killing each other..."

"Fuck," he said.

If it sounds like a load of crap in your head, imagine what it's going to sound like coming out of it!

But what else can I do? The police don't want to know.

Which reminded him: If Morrison was not interested in the potential apocalypse, then why would any other copper care?

"Get out of my bloody way!" he yelled.

The double-decker bus in front of him was driving irritatingly slow, yet, despite this, it was still managing to spray a perpetual dirty mist at Matt's windscreen, and had been doing so ever since he'd joined the road.

Just overtake him!

He had thought about it, but kept putting it off. Visibility was poor and they were driving up a steep incline; he did not want to find himself short at the summit. Yet, he could not afford the time. He dropped from sixth to fourth gear, gunned the engine, and proceeded to overtake the bus.

However, just as he was entering the shower generated by the vehicle's wheels and drawing level with the driver, he realised that he was no longer gaining, but instead was falling back.

His initial reaction was dread; he thought the car was breaking down. However, a cursory glance at the speedometer told him that his speed was good – 65 MPH.

Then why am I slowing...?

He glanced across; the overweight bus driver grinned back at him.

"What the fuck?"

The bastard's accelerating!

"Are you out of your fucking mind?" he shouted at the

passenger door window, but the bus, full of people, maintained its speed.

"HEY!" Matt protested as they sped, side by side, toward the crest of the hill.

But the driver didn't care. He just stared back with wild eyes and a deranged grin.

Oh my God. He's playing chicken with passengers on board!

Matt pushed on the accelerator, the car growled forward, and, slowly but surely, it started to gain just as both vehicles hurtled over the ridge.

75 MPH.

Matt's heart leapt into his mouth as the other side of the hill came into view.

They were no more than 100 yards ahead – an ocean of red and blue lights twinkled in the gloom of the darkening sky. Taillights blazed and police lights flashed as the traffic, at the foot of the hill, queued, bumper-to-bumper as Paramedics treated casualties laid out on the tarmac and police officers attempted to clear the road of the remains of two vehicles with the help of a tow truck.

There was no way through.

"NOOOO!" Matt screamed, stamping on the brake.

80 yards...

An old man in a rusty Ford Fiesta glanced in his rear view mirror and spotted the two sets of headlamps – one slightly higher than the other – gaining rapidly, and grumbled, "Slow down, you silly idiots."

He switched his hazard lights on.

"What's wrong, dear?" his wife asked.

The old man opened his mouth to speak, but the words didn't come out, for he realised that the headlamps were approaching much faster than he'd originally thought, and thus could only gape in stupefied horror.

50 yards...

Matt's car slid, tyres aquaplaning, toward the back of the Fiesta. He instinctively yanked on the wheel in an effort to avoid the collision. The car fishtailed several times, each action invoking a turn in the opposite direction.

25 yards...

The double-decker's brakes screeched as the world slid into

slow motion – the ambulance men, the couple squabbling over directions, the young woman fiddling with her radio... all turned around to watch the vehicles hurtling towards them.

"Fuck..." was all an officer could gasp, glued to the tarmac in terror.

15 yards...

Matt's car slammed and bounced off the central reservation, flipping like a pinball into a 360 degree spin, where it completed two full revolutions before propelling itself sideways, through the steel barrier and into the opposite lane, where it span one more time before skidding to a halt in the middle of the road.

Matt froze, eyes shut, heart pounding, hyperventilating, with both hands still clinging to the steering wheel as if it were life itself.

5 yards...

The police officer barely had time to shout, "Get off..." as the bus ploughed into the Ford Fiesta, mashing the old couple into the metal of their car and flinging it up and into the bus's windscreen, crushing the driver and squeezing his insides out of his mouth like tomato paste from a tube. It careened forth, shunting cars left and right, like skittles, towards the flashing blue lights of the emergency services. Ambulance crew members, who were still crouched over victims from the previous pile-up, barely had time to look up as a convoy of cars rolled towards and over them, steam-rolling their flesh and bones into the tarmac.

The metal landslide slid forward, smashing into the ambulance and flipping it onto its side, all to the soundtrack of bending metal, smashing glass and screams.

Eventually, the debris slowed the mangled monster's progress and, after bulldozing its way through a total of twenty vehicles, one ambulance and one police car, what was left of it screeched to a stop.

The scraping and crashing had barely finished when Matt heard the sound of another engine. It was getting louder as it rapidly approached.

Oh God, no!

He peeped over his hands to see a tourist bus, lights flashing, horn blaring hurtle towards him on a collision course.

Matt closed his eyes, once more, and prepared himself for the inevitable.

41

"Sir, the rain is continuing South, toward the city of Plymouth," the operator said, looking at the radar in front of him.

Williamson looked up at the giant map and the red dot that indicated the cloud mass' current position.

"It appears that Hudson was right," he said, watching a black and white image of Blake and Sky inside the laboratory on one of the wall monitors.

"About what?" the colonel asked.

"A football match is taking place in Plymouth. There'll be a concentration of thousands inside that stadium. The majority will be infected before the game even starts."

"So?" The colonel asked without turning. He was too busy scanning the various wall monitors for Peter Briem.

Williamson stared at the side of the colonel's head, eyes burning with resentment, but said nothing.

"Ah, there it is; the disdain," the colonel said, without turning, as if he could sense Williamson's glare. "You think that my disregard for human life is typical of such a blunt instrument. But tell me, Doctor, is that because I've become the proverbial monster, or more because you've suddenly developed a conscience?"

"Everything I have done has been for the benefit of the project, of science," Williamson snarled.

"You carry on telling yourself that if that helps you sleep at night. I'd sooner get on with the mission." He finally gave Williamson his eyes, and added casually, "If that's okay with you, of course."

Williamson wished he could slap the smirk off the man's face.

"Sir, Briem is approaching the A1 sector," the operator spoke, as if he was oblivious to the squabbling.

"Where the hell are your men?" Williamson clipped.

"They're approaching the engine room now," the operator replied, tapping his screen and transferring the image to one of the control room's larger wall monitors; it showed five armed men furtively making their way down a corridor.

The first two of the men flanked the door; three and four aimed their weapons at it while number five swiped it open.

"Colonel, did you not hear…" Williamson began.

"…I heard you, Doctor. How else do you expect them to stop him? And even if my men drop their weapons, it doesn't mean that your pet will drop his. At least, if they're armed, they'll have more of a chance of taking him out before he causes any damage."

"Or they'll be the ones initiating a chain reaction that will see us all blown sky high. Have you already forgotten what happened in Iceland? That's how this all started."

"My men are professionals. They know what they're doing. I can guarantee your safety."

"Well, be offended when I say that your guarantee means nothing to me. My work has already suffered because of the stupidity of others; I'd rather not lose my life to the same."

"Actually, now that you mention it, Doctor… Weren't you responsible for Iceland project, also?"

Williamson threw the colonel a look of utter contempt, but the colonel was feigning interest in the various wall displays. "There's that look of disdain again," he said. "Anyway, while we're discussing pets, what are you planning do with your guests?" he asked, nodding at the image of Blake and Sky.

"What I do with them is none of your concern." He pointed at the image of Peter skulking amongst giant tanks. "That man is the only thing you should worry about, along with the fact that those tanks are loaded with fuel. If you manage not to destabilise the core of the T100, I'd say they stand a pretty good chance of igniting one of them. The blast would tear a hole in this ship large enough to sink it before you even get the chance to haul your bulk out of here!"

The smirk on the colonel's face was replaced with a scowl.

Then he spoke into his headset.

Unlike the rest of the ship, the engine room was well lit and the noise level was uncomfortable. Although, most of the cacophony was generated by the crunch, grind and whooshing sounds of the engines, which were situated at the back of the ship. The T, for Turbine, 100 was actually relatively quiet, considering the machine's immense power-generating abilities.

Peter Briem moved cautiously through the giant fuel mountains, swapping the gun between hands.

He was not feeling well.

His head hurt, he was hot, his lips were parched, and he was leaking sweat from all over his body. He needed fresh air, and he needed to carve the bugs from his body and stop them crawling under his skin. They were everywhere, burrowing into the roots of his hair, scuttling through his veins, and tickling his mind.

Yet, he felt energised; eager to wreak havoc, and this tugged a mischievous smile from his lips as he clutched the gun and moved forward.

Twenty feet behind him, the colonel's men had made visual contact and were cautiously following the target's movements. Their orders were to disable and apprehend. The use of guns of any kind had been strictly prohibited.

The colonel controlled the advance by speaking through the earpiece inside the team leader's ear while monitoring their progress through images beamed back by micro cameras mounted on the men's helmets.

Peter arrived at the clearing in the heart of the engine room. A bank of six-foot-high cabinets formed a square, inside of which were four desks with computer consoles. Peter was about to step forward toward them, but stopped when he realised something was off.

There was nobody there. This room was rarely unmanned. Yet, now, the area was completely deserted.

Why?

He thought about this while tapping the side of his head with the gun. He was finding it hard to think straight and he could feel a pressure growing between his temples. He scanned the area around him. The corridors between the tanks, in front and behind, were deserted. He was alone.

Or am I?

Another wipe from the back of his sleeve dried up the sweat that was dripping off his nose.

He smiled.

From the control room, the colonel watched a wobbly image of the engine room as his men advanced.

"He is heading straight for the engine room computers. What do you think he's up to?" the colonel asked.

"I have no idea, other than the fact that he knows how volatile it is in there. He's most likely hoping that you'll send your men in after him. And you've played straight into his hands."

"Are you saying that he actually wants us to..."

"Open fire, yes. This is exactly what I've been telling you. He has nothing to lose. He's seen the effects of the toxin first hand. He knows he's infected, and he's probably deduced that the amount he was exposed to is incurable. He knows he's dying. In fact, by my reckoning, he should be dead already. Presently, he's experiencing the symptoms. Eventually, it will clog his arteries and cut off his blood supply. If he can kill all those responsible before that happens, then so be it."

"You mean he has a death wish."

"Kill or be killed – those are pretty much the symptoms."

"And yet, you were spouting all of that rubbish about suppressing gun fire and apprehending him alive."

"But that's exactly it. Don't you get it?" Williamson hissed. "He wants you to open fire on him and he'll make sure you hit one of those tanks in the process. He has no other reason to enter the engine room, other than to lure your men there. That's why you must order them to stand down and retreat immediately."

"What? And leave him to go on the rampage?"

"I've already explained what will happen. You just need to give it time."

"How long?"

The operator interrupted. "Sir. We've lost visual."

"What?"

A wavy image from the team leader's helmet showed that the men were on the move.

"It looks like they've lost him, too. It's imperative that we keep him in our sights. We must find him," Williamson insisted.

The operator tapped on his keyboard, and an album of images flickered on the main wall screen, but none appeared to reveal Peter's location. The engine room appeared to be empty, but for the colonel's men who could be seen skulking in between the fuel tanks.

Peter was gone.

42

Sky looked up at the speaker. It had been over five minutes now, and Williamson had said nothing. The silence was unnerving.

"What do you think he's up to?" she asked in a subdued tone, averting her face from the gaze of the prying camera.

"I don't know, but whatever it is, it won't be good. We've got to find a way out of here," Blake replied in the same hushed tone.

He looked around the room; the spacemen had grown tired with their visitors, and had returned to their jobs once more. To Blake, their indifference was surreal, but he didn't care; he had a mission of his own right now, and that was to get both him and Sky off this ship.

Unfolding her arms from him, he said, "Okay, time to go."

"Where?" she asked.

"I don't know," he said distractedly, scanning the room for an exit.

"What about the toxin?"

"What about it?"

"Well…" Sky didn't finish the sentence.

He looked at her. She was biting her lip. He softened his stance, "We don't even know if we're infected. For all we know, he could have lied in order to convince us to join the other freaks back there," he said reassuringly. "How are you feeling?"

She took a few moments, as if checking herself. "I think I'm okay. How about you?"

"Never felt better," he smiled. "Come on, I want to get back for that meal we never had."

He looked across at the space men who were surveying the area on the opposite side of the room. His eyes roamed over a network of benches, scientific paraphernalia and electronic gauges, but there was nothing of use.

Then he saw it, standing on the floor nearby – a large stainless steel dustbin.

He took Sky's hand and pulled her away from the door, before picking up the dustbin and trying it for weight; it was perfect. Then, with both hands and with a minute amount of exertion in his voice, he said, "Remember when we were running down that corridor and I stopped to kick that door panel in?"

She looked at him, perplexed.

He nodded at the red glow of the wall panel. "Remember how I thought that, by kicking the panel, I would engage the lock permanently, but instead I just broke the mechanism?"

His locked eyes with her and he grinned. "Watch yourself," he said, and then swung the bin at the panel with all of his strength.

The blow was so powerful that it sheered the control panel clean off the wall. The cavity spat sparks and puffed out a plume of acrid smoke. The spacemen stopped what they were doing, attracted by the fracas, and turned to the intruders.

"Hey!" one of them yelled, pointing, and then lumbered forward to intercept.

Meanwhile, Blake launched his full weight against the door; it gave easily, swinging open and slamming against the wall of the outer corridor. An alarm shrilled angrily. *"Attention, containment in main laboratory has been breached due to locking mechanism malfunction."*

The spacemen skidded to a halt.

Back in the control room, the colonel barked, "What the hell is that?"

"They've broken out of the laboratory door," Williamson explained. His face was impassive but, for the first time, the colonel thought he saw a flicker of concern in the man's eyes.

"I guess it's another mess I'm going to have deal with. I'll have my men pick them up," the colonel said dismissively.

"You've missed the point. They've breached a sealed area. If the toxin is airborne, it could infect the whole ship!"

"What do you mean, *if* – you mean you don't even know yet?"

"What do you think we're doing in there? They're trying to take readings now."

"I thought the computer was supposed to be able to monitor all of that."

"It does. But only in designated spaces, where the investment was made to build sensors into the walls and ceiling."

"Jesus Christ!" Now it was the colonel's turn to look worried. "You must be able to contain it."

"Of course we can. Providing no other locks are breached," Williamson snapped.

The colonel shook his head incredulously. "And you're the man who supposedly thinks of everything, huh? Everything but fucking tamper-proof doors!"

"Bring up a map of the ship," Williamson barked at the operator.

The operator tapped keys; instantly, a digital map of the ship appeared on the main screen.

"Superimpose possible contamination areas."

More keys clicked and then a red glow coloured in various sectors of the map.

Williamson sighed. "Sectors B and C could be exposed."

"What the hell does that mean in English?" the colonel asked, frustrated by all the computer imagery that meant absolutely nothing to him.

"It means that there are only another three more doors separating us from the toxin. If it is airborne, and if Hudson continues breaching doors between them and us, we'll be eating the toxin for supper."

"Another scenario you didn't take into consideration, Doctor?"

Williamson took in a deep breath, and spoke calmly, "Of course I did. All of the doors on this ship have been designed to create individual isolation chambers to contain flooding or contamination. What I couldn't predict was that we would have a pair of hooligans running amok, vandalising all of the door locks."

"I see. And whose fault is that?" the colonel asked as he spoke into his headset.

The man's patronising tone was enough for Williamson to want to snatch his gun from its holster and put a bullet in his head, but he resisted the urge because, truth be told, he needed the man, now more than ever.

"This is the colonel; we have visual on two intruders, one male, one female, in section B, heading aft, towards section A. Proceed to intercept. Rules of engagement are shoot to kill. I repeat, shoot to kill!"

43

Blake and Sky escaped from the laboratory only to find themselves inside yet another corridor within the labyrinth of the tanker. They stepped through another door that led to a junction.

"Where to?" Blake asked.

"What? You're asking me?" Sky panicked.

"Just thought I'd get a second opinion."

Blake scanned the area and found exactly what he was looking for: a handy you-are-here-type map that told him to continue straight for *SECTOR C and all other sectors*, left for *MAIN CORRIDOR, SECTOR A* and *EXIT*, or right for *SECTOR B2*.

"Here we go," he said brightly. "Left for main corridor and exit." They turned, but the door was glowing disappointingly red. "Can you take care of it this time?"

Sky just rolled her eyes.

Before long, the panel's cavity was choking sparks and they were running, hand in hand, down the main corridor.

"They are progressing down the main corridor," the operator announced from the control room.

"How long until your men intercept them?" Williamson asked.

"Don't concern yourself. They'll be stopped before they get to the elevator," said the colonel.

"Sir, something is happening," the operator said.

"What's wrong?"

"I'm losing visual in Sector A."

"What's happening?" the colonel asked.

"The cameras are just blanking out."

The colonel paused and then looked at Williamson – their exchange was telepathic.

"It's him! Bastard!" the colonel glowered.

Williamson, on the other hand, although he didn't realise immediately, was actually smiling.

"You think this is funny, do you, Doctor?"

"No, but you have to admit, it is impressive. He's managed to elude five of your men and make his way towards the exit."

The colonel scoffed. "There's no way out. Did you revoke the card he was using?"

"Yes, Sir."

"Then, how the hell is he still managing to make progress?"

"He must have managed to acquire other cards, Sir."

"Scan card usage in those sectors!"

"Already on it."

"How far, exactly, does he expect to get?" the colonel muttered.

"I would have thought that was obvious. He wants to get off the ship," Williamson said casually.

"And go where?"

"Home."

The admiration was clear in Williamson's voice, and it irked the colonel. Even now, the man was still thinking about his shitty project, rather than focussing on containment. That fell to him, as always, and he was ready. The child was no match for him.

"We'll be waiting for him," he said seriously. "Marcus, suspect is heading for the elevator at Section A. I want you to rendezvous there with Alpha Team. I want him stopped. I want him dead. Do you understand?"

"You won't get there in time," Williamson said challengingly.

The colonel glared at him and then barked at the operator,

"Seal that elevator!"

"It won't help," Williamson interjected.

"Do as I say!"

"It won't help," he repeated. "He has a key card with level 4 access. He's able to override any command we give the computer from here."

"What are you talking about?"

"Can't you see? He's been playing us this whole time. We've been revoking access to cards we believed he'd use in those sectors, but all along, he's actually been using a card that none of us had the foresight to consider. He's using Harket's card. His passing hasn't been fully processed. His clearance is still active."

"Do it anyway!" the colonel ordered.

The operator complied.

The colonel sneered. "So much for your safety protocols. All you've managed to do is lose control of your own ship."

"I think you'll find that this was a security feature requested by your own security team. They wanted the human ability to override commands issued by the computer."

"God damn it!" the colonel raged, slamming his hand against the nearby desks. "Check that fucking card! Revoke those rights now!"

The operator was about to respond, but instead pressed his headset to his ear. "I'm picking up gunfire in Sector A, Sir."

"He's reached the elevator," Williamson whispered, ominously.

No sooner had he uttered the words than the operator agreed, "Elevator is on the move, Sir."

The colonel spoke into his headset. "Alpha Team, report."

Silence.

"Alpha Team, sit rep, now!"

More silence.

Then, the radio burst to life. "Sir, this is Marcus. Haven't been able to get through to Alpha Team, Sir. Not since they engaged target."

The colonel frowned. "What the…"

"Your men are dead, colonel," Williamson said with icy casualness.

"That's impossible; he's just a lab rat, for fuck's sake!"

"Yet, he's managed to overpower them."

"Scan the area!"

"They're dead," Williamson repeated.

"On screen, now!"

"I'm sorry, Sir. I can't."

The colonel was actually trembling with rage now. "Do as I say or…"

"The cameras are out in that sector, Sir, I'm sorry."

Williamson could not have been more delighted. Fuelled by the toxin, Peter was able to evade capture by cunning or perhaps even brute force.

The radio crackled to life again. "Sir? Sir, this is Marcus."

"Marcus, situation report."

"They're down. All five of them, Sir. They're all dead." The man's voice faltered for a second, and then he added, "He butchered them."

In tandem, they all looked up at the main screen that was now projecting the wobbly image of the helmet cams as they panned across the bloody body parts of their fallen comrades who, true to the soldier's words, had been hacked to pieces with a fire axe, and strewn up and down the corridor.

The colonel could only watch in stunned silence until he finally found his tongue, and he uttered, "How in God's name is that possible?"

"I told you, it's the toxin." Williamson said.

"They did manage to squeeze off some rounds, though," Marcus' voice sombrely continued.

"And they probably hit him, but Peter is infected with the toxin. Right now, he's on a high. He could probably sustain several gunshot wounds and not even notice.

"Are you reciting this from your medical journal?" the colonel asked, disgusted.

"As a matter of fact, I am."

"Marcus, get up on deck and use whatever force you deem necessary to bring that fucker down!"

"Yes, Sir," came the scratchy reply. "Oh, Sir?"

"What is it?"

"What about the other two? They're heading this way."

"Don't worry about them." The colonel pulled out his gun. "I'm going to take care of them, personally.

Williamson looked at one of the wall monitors and watched how Blake and Sky were literally running towards their death.

44

The sound of squealing tyres came and went, and it took Matt Allen a long time before he dared look up and check whether he was still alive. When he did, he saw that the bus had screeched and swerved to a halt, missing the car by inches.

Now, as thunder boomed overhead and a gale buffeted his vehicle, he pulled on the door handle and stepped out.

The wind tugged at his clothes like a demanding reporter, eager to broadcast the carnage in the opposite lane, and brought with it the acrid smell of fuel, the groans of the injured, and the anguished wailing of those coming round to find their loved ones dead in the seat next to them.

Matt gaped at the devastation as he stumbled away from his car, struggling to process exactly what he had just survived versus the hellish nightmare he now found himself standing in the centre of.

Meanwhile, a group of bus passengers left the bus, with all of the eagerness of disaster tourists, and made their way towards the destruction. They chatted and gasped as they approached the central reservation, craning necks and averting gazes, all while the grumble of thunder and the strobe of lighting added an even more chilling dimension to the horrifying spectacle.

Then Matt noticed it – the black smoke, billowing out of one of the cars. It started as a small smouldering mass and rapidly turned into a bonfire, and he couldn't work out if the high-pitched squeal that accompanied it was the sound of melting tyres or that of a child being roasted in the blaze.

More people congregated by the central reservation, almost shunting and pushing each other in order to get a better view from which to film and photograph the event on their mobile devices. Then, before he even knew it, Matt was shouting at the top of his voice, "Get away from there!" he yelled. "Get away!"

But, it was too late.

A high-pitched sighing sound filled the air, shortly followed by a massive explosion that catapulted one of the cars into the air like a rocket, it crashed back down, seconds later, onto another car.

Then, there was more screaming, this time from the newly formed crowd of spectators; a woman wailed in agony as she clutched a jagged piece of metal lodged into her right eye. As blood dribbled down her face, creating a growing inky stain on her overstretched T-shirt, someone tried to help her; she slapped them away and turned to run, but tripped and fell, face-forward onto the tarmac.

Death was instant, although the body continued to twitch supernaturally.

More lightning flashed as Matt instinctively threw his hands to his mouth, both to stop the bile from erupting and to suppress the scream.

He staggered back to his car, where another group of onlookers had gathered at the much safer viewpoint. Then he heard her talking on her mobile phone – the girl couldn't have been more than eighteen years of age

"Yeah, it's great!" she said excitedly. "I was like, in the coach, thinking the trip was really borin' and then, well, I mean, I just thought some idiot had parked his car in the middle of the road and done a runner. I didn't even notice what had happened on the other side, but then I heard some people talkin' behind me, so turned my head and, OMG! No word of lie, I nearly threw up over the window. It's like something out of a film. Total and utter carnage! There are people crying, screaming, oh, and some woman just got a piece of metal stuck in her eye. It's bloody gross. I'm tellin' ya'. You haven't seen anything like it. Yeah, I've already filmed some; I'm gonna' see if I can get some money from the video, or upload it to YouTube; you know, some bloke got... HEY!"

She protested when Matt snatched the phone from her hand.

"Oi, you! That's my phone!" she whined.

Matt smacked her with an icy glare and angry clenched teeth. The girl fell silent and instantly backed away.

Then, as Matt's stance softened, she added, "It ain't mine, it's my boyfriend's, and he won't be happy…."

The girl's babbling faded into nothing as Matt walked away from the crackling blaze, the chattering, the screaming and the sobbing, to the side of the road.

He put the phone to his ear and heard the stranger at the other end of the call. Whoever it was was tucked up at home, probably sprawled out on the sofa, drinking tea as her friend recounted the grizzly details of the shattering of other people's lives. He pressed disconnect. His mind was numb. He could not digest any of the hideousness that had happened here. None of it made any sense. None of it was possible.

All of it was just a horrible dream, from which he would soon wake to discover that this day had not even happened. His friend had not been abducted; he had not spent hours at the police station being questioned by condescending, unhelpful police officers, and thousands of people were not gathered in a stadium where they were going to be exposed to some pathogen that was going to turn them into God knew what.

But it had all happened, and was happening. The police did refuse to help him and he was on his own. Morrison had been unequivocal; there was nothing they could do. *"Unless something happens, like a bomb scare…"* Morrison's words suddenly flashed into his mind.

That was the answer! Morrison had supplied him with the solution, but he had been too dumb to see it.

Of course!

He dialled 999.

"999 Emergency, which service?"

"Police, please." He was talking, but he didn't recognise himself. It was as if he was possessed. Matt Allen, the person he had lived with for all of these years, was gone, he busy recovering somewhere. He had nearly died in a car crash and had just witnessed some horrifying things. He needed some time to recover from that, but this guy, he was on a mission, and he wasn't going to stop until he had seen it through.

"Police, what's your emergency?"

Silence.

"Hello? Caller? Are you there?"

"Yes, I would like to report a bomb, please."

"I'm sorry, Sir. Did you say bomb?"

"Yes, I said that I would like to report a bomb!"

45

The wind tore at Peter's hair the moment the elevator doors slid open.

He stood for a few seconds, training the gun on the area in front of him, but there was nobody there. They were going to let him go home after all.

He relaxed, slightly, but remained wary.

Then he looked down and grimaced; there was already a miniature pool of blood at his feet, although most of it had soddened his clothing. He had sustained two gunshot wounds – one to his shoulder and the other to his stomach – but he didn't feel pain, and, although he felt light-headed from the loss of blood, he was still buzzing.

He could still make it.

He stepped out of the elevator, climbed through the porthole, and squinted into the floodlights. It was dark outside, but the star-spangled sky was nonetheless a welcome sight. He sucked in the fresh ocean air and felt a small boost. If only he could stop the drum pounding in his head, and the insects from scratching his veins.

He stepped behind a giant weatherworn pulley, and then cautiously peeked out.

Up ahead, he could clearly see the two well-lit helipads, although only one of the black helicopters was anchored there.

Beyond it, he could just about make out the group of men standing outside the entrance to the F Sector elevator.

He smiled to himself, and then stepped out from his hiding place, taking a few seconds to steady himself by clasping onto the side of the metal pulley, for the ship's sway was compounding his dizziness. He could feel the energy ebb as he lost more blood, and thus the associated boost he had been receiving from the toxin, but he could make it. He had to make it home, back to his family, and back to the farm where he'd been raised, and where he had made so many happy memories.

He thought about his mother, and the sacrifices she had made to provide him with the tuition that had eventually led him to winning this role and its lucrative salary.

However, now it was time to go home, and nothing and nobody was going to stop him.

46

Gun in hand, the colonel left the control room.

He was about to board the waiting cart, but stopped when he noticed something glistening on the floor in front of him. He paused to take a closer look; it was blood, and the trail led from the main corridor, past the control room and to the doors of the elevator. He touched the sticky substance with his finger, as if disbelieving what his eyes were already telling him.

It's his blood!

He tapped his ear and spoke, "Marcus!" There was a pause. "Marcus, here."

"Do you have anybody posted at F Sector elevator?"

"No, Sir. We were told, assumed that he'd be…"

"Forget what you were fucking told! He's played all of us. Get some men over there now! The bastard sneaked right by us and used the lift right under our fucking noses!"

"Yes, Sir!"

Cheeks flushed, body trembling, the colonel was so angry that he could feel a vein throbbing in his neck. Such was his rage, he didn't even bother boarding the cart, and instead, he ran forward. He had been made a fool of long enough. Now, somebody was going to pay. Somebody was going to pay very dearly.

Above him, the sign read *MAIN CORRIDOR LEADING TO A (& ALL OTHER SECTORS)*.

That was where he would find Blake and Sky.

47

Peter fought the queasiness as he scurried towards the helipads, and he was almost there when he heard shouting up ahead. He looked up to see the group of guards, previously gathered around the lift shaft, making their way towards him. Their calling had conveniently caught the attention of the two men – one in greasy blue overalls, the other in a pilot's uniform – who were standing around the helicopter.

Before either of them could follow the gaze of the approaching guards, the mechanic took a bullet to the back of the head and collapsed forward. The pilot spun around, but instantly held his hands up.

"Get in!" Peter ordered, motioning the gun to the helicopter. The startled man hesitated until Peter pointed the gun at his head and yelled, "NOW!"

The man complied, scrambled inside, and clicked himself into the pilot's seat while Peter slowly followed him, steadying himself against the doorframe as he went.

There was more shouting from the pursuers, someone ordering him to stop while simultaneously opening fire. Bullets rang and danced off the helicopter's shell, causing the pilot to duck impulsively.

"Jesus Christ!" the man cried.

"Get us out of here," Peter hissed, "or you'll be seeing him sooner than you think." He pressed the gun to the man's temple. "NOW! NOW! NOW!" he screamed.

The terrified pilot flicked various switches in quick succession. Meanwhile, like the lights on a car with a flat battery, Peter's vision dimmed. He feebly attempted to shake the grogginess away, but it remained. The engine turned and the blades slowly began to spin as a catatonic Peter shifted to the side of the open doorway and opened fire.

One of the bullets hit the first guard squarely in the chest, the impact propelling him backward. The action prompted his comrades to scatter and take cover behind nearby pipes, before regrouping and returning fire, showering the helicopter with miniature meteorites.

"GET US OUT OF HERE!" Peter ordered once more.

"But…" the pilot stuttered.

"…NOW!" Peter yelled through his haze, swinging the gun somewhere in the direction of the pilot's head.

The speed of the beating blades increased until the loud whir became a chopping sound, and the craft tentatively lifted from the deck. Another shower of bullets pierced the interior of the craft. One of them sliced through Peter's arm, and another burned its way into his leg, but he felt nothing. His senses weakened, his energy depleted. His body was slowly shutting down.

Then, the helicopter began to sway. To Peter, it felt as if he was back in his mother's arms and she was gently stroking his hair, rocking him to sleep, and caring for him in the same way she always had.

"I'm coming home, Mama," he murmured. "I'm coming home."

The men watched as the whirling machine hovered thirty feet above them, pulling and tugging at the steal safety harness that was still attached to its feet, straining to get away. The mounting tension caused the helicopter to swing from side to side, the engine growling and whining like a rabid dog as it struggled to break free. It whined, spluttered, and puffed smoke from the over-revved engine that the pilot involuntarily continued to gun as he lay slumped over the controls with a bullet in his lungs.

Then, there was a high-pitched twanging sound as the cable began to fray, and this was shortly followed by a loud bang as the exhausted engine cut out, expelling dark smoke as if it were its dying breath.

The guards ran for cover while, slowly, as if real life had switched to slow motion, the flying machine dropped out of the sky and plummeted towards the ocean until the cable yanked it back in one pendulum motion, crashing it against the side of the ship in a gigantic fireball, burning a hole the size of a small car.

The damage was above the waterline, yet the ship continued to take in large gulps of seawater as it dipped in and out of the Atlantic basin. The water did little to suppress the fire that had been ignited as a result of the crash that had ruptured the dual tank containing both the fuel to power the ship and the oil to disguise it.

While the crude oil could not be used to feed the turbine that drove the ship's engines, it could be used to satisfy any potential inspection by curious Coast Guards officials. This had all been part of Williamson's plan – to cruise international waters, testing and reproducing an array of experimental drugs while simultaneously circumnavigating any jurisdictional hurdles.

However, both the unrefined oil and the highly combustible fuel were now flowing and mixing freely into a deadly cocktail that was rapidly metamorphosing into a noxious lava that ebbed and flowed with the motion of the ship, spreading to various sectors... including the engine room.

"What was that?" Sky asked as she steadied herself from the quake.

"I don't know," Blake replied, somewhat perturbed. "It felt and sounded like an explosion."

"Should we be worried?"

"I would think so. Explosions are rarely good," he said, sardonically, "We should probably increase our rate of escape."

The doors in the main corridor had been closed, dividing it into two compartments. They were at its centre, where the door panel glowed red. They needed to get beyond it, back to the elevator, and out of there.

"Shit!" Blake swore, "It's locked."

"Well, just kick it in." Sky said casually.

Blake had already thought of that, but he had his doubts. Unlike all of the other doors, the panel on this one was displaying a warning message: *Containment Protocol. Biometric Access Only.*

Yet, he was still going to give it a try. "Okay, stand back," he said. He sized up the panel, and then kicked it. Nothing on the panel changed, but he yelped, 'Oh Shit!' as fracture pains shot up his ankle.

Sky looked at him, and then promptly rolled her eyes.

"Oh, why don't you give a try?" he said through gritted teeth.

"Who's the man here? Actually, don't answer that."

"Thank you," he said with a grimace as he summoned up the will to launch another assault on the door. "There are only so many of these you can kick in on any one day."

"Come on!"

He continued his attack until, eventually, the brutalised panel fell off with the usual sparks of protestation. He looked at her, pulled a smug expression, and tugged at the handle, but the door did not budge.

His smile faded. "What's going on?"

"Is it still locked?"

Using his foot as leverage, he tried again, "It certainly feels like it," he said through clenched teeth.

"I don't understand."

"Nor do I," he said, examining the burnt-out cavity.

Then, he checked the seals around the four edges of the door in an effort to establish what exactly was keeping it so tightly shut. He scanned it from top to bottom until he reached the glass panel, where he was horrified to find a face staring back at him from the other side.

"Fuck!" he shouted, jerking back and ducking down, pulling Sky with him.

There was a muffled explosion, then another, and then another.

"What's going on?" she cried.

"I think he's fucking shooting at us!" Blake uttered in disbelief.

"What?"

"Get away from the door!" he yelled, pushing her sideways as bullets punctured the doorframe, blasting debris into the air in front of them.

"He's trying to kill us!" she shouted over the blasts.

"Come on, we've got to go, now!"

In unison, they sprang up from their squatting positions and ran forward; back up the corridor from whence they'd come.

Seconds later, they heard the door's glass panel explode, shortly followed by the sound of bullets ricocheting off the walls behind them.

"Where to? Where to?" Sky asked frantically.

"The same way we came. There's nowhere else to go!"

The few minutes it took to reach the junction felt like hours. They ran past the laboratory, which had now been resealed, in the opposite direction, until they reached another door. The light was green.

"It's open!" Blake said, relieved that they wouldn't have to waste time kicking another door in. However, the relief was short-lived, for nothing could have prepared them for what they saw next.

The wall of heat slapped them as soon as they opened the door, forcing them to jolt back, grimacing and choking on the cloud of noxious fumes that instantly burned the backs of their throats.

"What the...." Blake couldn't finish his words; the scene in front of them was surreal.

A steady flow of what appeared to be burning black water was flowing down the corridor. The multi-coloured flames, like leaves on a stream, glided on the surface, licking at walls and clinging to doors. Neither had seen anything like it, outside of a disaster movie.

Sky's eyes filled with tears, both from the smoke and from the hopeless sight before her.

"My God, Blake. What are we going to do?"

"I don't know," he said, masking the fear in his voice, "But it looks like we won't be going this way."

From the control room, Williamson watched the scenes unfold with horror.

"What does that imbecile think he is doing?" he snarled as he witnessed the colonel shoot out the glass of the main corridor door, breaching the contained area.

If the toxin was airborne, nothing could stop it from reaching the control room now.

However, that was the least of his worries.

"Sir, the burning oil is running the length of corridor A, and through B1 and B2."

"But that's the whole width of the ship."

"We also have a fire in the storage area in one of those sectors," the operator added, seemingly immune to their ordeal.

"Why hasn't the fire system kicked in?" Williamson demanded, staring at the monitors.

"They work on a snuff system, Sir."

The snuff system worked by sealing the fire in a contained area and then depriving it of oxygen – crucial when considering that a good proportion of their cargo was fuel and oil, not easily extinguished with water.

"Yes, I know how it works," Williamson snapped. "Why has it not triggered?"

"We can't seal off the area, Sir. The explosion breached the hull. There are also a series of doors that we're no longer able to pressurise," the operator continued, referring to the various breaches caused by Blake and the colonel.

"Are we taking on water?"

"Some."

"Some? What in God's name does that mean? Are we or aren't we?"

The operator tapped on his keyboard; a map of the ship appeared on the wall monitor. "The amount we are taking on can be contained by sealing off," he nodded at the screen, "all functioning junctions between B and C sectors."

"Do it," Williamson ordered, involuntarily clutching the operator's chair.

In that moment, a red ceiling light flashed and an alarm sounded.

"Warning – The temperature in the main engine room exceeds recommended operating levels. Please correct this condition immediately."

"Oh no," the operator said, flicking switches and working the keyboard in front of him. "No, no, no… wait a minute," he said with dreadful realisation.

"What?"

The young man didn't answer. He keyed in commands, checked the information yielded, and then re-keyed the interrogation command once more.

"What's happening?" Williamson asked anxiously.

"The fire in Sector A," the operator began, checking more information on his computer. "It neighbours the engine room, and it's pushing up the temperature inside."

"What?"

"Also the flow of oil… Look!"

He tapped his keyboard. The main wall image changed to show a black and white picture of the engine room.

There was no mistaking the tide of dancing fire that was sluicing into the room and engulfing the metal stands of the fuel tanks. If the scene hadn't been so tragic, it would have been beautiful, but Williamson was not scared; he was petrified.

Blake pushed the door shut and they both retraced their steps once more; they had no choice but to go through the laboratory, but the door appeared closed and locked once more. It was as they were trying to pry the thing open that they heard footsteps; the colonel was running towards them.

They clawed at the door, but it wouldn't yield.

The colonel took aim…

Blake frantically looked for somewhere else to run, but Sky beat him to it, "In here, Blake! In here!" she shouted, pointing to an opposite doorway. She raced inside.

Blake was about to follow when a hail of bullets bounced off the doorframe and wall. Blake clutched his arm and crashed to the floor.

"Blake!" Sky screamed. She ran to him and, grabbed his other arm and dragged him to the far side of the room, where she knelt next to him, "Oh my God, Blake, you've been hit!"

"Are you stating the obvious again?" he asked with a grimace.

She battled tears, "Blake."

"I'm okay. Honestly, I feel – ahhh!" he wailed as she prodded his wound.

She hastily unbuttoned his shirt…

"Um, not sure we have time for that," he said, lifting an eyebrow while grimacing some more.

Yet, the closer inspection revealed that it was just a flesh wound. "Thank God," she breathed with an immense sigh of relief, before a knot of emotion suddenly formed in her throat, "Blake," she whimpered, "I love you."

He looked at her, curiously, and then, with a big smile, added, "Wow, you really do pick your moments, don't you?"

Blake's smile vanished the moment the colonel appeared at the door with the gun in his hand and a maniacal grin on his face.

48

Chief Superintendent Paul Connor, immaculate in his dark blue uniform, stood on the balcony of the control room and was startled by the boom of thunder overhead.

Why they didn't just call off this match is beyond me. Hopefully, the pitch will get waterlogged.

He did not like football, and with all these riots, he could do without redirecting precious resources here to mollycoddle a bunch of lager-swilling troublemakers.

"Sir?" An officer called from inside the control room behind him.

"Yes. What is it?" he asked without turning.

"Five more minutes until kick-off, Sir."

"Very well. How are the turnstiles looking?"

"Good, Sir. Most of them are inside."

Paul nodded, but said nothing. Instead, he surveyed the sea of multi-coloured bodies.

The football stadium was almost full, which meant that there were nearly fifteen thousand spectators out there, all eagerly anticipating the arrival of their favourite team with chants and whistles that echoed around the structure as random faces were beamed onto giant video screens.

"Sir…"

"What is it now, Constable?"

"I think you should see this."

Paul lingered, finishing his train of thought. Nothing Paul Connor ever did was in haste; everything was thoroughly thought out and meticulously planned.

Eventually, he turned and walked back into the control room. It was a small room with a balcony overlooking the VIP stand. It was packed with an array of monitors, computers, and communication equipment.

"Yes?"

The young constable handed Paul a slip of paper. "We've received another one, Sir."

Paul's eyebrows furrowed, and then he said, "Another bloody bomb scare. Have these people nothing better to do?"

The constable shrugged, but the question was rhetorical.

A minute or so went by before Paul spoke. "How long now?"

"About two more minutes, Sir," the young officer replied as the chanting outside grew louder.

Paul glanced at the balcony as a gust of wind blew in, tugging at the paper in his hand. Lightning flashed. Thunder responded and then rolled away.

"Alert all officers to report anything suspicious. Oh, and tell them to be discreet."

"Yes, Sir."

A cordless phone rang. It was a direct line. Used exclusively for communication between commanding officers. Paul calmly picked up the handset and pressed connect. "Chief Superintendent Paul Connor."

Pause

"Yes, Sir. I have the communication in my hand right now."

Pause

"Yes, Sir, it's unconfirmed."

Pause.

"Yes, it may well be another hoax. No, it wouldn't be the first time."

Pause.

"Yes, Sir, thank you, Sir. I will keep you informed. Goodbye."

He disconnected and became pensive while, unconsciously, tapping the phone to his thumb as the officer looked on.

"Call administration and tell them that the game is halted until further notice. Then notify all officers. I want the stadium searched." He pointed at the balcony, "And I don't want any of that lot knowing, is that clear?"

"Yes, Sir, but, Sir, what should we tell them?"

"Tell administration the truth, but not a bloody word gets out! Make that clear."

"Yes, Sir."

"And get Garrison and Parker up here right now!"

The officer, and his colleague sitting opposite him, busied themselves on the telephone and radio respectively as Paul stepped out onto the balcony once more. The gale was growing stronger, and it blasted him with the scent of rain as if irritated by his decision. As low-hanging black clouds drifted closer, the masses started chanting, *Why are we waiting? Why are we waiting? Why are we waiting?...*

However, Paul was not hearing them. He was deep in thought, considering his next move.

Cancel the game and incur the wrath of thousands, or play it safe, with all the logistical conundrums that would entail, not to mention the skirmishes, if not worse, that would ensue as a result.

Think, Paul!

What if there is a bomb? What if it's hidden somewhere in here, in the stadium, maybe even in the control room behind you? These could be your very last seconds on this Earth. If something happens and you knew about it...

..."Ladies and gentlemen. We are very sorry to have to inform you that, due to technical difficulties, the match is going to be delayed. Please bear with us. We'll be sure to make further announcements as soon as we know more."

The giant screens reinforced the announcement by beaming the message, *MATCH POSTPONED*, which invoked a roar of angry protest that swept around the stadium like a Mexican Wave before reaching Paul and punching him in the face.

"Sir?"

"Yes?" Paul answered irritably; he was trying to think.

"Administration wants to know how long the delay will be."

"As long as I bloody well deem necessary!" he retorted. "Christ, these people have no idea."

You have to make a decision.

He turned and shouted, "Where the hell are…" and stopped in mid-sentence as the door opened and two of his men walked in.

"At last," he said.

The sergeants, two of his most trusted advisors, joined Paul on the balcony.

"Sir?"

He handed the sheet of paper over to one of them, who read it and then passed it on.

"No one claiming responsibility, Sir?" asked Parker, the elder of the two.

"No."

"Hoax?" Garrison asked.

"Possibly. But can we take the risk?"

"Evacuating everyone would be a logistical nightmare, Sir. Not to mention the backlash," Parker shouted above the roar of the impatient crowd.

All men paused for thought.

"What if we told them?" Garrison asked.

"Surely, that's not an option," said Parker.

"It's the only way we're going to get them out of here without reprisal," Garrison continued.

"As a stampede," Parker retorted.

They both waited for Paul to comment, but he was still busy trying to figure out a solution. Then he said, "I don't think evacuation is an option. We don't even know if the bomb exists. I say, step up the search and then decide."

"Sir, there's no way we have enough manpower to cover this place," Parker lamented.

"We'd have to decrease the police presence we imposed after the riots," Garrison said.

"I think it's a case of needs must," Paul said. "Make the call, Garrison."

"Yes, Sir."

Garrison stepped back into the control room.

Paul turned to face the chanting crowds once more.

A minute went by.

Lightning blinked.

"You don't believe it, do you?" Parker asked casually, without taking his eyes off the swaying mass of people.

Paul shrugged. "Hard to tell. Nobody's claimed responsibility, and isn't that what it's all about? Grandstanding. Why would someone want to bomb a football match and then not take responsibility for it? And, it's not as if football matches have proved to be popular terrorist targets in the past."

"Maybe not, but if you think about it, it would make sense, especially at a game like this one."

"What, even with all the gate security?"

"We would have to assume it was planted before the match."

"At the risk of it being discovered?"

Lightning flashed.

Parker looked heavenwards. "It keeps threatening, and I wish it would just get on with it."

"Yes, the irony being, if it chucked it down, we'd at least be able to postpone due to *adverse weather conditions*. But then, I suppose, especially on a day like today, rain is the least of our worries?"

The disgruntled sky disagreed and spat at the two men.

49

The colonel stood in the doorway, looking down at the two intruders as they huddled on the floor at the far end of the room.

"Do you have any idea how much trouble you two have

caused?" he asked with a menacing growl.

"What do you want from us?" Sky screamed.

"I just want you do die!" The colonel said with all of the vitriol of a Bond villain as he aimed the gun at her.

"NOOO!" Blake shouted as he threw himself over her protectively.

The gun's blast was much louder than both of them had expected. In fact, it sounded more like an explosion.

And it was.

One of the fuel tanks had exploded, blasting through the reinforced walls of the engine room and punching out the door that then careened into the colonel, hurtling him ten feet down the corridor.

Then, there was the ominous, deep, guttural groan of bending metal, which was promptly upstaged by a loud siren and the computer's loud voice. *"Attention, evacuation protocol is now in effect. All personnel must abandon ship immediately and proceed to safety boat embarkation."*

Blake turned to find, to his astonishment, that the doorway and the colonel had disappeared, and in their place was a warzone of charred debris, crumpled metal and dust.

"What happened?" Sky gasped.

"I have no idea, and I don't want to stick around to find out," Blake said with a grimace as he hauled himself to his feet. "We need to go," he said, extending a hand to her. "Come on!"

The giant creature that was the ship moaned as if mourning the fact that its engines had been disabled, leaving it paralysed in the water, as Blake gingerly climbed over the mound of rubble that used to be the doorway. He was careful not to tread on any of the thick hot oil that smothered it, like syrup on ice cream.

Once he descended into the corridor on the other side, he reached out for Sky, glancing from time to time at the black, steaming slime that was still slithering towards them. As soon as Sky was safely on the other side, they ran, hand in hand, dodging chunks of fibreglass and metal until the percussion from another blast knocked them sideways, almost off their feet.

It was as they were steadying themselves to resume their escape that they noticed it – rumbling.

It could be felt underfoot, like a small earthquake, gradually growing in intensity until there was the loud hissing of a snake. No – it was not a snake; it sounded more like water on coal.

Blake pulled a face as they reached what was left of the colonel; he was lying there with part of the door across his chest. His face was charred, the skin melted and studded with chunks of glass that glinted under the now flickering lights.

The rumbling grew louder. So loud that it caught their attention and compelled them to look back when, like something out of the *Poseidon Adventure*, a five-foot wall of water exploded into the corridor, dredging with it a mountain of debris.

"Oh my God!"

"Run!"

"I am!"

"Faster!"

The black mass chased them down the rest of the corridor like some kind of primordial aquatic creature.

They were just a few feet from the door, but it was gaining.

Closer…

And closer…

Williamson watched the drama unfold on the monitor. "Seal the door!" he ordered. Then, as if justifying himself, he added, "Otherwise, we'll all drown."

"I can't, Sir," the operator said apologetically.

"What do you mean you can't?"

"It seems the colonel damaged the mechanism."

It took a few seconds for Williamson to absorb the information. Then, he slowly shook his head when he realised, "That fascist bastard. He wanted this all along."

He stared at the screen and watched as the water enveloped the two fugitives.

Blake and Sky gasped as the Atlantic's icy cloak wrapped around their legs, almost knocking them off their feet.

"Quick! Through here!" Blake shouted, ushering her through the junction door. He followed and pulled the door shut, leaving the water to fill the corridor behind them.

They paused to gather their thoughts and their breath.

The metal leviathan howled and moaned as it was rocked by another explosion. This time, the quake knocked both off them off their feet, sending them sprawling into a crumpled heap as the ship sunk into a backward list.

The water in the corridor had risen to the glass' level, filling it with the blackness of the oil. It pressed on the door, compelling it to creak under the pressure.

Blake caught Sky's hand and, the next thing she knew, she was being pulled out of the junction and into the corridor. He pulled the door shut, but he knew this would have little effect since the locking mechanism had been disabled by his own hand.

They ran down the main corridor, towards the control room and the lift Blake had spotted upon their arrival.

They were thirty feet from the control room when they heard the loud crash of the junction room door as it imploded, allowing the water to fill the area.

"Where are we going, Blake?" Sky yelled.

"Just keep running!"

It was less than a minute before the second junction room door gave way, exploding outward, unleashing a six-foot black liquid creature that instantly gave chase.

"Don't look, just run!" Blake ordered over the sloshing roar.

But the tidal wave was gaining fast, and the end of the corridor was too far away. It took seconds for the creature to reach out and wash them down the rest of the corridor, slamming and then pinning them both against the control room doors while freezing the breath in their lungs.

The corridor filled rapidly, and the pressure of the rushing tide was so great that neither of them could move.

Blake strained to look at the wall panel; it glowed a consistent red under the water, which was up to their waists now.

Another groan as the ship sank further backward. The action shifted the centre of gravity away from the control room towards the end of the corridor and beyond, where once locked doors yielded to the overwhelming pressure and, one by one, imploded inwards.

They seized the opportunity and staggered through the wash, panting with the exertion, but there was no time to recover.

"Which way?" Sky yelled, through gulps of air.

The ship wailed like a dying animal as the engine room slowly and reluctantly succumbed to the will of the ocean. The cacophony of bending metal and shattering glass was as loud as it was terrifying.

Blake didn't answer Sky's question, for he was too busy catching his breath; instead, he took her hand and they staggered through the water, toward the elevator, leaving the ship's control room behind.

Inside, Williamson sat alone; he had ordered the evacuation as soon as he learned that the fuel tanks were exploding, puncturing holes in the ship's hull. He knew it was only a matter of time before the tanker, years of research, and millions of dollars of investment sank, like many ships before it, to the bottom of the Atlantic Ocean.

The control room doors shook as the water gathered like a marauding clan outside, but Williamson was not worried. He knew that the contents of the injection would soon take hold. Soon, he would personally experience the effects of the toxin, and he welcomed it, for there was nothing for him beyond this – this, his biggest failure.

Outside of the elevator, Blake frantically pressed the call button as he steadied himself against the slant of the ship while the water circled around his knees.

"Come on… come on," he chanted as the lift descended, painfully slowly, from the deck.

Eventually, it arrived and the doors casually opened, unlike the water that rushed in ahead of them like an anxious puppy.

"…all personnel must abandon ship immediately and proceed to safety boat embarkation."

"In you go," Blake said, pushing Sky inside and then following her.

He pressed the blue button marked "F Deck" and then, and only after a dramatic pause, the doors closed and the lift climbed, draining the water away as it went.

Seconds seemed like minutes as they both stared upward, panting and shivering.

Then, another quake knocked them sideways, but they managed to maintain their balance by steadying themselves against the cabin walls. They remained this way as the lift ascended, staring at the triangular hatch in the ceiling as if it was a piece of art.

Blake willed the lift to move faster, but instead the petulant rebel decided to snuff out the light and shudder to a terrifying halt.

"Attention, evacuation protocol is now in effect. All personnel must…"

Sky screamed into the blackness, her voice resonating around the compartment and echoed by the whale-like lament of the sinking vessel.

"Oh My God… Oh My God…." she murmured repeatedly,

"Don't worry," Blake said, seeking her out in the gloom and holding her to him. "It's just a temporary power drain. It'll be back soon," he said reassuringly, as if he had witnessed this kind of thing all the time.

However, more seconds that seemed like minutes drifted by, and yet the blackness remained, giving birth to the now dreadfully familiar sound of sluicing and sloshing. The freezing shroud of the ocean returned, pouring through the cracks and wrapping itself around their feet.

"Shit!" Blake hissed.

The water was rising much faster than he'd thought it would.

They had to act quickly.

"Sky, climb onto my shoulders."

"What?"

"Climb onto my shoulders."

"Blake," she protested, "I can't even see where you are!"

"Then feel me!" he shouted, and then promptly laughed, "Bet you don't get an offer like that every day. Here," he said, "feel for my hands."

She complied, feeling for his shoulders, the muscles of his arms, his wrists, and then the stirrups he had made of his hands.

"Did you see that trap door in the ceiling?" he asked.

"Yes."

"Well, we need to use it."

The water was at their knees now.

"Hurry!"

"Can you feel anything?" he asked through grunts and grimaces as she stood in his hands and pulled at his wound.

"No, not yet," she grunted as she frantically groped for the latch in the darkness.

The water was at Blake's waist and rising fast, gurgling and bubbling like an icy cauldron of death.

A snapping sound, a hollow prehistoric groan, and both of them felt a swaying giddy feeling as they plunged with the motion of the ship.

Sky lost her balance and screamed as Blake stumbled through the water but, with clenched teeth, he retained his footing. "You're okay. We're okay," he reassured her through the exertion.

"I can't find it! I can't find it, Blake!" she yelled into the darkness.

"Yes, you can, Sky," he said forcefully. "And hurry up, because judging by this tableau, I'm going to be the first to drown!"

"Well, you could always get up here and try for yourself," she said.

"Now, why would I do that when I know that you'll do a much better job?"

"I see, even as we drown, you still haven't lost that patronising tone."

"Never."

"You can be so annoying sometimes," she grumbled as she finally flipped the catch and a slither of light sliced through the darkness, dazzling them both.

"At last," he said with deep satisfaction.

The water was above his chest and binding his limbs. "C...can... you climb through there?" He asked through chattering teeth.

"I think.... so," she said, hauling herself up and out of Blake's hands.

Suddenly, the cabin lurched sideways; Blake lost his balance and fell with a giant splash back into the water.

Sky heard the sound, but could see nothing.

"Blake?"

The only response was the loud sloshing of the water, echoing off the cabin walls.

"Blake?" She attempted again, straining to see in the darkness.

"BLAKE!" she yelled as her heart bounced around her ribcage.

Then, thankfully, she heard more splashing and the sound of his spluttering. "BLAKE? BLAKE?" she called.

"Yeah.... I'm... I'm ... okay." He had to force the words out through coughs and shudders. His body was being paralysed by the cold. Further, the water had reached his neck now, and he was finding it difficult to keep upright.

"Take my hand!" Sky cried, "Take it!"

He held his hand up to the sound of her voice, but they failed to connect.

"Where are you?" she shouted with frustration as she groped the darkness for his hand.

"I'm here!"

"Where?"

"HERE!"

"Reach for that shard of light, Blake! Into the light!"

He complied and she finally caught his hand. She gripped it so tight she could have crushed bones. "After three! One, two, and three!"

He jumped, she pulled, and, aided by his buoyancy in the rising flood, he climbed through the escape hatch with relative simplicity.

They both sat for a few seconds in a melee of breaths and shudders.

"Now where?" she asked. "Have we got to climb?"

"Yes. It shouldn't be..." he stopped when he noticed a slither of light through the slit in the wall. "What's this?" He pressed his eye to the crack and laughed with relief. "We're there, Sky! We're there!"

"Where?"

"On deck!" he exclaimed excitedly. "The lift has stopped just a few feet from the deck!" He pushed his clumsy, numb fingers through the crack between the two doors and attempted to pry them apart. "Help me," he grunted.

Sky moved to her knees with a splash; the water had reached them once more and was rising.

They strained to pull the doors apart, but their efforts were slow, the strain on their fingers immense. Sky clawed and pulled. He grunted and groaned; the pain in his arm now secondary to the task in hand.

Eventually, their work was rewarded; the gap in the door grew, revealing a dazzling floodlight. However, the moment was dulled by the fact that the water, from which they had been running, was now spilling out in front of them.

"Come on," Blake winced through gritted teeth as the doors inched further apart, "we... re... nearly there!" He strained.

A few more inches.

"Al...most!" Sky grimaced as the water rose above her chest and began to float her hair around her.

Then, with one final heave, the doors gave way, the water spilling out and rapidly filling the box-like room before them.

"Get out, Sky!" Blake shouted, still pushing on the doors as she crawled through.

"Come on!" she shouted once she was safe on the other side.

Blake followed her through, breathing in as much as he could, secretly thanking himself for rigorously sticking to his morning runs.

Once they were together again, they spontaneously hugged as the ever-present flood continued to swirl and pool at their feet.

Their eyes met and they caressed one another's faces, thrilled to be together, and alive. They lingered for a few more seconds until the sickly swaying of the ship reminded them of their ordeal.

"Come on!" he said, taking her hand and running out of the small compartment, up a few steps until they were on deck once more.

However, the sight that greeted them was much more terrifying than anything they had experienced thus far. They had emerged at the bow of the ship. Above them, a giant mast towered high into a starry sky.

The giant floodlight mounted to it, and several others bolted at various intervals throughout the length of the ship, were doing a chillingly good job of illuminating their predicament.

The oil tanker was at a slant. Most of the stern had disappeared beneath the waves, leaving just the T-shape of the original control tower above the waterline. Inside, lights flickered eerily through portal windows, revealing the tiny silhouettes of terrified people as they climbed the stairs in an effort to reach the highest point.

However, when Blake looked up, he could see that, like ants, a group of people were already clamouring and jostling for the best spot on the roof, but what they didn't seem to realise was that they were on the wrong side of the ship – the side that was going to sink first.

His instincts told him to call out to them, to warn them, but they were too far away. Nobody would hear him.

It was in that moment, as the cold Atlantic gale puffed around them, that Blake Hudson and Sky McPherson became aware of the insignificance of their existence out there. In the vast expanse of the ocean, the sinking tanker was nothing but a leaf on a lake.

Screams drew their attention, and they turned to see a group of people, about five of them, running from the growing surf as the ocean devoured another chunk of the ship.

"Where are the lifeboats?" Sky spoke, suddenly full of dread. If there were still so many people on board, it could only mean one thing.

Blake said nothing. He had already come to that dreadful realisation the moment they had emerged.

Suddenly, there was a whale-like spurting sound as water and air were pushed up through the control tower, killing the lights and punching out the windows to a cacophony of smashing glass and hysterical screams. Blake could feel Sky shuddering against him, and he thought about what he would give to fill the empty helipad and reappear the absent lifeboats.

Yet, there was no escape.

The oil tanker was sinking. There wasn't much left of the control tower, and those who'd once been huddled on its rooftop were now jumping into the water and attempting to swim while simultaneously grabbing anything and anyone to stay afloat. The others were now either climbing onto the giant winches at the centre of the ship or running towards them, which prompted Blake to look up.

"Up there, Sky!" He pointed at the mast.

"No, Blake," she said.

He looked at her in bewilderment.

"I can't do this anymore," she added through shivers. "I just don't have the strength."

"Come on, Sky," Blake said, pulling her arm as if she was just messing with him, but she resisted.

"What's the point?" she screamed. "What is the point, Blake? We're just postponing the inevitable! There is no way off this thing, and even you can't joke your way out of this one!"

She was angry. She actually wanted to cry, but she was all cried out. She was done. The adrenaline that had kept her going all this time had disappeared, washed away with the realisation that it was all for nothing. They were going to die out there, in the middle of nowhere. Now that she had rediscovered the only man she had ever truly loved, she was going to lose him again, to this!

Blake shook his head, and said sternly, "Oh no, you don't. You're coming with me, and you're coming now."

"I can't!" she shrieked.

"You are not giving up now," Blake warned.

"Try me!"

"Sky…"

"No, Blake. Look at us! Look at us!" she said, throwing her arms about and pointing at the peaks of the swell that was gradually making its way towards them. "There is nowhere to go, nowhere else we can run or hide! It is over! We have to face the facts."

"I am facing facts!" he retorted. "Everything I've ever done when it comes to us is face facts. I've faced them, Sky, and I know I can't be without you." His voice faltered. "I can't and never want to imagine a life without you. And believe me, if I was alone, then, well, if I was alone, I would have fucking given up back there, but I'm not alone, Sky, I'm not alone; I'm here, with you…"

He choked on a mouthful of emotion, and then continued with determination.

"… I'm here with you, and I can't, I won't stand here and wait for the fucking water to drown you. I can't! I won't! I fucking won't let that be the last image I have of you. No, I'd rather die knowing that we tried, and that we didn't just give up like we did all those years ago. In fact, that day I met you again at the college, I made a vow. I made a vow that if you and I managed to hit things off again, I would never give up on us, never, at least not without fight, and I'm not about to start now. So, you either climb this fucking thing or I swear to God, I'll drag you up there!"

Angry tears leaked from his eyes, but he didn't wipe them. He just stood there, legs tense, jaw clenching as the tide inched closer.

Sky was speechless for several seconds before she blinked back tears she'd believed she no longer had, and said, with a smile, "All right, you don't have to get all *Last of the Mohicans* on me."

He stared at her.

"What? You think you and Matt are the only two who can make movie puns?" She asked casually, before reaching out to touch his cheek.

He held her hand there for a while, and they knew then, in that moment, that they were ready for this.

The surf rumbled and fizzed closer.

"Up there, quick!" she reminded him, pointing at the mast, and then took his hand.

They splashed through the water and climbed the metal ladder that scaled the facet of the mast, ascending as fast as they could.

"Hold on tight, Sky!" No sooner had he finished saying the words than the dying metal monster lunged backward, pulling her from the rungs.

Blake looked down, panic-stricken.

Yet, she clung on, and even managed to smile up at him, squinting into the floodlight that was still shining brightly and spotlighting the watery hell beneath them. "Right until the end!" she shouted.

They climbed to the summit and gripped onto the railing as the bow of the ship gradually lifted from the water like the snout of a prehistoric monster, spluttering and wailing, as if protesting against the watery darkness that was eating it alive.

Most of the deck was submerged now, and the other stranded few had abandoned their hasty islands to make their way to the mast.

Blake and Sky looked at each other as they clung on, literally, for their lives.

"Nothing else matters, Blake. As long as we're together," she said encouragingly, with one hand on the railing and the other on his.

There were screams as the mast's floodlight blinked several times before finally plunging their world into darkness.

Blake and Sky prepared themselves for the inevitable. In their heads, both of them had reconciled that there would be no surviving this. Even if they endured the actual sinking of the ship, they would never survive the water temperature.

The mournful cries of the imploding tanker and the squealing sound it made, as it exhaled its last breath of air through any remaining orifices, was so loud that neither of them heard the beating sound in the distance.

It was only when the fireflies appeared on the horizon that they noticed them. Even then, they had to look at each other for confirmation that what they were seeing was not in fact a hallucination.

However, as they drew closer, their engines louder and their searchlights more distinctive, it became clear that the fireflies were in fact a pair of fluorescent yellow RAF Sea King helicopters, and that they were heading directly to the sinking ship.

Could this be possible? Could they really be saved?

There was a violent shudder, as if the ocean had delivered its deathblow, suggesting the tanker was ready to surrender to the will of the deep. The turbulence rushing at their faces told them that this was indeed the case.

"NO! Not now!" Sky screamed.

However, there was no stopping it. Over half of the ship had disappeared beneath the water, the waves reaching the few survivors who were pointlessly holding onto parts of the giant winches – and washing them away like ants.

"NOOO! NOOO!" Blake protested, powerless against the vertical dive as one of the searchlights found them, and the helicopter buzzed overhead.

"Should we jump?" Sky yelled over the opposing turbulence of the downdraft from the chopper and the updraft of the sinking ship.

Blake considered the question, quickly shook his head, and then looked up into the searchlight, willing it to drop its lifeline as he considered what would happen in the ship's wake. He had no doubt that the displacement of water would generate strong, swirling currents. If they didn't make it off the ship before it sank, he doubted they would survive.

He glanced, desperately, at the other helicopter; it was hovering several yards away as its searchlight found a clutch of survivors bobbing around on the ocean surface.

He looked up again, and finally, he could see a single under-arm fluorescent harness descending towards them, and he felt both relief and dread.

The ship was sinking fast. Giant bubbling waves exploded and fizzed under the searchlight while the helicopter's engines laboured deafeningly loud as it hovered overhead.

"Sky, I want you to grab it soon as it reaches us," he yelled over the whirring dissonance.

"What about you?" She asked, alarmed.

"I'll be right behind you."

"No, you won't." He was avoiding eye contact with her and that only meant one thing.

"Sky…"

"No, Blake, not without you!"

"We can't go at the same time…"

"Then you go first!"

The harness dangled closer. It was almost within reaching distance.

"Grab it, Sky!" He shouted.

"Not without you!"

"For once in your life, girl, do as you're bloody told!"

He caught her hand and thrust it upward as the harness came into reach.

"GRAB IT!" he ordered as the ship plunged a few more feet, squeezing his stomach with dizzying fairground queasiness.

The lifeline drifted up and away once more. The ship's variable descent was making it difficult for the pilot to compensate. Then, as it gradually drifted closer again, and while Sky was busy stretching to reach the harness with one hand whilst clinging on with the other, Blake anchored his leg around the railing, grabbed her waist, and lifted her as high as he could.

She instinctively looped her arms and interlocked her fingers.

"BLAKE!"

"DON'T LET GO! I LOVE YOU!" Then, before she had a chance to protest further, he squinted up into the spotlight and gave the thumbs up.

"NOOOO!" Sky screamed as she was instantly hauled up and away from him. "NOOOO!" She continued as the chasm between her and the man she loved grew wider.

Blake watched her disappear into the light as both joy and abject misery sucked the life from him as he contemplated the watery grave below; the ship was sinking too fast. There wasn't enough time to send the line back down.

The journey up into the helicopter took seconds, but it may as well have been hours. Sky was greeted by two crewmembers, one of whom attempted to wrap her in a tinfoil blanket, but she slapped him away and turned to look out of the door once more. Blake was still clinging to what was left of the mast as gargantuan water bubbles rose and snapped beneath him like the angry jaws of a shiver of sharks. He was just seconds from the rising tide of oil, foaming water, and floating debris.

"Hurry, please hurry!" she shouted, anxiously at the winchman as the line unravelled with sadistic slowness.

The helicopter dropped, bringing the harness to within fifteen feet, but the white ocean froth salivated closer than that.

Blake looked up as the line dangled temptingly close.

10 feet.

"Down! It's too far up! He can't reach it!" Sky screamed, but the winchman could do no more; the cable was fully deployed.

8 feet

The helicopter dropped.

5 feet

The ship sank, the mast peeking out from the ocean like a periscope. It was all that remained of the metal giant, but it was sinking fast, much faster than the pilot could negotiate.

Blake instinctively stretched as far as he could without letting go, but the lifeline remained tauntingly out of reach, by just inches, as he was slowly being fed into the mouth of a giant leviathan. He could already feel the spittle of the waves and the fetid breath of the crude oil.

He was out of time.

"NOOOOO! BLAAAAAAAKE!" Sky screamed, leaning out of the door as if she could catch him, but the winchman pulled her back in. "NOOOOOO!"

The helicopter lurched one final time as Sky felt hands on her shoulders. The crewmember pulled her away from the open door, despite her protestations, wrapped her in a foil blanket, and strapped her into a seat. It was only in that moment, when she stared into the sad grey eyes of the middle aged weathered-faced man who was gently resting a restraining hand on her shoulder that she understood; he was gone. Blake was gone, and no amount of screaming or hollering was going to change that.

He was gone.

So, she stopped protesting, stopped making a fuss and began fading into a painless altered state as her mind attempted to process what exactly had just happened.

The world shrank away, the whirring of the helicopter blending, the animated voices of the crewmembers diluting into nothing but hollow echoes somewhere in the distance. Slowly, the fear dissolved, the cold thawed until there was nothing left, but emptiness.

He's gone.

The concept was as incredible as it was unfathomable, yet it was true, but it could not be. And so, the mind loop continued until the sickly swaying of the banking helicopter made its presence felt.

Are they leaving already? No, wait! Blake is down there. He's waiting for us. Stop!

She tried to speak; she tried to verbalise the thoughts in her head, but she couldn't and yet the helicopter continued to climb.

Stop! Stop! Wait!

That was when she heard them. Distant, at first – just echoes as her mind, like a faulty radio, began to tune into the signal of reality once more; the crewmembers were cheering.

Cheering? Blake is gone and you're cheering? What's wrong with you people?

Slowly, as the smeary echoes dissipated and reality gradually came back into focus, she felt the winchman's hand on her arm once more; he was tucking the blanket around her. It was only when the man moved out of her line of sight that she saw him; he was wet, shivering, white as a ghost, but alive, and wearing the feeblest of smiles as he was bundled into a foil blanket and guided into the seat next to her.

She pulled at her belt as the volume of the world was gradually turned up into reality once more.

The grey-eyed crewmember was smiling warmly at her while placing a restraining hand over the buckle of her belt; she needed to stay strapped in.

"How…." She uttered, touching Blake, and looking him up and down as if to reassure herself that it was actually him, that he was actually sitting next to her and that he was still alive.

Grey-eyes responded for him. "Our pilot's nickname is Maverick, you know, the character from…" they both nodded. "Well, we call him that because sometimes, well, he can be bit crazy. He dropped the chopper so far the harness nearly hit the water, and this guy, well, he must be just as crazy, because he made a jump for it right at the last second!"

Grey eyes shook his head, incredulously, and patted a shivering Blake on the shoulder. "Well done, mate," he said, sincerely, and then added, seriously, "Don't unbuckle those belts," before he left the two survivors to join his crewmates.

"You *are* crazy," Sky said, shaking her head.

"Yeah, yeah… about…you," came his quivering reply. "And I'm never going to let you forget it," he said.

She cocked her head, "Is that a veiled proposal?"

"M…Might be." He said, forcing another grin.

She threw her arms around him and squeezed him tight.

"I love you," she said sincerely, clinging to him. "I love you so much."

He waited for a few seconds, enjoying the sound of those words, then quipped, "B…. blimey…. T…. twice in one day. Does that mean your answer's yes?"

She emerged from the embrace and looked him in the eyes; his lovely eyes that, despite his ordeal, were still sparkling in that handsome face of his.

"Might be," she said, echoing his earlier sentence. "All depends on where you're thinking on taking me for our honeymoon."

He didn't even have to think about that, and said quickly, "Anywhere there isn't water."

"You're on!"

She held his face and then they kissed for the longest time as the helicopter dipped and made its way through a star-filled sky back to land.

The End

Epilogue

"... And the headlines today.

The extraordinary riots that besieged most of the Southwest of England last week appear to be over as local authorities report a second week of calm.

An investigation has been launched after it emerged that local police received a bomb threat ahead of last week's highly anticipated football match between Cambridge and Plymouth Argyle, yet refused to call it off. Some MPs have gone as far as accusing local authorities of putting the beautiful game before human lives.

One of the Environment Agency's top executives, Christopher Hamilton, has been arrested amid allegations of corruption.

Now, just before we go, a look at the weather with Andrew Jarvis."

"Hello, Elena. Yes, good news all round, as it seems that this mild dry front that we've been experiencing over the past few days is here to stay. This will undoubtedly come as welcome news to many, just as it did to the thousands of fans at last week's game, who were spared a washout when the deluge that threatened the match fizzled to nothing. In fact, that very large band of cloud that was going to be responsible for that has pretty much dissipated. This means we can expect nice sunny spells for most of this week, but make the most of it because we all know how unpredictable the British weather can be. "

"Too right, Andrew. Thanks for that. Well, that's all from us today; the next main news will be at six o-clock, but in the meantime from Andrew and me, Elena Parker, for Southwest Radio, goodbye."

ALSO BY TONY MARTURANO

More fiction by Tony Marturano

A supernatural thriller

*"Fear the living, fear the dead,
fear the Unspeakable."*

PAPERBACK AVAILABLE FROM AMAZON.

**AUDIOBOOK AVAILABLE FROM AMAZON,
AUDIBLE AND ITUNES.**

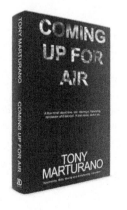

Non-fiction by Tony Marturano

True stories you'll have to
read to believe.

*"If you are, or were in a relationship, this
book is not only
for you, it's about you!"*

**PAPERBACK AND HARDBACK AVAILABLE NOW
FROM AMAZON. AUDIOBOOK OUT APRIL 2016.**

Acknowledgements

I'd like to thank (in no particular order) the following people for their help during the writing of this novel:

Dr Ed Uthman, MD (For all the grisly details)

Derek Hardy, UK Met Office. (For the hard time you gave me in the name of realism!)

Gareth Bates, UK Environment Agency. (For Blake.)

Nimbus Focus Group: Marina Coleman, Glenys Shaw, and Bill Ratcliffe. (For help in orientation.)

Bella Coleman. (Without you, there wouldn't be a Nimbus. You are and always will be my inspiration.)

You, the reader. (If you are reading this page, it is probably because you bought this book. Without you, all my work would be worthless. Thank you.)

Discover more at
www.tonymarturano.com

Made in the USA
Monee, IL
29 December 2022